A DEBT FREELY PAID

"I always believe in collecting on debts owed," Locke murmured in a husky voice.

"You do?" Cornelia whispered as he pulled her into his arms.

"Always. Especially when the debt owed is from a certain special lady," he murmured. With the crook of his finger he lifted her chin and bent his head.

He gently kissed her. Her lips were soft and warm, silently inviting further exploration. Without wasting the moment, he deepened the kiss.

"Locke," she moaned, helpless to stop the heightening pleasure that dulled any further thoughts of protest. She was still in a daze when she felt him bend down and swoop her up into his arms . . .

GWEN CLEARY
COLORADO TEMPTATION

ZEBRA BOOKS
KENSINGTON PUBLISHING CORP.

This book is dedicated to all my readers who have traveled down the same rough road as my heroine in this story and emerged stronger and more fulfilled.

And to all of you who have been fortunate enough to be spared the trials and tribulations.

May all your lives be filled with happy endings . . .

ZEBRA BOOKS

are published by

Kensington Publishing Corp.
475 Park Avenue South
New York, NY 10016

First printing: August, 1991

Printed in the United States of America

Chapter One

The harsh voice of the ferret-faced court clerk rang out in censuring tones around the courtroom. "The court calls Cornelia Lloyd Talbot to the witness stand."

All eyes in the packed room swung toward the far rear corner as the gaunt young woman with the lifeless, honey-brown curls shifted in her seat. "And to think that my Herbert was heartbroken when she married Linley Talbot. She is not the beauty she once was considered," commented an older matron, who had squeezed into the courtroom to enjoy the public airing of the young woman's scandalous affair.

"She may have been a beauty, but I always knew she was not the sweet young thing everybody thought her to be," returned the woman's companion. "I knew there was the devil in her from the first time my Gerta got in trouble as a youngster. She always insisted that it was the Talbot girl who was responsible. Now folks finally believe me, after all my warnings that that woman would come to ruin."

Cornelia huddled in the last row of the paneled

5

room, trying to ignore the cruel remarks. She had attempted to appear as inconspicuous as one of the marble pillars lining the walls, but the grating voice of the court clerk made it impossible.

Her first inclination had been to drop her eyes and wish she were back in her cheery kitchen, even though she knew that no matter how hard she wished, this dreadful scene would not disappear as if nothing had happened and the pieces of her marriage would not snap back together as easily a child's puzzle.

That was the most trying part about this horrible muddle: Nothing had happened. Only no one believed her, which was how her troubles all began.

The clerk's hard eyes fastened on her, and his brows drew together in sanction of a verdict she feared had already been passed down. "Cornelia Lloyd Talbot to the witness stand."

Determined to retain her composure, Cornelia breathed in a deep gulp of air and smoothed her somber gray skirt as she rose to take the witness stand. She inched her way down the row, and the heel of her shoe caught on the chair leg next to her. She tripped, yet refused to be robbed of another bit of dignity as she valiantly fought the urge to turn and flee under the censuring stares. No, she was not going to take flight. She bit her lip. She would not let these people think she was backing down and accepting the judgment without a fight.

Quickly recovering, she raised her chin and walked up the center aisle until she stood in front of the clerk holding a Bible in his bony hands.

"Place your right hand on the Good Book," the man instructed.

A nervous wreck, Cornelia removed her gloves and placed her left hand on the worn Bible. The simple, wide gold band on her ring finger gleamed, causing a murmur to buzz around the room.

"Your right hand, Mrs. Talbot," the man admonished.

"Sorry." Cornelia pulled her hand back and hid the ring that she had refused to surrender within the folds of her skirt.

As she woodenly listened to the clerk swear her in, her mind relived the mistaken incident in which her husband had caught her in the arms of another man. The truth was she had not actually been embracing the man. If only Linley had come along a moment later, he would have seen how utterly innocent the situation had been.

"You may take the stand now," the clerk directed, forcing her mind back to the present.

From the raised witness box Cornelia's vision caught with Linley's.

He shook his head and glanced away.

Her heart sank. She had shamed her husband and forced him into this divorce action all because she had been unable to locate the stranger and have him corroborate her story.

She ventured a glance around the room. Condemning faces stared back at her. It seemed that the entire community had squeezed into the room to hear the sordid details; she would never be able to hold her head proudly again until she had exonerated herself.

After stating her name and place of residence, she was asked to step down. To her horror she was forced to sit up front in full view of everyone for hours. The remainder of the day, witness after witness testified against her. The entire town must have seen that mistaken embrace. At the end of the day she was recalled to the witness stand.

"Do you understand the gravity of the charges and testimony leveled against you?" the judge questioned.

Cornelia swallowed hard as she kept her gaze steady toward the black-cloaked jurist. "Yes, Your Honor. But I—"

"All you are to do is answer the questions, Mrs. Talbot."

Cornelia hung her head, realizing that she was about to be erringly branded an adulteress. "Yes, Your Honor."

The judge went on to summarize the charges and review the testimony. It seemed like an eternity before he finally concluded with, "Under the circumstances and in view of the facts, it is the decision of this court that divorce is to be granted to the plaintiff, Linley Horton Lloyd." The judge handed Cornelia a stack of legal papers to sign.

Stunned, Cornelia took the papers and in a burst of emotion bolted to her feet, crying, "Please let the record show that this is all a dreadful mistake and I do not accept the ruling of this court or the divorce willingly."

Tears streaming down her cheeks, Cornelia stepped down from the stand, the drumming of the judge's gavel in her ears. With all the dignity she could garner, she endured the gauntlet of condemnation as she strode from the courtroom in shame.

Outside, she leaned against a post and took in big gulps of air. Once she had caught her breath, she straightened her shoulders, raised her chin, and headed home. Despite the weight of guilt cast upon her, she was going to prove them all wrong!

Chapter Two

Cornelia stiffened her stance and smoothed back an escaping honey-brown curl as she listened to her long-time friend drone on with unwelcome advice. Cornelia's gaze shifted around her tidy childhood bedroom in an attempt to ignore Lucretia until it became evident the plump woman lounging on her bed had no intention of ceasing her prattle in the near future.

"Lucretia, I appreciate your concern, but I have already made my decision, and I have no intention of changing my mind."

Lucretia's eyes widened. "You can't be serious!"

"I am very serious," Cornelia said and turned from Lucretia.

Cornelia took a dress from the wardrobe and, folding it, carefully tucked it in the bag sitting next to the others already neatly packed.

Lucretia climbed off the bed and hovered over Cornelia while she continued to pack her belongings. Wringing her hands, Lucretia said, "But Nellie, do be practical. If you accompany your brother to Colorado, you'll never be able to prove that you're innocent and convince Linley to take you back. And your family will continue to suffer your disgrace."

Cornelia swung around and dropped her gaze for a moment before lifting green eyes and meeting her friend's probing blue stare. "Perhaps my absence will allow the community to forget *my disgrace* and let my family get on with their own lives."

Scandalized, Lucretia grabbed the bow at her double chin. "You know I only mean to be of help."

Taking a deep buoying breath, Cornelia said, "I know, but my mind is made up." Despite the inclination to ask Lucretia to leave her alone to finish packing in peace, Cornelia was glad she had held herself back. Lucretia was the only friend she had left.

"Blessed be. Whatever has gotten into you? You were the model daughter for twenty years and then the model wife for four years. Everyone always looked up to you . . . until that dreadful *situation* came up."

"You mean, until I was mistakenly presumed to be having an affair with a man I was accused of embracing, and thereby breaking my marriage vows. That is what you were attempting to say, isn't it, Lucretia?"

Lucretia stepped back at the vehemence in Cornelia's voice, and she blushed down to her red roots with shame for her adulterous friend.

A long moment of silence lapsed.

"I thought so," Cornelia said with a disappointed sigh. She was stung that her childhood friend also had deserted her, despite her presence, and believed those horrid accusations.

"Oh, Cornelia, you know that deep down no one truly believes you could be capable of such a sin," Lucretia blurted out belatedly, knowing that everyone believed quite the opposite and Cornelia knew it.

"Then why is it I have been made an outcast in the community, and the church has turned its back on

10

me as well? And why is it that my family has been made to feel that they have reared a pariah?"

Lucretia grabbed a skirt out of Cornelia's hands and hung it back in the wardrobe. As if she were speaking to a naughty child, she chided, "Yours is the first divorce people remember occurring here. It is not as if we were living in New York City or one of those other large cities where *that sort of thing* happens everyday, you know. Divorce is simply unheard of in our community with its strict Puritan ethic. All the gossip will die down eventually. I know it will. Then perhaps you can convince Linley to forgive you and even take you back."

Cornelia huffed out a breath. "There is nothing to forgive me for," she insisted. "And quit hovering over me." She snatched the skirt Lucretia had taken from her back off the rod, folded it, and tucked it in the corner of her bag.

Although she did not look at all convinced, Lucretia said, "I believe you, truly I do. But it is hard to convince people when there were so many witnesses."

Cornelia shook her head in exasperation. "I have explained what happened a thousand times. The stranger mistook me for someone else." She sighed. "I thought Linley at least would believe I was telling the truth. I was wrong. Even he believed the worst."

"Nellie, I'm certain he never wanted the divorce in the first place. He was forced into it to save face."

Cornelia gave a bitter laugh. "I know. Public appearance always has been of foremost importance in the Talbot family." Ignoring the ache in her heart, Cornelia lifted her cleft chin. "Eventually the truth will come out, and Linley and I will be man and wife again," she said with conviction.

"Then why run away like you're doing?"

"I am not running away! My brother is very ill,

11

and I am sure that if I accompany him to Colorado and see that he is settled properly, he will fully recover from his consumption."

"It is the Great White Plague, you know. People don't recover from it," Lucretia said softly and laid a comforting hand on Cornelia's arm. "Not even if they are very special to you, like your brother is."

Her features set, Cornelia retorted, "I have read about cases in which the dry mountain climate has helped sufferers afflicted with Paxton's illness. And I have selected the perfect location where Paxton will get the rest he needs."

"If your father hadn't purchased those silly reading glasses for you, you probably wouldn't be in such a muddle now because you wouldn't have been able to read that note you insisted was delivered to you by mistake. And you wouldn't have ended up in that stranger's arms in front of that restaurant that you insisted the note, which was so inconveniently taken from you, instructed you to go to meet Linley. And you wouldn't be leaving town for some wilderness settlement."

Cornelia snapped her bag shut. "Well, Father did purchase the glasses for me, and I am grateful he did. *And* I shall continue to swear that the note was written in a familiar hand, instructing that I meet Linley. Although I admit now that I must have mistaken the script," she added with a sigh of regret.

"If you only could find the note to show people."

"I told you the same thing I swore to on the witness stand: I showed the note to the stranger and he took it from me."

"You should have insisted he return it."

Cornelia's fingers tightened around the luggage handle. "I told you, I did not think it would have any importance, since it was all a dreadful mistake."

"Oh, Cornelia, if only—"

"If only," Cornelia echoed in exasperation. "If only. It does not do any good fretting about something that is already done. So quit worrying. As soon as Paxton shows improvement, I intend to return and exonerate myself. Then everything will return to normal, the way it should be. Linley and I will be remarried and I shall be able to get on with my life."

Not waiting for her friend to protest further, Cornelia toted her bag from the bedroom. She closed the door behind her, effectively shutting out Lucretia's protests, and went outside in the morning sun to wait for her father to bring the family carriage around. For the first time in months, her life was filled with direction again and she was resolved not to be deterred.

As the carriage jolted and jarred along the neat tree-lined street toward the train depot, Cornelia's withered mother kept her eyes downcast and maintained a silent frown. Her father wore a tight-lipped expression, and though he made no effort to respond to Cornelia's attempts to carry on a conversation, he winked over her mother's head.

Cornelia knew her mother had taken her back into the family home despite the disappointment she felt. Her mother did not believe her any more than the rest of the community. At least her father had not deserted her, although she knew he would not openly support her against her mother.

The brilliant sun glinted off the train engine as they approached the station. Cornelia brightened when she caught sight of her brother sitting on a bench, waiting. Despite his growing weakness, Paxton had insisted on making the last-minute prepara-

13

tions and doing the necessary errands. He had always stood up for her, and now he was the only one who truly believed her story. He had stood by her in her time of need, and she would stand by him in his, regardless of what others thought.

Not waiting for her parents to accompany her to the train, Cornelia alighted from the carriage the instant it stopped. She lifted her skirts and ran toward the emaciated shadow of a man who rose, leaning heavily on a cane, and opened thin arms to receive her.

Cornelia flew into Paxton's embrace and hugged him. He wheezed before choking spasms racked his chest. She was patting him on the back in an attempt to help him catch his breath as their parents joined them.

"Won't you listen to reason, Paxton?" Hattie Potter Lloyd reached a gloved hand to caress his hollow cheek. "When you returned from Europe a couple of weeks ago, I thought you had finally come to your senses and realized that you belong at home with your family where you can be cared for properly. You are much too ill to make this trip. If you stay home, when you start feeling better you can return to your studio and start painting again. I've kept it just the way you left it, Son."

Cornelia garnered her last ounce of fortitude. She had always been the pliant daughter, acceding to her mother's wishes without question until now. A measure of guilt assailed her and she had to fight against the urge to beg her forgiveness.

"Please try to understand, Mother. Paxton and I are making this trip because he is ill. We are going for what I read is the 'camp cure.' The dry climate in Colorado will help him grow strong again so he can return to his painting. And we do not need money. I am using the money Grandmother Potter left me to support us while we are there."

Jonathon Lloyd cleared his throat. "You know this is difficult for your mother." To Cornelia's crestfallen look of pain, he added, "Perhaps if you had allowed your mother to try to get you and Linley together like she wanted to, this trip would not be necessary."

"Listen to your father and repent this shameless behavior before it is too late," Hattie urged.

Cornelia felt the urge to break down and cry. But in her heart she knew that taking Paxton to Colorado was the right thing. So she fought back the tears and raised her chin.

"I have done nothing to be ashamed of, Mother."

"Nothing to be ashamed of?" Hattie Lloyd cried. "It is bad enough you refuse to beg Linley, God bless his noble heart for standing against the community for as long as he did, to take you back, but to deny your guilt, before God no less. It is a sin!"

Jonathon grasped his wife's arm. Although he secretly was glad and prayed his daughter knew it, he had learned long ago what hell his life could be if he went openly against his wife where the children were concerned. "Hattie, perhaps it would be best if Cornelia went away for a while."

Her eyes blazing, Hattie swung on her husband. "If she leaves, she won't be able to make amends to Linley before God and the community. And why must she take Paxton away with her?"

Noting Cornelia's tightening lips, Paxton said, "Mother, I asked Cornelia to accompany me. She has been kind enough to set aside her own troubles to offer me her help. The least we can do is to continue to support her."

Hattie's face colored, and Jonathon put his arms

around his wife to offer his comfort. "We have supported Cornelia through this terrible ordeal."

"Of course you have, Mother," Cornelia said.

"Then don't you think you should have some consideration for your poor mother?" she barked out. "Do you want me to lose both my children?"

Cornelia dropped her eyes. "No."

Paxton was amazed at Cornelia's forgiving nature in face of such an indictment. Although he knew his mother wasn't to be blamed for her intolerance—she was a product of the community—he was not going to allow her to continue to rule Cornelia's life by wielding platitudes of guilt.

Just then the train whistle sounded.

Saved from what was becoming an increasingly difficult scene, Paxton urged, "Come along, Cornelia, we'd best board."

Cornelia glanced at her parents. Their faces beseeched her to remain. Her vision trailed to Paxton. He, too, was relying on her. He had supported her and now she must offer him her support. Despite a last stab of guilt, she was going to accompany him to Colorado. Her parents were just going to have to understand. Of course, once Paxton returned, cured, she was certain they would thank her.

Realizing the futility of trying to change her children's minds, Hattie begrudgingly relented at the silent pleading in her husband's eyes and hugged Cornelia to her bosom. "In spite of everything, we do love you, child. Take good care of your brother."

"I shall. And don't worry. By the time Paxton and I return, I'm sure Linley will have come to realize that this dreadful muddle was nothing more than a terrible mistake. Then we shall be together once again," she said bravely.

16

"When are we going to be together openly?" demanded Margo, wrapping her generous thighs around Linley's naked flesh. She nibbled on his ear. "I am tired of sneaking around."

"It won't be long, Margo, honey." Linley groaned and squeezed her overripe breasts. "I divorced my wife, didn't I?"

"Yes, but I am getting tired of waiting."

"Quit worrying. Now, no more talking. Put those delightful little fingers around me the way I like and show me how much you love me."

Margo giggled and edged down over Linley's ready body, her auburn curls draped over her head. She stroked him. "This is only the beginning," she cooed.

"This is going to be a fresh beginning for both of us," Paxton said as they found their seats on board the train.

"Yes, a fresh beginning," Cornelia echoed.

Cornelia settled next to Paxton and directed her attention out the train window. Her heart pounded with a mixture of sorrow and excitement. She looked back toward the little town that had always sheltered her. The quaint village was her past. Then she directed her attention westward. Out there, in the west, was her present. She had made a difficult decision, but she had no regrets. She only wished that she was as sure of her future as she had led her friend Lucretia to believe.

The train gave a jerk. They were underway. Cornelia opened the window and leaned out. Her parents were huddled together, waving. She waved back before a cloud of steam billowed from the engine and created a heavy fog, which swirled up and encased the aging couple who were now clinging together and shaking their heads.

Cornelia settled in her seat, leaned back, and closed her eyes.

"I think Father would like to have taken your side this time," Paxton offered.

"Yes," she replied and said no more. What else could be said? Her father had never crossed her mother in his life.

Cornelia took a deep breath. She was going to see to it that Paxton found his health again, and then she was going to return and pull her own life back together. Her dear sweet Linley would take her back, and she would make her parents proud again.

Chapter Three

When Cornelia had helped Paxton disembark from the train, she looked about the station that was was abustle with activity. Despite her troubles she felt a renewed energy and vitality fill her as she thought about the train trip.

The trip westward had been uneventful. Every mile of track had proved a healing balm to Cornelia. No silent, accusing eyes had stared at her. No one had whispered about her behind raised palms. No one had refused to acknowledge her presence, and she had been welcomed into conversations and treated with the same respect she had been afforded before the divorce.

"Cornelia, are you listening to me?" Paxton asked, interrupting Cornelia's reflections.

"Oh, sorry. Guess I was woolgathering."

"Now that you are finished, go hail a carriage while I see to the luggage."

"Why don't you sit over there—" Cornelia motioned to a bench against the wall "—and allow me to start taking care of you for a change?"

19

"I am not a total invalid. I'm afraid if you have your way, you'll pamper me right into a wheelchair before long." He laughed at her shocked expression.

"I want to take care of you," she protested. She felt a new strength, a surge of independent determination and pride overtake her. She was going to take care of her brother and demonstrate to her family that she was capable!

"By coming here with me you *are* taking care of me. But do try to allow me to keep active. You know I have never been able to sit still for long, and I intend to regain my health very soon."

"All right, if you insist. You can see to the baggage while I hail a carriage to take us to a hotel so you can rest."

Her spirits lifted by her brother's tenacity to get well, Cornelia trotted off, oblivious to the hustle and bustle of her surroundings.

Next to the station, the swarm of carriages dwindled fast as harried passengers claimed them and hurried off toward their destinations. Watching the carriages engaged and depart from the station one by one, Cornelia stepped up her pace. There was only one coach remaining as she neared the platform and she rushed toward it.

From the facing direction, Locke Breckenridge was also rushing toward the only available coach. He was anxious to get back to his mountain retreat after making a final, necessary trip to Denver to pick up the last of his belongings that he had sent for. Nearly dropping one of his bags, Locke cursed his luck that his sister had sent more than he could pack on his waiting horse, forcing him to hire a coach.

"Oh!" Cornelia cried as she found herself suddenly slammed to the ground.

The unexpected impact sent Locke's burdens flying, causing him to lose his balance. He swayed precariously before he went down with an "oof."

The wind was knocked out of Cornelia. She blinked at the heavy burden that lay on top of her, pinning down her heaving bosom. The warmest brown eyes speckled with silver flecks stared back at her. She was momentarily taken aback by the strength of the features and the perfection with which the line of jaw and nose had been drawn until she attempted to take another breath and found the man's weight made it very difficult.

"Get off me, you imbecile," she snapped and tried to push against the broad width of hard chest pinning her beneath him.

"As long as you put it so politely, how can I refuse?" He gave her an easy grin that featured a deep set of dimples as he crawled to his knees and retrieved his hat.

Cornelia sat up and filled her lungs with air. She smoothed down her skirt and straightened her hat. "Why didn't you watch where you were going?" she demanded, forcing herself to ignore his enticing, white-toothed smile.

He cocked his brow, and she noticed that he, too, had a cleft in his chin. "I was quite cognizant of the direction in which I was heading."

"Then I certainly hope that in the future you will be even more *cognizant* of your surroundings, or do you make a habit of accosting poor unsuspecting ladies who have the misfortune to be in the same general area?"

To Cornelia's consternation, the man threw back his head and laughed in response. "What is so amusing?" she demanded.

Locke immediately sobered. "One never knows when one might run into a pretty lady, but I never

21

thought about it in terms of such a literal nature before." He climbed to his feet and offered a hand. "Miss?"

His referral to her as "miss" made Cornelia glide her fingers along her ring finger, and a wave of sadness washed over her. The simple gold band no longer adorned her left hand; Linley had demanded its return after the divorce. Her gaze shot down to where a white strip of skin bespoke of her recent change in marital status, and her momentary thoughts of the man standing over her as attractive faded from her mind.

"I can manage."

Despite the lady's insistence, Locke was a gentleman. There was something about her expression that gave him pause. A certain vulnerability encased within a hard veneer stopped him from simply leaving her where she sat.

Over her protests, he helped her to her feet. The lady's hand was warm, smooth, and inviting. For an instant he was reminded of the first time he had touched his ex-wife, which caused Locke to release her and step back. He studied her thin figure. She looked nothing like Margaret, but her touch momentarily reminded him of the reason why he had left Leadville and moved to Estes Park: to get away from all women. With that in mind, Locke turned from the lady toward the coach.

Cornelia was an astute observer and wondered about the pain she noticed flicker in the man's eyes before she realized what he was about.

The tall, ebony-haired stranger built like the towering pines that grew along the Colorado hillsides was going to try to engage the last remaining coach!

She surged forward and tried to elbow past the man. He was not going to reach the coach first if she could stop him! She needed that coach for Paxton; he had looked so exhausted despite the brave front he tried to set forth, and she was determined to get him to the hotel as soon as possible.

"What do you think you are trying to do? That is my coach," she called out. "Find yourself another one." She inched past him.

"Only if you get there first," he said in response to her order. He moved forward, past the insistent woman.

Whatever had made him think that pushy broad was a cultured lady, he could not fathom!

"I knew you weren't a gentleman," she hissed to his back and stepped up her efforts to get to the coach before the frontier bully.

"Look, lady, why can't we share the coach?" Locke stopped and offered to end what was becoming a contest.

Cornelia also stopped. Other passengers passed her as she moved toward the irritating man to put an end to the exchange once and for all. "There is not enough room."

"You don't look like you'd take up that much space, such a scrawny, little thing like you," he said and gave her a grinning perusal.

"Scrawny little thing?" she echoed. Cornelia sucked in her cheeks. She was not used to being inspected as if she were a wanting round of cheese. Marriage to Linley had protected her from men as brazen as the one who stood before her now.

"Well, actually, with a little meat on your bones, you probably wouldn't be half bad."

"How dare you refer to my anatomy!"

Locke studied her for a moment. Despite knowing he had forgotten himself, Locke found he enjoyed engaging horns with the woman. "I beg your pardon.

It seems I forgot myself. Meat or no meat wouldn't amend your disposition."

She crossed her arms over her chest as she had seen her mother do hundreds of times when the woman expected and got her own way. "Are you going to do the gentlemanly thing and wait for the next coach or not?"

Locke's eyes shot past the lady for an instant before he returned his attention to her. His dimples never once disappeared when he said, "If you insist."

Cornelia straightened her stance. She was proud that she had taken the initiative and faced down the stranger. It was a good feeling, to speak her own mind without regard that she had said the wrong thing and Linley would disapprove as he had so often during their marriage.

Cornelia raised her chin in triumph. "It is about time."

As she pivoted around to claim her rightful acquisition, her radiant inner glow of success faded and was replaced with disbelief, then fury.

Her victory had been short-lived. One of the passengers who had passed her while she was distracted by exchanging insults with the stranger had just engaged the last coach!

Her fists balled, her teeth clenched, and her face took on a heated flush as she slowly pivoted back to the man. Her eyes fastened on the crater in his chin, she saw him shrug his shoulders. Before words befitting the situation formed on her tongue, she blurted out, "How could you?"

"How could I what?" the man answered.

"How could you what?" she echoed, her voice squeaking in disbelief. "You let someone else claim the last coach after you so *graciously* agreed that I could have it."

24

The woman was blaming him for missing the coach! What nerve!

"Lady, if you hadn't spent so much time berating me for something I have no control over, you probably wouldn't have missed your precious coach. You have no one to blame but yourself."

"I have you to blame!" she retorted and crossed her arms over her chest again. To her added fury, the man nodded with a mock tip of his hat, picked up his bags, and sauntered away. "Where are you going?"

He threw back over his shoulder, "To my hotel."

"What am I to do now?"

"I'd say you'll have to wait for the next coach."

"You are intolerably rude, sir!"

Locke shrugged. "Some think so, some don't. At least you won't have to concern yourself with my intolerable rudeness any longer," he drawled with all due sweetness and left the woman to stew. Why he had ever given even a passing thought to such a disagreeable woman he'd never know. Thank goodness he would never see her again!

Minus a victory over the stranger as well as a victory of securing the last coach, Cornelia stood at the end of the platform alone, perplexed as to what to do next.

She was still standing there fuming over the nerve of the stranger when Paxton, followed by a boy carting their bags, joined her.

"Where is the carriage?" he asked before he noticed his sister's flushed face. "That bad, huh?"

"Worse."

"Anything I can do to help?"

"Not unless you care to lend me a gun."

"I beg your pardon?" he said, quite perplexed by Cornelia's sudden strange behavior. She had always been a lady of the most proper decorum and even temper. Now, he had to admit to himself, he rather found the emerging streak of independence Cornelia had recently begun to display a most refreshing bit of behavior.

"Cornelia?" he prompted when she did not respond.

She snapped her attention away from her murderous thoughts. "Yes?"

"Would you care to explain your comment about a gun?" he asked.

She cast him a sheepish look. "It was nothing, really."

"It didn't have anything to do with Linley, did it?"

"Of course not! Although I may be divorced legally, I continue to consider myself married in the eyes of God. As soon as we return home, I intend to make sure Linley realizes what a dreadful mistake our divorce was. Once he does, we shall be remarried and my life will return to normal again."

Paxton kept his face impassive although secretly he did not like Linley, never had. Though he would never admit it to Cornelia, the reason he had let her talk him into coming to Colorado had been his hope that she would forget the wastrel and start a new life away from their mother's urgings to return to the man.

"Yes, well, in that case where is the coach?" he asked, the conversation having come full circle.

"The coach?"

"Yes. Remember, I was to collect the luggage while you went for a coach to take us to the hotel."

"Yes, I remember. Unfortunately, before I could reach the last available carriage, some frontier bully claimed it. I am sorry, Paxton. I fear we shall be forced to wait until the next one arrives."

Paxton gave a laugh, but the effort sent him into a coughing spell. Cornelia quickly paid the boy and sent him away. She arranged their bags near where the carriages would return and had her brother perch atop the luggage so he could rest.

Once she got Paxton settled and the strangling spasms had subsided, she left him to search for a restaurant at the station to get him something refreshing and hot to drink.

She hunted up a restaurant and then waited for the waitress to fill her order, all the while silently cursing the stranger who had delayed their departure from the station. At the same time she was grateful that she would not have to be subjected to that horrid bully again!

After she returned to her brother, they waited over an hour for another coach, and finally they were on their way to the hotel. Cornelia let the unsettling incident with the man drop into the back of her mind as the coach rocked along Seventeenth Street from the train depot toward the hotel.

Denver was a magnificent city and she was charmed by the civilization out west. The multistoried brick buildings impressed her, and the sheer sprawl held her in awe. Only the vast numbers of street urchins gave her pause, but she forced them from her mind; she had a mission and that was to focus her attention on her brother's needs.

The air was dry and the streets had been sprinkled to keep the dust settled. Once she had Paxton in the fresh mountain air, he would be in the proper surroundings to restore his health. Her hope for his recovery buoyed, Cornelia leaned back in her seat.

A couple of nights' rest at the hotel and Paxton could continue their trip. They would both be refreshed. She had made reservations at a fine hotel where the clientele was only the most refined and she and Paxton need not concern themselves with any more unpleasantries before embarking on the last leg of their journey.

Chapter Four

Locke had to trudge nearly a half mile, toting his heavy load, before he was able to locate a carriage to carry his possessions to the hotel where he was staying. All he could think of as the carriage rolled through town was getting back to his mountain retreat and out of the aristocratic city plagued with black smoke and coal dust, which often obscured the view of the mountains.

As the carriage lumbered along the street toward the hotel, Locke glanced out the window at the distant mountains now visible. Those peaks conjured up memories of how he had ended up living alone in a mountain cabin. Locked leaned back and shut his eyes as those thoughts clarified in his mind.

He had spent five years with Margaret in Leadville attending fancy social balls while she tried to outdo all other society matrons. It was a life he had endured until the breakup of his marriage two years ago. Afterward, the desire he had always had to experience life far away from the turmoil could not be ignored and he had left his business to be overseen by his sister and set out away from civilization.

The carriage jarred to a halt, forcing Locke back

from his musings as the driver's deep voice assaulted his ears. "Here we are, sir."

Locke gave the driver a good tip and instructed him to see to his horse. He collected the key to his room, then hunted up a bellboy to take care of his baggage.

Not more than two hours later, as Locke walked through the lobby, he nearly tripped over a frail man's cane.

Paxton had noticed the big man dressed in leather pants, a plain white shirt, and fringed jacket just in time to be spared being knocked to the ground by the man.

"Sorry. Are you all right?" Locke asked, cursing his luck for the second time today.

"Yes, I am fine," returned Paxton leaning heavily on the cane. "I apologize for nearly causing you a mishap. I am afraid being an invalid of sorts is still quite new to me."

Locke immediately liked the man. "I have to say that I fared better this time than I did earlier." To the man's look of questioning confusion, Locke elaborated. "I was knocked off my feet earlier by one of the most unpleasant woman I have ever had the misfortune to come in contact with. Then, to add insult to injury, she proceeded to accuse me of purposely attempting to accost her."

As Paxton listened to the man relate his story, Paxton found a growing sense of camaraderie. "Sounds like you have had quite a morning."

"That's for sure. But that is not the all of it."

"I was just going into the dining room for a cup of coffee, would you care to join me?"

"I could use a glass of something cold to help cool me down."

"Good. Then you can tell me the rest of what happened." Paxton held out an unsteady hand. "The name's Paxton Lloyd."

Locke nodded, pumping Paxton's hand. "Locke Breckenridge."

Locke had immediately taken a liking to the man and found that despite Paxton Lloyd's obvious illness, he had a firm handshake, which Locke had always considered a sign of a good man.

Paxton, too, judged a man by the strength of his handshake. Locke Breckenridge was no pantywaist. This man was so unlike his brother-in-law, who had presented Paxton with a limp hand when they were introduced. Paxton's regard grew for this Westerner. And the thought assailed him that his sister would probably find Locke Breckenridge a refreshing change from the men back East.

Locke swung out his arm. "Lead the way."

The two men settled at a table in the corner of the tidy little dining room and placed their orders. They exchanged small talk, Paxton relating the story of his illness and how his sister had brought him west, Locke only describing his mountain retreat, carefully not mentioning the details of his life.

When Paxton learned that they would be neighbors, he was delighted and promptly invited Locke to visit him and his sister once they were settled.

Once their orders had arrived, Paxton took a sip of his coffee, set it down, and leaned his elbows against the table. "I am waiting to hear the rest of what happened with that bossy lady you encountered this morning. By the way, where did all this take place? If it was here at the hotel, I had best be on the lookout. I wouldn't want her to try to run me down in my condition. I might not be able to get out of the way in time."

Locke laughed at Paxton's sense of humor. "You

31

needn't worry about that. It occurred back at the train depot."

"My sister and I came in just this morning. I suppose we were lucky we didn't run into her there."

"That's for sure," concurred Locke, who was beginning to see the humor in the whole episode now that he had time and distance between himself and the incident.

"You must finish telling me your tale. You have captured my interest now," Paxton urged, his interest piqued after hearing that the man's misadventure had occurred at the train station.

"Sure you want to hear about it? It seems of little importance now."

"Positive," Paxton answered, leaning on his palm.

"Well, after the pushy broad proceeded to argue with me over whose fault it was, she continued to lambaste me and demanded that the last available coach was hers, can you imagine?"

Paxton leaned forward now and nodded. "I am definitely beginning to be able to." There was suddenly something strangely familiar about the tale Locke was relating. Surely it was no more than a coincidence. "What did you do?" Paxton asked, keenly interested in Locke's answer.

"I did the gentlemanly thing and deferred. But do you think that satisfied her? Oh, no, not that broad. Another passenger engaged the carriage while she was busy trying to shred me with her sharp tongue, and the broad goes and blames me for that, too!"

The two men chuckled together. But Paxton was certain that Locke was enjoying his tale much more than Paxton was. Paxton now had quite a different vision of the entire incident.

Paxton listened patiently as Locke finished his story with, "With her disposition, she is probably

32

still at the station waiting for another coach."

Curious about how Locke would answer his next question, Paxton leaned forward. "Was she as ugly as she sounds?"

Locke thought for a moment. "No, not actually."

"What, actually?"

"Why do you ask?"

Paxton was not expecting the question and was taken aback for an instant before he quickly recovered himself. "No reason, really. Just in case she shows up here, I wouldn't want to take the chance that she might run over me. If I know what she looks like, I might be able to get her first." He patted his cane. "If not, at least I'd be able to stay out of her way."

Locke found that amusing and let out a hearty laugh. "Can't blame you there. As scrawny as she was, she sure managed to pack quite a wallop. If she had a little meat on her bones, she probably wouldn't have been half bad looking."

"But what did she look like?" Paxton urged. He wanted Locke to confirm his suspicions.

"She had warm honey-brown hair and snapping green eyes, and the cutest upturned nose with a smattering of freckles. Pity she had such a rotten personality. Probably why the woman was still single."

"I see," Paxton said and scratched his head. The incident Cornelia had described to him earlier and the one Locke had just described were identical, only told from two very different points of view. There was no longer any doubt in his mind, the "pushy broad" Locke was talking about was Cornelia.

"Why don't you and your sister join me for supper tonight? I'm not pulling out for home until tomorrow morning and I'd like the company."

"My sister made me promise to rest tonight. You see, I convinced her to leave for Estes Park tomorrow morning, and she worries about me."

Locke usually traveled alone; he liked the freedom of his own company. But he also liked Paxton Lloyd. Despite the man's illness, Paxton possessed a positive attitude and a quest to experience all the glorious things that Locke had already found the West possessed. So before he could catch himself, Locke said, "Since our destinations are the same and we both plan to leave tomorrow morning, why don't we travel together? It will save you some of the expense, and I'll have the pleasure of your company, and that of your sister as well, of course."

"The pleasure of Cornelia's company," Paxton muttered under his breath. "That truly might be interesting, if not entertaining."

"Beg your pardon?"

Paxton hid the calculating smile lurking about his lips. "My sister and I shall be delighted to join you in the morning. What time would you like us to be ready?"

Locke's estimation of the man grew further. Paxton Lloyd and his sister would not keep him waiting for hours in the morning. Locke stood, a big smile on his face as he offered his hand. "I'm glad we met. I look forward to meeting your sister. See you out in front of the hotel at six."

"Six it is. We'll be ready."

"Good."

Paxton watched Locke stride from the room and for the first time, noticed the six-shooter strapped to the man's hip. From the description Locke had offered about his encounter with Cornelia, Paxton wondered why he hadn't threatened to use the gun on his sister. Because Locke Breckenridge was a true gentleman underneath his hard exterior, that was why. The realization made Paxton smile. Tomorrow morning certainly was going to be the beginning of a most interesting journey.

Paxton drank the rest of his coffee before he returned to his room, humming to himself. He had always enjoyed a challenge, and this trip just might prove to be as beneficial to Cornelia's health as it would be to his.

Cornelia and Paxton were out in front of the hotel and waiting a half hour early. Cornelia stood shivering for ten minutes before she bundled Paxton back inside the hotel to wait while she returned outside. She had questioned the wisdom of traveling with a man Paxton had just met but had conceded to his wishes after a lengthy discussion. Since her brother had returned from Europe, he had not made many friends; people had shunned him because of his illness. Paxton was so excited about meeting the man in the hotel that she just could not refuse.

She inhaled the fresh early morning air. Paxton was certain to get well in such surroundings. The atmosphere was dry and fresh, and Paxton had already made a friend. Despite misgivings, Cornelia decided to give the man the benefit of a doubt. She owed Paxton that much. The man had to be a good man after Paxton had spent all evening singing his praises.

She had not been waiting more than another ten minutes when a man all bundled up and driving a wagon pulled up in front of the hotel. He climbed down and was tying the horses to the hitching post with his back to her when she approached him.

"Excuse me, I am Cornelia Talbot. Would you be

Mr. Locke Breckenridge, per chance, here to meet my brother, Paxton Lloyd and me?"

The big man wrapped up to his nose swung around as he removed his hat. When he caught sight of the lady, his wide smile immediately disappeared.

Cornelia, who also had been wearing a bright smile, lost her smile, too. "You! What are you doing here?" she demanded. A sudden concern overtook her that the man might have followed her to the hotel.

"I think the question should more appropriately be, what are *you* doing here?" he shot back.

Cornelia raised her chin. "My brother and I are meeting a Mr. Locke Breckenridge here shortly. If you will move your wagon out of the way so he will be able to load our luggage when he arrives, I shan't detain you any longer."

Locke's first inclination was to get back up onto the wagon box and drive as fast as he could away from the pair. But since he liked Paxton and they were going to be neighbors, he decided that he would make peace with the disagreeable young woman.

He studied her. So the "pushy broad" was the sister Paxton had raved about yesterday. Locke wondered if the man had any inkling that they had been speaking about the same woman. He thought about how he had described her and hoped the man had a sense of humor; it was certainly going to take one to make this trip!

"I'm afraid I'm not going to be leaving your sight any time soon," he said with a smirk.

"I thought I fully explained the necessity for you to move your wagon, Mr. —"

Locke plunked the hat back on his head. With a big, dimpled grin he said, "Mr. Breckenridge. Locke Breckenridge to be more precise."

The distinct feeling of horror spread through Cornelia's veins. *"You* can't be Locke Breckenridge!"

"Well, afraid last time I looked, I was," he drawled.

The scene at the train depot rose up before her. "There must be some dreadful mistake," she cried.

"Can't say as I disagree with you about that. But fact is, I am Locke Breckenridge and you have to be Cornelia, Paxton's sister."

She wanted to choke the intolerable grinning brute. "If you had been listening earlier, I did mention my name." He merely smiled at her, which caused her to pinch her lips. "Are you sure you are Locke Breckenridge?"

"One and the same." He motioned to her bags. "Those the bags I am to load?"

"Yes . . . ah, no. I mean no!" she practically shouted. "Paxton and I are not going anywhere with you!"

Locke leaned against the wagon wheel. "Suit yourself."

Cornelia swung around to confront her brother and caught sight of him coming out of the hotel to join her. "Oh, I see you two have already met. Are we ready to leave?" he said with an air of innocence.

"No," Cornelia said flatly. She pointed an accusing finger toward Locke. "That is the man from the train station whom I told you about. We aren't going anywhere with him!"

"Didn't you ever learn it's not polite to point?" Locke interjected.

She sent Locke a daunting look, then settled her frown on Paxton. "You didn't know anything about this, did you?" she probed.

"Of course not," he lied. He was not about to admit to his treachery or she would never relent, and he

37

did not want to lose a friendship he had just made.

Paxton's face fell into a forlorn expression. That always worked to get his own way with Cornelia. Once he was sure that Cornelia had reaped the full benefit of his pitiable look, he turned to Locke. "You mean my sister is the 'pushy broad'?"

Cornelia gasped and watched Locke's impassive mien. *"Pushy broad?* You referred to me with as a 'pushy broad'!"

He shrugged. "I'd say, if the shoe fits . . ."

Paxton was enjoying watching the fight come into Cornelia's eyes. "You did refer to Locke as a 'frontier bully,' if I recall correctly, didn't you, Nellie?"

Horrified at her brother's revelation, Cornelia shot Locke a glance of mortification.

"I'd say I was much more accurate in my assessment," Locke crooned.

"Why you —" She broke off and stormed back inside the hotel with Paxton trailing on her heels.

Cornelia stomped up to the desk and demanded their rooms back. To her added horror, the clerk informed her that he had already given their rooms away and the hotel was full.

"Cornelia, do try to be reasonable. Locke is going to be our neighbor, so don't you think it would be a good idea if you two made peace?" Paxton said and was grabbed by a choking cough.

Although Cornelia would have preferred to hunt around for another hotel, she could see her brother tiring. And he had looked so disappointed and crestfallen. His health was more important than her personal feelings toward that frontier bully. Paxton's needs came first.

She patted him on the back. "I suppose I was a little hasty calling the man a frontier bully," she conceded for Paxton's benefit. "Of course, we'll be able to come to some sort of satisfactory agreement."

"Then you no longer object to traveling with Locke? After all, he is the first friend I've made since returning from Europe."

She could not let Paxton down. Admitting defeat, she took his arm and helped him toward the door. There she adjusted his scarf more snugly around his neck. "Don't worry yourself, I am certain Mr. Breckenridge and I will be able to come to a mutual understanding. After all, we must get you settled so you can get lots of rest and grow strong again," she said sweetly. Secretly, she dreaded the journey ahead with that insufferable bully and worried that what the trip held in store would not be to her liking.

Chapter Five

Cornelia was grateful that the weather cooperated. Once the sun rose, it was no longer cold and Cornelia left the wagon seat where she had been boxed in between Paxton and Locke. Locke's hard-muscled leg had been pressed warmly against hers, and she had no desire to sit so close to a man who caused her pulse to beat so irregularly.

She walked alongside the slow-moving wagon, taking in the flat stretches of land bursting with grasses and blooming wildflowers. The mountain peaks blanketed with snow glistened fresh and clean, and gave her downtrodden spirit a sense of being cleansed.

Locke, too, had felt the warmth pressed against his leg and was relieved when she left the wagon — at first. He was beginning to feel that her assessment of him as a "frontier bully" might have some accuracy. A gentleman did not allow a lady to walk. "Will you take the reins?" he asked Paxton.

Paxton had noticed Locke sneak glimpses at his sister out of the corner of his eye for some time. Secretly, it gratified him. "Of course. But I warn you, if you are thinking of joining my sister, you have your work cut out for you."

"I only want to be neighborly. I don't plan on trying to court the lady."

Paxton laughed. He thought briefly about warning Locke that Cornelia had been deeply hurt, which was undoubtedly the reason why she had her defenses up around anyone of the male gender, but something held him back. If Cornelia wished to share her pain with anyone, she would when she was ready. Of course, he felt it was his duty as her older brother to watch out for her and if she needed a nudge, he would be there to provide it.

Cornelia had been enjoying her walk until the male presence fell in step beside her. She attempted to focus her attention on the countryside, but the man's nearness made it impossible. So she forced herself to not look at him.

His hands shoved into his pockets, Locke walked quietly by her side for some time. Finally, when it became obvious she was not going to acknowledge his presence, he said, "Thought you might like some company."

"Mr. Breckenridge—"

"Locke, please."

Back home, Cornelia would not have considered calling the man by his given name. She hesitated.

"You needn't worry if you are concerned that my intentions are to further our relationship beyond your being the relative of a new acquaintance of mine."

For an instant, Cornelia was taken by surprise at his need to mention his intentions toward her, but she quickly recovered. She was being silly. Of course, he had no interest in her. "Well, I suppose there would be no harm in using your given name. But do not think that I have any intention of forgetting your unforgivable behavior at the train depot."

Locke tipped his hat. "I would never think of asking you to overlook such behavior on my part . . . Miss Cornelia."

"You may drop the use of Miss," she said, uncomfortable with the misnomer and not about to offer an explanation of why.

"If it pleases you, Cornelia."

"It does."

For some reason, she was sure he was trying to goad her, but for the life of her she could not figure what kind of ulterior motive he had in mind—that was, until they stopped for the evening. Cornelia had expected to spend the night at an inn or some other accommodation. Learning they would be camping out in the middle of nowhere was a complete surprise, but she sagely kept her tongue despite her rising ire.

Locke unharnessed the horses, watered, and hobbled them while Cornelia collected a stack of blankets and got Paxton settled against four rocks grouped at right angles around their campsite. Cornelia then settled down next to Paxton and watched Locke build a fire.

"What are you fixing for supper?" she asked the second time her stomach issued a rolling growl.

Locked looked up. The gall of her! The soft city woman had been just sitting there for nearly an hour while he readied their camp for the night. But then, he hadn't bothered to tell her that Paxton had requested that they camp out under the stars instead of staying at a roadside inn as was Locke's usual custom on his trips to Denver.

Locke's gaze trailed to the man. "Paxton, didn't you explain to your sister what we discussed earlier?"

Cornelia shot Paxton a look filled with suspicion. He slouched down, warning her that she probably was not going to like what was about to come. Taking a deep breath, she asked, "Paxton, would you care to explain what Locke is referring to?"

Paxton's eyes shifted from Cornelia to Locke and back again. "Not actually."

"Paxton?"

"I asked Locke if we could camp out," he admitted sheepishly. He went into a spasm of coughs before she could chide him.

"It's all right," she cooed, rubbing his back. "This might even be fun," she added less than enthusiastically. Once his chest quit heaving, she turned to Locke. "Paxton needs a hot meal."

"Then I guess you'd best get busy."

Cornelia climbed to her feet and faced the man. "I beg your pardon."

"No need. The gear you require is in the wagon."

"Gear?"

"To cook supper with. Your brother offered your services until we get to Longmont."

"My services?" she said and swung Paxton an annoyed frown.

"Paxton wanted to camp out, so we made a deal."

"Cornelia, I hope you don't mind. I wanted to experience sleeping out under the stars and knew that you would never stand for it, so Locke and I reached an agreement," Paxton informed her repentantly.

"An agreement?" she huffed out.

"I agreed to make camp if Paxton had you do the cooking," Locke supplied with a grin that told her he had no intention of making any other arrangements.

Cornelia's eyes rounded. "Is that true, Paxton?"

Paxton gave another round of coughing before he managed to say, "Nellie, it is the least we can do since Locke has been so gracious as to provide the transportation."

"Gracious?" she muttered.

"Yes, gracious," Locke reiterated, then smiled. "Nellie. I like that better than Cornelia. Sounds much more down to earth, like someone you would expect to find cooking out under the stars for her ailing brother if he asked."

Cornelia's lips tightened in defeat. Arguing over her name was not worth the effort since it was quite apparent the man was used to having his way. She had no desire to cook for him, but she could not refuse Paxton; Paxton knew it and that frontier bully knew it, too. "If you'll be patient, supper will be ready as soon as possible."

She expected Locke to sit back and watch her struggle as she yanked the supplies from the back of the wagon. To her surprise, he was right behind her, helping her unload the heavy crate.

"Where do you want me to put this?" he asked, holding the crate.

Her smile was playful when she muttered, "You need to ask?"

"I'll rephrase the question since I would not want to put a lady such as yourself in the position of having to describe the part of anatomy I have the feeling you were alluding to." At her look of shock, he asked, "Do you want it over by the fire?"

"That will be fine."

To her further amazement, he proceeded to help during all the preparations. And what was more, Cornelia realized that the man did indeed have a better side, despite her earlier assessment of him as a two-dimensional character past redemption.

Cornelia fixed Paxton a plate of beans, bread, and bacon, then took a seat next to him. In companionable silence they ate. Locke stared across the fire at the pair. He liked Paxton Lloyd and at odd moments

44

found the man's disagreeable, pushy sister quite human. It was those other times in which he had encountered her that made him understand why the woman was still single: she was two different women rolled into one.

The next morning they passed the town of Boulder, and Cornelia gritted out, "Why didn't we just travel a few miles farther last night and stay at one of the inns? We were so close."

"Yes, I know we were," Locke said.

"Then, why did we *all* have to camp out on the cold, hard ground?"

"Thought you might enjoy it."

Whatever had given her the idea that he had any redeemable qualities? She sucked in her cheeks rather than give that horrible man the satisfaction of seeing her lose her control. Instead she smiled sweetly. "I did, actually. Thank you for the experience." Then she climbed down from the wagon and scampered away before he could respond.

The remainder of the trip went without incident. Cornelia made every effort to be civil to Locke Breckenridge because her brother found the man interesting, but she silently vowed to keep her distance once they were settled at Estes Park; she did not need to endure the man's questioning gaze any longer than necessary.

To her relief, once they reached Longmont, Locke Breckenridge left them at a delightful inn and continued his journey alone. Paxton had tired and needed several days to recuperate, and Cornelia needed to stay away from Locke.

At the St. Vrain Hotel, Paxton encountered his old friend Lord Dunraven, who, to Paxton's delight, had invited them to be his guests at his home in Estes Park, where he'd taken up residence years ago.

From Longmont, it took them a day's journey by stage to travel up the mountain to Estes Park. Paxton seemed to be in his glory sharing times past with Lord Dunraven while all Cornelia could think of was getting to their destination away from the black flies and soaking the blisters she was certain adorned her backside from such a jarring trip.

Estes Park exceeded all her hopes for Paxton. It was grandeur with its winding river and far-reaching pines, and there was health in every breath of fresh air.

Lord Dunraven's lodge was a sprawling single-story affair, and Cornelia was pleased that, although she and her brother had chosen this wilderness site, they did not have to reside in some canvas tent.

She got Paxton settled in a delightful four-room cottage complete with pianoforte next to the main lodge so he could rest and then went back to the main house to join the earl.

Lord Dunraven was sitting on a porch swing, enjoying a smoke. "Your brother looks a little worse for wear. Colorado will do him a world of wonders, you'll see."

"I hope so. You know, he has always taken care of me. I hope I can take good care of him." She paused for a moment and took a chair near the swing. "I do want to thank you for your offer of hospitality."

"Think nothing of it. I enjoy the company. And you know, Paxton and I have a lot in common. We met while hunting in Africa."

Cornelia listened politely to the earl's tale although she did not have the stomach to harm any of God's creatures and was glad when he was called away. Before he left her, he suggested, "Why don't you enjoy a tour of the estate? The weather is delightful."

"Yes, thank you, I think I shall." She watched the distinguished middle-aged gentleman head toward the barn. She had many questions to ask about how he had come to be at Estes Park and looked forward to enjoying the company of such a respected world traveler.

Cornelia went back to the cottage, got a shawl, and strolled from the house.

She marveled at the beauty of the valley nestled in the midst of high-rising mountains dotted with enormous pines. She walked to the edge of the Thompson River. The icy waters ran swift and deep. Turning from the bank of the river, she started picking wildflowers, following the clusters up the side of a hill.

A high-pitched whine assaulted her ears. Following the sounds of anguish of an animal in pain, she picked her way through the underbrush until she came to a clearing where a young mountain lion cub was caught in a trap.

"You poor little creature," she said and knelt down to help it, not giving thought to the fact that it was a wild animal and its mother was probably nearby. Using her shawl, she managed to pry open the jaws of the trap.

"What do you think you're doing?" Locke demanded, standing over her.

She was startled to hear the familiar voice. "What does it look like?"

Although Locke would have released the young animal, he watched the cub try to stand, then said, "It looks like you first try to break my neck in Denver and now you are trying your darndest to ruin some fool's livelihood." He did not mention his suspicions that the trap had been illegally placed on Dunraven's land since he knew how Dunraven felt about his private estate.

Cornelia got to her feet before the big man now dressed in buckskins and dropped balled fists on her hips. "If you mean that someone makes his livelihood from traps like that"—she pointed to the steel jaws "—the answer is yes. You aren't responsible for causing the creature's pain, are you?" she blurted out, not sure why it was important to hear that he could not do such a cruel thing.

"You can take the look of horror off your face. I don't trap animals."

"That, at least is a relief," she said sharply. Locke grinned at the lady with her hackles up and bent down and checked the cub's leg. "Looks like it has a broken leg."

Cornelia watched in horror as he took out his knife. "What do you think you are going to do with that? You aren't going to kill it, are you?"

"Quit worrying, I'm only going to cut a strip off your petticoat and—"

"You most certainly are not!" she screamed and jumped back.

"I would have thought you would prefer that I bandage the creature's leg rather than skin it."

Cornelia took a hesitant step forward. She tried to examine the creature's leg, but it swung at her, claws bared.

"Even though it's young, don't forget it is still a wild animal," he admonished.

She bristled that he could consider her to be without common sense. "I know that."

"What do you want me to do? Do I bandage the leg or skin it?"

"Don't be ridiculous, bandage it, of course."

When she just stood there, he prodded, "Well?"

"Well, what?"

"What are you standing there for, cut a strip off your petticoat."

"Then turn your back."

Locke rolled his eyes but complied. "However is a prude like you going to survive out here? This isn't one of your Eastern cities, you know."

Cornelia tore a length of petticoat and handed it to Locke. "How well I know. I can hardly wait to get back once Paxton is feeling better."

As she stood and watched the big man minister to the small creature with such gentleness, she had to admit that what she said was true: She could hardly wait to get back home. Despite the calming salve Colorado had been to her life, she had to get back and exonerate herself. She knew that her husband was home, facing the community by himself and pining away. She could not allow poor, dear Linley to bear the brunt of chastisement alone.

Chapter Six

Linley Horton Talbot, looking sad and forlorn, stood encircled by a cluster of society matrons. His narrow shoulders slumped forward, his weak chin pointed toward the ground, and his eyes were downcast.

"You must come to Sunday dinner, Linley. I know you could use a hot meal after what you've been through," Mildred Conover insisted. "You are looking much too thin and haggard, having to bear the brunt of Cornelia's sin all alone."

Linley heaved a deep sigh and shook his head. "It has been a difficult time, learning that Cornelia was not the sweet, innocent young woman I thought she was," he said.

"We were so wrong. Can you ever forgive us for not realizing what you have had to suffer with that scandalous woman for four years?" Mildred said and set a comforting hand on his shoulder.

He sent the circle of old biddies his most desolate look. "I was hoping Cornelia would reform."

"Of course you were, dear boy. Now, you will come for dinner Sunday? I won't take no for an answer."

From the size of the old crow, there was no doubt she was a good cook. And Linley always had enjoyed the meals Cornelia prepared. "I could use a hot meal—I'll be there. I must be going now. Thank you for all of your support during this painful time," he said and hurried up the gated drive toward his mother's foreboding mansion.

It had taken him nearly a year of planning, but Linley was sure he had seen to every detail. He was ready for the interview with his mother. This time he was sure he would succeed. This time his wealthy mother would not deny him the money from his father's estate that should have been his all along!

Instead of knocking at the heavy carved door as Linley had become accustomed to doing, he barged into the house, past the astonished butler, and into the opulent parlor where his mother regally sat behind his father's ornate walnut desk.

Mona Talbot raised silver-arched brows. "I see you are feeling more sure of yourself," she announced.

"It has been very difficult, but I am beginning to accept Cornelia's scandalous affair."

"No doubt such behavior is quite foreign to you," she commented with sarcasm.

Linley bit back a retort. "It has been foreign to most people in the community."

The silver-haired woman looked down her nose at her sniveling son. Cornelia was the best thing that had ever happened to the weakling, and Mona continued to have difficulty believing that such a dear girl like Cornelia could commit adultery. If only the girl hadn't left town.

"And what is it you want to speak with me about?"

"You might ask me to sit down first," he said. Gawd, how he hated standing at attention before the woman; it made him feel that she was holding court and he was just another one of her poor subjects.

"Sit if you must. But if you have come for some specific reason, I suggest you don't waste any more of my time."

Linley settled gingerly on the green leather couch and crossed his legs. "I—I thought that since I have truly tried to hold my marriage together and made every effort to fulfill the requirements of Father's will, you will set aside the requirement that I produce an heir. So—"

"So you thought you would come and beg that I release your inheritance. Is that correct?"

Linley frowned. The old hag was the most uncooperative person on the face of the earth! Even when he was growing up, it was his mother who curtailed his activities. He could manipulate his father but not the old hag who sat so regally before him now. "Well, yes. I think it is time that I get on with my life. I want to put Cornelia's sin behind me."

"Can't you get on with your life without tapping into your inheritance? Although I realize the idea is probably most *foreign* to you, you might try seeking gainful employment. You know that your father's will specifically states that you must produce an heir in order to inherit from his estate."

He ignored her suggestion that he work for a living. Working was for the lower classes, certainly not for a person of Linley's position in life. "I have tried to produce an heir for four years, but that barren, prudish woman I married could not give me an heir," he whined.

Mona rolled her eyes. "But you took care of that, didn't you?"

"Me? She was the one who strayed, not me!" he bellowed.

Mona huffed out an exasperated breath. "No. Of course not you, Linley."

"What about my inheritance?" he pressed. "I shall remarry and produce an heir. If you will read the fine print, the will specifically states that I had to have made an honest effort. I've done that, and the divorce clearly shows that what happened with Cornelia was not my fault."

"No doubt you have spent hours studying the document," she snapped, "as has that sleazy lawyer you hired to pay me a visit. You will not inherit your father's estate without an heir." She hesitated. She studied his trembling chin, wondering if there could have been a mix-up somehow when he was born. She truly could not understand how she could have produced such a weakling. But she had to face facts; Linley was her son. "I may consider releasing a portion of it after I have reviewed the final divorce decree. Bring me a copy of the decree to review," she said. She wanted nothing more than to end this disagreeable interview.

"I'll go directly to the court and get you a copy," he said and stood.

Without offering the customary good-byes, Linley left the old hag surrounded by her wealth and headed directly to the courthouse. Once he took care of the details, he would finally be free of perfect Little Miss Cornelia. Then he could be with Margo, produce an heir, and finally live in the style to which he was rightly entitled. He had had to do without for far too long with all Cornelia's frugal habits!

When Cornelia walked to the barn next to Dunraven's lodge with the mountain lion cub wrapped in her shawl in her arms, she was met by Dunraven's ranch manager.

"What do you be having there, ma'am?" the red-haired man crooned. Keeping his face impassive, Sean McCurdy gave Lord Dunraven's latest guest a very favorable assessment.

Cornelia scratched the cub behind the ears. "An injured mountain lion, sir?"

"Sean McCurdy, ma'am, his lordship's foreman," the brawny Irishman said. "And you be?"

"Cornelia Talbot."

"Such a pretty name for such a pretty lass." He expected her to practically swoon into his arms, and it annoyed him when it appeared that the fine lady was ignoring him for the lowly animal.

"Mr. McCurdy, could you find this cub a warm corner where it can mend? I released it from a trap nearby and it has been injured."

Carefully masking his irritation, since she had no doubt robbed one of his traps, he took the filthy little beast from the lady and, forcing a smile, said, "Don't you be worrying; I'll take proper care of it. Would you like to see where it'll be?" he asked, a sly smile spreading his lips.

Cornelia nodded and followed the man into the barn. She watched him settle the cub in a box. "However can I thank you?"

Sean leaned on a post next to Cornelia, blocking her exit. With a lazy grin curling his full lips, he said, "I'll be thinking of some way."

Cornelia fidgeted. The man made her feel instinctively uncomfortable, and he made no effort to step aside so she could pass.

He leaned closer toward her, and she could feel the crawling warmth of his moist breath on her neck. She glanced around him, looking for a way to flee when Paxton entered the barn.

"There you are," he said and came forward with great effort.

To her relief, Sean stepped back and went to greet her brother. Cornelia stared after the man. Despite her trepidation, she had to admit she was probably just being foolish, although something in the back of her mind warned her to be wary of him. He had a devil-may-care walk, a proud carriage, and he undressed a woman with those cold silver eyes of his. And worst of all, it was obvious that he seemed to think she welcomed his less than honorable intentions even though she had done nothing to encourage him. Cornelia swore to herself that she would keep her distance from the foreman from now on. Carefully maintaining a respectable distance from Sean McCurdy, she moved to her brother's side.

"Cornelia, I came looking for you because Locke was nice enough to stop by and told me about your encounter with the mountain lion. He said you were out here, and I thought you would want to see him before he leaves."

"Yes," she said weakly. "Locke Breckenridge is just the person I want to see." What she didn't say was that she only wanted to get away from the foreman.

She took Paxton's arm. "Did you rest well?"

A cough escaped him. "Yes, and now I am ready for some of Colorado's pure, healing fresh air. Since Lord Dunraven had pressing matters elsewhere, Locke has graciously agreed to accompany me on a brief walk about the grounds, and I thought you might also enjoy exploring this beautiful land."

"Of course, I would."

Ignoring Sean McCurdy's penetrating gaze, Cornelia helped Paxton back toward the cottage where

55

Locke was lazily leaning against the rustic pine post, a wide grin on his face.

"Nellie, I'm glad that you have decided to join us," Locke said as the three set out on their walk.

"I wouldn't miss the opportunity to explore Lord Dunraven's estate." She looked pointedly at the broad-shouldered man. "One never knows what one might discover. Isn't that true, Locke?"

"That is true. And one must also be careful to guard against misconceptions."

Paxton shook his head. "Misconceptions?"

"What Locke means, Paxton, is that one should be on guard against others who might attempt to *misconstrue* their intentions. Unsuspecting people could be deceived."

Paxton scratched his ear. "Misconstrue . . . misconceptions . . . deceived? Whatever are you two talking about?"

Cornelia glared at Locke. "Nothing, really, dear," she said.

"Somehow I think I have missed something," Paxton said. Secretly, he had not missed a thing. Cornelia and Locke were verbally sparring with each other. That meant that they were not impervious to each other even if they, themselves, didn't know it yet. Cornelia deserved happiness after putting up with the likes of Linley Talbot for four years. And Paxton was sure, after talking with Locke, that the man was genuine.

After a lengthy silence, Paxton observed, "The landscape is even more beautiful than I could have imagined."

He pointed out huge trees in the distance. "I wonder what the first settlers thought when they saw this magnificent valley."

"You mean Joel Estes," Locke supplied.

"Joel Estes?" Cornelia asked.

"The Park is named after him. 'Park' is a Western term for mountain valley. Estes was a man who liked to be away from people and wandered into Colorado in '59. He first glimpsed the valley while he was hunting."

"Hunting. Humph!" Cornelia gave a disapproving grunt.

"Unlike some city folks, most of us realize that if we are going to eat out here in the wilds, we must hunt."

Cornelia cocked a brow. "Indeed."

Locke ignored her. "Well, as I was saying, Joel and his wife moved into the Park and built a log cabin along Willow Creek. Estes and his family lived in the Park quite happily for three years before some tourist campers visited him and others started moving in. It wasn't long after that that Estes began to long for a land more remote and so they moved. Estes's claim passed through several folks' hands until a few pioneers came and stayed."

"And you were one of them, I suppose?" Cornelia said.

"As was Lord Dunraven. But I don't consider myself a pioneer, if that's what you mean."

"Then what do you consider yourself?"

"A man content to live a simple life here in the Rocky Mountains," he answered, effectively cutting off any more comments.

"Then you have no aspirations, Locke?" she asked much too sweetly for it to be a simple question.

"Aspirations are a matter of definition, Nellie. What about you, what are your aspirations? To marry and have children?"

Cornelia fidgeted, and her expression tightened before it became hooded.

"Locke, I think you had better know that Cornelia has recently suffered through a devastating divorce," Paxton offered in Cornelia's defense despite an earlier decision to allow Cornelia to make her own admissions.

"Paxton, please!" Cornelia cried, horrified that her brother was about to reveal her shameful secret.

The expression on Locke's face transformed into one of sympathy, which only served to horrify Cornelia further because she had not expected it from the man. In her own defense, she said, raising her chin. "You needn't feel sorry for me, Locke. When I return home, everything will be remedied."

Not waiting for the man to delve further into her private life, Cornelia turned on her heel and marched away from the men, calling back over her shoulder, "Please see that Paxton gets back to the cottage safely."

Once Cornelia was out of sight, Locke turned to Paxton. "What was that all about?"

"I think it'd be best to let Cornelia tell you when she's ready," he answered cryptically, wishing he hadn't said anything in the first place.

Back at the lodge, Lord Dunraven was in the barn preparing to go riding. "What is that mountain lion cub doing in here?" he demanded of Sean.

"Miss Talbot found it and asked that I nurse it back to health." He didn't say that it had been caught in one of his traps and he had intended to finish it off and sell the skin before the earl had seen it.

"She has a kind heart, that lady. I hope she did not find it in some poacher's trap on my land."

"No, Your Lordship," Sean answered.

"Good. Good. Perhaps we have seen the last of

whoever has been trapping game on my land. But just to be sure, I shall post a handsome reward in town. Therefore, the town's people will also be watching for any poachers. That should help put a stop to it."

Sean's lips tightened. Trapping animals on the earl's land had been profitable. Now he would have to stop. He could not take the chance of getting caught.

"See that the animal is well cared for and then release it back into the wild," the earl ordered.

"Miss Talbot should be liking that," Sean said without enthusiasm. Now he would have to nurse the filthy thing back to health instead of dispatching it. He could not chance the earl finding out otherwise.

"She is *Mrs. Talbot,*" the lord corrected.

"I haven't seen the likes of a husband," Sean said, which shifted his attention from the beast to another kind of prey.

"Her brother tells me that she brought him out to Colorado for his health. But I think she accompanied him because, as Paxton accidentally let slip, she was divorced for adultery. He insists that it was all a dreadful mistake, and she plans to return home and exonerate herself."

The earl continued to drone on, but Sean was no longer listening as he saddled the lord's steed. All he could think of was that the earl's attractive guest had been divorced due to her adultery. So, the lady wasn't such a lady after all.

Sean considered himself quite a ladies' man and had been perturbed when Cornelia Talbot had spurned his advances since he did not bestow them on just any female.

"So you are not the lady you pretend to be," he muttered as he pulled on the cinch.

"Beg your pardon?" the earl said.

"Forgive me, milord, I be merely saying that your mount is about ready."

"Good. Good."

Sean watched the earl mount and ride from the barn. But his thoughts continued in only one vein: No woman who would cheat on her husband was going to act like the outraged lady with Sean McCurdy and get away with it. A calculating smile crept around his lips. He was determined to make the woman see the error of her ways. Once she got to know him, Sean was certain that she would fall into his bed with relish. He was not about to be spurned by a common adulteress who set herself above her kind and had cost him a good profit in hides on top of it. Before she returned home, she would give him a taste of what she had been giving away back East!

As he was thinking about the lady, she appeared, heading toward the cottage, as if it were Fate. She was much too thin, but it didn't matter. Sean liked his women in all shapes and sizes. Most of all, Sean liked his women beneath him. And Cornelia Talbot was going to become the next notch on the Irish shillelagh he had brought over from the old country with him.

Chapter Seven

Paxton returned from his walk winded but jubilant. "Locke has invited us to dine with him tonight, and I have taken the liberty of accepting for both of us," he announced once he located Cornelia in the tidy little parlor.

"Don't you think we should dine with Lord Dunraven this evening? After all, it is our first night here, and we are his guests."

"The earl told me that we should feel free to come and go as we please while we are here." To Cornelia's horrified expression, he added, "Furthermore, he told me he is leaving this afternoon for an expedition to Grand Lake and will be gone for several weeks. So we have the run of the place in his absence."

"But I don't think—"

Her objections were cut off when Paxton turned white as a puffy cloud and went into another bout of coughing. She rushed to his side and helped him to his room.

Her brother settled, Cornelia went to her room with the intention of keeping to it. It was a cheery room, rustic in its decor with rough-hewn bedposts, patchwork quilt, and a braided rug. The only piece that disturbed her was the elk head positioned over the dresser.

In an effort to keep from thinking about the upcoming supper with Locke and how the thought of it bothered her, Cornelia busied herself by putting away her clothes and rearranging the room. All the while she worked, the elk head seemed to be gazing at her until she could no longer abide its soulful gaze.

Determined to locate someone to remove the piece, she left the room to talk to the servant Lord Dunraven had said he would send over to assist them in getting settled.

She found a young woman, who appeared perhaps five years younger than Cornelia's twenty-four years, baking bread in the well-equipped kitchen.

"Excuse me, I wonder if you might be able to help me?"

The young woman looked up and started. She wiped the flour from her hands on her apron and smoothed back greasy strands of hair the color of mud. Cornelia hid her horror at the girl's unkempt appearance.

"Howdy, ma'am," She offered her hand with an open smile on her face.

Cornelia did not hesitate. She shook the girl's hand. "Cornelia Talbot."

"I'm mighty pleased to make your acquaintance, ma'am."

"Please, call me Cornelia."

The girl beamed. "Thank you, I'll be mighty pleased to. Lord Dunraven told me he had guests. I'm Annabeth Mills, but most folks jes' call me Annie 'cuz Pa says I ain't got what it takes to fit such a fine name what Ma called me when she birthed me, like she done. 'Course, Ma didn't have no chance to

62

see how I growed up. She passed on back in Alabama when I was a young 'un."

Annie noticed the expression of sympathy come over the proper lady's face. "Don't you go feelin' sorry none now, you hear? Ma went to heaven to be with God. A body can't ask for nothin' better. And me and Pa's done all right. There ain't no better place to live on earth than Estes Park. This is God's country. We got a good, sturdy house. Pa's learnin' code to take over a job in town. I got a good job cookin' and cleanin' for the earl. Our guts is always full. We don't want for nothin'.''

Cornelia beamed back, fascinated by such a lengthy outpouring. "Of course you don't." She immediately liked the backwoods girl. But Annie didn't give herself enough credit. She was a delightfully honest, friendly young woman. And if cleaned up, she would undoubtedly be a beauty.

The girl leaned forward. "Was there somethin' you needed?"

"I was looking for someone to remove the elk head from my room. Its soulful eyes drive me to distraction."

"I know jes' what you mean. When I'm in there cleanin', my heart goes out to the beautiful creature. But when I'm at the supper table, I'm thankful for the bounty." A coy grin dimpled her cheeks. "Not to mention the good eatin'."

Theirs was an easy camaraderie, and Cornelia found herself laughing freely for the first time in months. "I have to admit that I agree."

"Speakin' of mighty fine eatin', how 'bout some juicy elk steaks for supper tonight?"

"I would love it, but my brother and I have been invited to dine with Locke Breckenridge this evening."

63

"Well, I'll be." She sighed. "Locke Breckenridge. He sure is goin' to make a mighty fine catch." Then she sobered. "But he keeps to himself most of the time. However did you manage an invite?"

"The man is a friend of my brother's."

"Oh. That explains it." Concern muted her features. "I heard your brother's got a sickness."

"He'll be fine once his lungs are cleansed by the pure, dry air here in Colorado."

"Livin' out here will do it, if anythin' can," Annie said. She glanced at the clock. "Oh dear, I been talkin' your head off. I got work to do, and you'll be wantin' to rest up before tonight. You jes' sit down over there—" she motioned to a chair next to the work table "—and I'll get someone to get that elk head out of your room."

Annie was not gone more than five minutes when she returned with Sean McCurdy in tow. Cornelia hid her dismay that she was about to lead that man to her bedroom. So in order to protect herself, she asked Annie to accompany them.

Mr. McCurdy was appropriately polite and took down the elk head while Cornelia listened to Annie babble until the big Irishman asked her to get a hammer so he could drive the nail into the wall. Before Cornelia could protest, Annie disappeared.

Once she was alone with the man, his grin widened. Before he could say anything, Cornelia suggested, "I think it would be a good idea if you removed the elk head from the room before it gets too heavy for you."

To her dismay, he cocked his brow. "I've handled more livelier ladies than this little gal—" he stroked the elk head with suggested intimacy "—and I never be having a complaint."

"Then I suggest you take the lady elk back to your

quarters with you . . . now."

Sean gave the elk head a smacking kiss. "I just might be doing that. I never be letting even the most stubborn colleen get away without giving her every opportunity to find out what she be missing."

She fought down the urge to flee. The man was not going to frighten her with his innuendos. If she did not stand up to him now, he would be forever making improper advances toward her. In a bold move, so unlike her usually reserved self, she walked over to the head and petted the elk's nose. "I would say that it no doubt lived a perfectly contented life without ever knowing."

To her further dismay, her efforts did not serve her intended purpose. McCurdy threw back his head and laughed with a rollicking roar. He toted the elk to the door, cooing to the head. "I don't intend to be letting this one get away. I think I might just nail her to my wall. She'll become one of my willing *trophies* . . . sooner or later."

"You best be careful that you don't end up being the one nailed to the wall," Cornelia said more harshly.

She should have known better than to try to parry words with such a man. He'd have no qualms about using a lady. The man was totally without honor.

"Here's your hammer," Annie said, coming into the room.

Sean kissed the elk head again and smirked. "Give it to the lady. I think she may be having need of it." To Annie's confused expression, he added, "She may be wanting to practice nailing."

"What was all that about?" Annie asked after Sean had left.

Cornelia smiled weakly. "Nothing, really."

"Well, you jes' stay far away from Sean McCurdy.

He thinks of himself as a real ladies' man. So you watch out for yourself. He collects girls' favors as trophies like Lord Dunraven collects them animal heads."

The girl's comment about trophies made Cornelia gasp, but she quickly recovered herself. "I shall never become any man's trophy. I am a married woman."

Surprise lifted the girl's brows. "Where's your man, then?"

Flustered, Cornelia felt her cheeks grow warm. She had not meant to share her shame with the girl. "He's back home, and as soon as my brother is feeling better, I shall be reunited with him," she said with conviction.

Bemused by the lady's force of words, Annie said, "Of course you will. I had best get back to the kitchen. Is there anything else I can do for you before I return to the lodge?"

"Thank you, no. I think I shall be able to rest now until it is time to leave for Locke Breckenridge's home."

Cornelia fretted all the way to Locke's cabin. She did not want to spend any more time with the big man, particularly after Paxton had slipped and told Locke she was divorced. Deep down, she had to admit she was worried that he would think less of her although she could not fathom why it should matter to her.

By the time they reached the cabin deep in the woods, the sun was sinking to the west, lending a pink glow to the jagged outline of the high mountain rising in the distance before them. "Oh, Paxton, look at that mountain. Isn't it magnificent?" Cornelia observed, mesmerized by the majestic giant.

"It looks rather foreboding to me," Paxton said.

"Foreboding? It has an incredible strength to it. I find it rather inviting."

"What do you find inviting?" Locke asked, leaving the house to greet his guests.

"Cornelia was just commenting about that mountain over there—" Paxton motioned to the peak "—she seems to find it fascinating."

"It is," Locke said. "A real challenge."

"You've been up it?" Cornelia asked, all anxiety banished by her interest in the mountain.

"Yeah."

Paxton coughed, reminding Cornelia that there was a chill in the air. She turned to her brother and said, "Let's get you inside before you take cold."

"You don't have to treat me like a complete invalid," he complained. But the drive over had been tiring, and Paxton was wheezing by the time he was seated in the small one-room cabin.

Cornelia's momentary comfort was short-lived. When Locke got a blanket for Paxton's lap and was handing it to Cornelia, their hands touched. She quickly pulled her hand back with a jerk and dropped her eyes as she withdrew and took a chair a safe distance from Locke.

Locke, too, experienced the touch with a strange sensation. He shot her a look, but she was making a study of the floor and refused to meet his gaze. Despite her thinness, she was attractive in her flowered skirt. In an effort to make her feel more comfortable, he said, "Well, what do you think of my place?"

Cornelia cast a quick glance about her. "I think I am beginning to understand why you like the simple life." Then she caught sight of the rifle propped up in the corner.

"Everyone in these parts owns a Beecher Bible," Locke remarked at her shocked expression.

"Beecher Bible?"

"The Sharp's rifle you are staring at."

"How can you refer to a gun as a Bible?" she asked with just a hint of outrage in her voice.

"Because it has affectionately been called that since Henry Ward Beecher, a fire-eating abolitionist from Connecticut, suggested every man grasp a Bible in one hand and a rifle in the other and head for Kansas."

"Oh," was all she responded under his probing gaze.

In an attempt to avoid his continuing piercing stare, she let her eyes go about the room again. The cabin was small but tidy. A potbelly stove stood in one corner. Three pots sat on top of it, their contents sending a fragrant aroma about the room. A small table, obviously handmade by Locke, adorned the middle of the room; a rough-hewn bed with a bear pelt pulled over the mattress was off in a corner. Cornelia blushed at the sight of the bed and moved her gaze to the stacks of books.

"Does it surprise you that a man such as myself is interested in books?" he asked, noticing her gaze linger on the numerous volumes.

Her discomfort passed and Cornelia stiffened. "I'm sure you are a voracious reader."

To Cornelia's chagrin, Locke went over to the bed and sat down. He picked up a book and opened it. He patted the place next to him. "Come here and let me show you one of my favorites."

Cornelia looked to Paxton to rescue her, but in his exhaustion he had nodded off. She hesitated, fearing the closeness of Locke with a new heightened sensitivity toward the man.

"What's the matter, Nellie?"

Cornelia held her breath. The man was going to make a terrible comment just the way that dreadful McCurdy had. A feeling of panic came over her, and she had to fight down the urge to run as she had earlier today when Paxton had told Locke that she was a divorced woman.

"Nellie?"

Cornelia took a breath and looked over at Locke. To her amazement, there was no scorn, no silent mocking, no lewd expression on his face. And to her further surprise, he got up and pulled a chair over next to her and handed her the book without commenting on her hesitation.

"It is a photo story of the westward movement."

Cornelia glanced down at the book, then rummaged through her bag, fished out her glasses and put them on. She marshaled her defenses, expecting him to make a negative comment as Linley often had about her spectacles, but he said not a word.

Relieved, she opened the book to a photo of an attractive young woman perched atop the most photogenic camel with a covered wagon in the background. Cornelia's fear subsided and a wide grin spread evenly over her lips.

"This is a marvelous book," she said, turning the page. "My mother has an autographed copy on a table in the parlor back home."

Locke looked at Cornelia's face; it was glowing. She was a most attractive woman when she allowed herself to relax, he thought. "I understand that it was a very popular book in its day."

"It made Uncle Cornelius a world-renowned photographer," Cornelia said.

"The author's your uncle?" he said, realizing the

69

similarity in their names.

"I was named after him. He is my mother's only brother. Have you seen any of his other works?"

"I'm afraid I can't say that I have."

"One of his works involves photos of unique weddings. It included the wedding of U.S. Senator Chandler in Montana. What makes that wedding so interesting was that the senator married the young woman twice within a couple of months. A couple of months later my uncle was asked to photograph Chandler's maiden aunt who married Addison Rutcliff, one of the country's wealthiest business men. Then he was asked to photograph Rutcliff's daughter's marriage to a gambler whom he had rescued from jail. Uncle Cornelius said theirs was one of the most diverse families he had ever worked with.

"Uncle Cornelius also photographed President Arthur's attendance at the Colston wedding in Wyoming. That couple, according to my uncle, feuded right down the aisle. It was sort of a book on the weddings of the rich and the famous and won acclaim throughout the country because of the candid shots."

"He's renowned for his candid shots. Is he working on another project now?"

"Uncle Cornelius is retired now and living in San Francisco. Although I'm sure it wouldn't take much to bring him out of retirement."

They shared a companionable time looking through the book. Cornelia related many anecdotes she remembered her uncle telling about the trip. And she spoke openly of her beloved uncle as they flipped through the pages.

"Would you like to look at another book?" he asked, caught up in her enthusiasm.

She ran her hand over the last picture they had

70

looked at. "I never tire at looking at this one. There are so many amusing stories that go with each photograph." She turned the page and giggled.

"Look at this one." With her finger, she outlined the photograph of three sodden men and a camel standing next to a swollen river.

"That man looks like he almost drowned, the other one is standing so stiff, but that camel, it's smugly posing!" Locke observed.

"The man almost did drown in the Platte River. The camel saved his life."

For over an hour while Paxton slept, they buried themselves in the book, laughing and sharing a camaraderie that Cornelia had never known before with any male, other than her brother. She let those first anxious moments slip to the back of her mind, but she was careful to keep their fingers from touching again.

Their enchanted moments ended when Paxton awoke with a bout of coughing. Cornelia rushed to his side and rubbed his back. "Are you all right?" she asked when he had stopped.

"Yes," he said. He noticed that the gray shades of night had come as he watched her tuck her glasses away. He had rarely seen her wear them, and he was gratified that she had felt comfortable enough around Locke to put them on. "I hope you will forgive me, Locke. I must have fallen asleep."

Locke went over to the potbelly stove and began dishing up supper. "Nothing to forgive. Ready for some food?"

After they had eaten, Paxton suggested that Cornelia remain and enjoy Locke's books as she had told him all about finding their uncle's book. Paxton was feeling drained and weary and longed for bed.

"I think we should get you back to Lord

Dunraven's," Cornelia said, noticing her brother's pasty-white face.

"I hate to tear you away from Locke's library. It seems as if you two were thoroughly enjoying yourselves."

Locke glanced at Cornelia. In the lantern light, her honey-brown curls reflected a halo. He wondered about what her brother had meant by her devastating divorce, and he puzzled over why he hadn't seen her pain before. Now, the circles under her eyes, the hollows of her cheeks were obvious and the looseness of her dress, he was certain, she must have once filled out. At that moment, he realized the divorce must have made her guarded around men.

Wanting to learn more about her, Locke suggested, "If you'd like to remain and browse through my library, I shall be happy to drive you back later."

The moment the words left his lips, Locke knew he had said the wrong thing. Cornelia's face underwent a transformation back to the suspicious, doubting woman hiding behind a protective layer of shrewishness he had encountered at the train depot.

"I hardly think it would be proper," she said stiffly. She turned to Paxton. "We have taken up enough of Locke's time, Paxton. I think it is time I get you back to the cottage. You need your rest."

"Feel free anytime to come back and borrow a book if you'd like," Locke heard himself offer. Hell, he should have known better. What was wrong with him? She was the first woman he had invited to his cabin. Having vowed to live without female companionship of any kind after his wife had left him, he had found it was not so painful after all to sit next to a female and enjoy her company. The thought gave him something to think about. Colorado really was a place where people came to heal. And not just from physical ailments. He was healing, too. The reflection made him smile.

Cornelia thought he was grinning at her the same way that dreadful Sean McCurdy had earlier. All men were alike. They had only one thing on their minds. And Cornelia had no intention of falling victim.

"Thank you for the offer of your library. But I don't think I shall have another occasion to return. Lord Dunraven has an extensive library. I'm certain he has enough books to meet any needs I may have for reading material," she said stiffly.

"Feel free to change your mind," he said, rising to the situation.

"I rarely change my mind."

"Perhaps you should try it sometime. You might just find that it will allow you to get on with your life."

Cornelia sucked in a breath at his all too close perception of what Paxton had been saying to her since her troubles had started with Linley. But she was not about to let Locke have the last word.

"You needn't concern yourself with my life. Thank you for supper," she said, changing the topic before he could make an attempt to probe into her shattered life.

"Next time I'll let you do the cooking."

"Sounds like a good idea to me," Paxton interceded to stave off his sister's rising ire.

Locke helped Paxton into the carriage, Cornelia taking her place before he could offer his assistance. It was obvious that the lady did not want him to touch her, and he could not help wondering exactly what had made her so stiff.

He watched the pair drive away from his cabin with narrowed eyes. He should have known better than to try to put a stop to the bickering between himself and Cornelia Talbot. No wonder she was divorced; she was an impossible shrew! he thought as he turned to go back inside. Yet, as he closed the door behind him, he could not quite get off his mind the flicker of pain or the unguarded smile he had noticed flash into her eyes when she let her defenses down without knowing it.

Chapter Eight

Cornelia and Paxton were halfway back to Lord Dunraven's estate before either one spoke. Night had closed in, and the pines were silhouetted black against the silvery moonlight that lit their way.

"Locke was only trying to be neighborly," Paxton said quietly in the man's defense.

Cornelia took a deep breath and snapped the reins over the horse's rump. "Perhaps. But it hardly would be proper for me to remain in his cabin alone with him, now would it?" she said in her own defense.

Paxton patted her hand. "No, sister dear, it would not have been proper, but you might have enjoyed it." To Cornelia's gasp, Paxton added, "We are no longer back home surrounded by all those stiff-necked old biddies. I am sure people out here are more liberal in their thinking. Besides, no one even knows you in Colorado yet, let alone branding you as a loose woman."

Cornelia's head snapped up. "And no one is going to either!"

For three weeks Cornelia remained on Lord Dunraven's estate, making no effort to go into town or to get to know any of the area's residents. She was careful to avoid the staff at the lodge, except for Annie, the delightful mountain girl who worked in the kitchen and cleaned their cottage. Cornelia spent her mornings overseeing Paxton's care. In the afternoons while Paxton rested, she walked in the warmth of the sun, discovering many winding trails. She climbed some of the nearby hills and spent hours sketching the beauty that was the valley. She delighted in the pine-scented air. And she began carrying crumbs to feed the many squirrels, chipmunks, and birds that flocked around her. When she had free time she spent it with Annie.

Cornelia developed a close kinship with the backwoods girl. Annie was a big help with Paxton, often sitting on the porch with him and listening to him read in the morning sun.

"You really like living out here, don't you?" Paxton asked Annie one morning as he rested in the big rocking chair on a sunny spot outside the cottage. Annie was sitting comfortably on the pine flooring, her legs nestled beneath her.

"Guess I couldn't rightly cotton to livin' no place else on earth."

Paxton enjoyed the time he spent with the girl. She was generous with her time, considering the many duties the earl had her perform and that often took her until long after dark. He would look out his bedroom window and see her making her way to the forest toward her home. He wondered whether she had any male friends.

"Do you have a beau?" he boldly questioned, unable to contain himself any longer.

"Ah heck, no. There ain't nobody what takes my fancy." She shot him a glance from beneath her long, thick lashes. Luckily, his vision seemed to be focused on a crested jay perched on a nearby branch. "I like doin' for myself."

Paxton's gaze ambled back to the girl. Sitting on the steps at his feet with her knees pulled up to her chest, she was smiling sweetly up at him. She was so unassuming, so fresh and delightful that Paxton found himself drawn to the waif of a young woman.

"Surely there are young men who take a fancy to you."

"A few I guess. But none what counts."

"Oh," he said. Her response quite satisfied him that she was not already spoken for. He had deigned to remain a bachelor like his Uncle Cornelius, but this girl sent his thoughts in an entirely different direction.

She crunched up her nose. "Why you askin'?"

Paxton kept his face impassive when he answered. "You are so pretty that I can't imagine why you haven't been spoken for, is all."

To Paxton's amazement, she said, "Then you ain't interested?"

Taken aback by her candidness, he choked out, "Me?"

"There ain't nobody else out here on the porch with us, is there?"

"I-I am in no shape to even consider such a thing," he stammered.

Her face dropped. "Oh."

"Did I say something wrong?" he asked, not wanting to cause her any pain. But secretly his heart was dancing a polka inside his chest.

"No, 'course not." She returned her attention to the simple words in the book that Paxton had picked out for her.

"Are you enjoying the book?"

"Ever so much. It gives me pleasure to be able to

decipher the marks on the page. I'll always be beholden to you for takin' so much time to teach me as much as you done. To be able to book read is important. My pa let me get a little schoolin' years ago. But there was too much to do to help out, and I had to quit."

"I'm glad that I could help you learn."

She smiled up at him. "Me, too."

Paxton listened attentively as Annie returned her attention to the book and read aloud. He had carefully selected a book he was certain she would be able to read with her limited knowledge of the printed word. It gave him a great deal of pleasure to feel useful and help someone else, not to mention that he especially liked having Annie around him.

"Paxton," Cornelia said, joining the pair. "It's time for your nap." She took a step closer to him. "Let me help you up."

Before she could reach Paxton, Annie jumped up and grabbed his arm. "I'll take care of him. Don't you worry none. Why don't you get a little sun. You could use some color in those pale cheeks."

Paxton gave a weak burst of laughter. "I have to admit I am rather enjoying having two beautiful women fight over me." To Annie's look of misunderstanding, he quickly added, "Cornelia, I am afraid you have lost this time." He turned to Annie, "I'm all yours."

The girl immediately brightened.

Cornelia watched them go into the house, then settled down on the steps. It was obvious that her brother was exhibiting more than just a passing interest in the girl and the interest was returned. Cornelia smiled to herself. Paxton had not shown much more than a passing interest in the girls back home since Mary Ellen Seward had left him standing at the altar to run away with his best friend. It had devastated her prideful brother and sent him off to Europe for three years before the consumption forced him to return home where he could be cared for.

"You look like you are miles away," Locke said, joining Cornelia on the porch.

The deep timbre of his voice snapped Cornelia back from her reminiscences. She looked up. Locke was standing over her, a book in his hand. From her position on the steps, he appeared to be ten feet tall. Locke's legs looked like towering tree trunks, his hands and arms the size of mighty branches, and his shoulders spread out wide and proud.

The resonance of his voice hummed through her, and she shook her head to clear it. "Paxton is inside," she said.

"I didn't come to see your brother."

"Then why did you come?"

"To see you."

"Me? Mr. Breckenridge—"

"Locke. Please. Remember?" he corrected and knelt down, his knees cracking as he joined her.

There was an aura, a strange electric magnetism Cornelia could feel emanating from Locke when he moved closer to her, and she scooted a safe distance away from the drawing aura of him. "Locke, why did you come to see me?"

"Haven't seen either you or your brother out and about for some time. No one in town has seen you either. So I thought I'd drop by and make sure you're both still in one piece. I heard Dunraven had a change of plans and won't be returning for some time."

"You asked the people in town about me . . . us?"

Locke noticed a strange glint of wariness spark into Cornelia's green eyes. It was as if she was hiding some shameful secret that she did not want people to know. Then he realized that the divorce must have taken a heavier toll on the lady than he had originally suspected. A sudden urge to protect her flooded through him.

"I was thumbing through my books and thought you might enjoy this one." He held out the worn leather volume. "It is by a native of Colorado."

Despite her resolve to go inside and get away from the unwelcome feelings that the closeness to the man elicited, Cornelia put out her hand and took the book.

"Aren't you going to put your glasses on so you can read the captions?" he asked.

"They are inside."

"Then go get them. I'll wait."

She hesitated, causing him to add, "Go ahead. Unless, of course, you have plans I'm interrupting."

She had been going to take her usual afternoon stroll. But she could not tell him about that because he would undoubtedly invite himself to go along. So she said, "You aren't interrupting any plans."

"Good. Then go get your glasses."

She reluctantly went inside and retrieved the spectacles. When she returned, she found Locke sitting on the steps with his legs sprawled out in front of him, leaning against the railing. He was staring off toward the towering pines, unaware that she had returned. She studied his profile. He had a strong chin with a masculine line to his cheekbones and long thick wisps of lashes, which should have belonged to a woman. An ebony curl shone auburn in the sun and just the hint of a beard lined his face.

As if he suddenly sensed her presence, he snapped his head around. When she headed for the rocker, he said, "Come, sit on the steps with me."

"I—"

"Don't worry, you won't get your white dress dirty." Then in a move that surprised Cornelia, he took out a handkerchief and laid it next to him.

"Quite the Sir Walter Raleigh, aren't you, all of a sudden?"

"It isn't all of a sudden," he said. "Besides, you had been sitting here before I came. If you would give me half a chance, you might find out that I can be rather gallant all the time."

"Yes, like you were back at the train depot?"

"Why don't we chalk that up to the past and call a truce?" he suggested.

"Said the spider to the fly," she mumbled.

"Pardon?"

"I said I'll try."

"Good. Now come and sit beside me so we can enjoy the book I brought."

Cornelia took a buoying breath and sat a respectable distance from him.

Locke smiled inside. She had made another minor concession. Despite her trepidation, she was sitting next to him. He opened the cover of the book.

Inside were numerous descriptions of the terrain and the animals of Colorado. Several cities were highlighted, and, in spite of herself, Cornelia again found herself poring through one of his books, marveling at the various mining towns and secretly wishing that she could be part of the fascinating hustle and bustle that reached out to her from each page.

"Have you ever been to any of these towns?" she asked.

"A few."

They turned a few more pages until one particular scene caught Cornelia's eye. "This one—" she pointed "—looks fascinating." It was a photo of a main street aswarm with people.

Locke leaned closer to get a good look, and she inhaled the aroma of pine and wood chips. It was an inviting fragrance that mingled with his own masculine scent.

"Leadville," he said. "I used to live there. As a matter of fact, I usually make several trips back each year to oversee my business." Silently, he made a note of her interest in the town as a girlish delight encircled the lady. Her eyes shone and her face lit up as it had a few weeks ago when she had accompanied her brother to his cabin for supper.

"What type of business—mining?" she asked before she could stop herself. It was not polite to probe into his private life, and she did not want to give him the opening to start probing into hers.

"Supply," he answered simply. "My sister takes care of the day-to-day details."

"Well, it looks like it would be a fascinating place to visit."

"Perhaps you and your brother might enjoy accompanying me on my next trip."

"Thank you for the generous offer, but Paxton is in no condition to travel for some time."

"It was just a thought," he said, wondering why he had made the offer in the first place. He turned the page.

They were just beginning to relax again when Annie bolted from the house. "You gotta come. Hurry. It's Paxton. I got him all settled in his room, and when I left I heard this awful thud. Oh, Cornelia," she cried, "he's laying on the floor, out cold, and he's deathly white."

Cornelia shot to her feet with a cry of anguish and fear for Paxton. With Locke and Annie right behind her, Cornelia raced to Paxton's room.

He was lying on the floor, his thin body crumpled into a heap. She knelt beside him and cradled his head. His face was white, and his breathing was shallow and labored.

"Oh, dear God, Paxton," she cried.

Locke bent down beside Cornelia. "Here, Cornelia, let's get him on the bed.

Cornelia reluctantly moved aside and allowed Locke to lift Paxton's limp body. Quickly, she threw back the quilt, and Locke set Paxton on the bed. Paxton lay deathly still. She loosened his collar. Fighting down a helpless feeling, she turned to the bewildered girl. "Annie, fetch water and towels, and hurry," Cornelia ordered.

Annie's heart raced as she sped to get the things that Cornelia needed. While she gathered the supplies, all she could think about was that Paxton had to be all right. He just had to.

"Here—" she handed the materials to Cornelia "—What can I do?"

"Thank you for offering. I'll let you know if I need anything else," Cornelia said quickly.

Annie stepped back and watched the lady nurse Paxton.

Annie had immediately liked Paxton Lloyd from the first time she had met him. He was thoughtful and considerate and never treated her like a servant. He was helping her learn to read, something that Annie had always wanted to learn but her pa had felt a female did not need to know. But most important was that he did not attempt to take advantage of her or woo her with pretty words and empty promises.

Annie's gaze shifted to Locke Breckenridge. He was such an enigma. He had kept to himself since he had arrived in Estes Park, and now here he was hovering over the lady. Annie shook her head. Those two had a lot more in common than even they realized. Two people full of pain, she thought.

"He's in pain," Cornelia cried when Paxton winced as she swabbed his chest. "And he is burning up."

Chapter Nine

Despite Cornelia's efforts, beads of sweat continued to break out across Paxton's face. A few minutes ago, he had been pasty white, and now his face was turning bright red. Annie slapped her hands to her cheeks. "I hope it's not the fever. In his weak state he could die," she blurted out.

Frantic, Cornelia turned to Locke. Her eyes were overly bright and her lip was trembling. "Please, is there a doctor in town?"

"There's Doc Jones."

"He's visitin' relatives in Longmont," Annie cried.

"He needs a doctor," Cornelia insisted. "Oh, I never should have brought him out to the middle of nowhere. If he dies, I'll never be able to forgive myself."

Locke placed a comforting hand on Cornelia's shoulder. "Paxton's not ready to die yet. Try to keep him cool. I'll go." Locke gripped her shoulder, then rushed from the house to the stables.

McCurdy was pitching hay to the horses when Locke entered. "You be enjoying your visit with the lady?" he snickered.

Locke balled his fists. If he weren't in such a hurry, he would have gladly punched the man out for the implication. Instead, he said, "Which is the earl's fastest horse?"

Worried about his job, Sean narrowed his eyes. "Why you be needing to know?"

"Unless you want to be held responsible for the death of one of Dunraven's guests, I suggest you get busy and help me saddle the horse."

The man's tone brooked no argument. Sean immediately grabbed a bridle and opened the door to a shiny black stallion.

In less than five minutes, Locke was charging out of the stable and heading toward Longmont. He rode the mighty animal as if marauding Indians were chasing him down the narrow, winding road. Branches slapped him in the face and scratched his arms, but he only stopped to give the horse brief rest periods. Paxton was his friend, and Locke feared that Cornelia would never get over it if anything happened to her brother. He admired Cornelia for her devotion.

It was after dark by the time Locke reached Longmont and located the aging doctor. Over the man's objections, Locke insisted that they start back immediately. Locke rode ahead of the doctor's buggy, holding a lantern to help illuminate the way. He had a feeling that somehow Cornelia's former husband had let her down, and Locke had no intention of adding himself to that list.

Meanwhile, Cornelia had spent the remainder of the day hovering over Paxton and worrying. Even when Annie offered to relieve her, Cornelia had refused. She was sitting by his bed, holding his hand, when he finally came around.

"What are you doing?" Paxton asked.

His face was beaded with sweat and Cornelia

gently swabbed his brow. "You fainted. But you are going to be fine," she said despite his labored breathing.

"I feel like a carriage has run over me," he rasped and closed his eyes.

"Paxton?" She feared that he might drift off and not awaken if she didn't keep him aware.

Slowly his eyes fluttered open. With all the strength he could muster, he took hold of Cornelia's hand and squeezed. "Don't worry, Sister dear, I am not going to leave you. I have much too much living to do yet."

Cornelia smiled gently. "I'm glad you have come to realize that."

Paxton gave her a weak smile. "Now, if you, too, would come to realize the same thing, we would both be on the right road."

Cornelia placed her free hand over her brother's. "I think I am coming to realize that I am much stronger than I ever thought I could be."

"Do you mind explaining what you mean?" he said with great effort and closed his eyes.

Trying to maintain a stiff upper lip and not let her voice quiver with worry over her brother, Cornelia said, "When the judge granted Linley a divorce, I thought my life was over. I couldn't believe what was happening to me. I thought if I closed my eyes, it would all go away like some nightmare. Then I was angry that no one believed the truth. I even tried to make a bargain with God that if He would make everything all right, I would be the best wife Linley ever had."

Despite his exhaustion Paxton made a major effort to comfort his sister. "You are the best wife Linley ever had or could have."

Cornelia pinched her lips. Inside, she still had difficulty believing that if only she had done something differently, Linley would have been here with her now. But she said, "Thank you. You have always believed in me."

"If only you would try believing in yourself."

"Yes, well . . ." she said and let the words trail off before she changed topics. "Enough about me. Let's concentrate on you now."

Annie entered with a glass of water, effectively cutting off Paxton's intention not to let Cornelia refocus the attention from herself. "He's awake." Annie rushed to Paxton's side. "You got your eyes open. Thank God." She turned to Cornelia. "He looks much better. Guess he ain't got the fever after all."

"The fever?"

"Spotted fever. It kills. But I knowed it wouldn't get you. I been prayin' real hard."

Despite his fatigue, Paxton tried to sit up. When Cornelia pushed him back, he said, "Sister dear, why don't you go make us something to eat? I could use something nourishing to fill my stomach."

When Cornelia noticed Paxton's eyes trail to Annie, she nodded and left the pair alone. In the kitchen Cornelia collapsed at the worktable and put her head down on her arms. She suddenly felt bone weary now that the crisis had passed. No longer able to fight against the heaviness of exhausted sleep, she drifted off.

The sound of buggy wheels crunching against the gravel in front of the cottage jerked Cornelia from her slumber. The first gray streaks of dawn were streaming through the windows. She sat up. Someone had placed a blanket around her shoulders. She threw it off and rushed out to the porch. Locke and a withered old man in a black overcoat were heading toward her.

"Doctor Jones?" she asked, rushing forward.

"Yes. How is your brother, my dear?"

"He seemed to be feeling better late yesterday afternoon. I went into the kitchen to fix him some soup, but I'm afraid I fell asleep."

"In that case we'd best go have a look at him," the doctor said. "Lead the way." As they headed through the cottage, the doctor added, "Locke said your brother was awfully sick and insisted we drive up the mountain last night instead of waiting until morning."

Cornelia's gaze shot to Locke, who had remained in the background but kept pace close behind them. She was amazed that he had driven himself so hard. And at the same time, a feeling of pleasure and gratitude warmed her.

Outside the door, the doctor turned to Cornelia and suggested, "Why don't you give me a few minutes to examine your brother?"

"But shouldn't I—"

"No, you shouldn't," Locke supplied.

"Why not put a pot of coffee on? It's been a long night, and we all could use something hot," the doctor said.

"Yes, yes, of course."

The doctor went into the room and closed the door, effectively shutting Cornelia out. "Come on, I'll make the coffee," Locke offered. "You must admit that I make a pretty good cup of coffee."

Fighting down her fears over Paxton, Cornelia allowed herself to follow Locke into the kitchen. She sat down woodenly and watched him get the coffee started before he joined her.

"Don't worry, Doc Jones is just mean enough to save your brother."

Cornelia's attention snapped away from her concern over Paxton. Locke had a sympathetic smile on his face, and he reached out and placed a comforting hand over hers. His hand was warm and his touch was tender.

"Thank you for riding to Longmont," she said softly. "I want to apologize for being so insufferable toward you when we first met. You went out of your way for me and my brother."

"Cornelia, it isn't something another wouldn't have done," he said.

"I suppose not. It is just that I guess I have lost my faith in Man."

"In Man or in all men after your divorce?" he asked.

Her first inclination at hearing him bring up the topic of divorce was to flee, but he had just ridden all night on her brother's behalf. She took a deep breath to steel herself. "Both, I suppose."

Locke watched her face undergo the pain of having to face her anguish. "I'm sorry if I am dredging up painful memories," he said.

"We all have painful memories to endure."

"How true."

"And what are your painful memories?"

Locke stared at her. She had managed the turn the tables on him and was now doing the questioning. He had not spoken about Margaret to anyone since he had moved to Estes Park. "I'm also divorced, Cornelia," he stated simply.

She was astounded by his openness and sat there gaping until he rose and poured two cups of coffee. He set her cup in front of her and sat back down across from her.

"You needn't look so surprised."

"I never dreamed. I'm sorry."

"No reason to be sorry. Divorce is not a subject

that you bring up readily. I learned a long time ago that life goes forward and I've made peace with myself. If you'd let me, I'd like to help you make peace with yourself."

"Thank you for your concern, but I shall be quite all right once I return home and prove I am not guilty of anything."

"Guilty?"

"If you must know, I was accused of adultery." To her surprise, his expression did not change. There was no condemnation in his eyes, no registered shock. She relaxed. "It was all a mistake, and my hus—former husband will realize it after I return."

He was beginning to understand why she had behaved as she had in Denver. "I'm certain he will."

"I can't actually blame Linley," she said. Now that the subject had been broached, Cornelia poured out the sordid tale of how she had been mistakenly accused of adultery.

Locke listened intently until she was through, his admiration for the young woman's determination growing. He could not help but admit to himself that he would be sorry to see her return to a man who had not stood beside her and believed in her. And he found himself thinking that if she were his wife and had been accused of such a thing, he would not have been so quick to destroy their life together.

To Cornelia's relief, the doctor entered the kitchen, saving her from answering any questions that Locke might have posed. "Sure could use a cup of that coffee," he said.

Cornelia rose, but Annie interceded, coming in from the parlor where she had spent the night on the sofa. "You jes' stay right where you sit. I'll fix the doc up." She motioned to an empty chair at the table. "Sit yourself down, Doc."

"Don't mind if I do," he said and pulled out a chair.

Cornelia leaned forward. "Doctor Jones, how is my brother?"

"He's resting peacefully. He'll be fine."

Cornelia sighed. "Thank goodness. What about the fever?"

"He doesn't have the fever, but he does need to take it easy. A man in his condition needs plenty of rest. I've given him a sleeping draft. He's sleeping peacefully now."

"Doctor Jones, he will get well from the consumption, won't he?" Cornelia allowed herself to come right out and ask for the first time since Paxton had taken ill.

The doctor blanched at her question but quickly recovered himself. It was not his place to break a patient's confidence. "I've seen a case or two like your brother's. It's not usually fatal for a man like Paxton. He's sick, but if he is going to get well, there isn't a better place than up here in the fresh air of the Colorado mountains."

The doctor seemed nervous, and his remark a little queer, but hearing that Paxton had a good chance of getting well superseded a momentary suspicion. "Thank you, Doctor."

He accepted the cup from Annie and took a sip. "Well, I'd best be getting on home now."

"Won't you stay for a meal?" Cornelia suggested.

"Another time."

"What about your bill?"

"You can pay me when your brother is well enough to have me over for that meal, young lady."

"If the doctor won't stay, I will," Locke said.

"I'll see you out, Doc," Annie announced. "Why don't you and Locke take a walk in the fresh air, and

I'll have breakfast ready in an hour." Cornelia opened her mouth to protest, but Annie raised her hand. "Don't you worry none. I'll keep watch over Paxton."

"Sounds like a good idea," Locke answered. "Are you game, Nellie?"

Cornelia only hesitated a moment before she said, "Give me a minute." She went to the pantry and pulled out five aromatic crusts of bread and tucked them in her skirt pocket.

Locke watched her with a questioning gaze. It was obvious she was not packing a picnic snack. He decided that she might be hungry, so he said, "Honey would go well with the bread."

"You think so?"

Locke just shrugged, having no idea what she had in mind. She hurriedly took out the crusts, slathered them with honey from the cupboard, wrapped them up, and returned them to her pocket. "I'm ready."

"In that case lead the way and I'll follow."

McCurdy stood in the doorway of the barn watching the couple stroll off toward the path leading to the river. It infuriated him that that woman was being so friendly with the likes of Breckenridge and had spurned all his attempts to even speak to her for the past three weeks.

Hell, he could have his pick of the girls around these parts, and the one whose husband threw her over was acting as if she was better than her kind. He punched the wall. No common doxy was going to treat him as though he was worth less than the dirt on her heel and get away with it!

"You can play the high and mighty lady now, little colleen. But just you wait. My time will come, Mrs. High and Mighty. My time will come."

Chapter Ten

The sun glistened through the pines and the birds chirped as Locke and Cornelia strolled up the hill west of the cottage. Squirrels and chipmunks appeared and sat up straight with expectant looks.

Cornelia stopped and pulled the crusts of bread from her skirt pocket.

"What are you doing?" Locke asked.

"I often feed the animals on my walks."

"That can be dangerous," he advised.

"Nonsense," she said with a flip of her hand, ignoring him.

Disregarding her stubbornness, Locke decided to appeal to her obvious concern for the wild creatures. "Those animals are going to grow dependent on you. Then what are they going to do when you leave? They should be foraging for the winter."

"I don't feed them that much," she protested, again ignoring his advice and tossing a few more crumbs. "You know, just yesterday when I was out for my walk, I saw two young fawns playing in a meadow. They were having such a grand time. Come—" she held out her hand to him "—and let me show you. I'll bet they will love the honey."

Locke was surprised by the gesture coming from a lady who had been so badly scarred. Forgetting his advice about feeding the animals, he did not hesitate and took her hand. It was warm and velvety smooth. Her fingers were long and slender as they curled around his, and he wondered if she played the piano-forte like the one he had noticed in the cottage.

They reached the meadow in short order and she kneeled behind a large fallen tree, pulling him down beside her. "Over there—" she motioned "—if we wait quietly, perhaps the fawns will come."

Locke waited quietly by her side. He was amazed at how girlish she could be once she had unburdened the secret she had been carrying. He decided to wait until she broached the subject of her divorce again before saying anything more. He wanted to reassure her that it made no difference to him whatsoever.

They had waited less than ten minutes before two fawns appeared. The pair leaped and made high-pitched squeaks as they romped and frolicked, chasing each other.

"Aren't they adorable?" Cornelia whispered. She forgot herself and squeezed his arm. Immediately, she withdrew. "Forgive me."

"Cornelia, there is nothing to forgive," he murmured, gazing directly into her warm green eyes.

Cornelia smiled weakly, then turned away from his all too probing gaze.

Locke forced himself to focus on the fawns although he would rather have focused his attention on the lady next to him. He felt a kindred pull toward her. The snap of twigs and crunching of fallen, dried leaves broke into his unsettling thoughts.

Locke looked back over his shoulder and immediately froze. The largest black bear he had ever seen was within twenty feet behind them, sniffing the air.

He groaned inwardly. He had known better than to let her bring that damn honey!

With great care, he turned to Cornelia. "Don't move a muscle," he whispered. "Don't even breathe hard." She opened her mouth to question the man's strange behavior, but he quickly brought his finger to her lips.

She swatted his hand away. "What do you think you are doing?" she demanded.

"Hush!" He put his hands up and slowly twisted her head until Cornelia's vision caught on the bear.

She gasped, her heart thudding. The bear sniffed the air again and slowly approached them. Cornelia closed her eyes.

The next thing she knew a heavy weight was pressing her into the bed of pine needles beneath her. Her eyes flipped open. She was nose to nose with Locke. She could feel his breath on her neck, and goose bumps rose down her sides. She pushed at his chest, but he remained pressed against her.

"What do you think you are doing?" she breathed, frightened by the sudden intimacy.

"Protecting you."

"Protecting me?"

"Yes, protecting you," he reiterated.

His legs pushed against the flimsy fabric of her skirt, and his heat flamed her cheeks. "Well, must you protect me so well?"

"Would you prefer I leave you to the bear's mercy?"

"No, but why don't you just shoot it or something?"

Despite the seriousness of their precarious situation, he could not help himself. He smiled at her naïveté. "No gun."

"Why not?"

"I don't usually accompany a lady out into the forest who carries tidbits to attract the wild creatures. Now, shhh."

Cornelia could hear the huge animal lumbering closer. "But what shall we do?" she rasped, wide-eyed.

"No matter what happens, lie still and make no attempt to flee, understand?"

Cornelia nodded. She opened her mouth to speak.

"No more talking, if we're going to get out of this unscathed."

Cornelia held very still, barely breathing. She felt a cold nose nudge her leg. Panicky, she looked up into Locke's eyes.

Locke smiled back in an effort to reassure her. He kissed the tip of her nose although he longed to taste those trembling lips. Instead he winked and concentrated on making sure the lady did not lose her head and do something foolish, such as trying to escape the bear.

The urge to run was nearly overwhelming as the bear continued to sniff its way up her leg. It pushed at her skirt pocket and pawed at the crusts of bread and honey hidden there. Cornelia felt the tug of her skirt and heard the seams give way as the fabric ripped. She was certain that within the next few moments they were going to be torn to pieces.

Locke covered her head with his arms and put his head in the cradle of her neck and shoulders. They remained that way for long minutes while the bear munched on the bread and honey with great noisy enthusiasm. Finally, when she did not hear any sounds other than the rapid thudding of Locke's heart for a few minutes, she ventured to ask, "Has it gone?"

Locke inched up on his elbows and glanced behind

them. "No, it is sitting back there, licking its chops."

"Do you think we could get away?"

"Not yet."

Her chest was rising and falling at an alarming rate, and Locke almost felt a twinge of guilt about having lied. The bear was nowhere in sight, but he could not bring himself to tell her the truth because she would again put a respectable distance between them, and Locke found that he liked to be close to her.

Cornelia waited. The only time she had been in this position, other than the episode at the train depot in Denver when she and Locke had collided, was with Linley in their own bed in the dark. It was terribly improper, and she did not want Locke to get the wrong idea about her as the people back home in Connecticut had. "How about now? Is it gone?"

Locke looked back. Then looked at Cornelia again. "What would you say if it were gone?" he whispered in that full, deep voice of his.

"I would say that you had best get off me."

"Then it's still there."

Cornelia looked deep into those silver-brown eyes. He was not being truthful with her; she could see it in those dancing silver flecks. Her breasts were rubbing against his chest and despite her efforts to still a feeling of excitement, her breasts were cresting beneath the yellow muslin fabric. Women were not supposed to have any of the strange feelings she was experiencing now, and in spite of her fear that the bear could indeed still be there, she shoved with all her might.

Locke landed on his side with an "oof"!

Cornelia sat up. The bear was nowhere in sight. "It's gone," she said in an accusing voice. Trying to smooth what was left of her skirt down over her ex-

98

posed thighs, she said, "How long has it been gone?"

A guilty look lent his features a becoming roguish cast. He shrugged. "Not more than five minutes."

"Five minutes! Then why didn't you let me up sooner?"

"Would it frighten you if I said that it was because I couldn't *bear* to?" He flashed his brows.

She rolled her eyes at his attempt at humor. "Very amusing. But if you think just because I am a divorced wo—"

"Stop it, Cornelia!"

"Stop what? That since my divorce, men look at me differently, that women snicker at me, and the good, honorable people at home have turned their backs on me? I have been branded a scarlet woman, and until I can prove I am innocent, people think the worst and treat me that way," she cried.

"Stop treating yourself that way," he said softly. He scooted next to her and grasped her shoulders. "You don't have to fight the whole world."

She let out a cry of misery, and he pulled her into his arms and let her cry softly until the racking sobs finally stopped. Stroking the silken strands of her hair, he murmured, "No one is going to ever make you feel that way again. And no one is going to take advantage of you. So you can quit fighting, Cornelia. You can let your guard down because no one is going to think less of you for it. We all have pasts, and many people out here have come to start over. So relax. And if you prefer, I'll stay far away from you."

Cornelia pulled back. Tears had run down her face, leaving dried streaks. She sniffled and wiped at her cheeks. For a long moment she studied his face. There was only sincerity there. There was no hidden agenda, only an honest openness.

To Locke's horror, she broke out into another round of sobs. "I'm sorry. I didn't mean to upset you further," he said, not knowing what to do.

Cornelia smiled through her tears. "It's all right. I am crying because you have no idea what a relief it is not to feel that I have to hide any longer because I was afraid you had told the town's people."

"I wouldn't do that. If you want anyone to know, it is up to you to tell people."

Cornelia started to laugh and cry.

He tentatively reached out to her. "Are you sure you're all right?"

"Yes, for the first time in a long time, I think I am truly all right. And I owe it all to a bear."

"A bear!"

"Yes," she said, gathering what was left of her skirt up closer around her. "That crazy black bear. From now on, I am going to bring it honey every day."

"Oh, no, you're not. We may not be so lucky next time. I have never heard of a bear coming so close to a human before without causing a great deal of harm."

Cornelia clutched her throat. "You mean to tell me that we *really* might have been killed or worse?"

Without answering, Locke jumped to his feet, grabbed her hand and pulled her up beside him. Dragging Cornelia along with him, he strode back the way they had come.

"Where are we going?" she squealed, trying to keep the tattered pieces of her skirt decently together.

"To my place," he threw back over his shoulder.

"But I can't . . . we can't go there."

"Yes, we can and we are."

"Why?"

"Because I am going to get you a book on bears.

If you are going to be living up here, it is time you learn about the dangers as well as the beauty. And bears, my dear young woman, are very dangerous creatures. They are not cute little animals to be fed."

Once they reached Locke's cabin, Cornelia hesitated to go inside.

"Come on, this is no time for you to change your mind. I thought we had made our peace."

"We have, but—"

"No buts. We are friends, and as soon as I get you a book on bears, I'll take you back to Dunraven's cottage."

She looked down at her appearance. "I could use something to put over my skirt."

"Don't worry. I've got it covered," he said, causing her to relax and smile as they entered the cabin.

She laughed and tried to adjust her shredded skirt. "Covered, huh?"

"Make yourself comfortable while I get you a shirt and that book. You hungry?"

"Annie no doubt has been waiting for us with breakfast long prepared. I think it would be wise to return to the cottage for something to eat."

"Then you are still including me?" he asked, rummaging through his stacks.

"Yes, I am including you . . . my friend."

Locke's face beamed as he came toward her. "I like the sound of that . . . *your friend,*" he said, rolling their new relationship around in his mind. But secretly he was thinking that he would like the sound of her calling him something other than friend. It was a change in his thinking, wanting to get to know any woman again, let alone as a friend. Inside he knew that he had no intention of settling for friendship. He wanted more from Cornelia.

She had managed to help him through a difficult

time that had plagued him since his own divorce. And he had helped her let go of some of the pain she had been harboring.

"Here's the shirt. It ought to provide you with a little modesty until you can change."

He held the shirt while she slipped into the sleeves. Before she could button it herself, he pivoted her around and did the honors.

He grinned. "I have to say, my shirt never looked better."

For an instant Cornelia thought he was flirting with her. But instead of saying something scathing this time, she merely laughed and swirled around. "Who knows? I may start a new fashion."

She giggled. And Locke laughed with her. She was obviously pleased with herself, and he delighted in seeing her relax. She was an altogether different person than she had been. And Locke planned to be around as the scrawny chrysalis turned into a butterfly and spread her wings. She had the potential of being a real beauty, both inside and out. That former husband of hers was a fool, and Locke had no intention of letting her return to such a man if he could help it!

Chapter Eleven

It was almost noon when Cornelia and Locke returned to the cottage. Cornelia was sitting next to Locke on the seat of his wagon, and they were laughing at something that Sean McCurdy could not hear from his hiding place behind the hedge at the side of the house.

Sean burned inside that that woman was being so friendly with Breckenridge — even friendlier than when they had left earlier in the day. Hell, they had been out for hours. His mind conjured up all sorts of scenarios, imagining what they had been doing together.

Watching Annie rush off the porch to greet them, Sean stepped back so he wouldn't be detected. He was astounded when the Talbot woman alighted from the wagon. Her skirt was tattered and a glimpse of slender ankle hinted at the shapely legs that the woman hid under Breckenridge's shirt. Sean gasped and shrank farther back into the bushes at the shamelessness of the woman.

The leaves rustled drawing Cornelia's attention.

"What is that?" she asked, looking around. "Who's there?"

"Probably just a squirrel," Locke said. But his keen eyes had not missed the shadowy form lurking in the shrubbery.

Annie plucked at Cornelia's shredded skirt. "My goodness, whatever happened to you?" Her gaze shifted to Locke, a questioning look in her eyes.

He held up his palms. "Not guilty."

"Annie, we were accosted by the fiercest bear," Cornelia answered to dispel any misconceptions the girl might have.

Annie cocked a skeptical brow. "A bear?"

"Yes. I had bread with honey in my pocket to feed the fawns I told you about. The bear must have sniffed it out. Locke protected me, or God only knows what might have happened."

Annie's gaze shifted from Cornelia to Locke and back to Cornelia. "That's how your skirt got that way?"

"Yes, the bear tore it."

"The bear," Annie repeated, scratching her head. "I ain't never heard the like."

"It's true," Locke said.

"Guess you two were lucky, considerin' that you been feedin' those animals for weeks now."

"We stopped at my place so I could loan Cornelia a book about bears. Perhaps it will help her to be more careful from now on."

Cornelia flashed Locke a look of annoyance. "You needn't worry about my attracting any more bears. I've learned my lesson."

"Good."

Annie did not miss the attraction that sparked between the pair. In an effort to put an end to the tension, Annie wrung her hands. "Well, how about somethin' to eat? Paxton is waitin' for us."

Cornelia's attention immediately snapped from Locke. "How is my brother?"

"Jes' as ornery as he's ever been."

Paxton was seated in the kitchen at the long, pine-wood table. Cornelia went to his side and kissed him on the cheek.

"Did you rest well today?"

His eyes roved over his sister. "My goodness, what happened to you?"

Annie interceded. "You jes' take your seats, and you can tell your brother all about it while I dish up the food."

Annie scurried around the kitchen while Cornelia hurriedly changed. After she returned, she and Locke filled Paxton in on their encounter with the bear. To Annie's delight, Paxton insisted that she join them, and the remainder of the afternoon and into the evening was spent in companionable conversation.

The clock chimed nine o'clock and Annie jumped. "Land's sakes, I'd best get the kitchen cleaned up and go on home before Pa comes lookin' for me with a switch."

"I'll help," Cornelia offered.

The two women gathered the dishes from the table while the men adjourned to the parlor. Paxton settled into the overstuffed chair near the window and put his feet up on the ottoman while Locke laid a fire in the fireplace.

"This should take the chill off," Locke said.

"Thanks." Paxton adjusted a lap robe over his lap. "I couldn't help but notice that you and my sister finally seem to be getting along. You two reach a truce?"

Locke's attention snapped up. The faintest of

smiles turned the corners of his lips up. "We're no longer at each other's throat, if that's what you mean." He had no intention of divulging anything else.

Paxton looked over his shoulder toward the kitchen. He could hear laughter echoing from the room. "The girls seem to be getting along well."

"Annie doesn't know a stranger."

"She does have a way of making people feel at home."

"Even Cornelia," Locke said, thinking how difficult it had been for Cornelia to let down her guard.

"I have no right to be telling you this, and Cornelia would probably skin me alive if she knew what I'm about to say, but I want you to understand her."

Locke set a log on the fire, then took a seat near Paxton. "You don't have to tell me anything about Cornelia, I—"

"I want to," he interrupted. "Cornelia is a very special girl. She's been through a hard time that she didn't deserve, and I don't want her to be hurt again."

"You needn't worry that I would cause her any pain," Locke said in his own defense.

"I believe you," Paxton said. "I suppose I want you to understand her because she is very special to me. Bringing me out here is the first independent thing my sister has ever done. She has always been the pliant, obedient daughter and wife. So you can see she is just starting to test her wings."

"She told me she was accused of adultery."

Paxton furrowed his brows. "I'm surprised she told you about that part."

"I don't think she planned to. It just happened."

"She's innocent, you know," Paxton said

106

staunchly.

"I never thought otherwise."

Paxton looked deep into Locke's eyes. The man did believe in Cornelia's innocence. A spell of coughing grasped Paxton before he managed to say, "You really do believe she's innocent, don't you?"

"Yes, I do."

"You're one of the few. That ex-husband of hers jumped at the chance to get the community's sympathy, the cheating bastard."

Locke listened intently as Paxton poured out the whole sordid tale, and his heart silently went out to Cornelia. Even her so-called friends had deserted her.

Once Paxton had finished, Locke asked, "Why is she so insistent on returning to the man?"

"It's hard for some people to let go of an image. Our parents ingrained in Cornelia the importance of honor and suppressing her own needs. I don't think she's ever had the chance to think for herself before she brought me out here."

"She sure picked up the skill quickly." Locke laughed, thinking how she had been able to give him a good dressing-down without much effort.

"She's finally finding out there's more to life than meeting everyone else's needs."

"What about everyone's needs?" Cornelia asked, coming into the room.

"Everyone needs to have some fun in life," Locke said.

"Fun?"

"Yes, doing the things that gives you pleasure."

Annie was right behind Cornelia and chimed in, "I know what I like to do for fun and pleasure."

At the sight of Annie, Paxton brightened. "What

107

do you enjoy?"

"Dancin'. We have a dance every week in town along with a basket supper, you know."

At Paxton's crestfallen's face, Annie quickly amended, " 'Course, I like readin' awfully well, too."

"Do you like to dance?" Locke asked Cornelia as she quietly took a seat near the fire.

"I—"

"She used to love to dance before she married Talbot," Paxton inserted.

"Paxton!"

"You know it's true. That person you married—"

"Linley," she reproved.

Paxton rolled his eyes. "Yes, Linley. He didn't like to dance, so Cornelia gave it up."

Cornelia dropped her eyes for a moment. "I didn't mind, truly."

"Why don't you and Locke go to the next dance?" asked Annie, who was excited as a child with a new toy. "I could help pack you a supper basket."

"Annie, Locke hasn't asked me. Furthermore, I don't think that it would be proper," Cornelia protested.

"Nonsense," Paxton said. "But just so you'll feel comfortable, Annie and I'll accompany you."

Annie's excitement soared at the thought of attending such a social with Paxton although she kept her tongue when Cornelia said, "But you are in no shape to go dancing, Paxton."

"I may not be able to kick up my heels, but there is no reason why I shouldn't get a chance to meet some of the townspeople. And I can enjoy some of the scrumptious food that Annie fixes."

"I don't think—"

"Sounds like a good idea," Locke interceded. "You've been doing way too much thinking. Haven't I told you that before?"

"Yes, but—"

"You needn't worry, Sister dear, I won't overdo it," Paxton said, interrupting. "I'll get lots of rest before we go, and we don't have to stay late."

Cornelia searched their faces. They were expectant. It was obvious that Annie was excited by the prospect of going to the dance with Paxton. Paxton had been practically a recluse since they had arrived in Estes Park and deserved to get out. Locke was the only one with a curtained expression. She could not read whether he really wanted to go along or not. Of course, it wouldn't be as if he were escorting her. They would be going as a group. Perhaps it would be all right.

Paxton noticed she was wavering and decided to settle the issue before she could say no. "Good. Then it's all settled." Paxton turned to Annie. "When is this dance and basket supper?"

"Next Saturday."

"Okay, next Saturday it is," Locke said.

Cornelia's eyes shot to Locke, but before she could beg off, Paxton laboriously rose to his feet. "At last, I can get out of this house and be around people. I feel better already. Annie, would you help me with my blankets before you leave?"

Cornelia swallowed her protest and waited while Annie helped Paxton to his feet and escorted him down the hall. Once Cornelia was alone with Locke, she turned a steady gaze on him.

"I did thank you for protecting me this morning, didn't I?"

Locke smiled. "Yes, you did."

Awkward moments passed until Cornelia said, "About that dance. You really needn't attend if you'd rather not."

"What makes you think that I don't want to go?" he asked, suddenly taken aback by her shy demeanor. Now that they no longer were adversaries, she was retreating into a protective shell.

"You didn't seem particularly anxious."

"I have a confession to make."

Cornelia scooted to the edge of her chair and steeled herself. She told herself that it didn't matter if this man rejected her company. After all, his opinion was not important, she repeated silently. Yet she sucked on her lower lip.

"A confession?"

Locke shrugged. "Dancing has never been one of my strengths."

Cornelia breathed a silent sigh. "I haven't had the opportunity to put Miss Goodhue's strict dance lessons to use for over four years, but I am willing to teach you if you're interested."

Locke couldn't help himself, he smiled. She had misunderstood. How was he to correct her? Paxton had said that she was just trying her wings. It had to help her feel good if she thought she was teaching him something. He had to admit that this morning she had felt real good in his arms, and a dance would prove the perfect opportunity to hold the lady again.

Cornelia waited a reasonable length of time for him to answer. Growing impatient and feeling awkward, she said, "It was only a suggestion."

"Cornelia, if you don't mind spending the time with me, I would very much like to have you share your dance education with a most willing pupil.

110

When do we start?"

"I would have time while Paxton is resting. Tomorrow afternoon?"

"Tomorrow afternoon would be fine." Locke rose. "Guess I ought to be heading on home now. It's getting late."

Cornelia rose to her feet. "I'll escort you to the door."

"Thanks, but I know the way out. See you tomorrow afternoon," he said with a nod. He grabbed his jacket and slid his arms into it.

"Wait, I'll get your shirt."

Unable to stop himself, Locke blurted out in his deep voice, "No hurry. You can launder it first. That way it'll be in the same shape that it was when I gave it to you."

Cornelia at first thought of retorting, but she noticed that he was smiling. "Oh, no, Locke, it won't."

He cocked a brow. "Oh?"

"It will be in better shape. I'd never allow a man of mine to wear anything tinged gray like that one was."

The minute the words left her lips, she could have bitten her tongue. She blushed down to her toes. "I mean—"

"Good night, Cornelia," Locke said, saving her the awkwardness of making an explanation. "See you tomorrow afternoon."

Cornelia watched him walk down the hallway toward the door. She had noticed his size and strength before, but now her senses were heightened and her awareness took on a new and different shape when she thought about his holding her against his hard chest.

Determined to put such unbidden thoughts from

her mind, Cornelia extinguished the lamps in the parlor, and as she headed toward Paxton's room to say good night, she forced herself to think about Linley. Yet as she opened Paxton's door, Locke Breckenridge kept intruding into her mind.

Chapter Twelve

Cornelia was preening before the mirror when Paxton stopped in the doorway on the way to take his afternoon nap. He smiled to himself. It was the first time he had seen her take much time with her appearance since his return from Europe.

"Glad to see you fussing with your hair again," he said.

Cornelia swung around, a gilt-handled mirror in her hand. "I'm not fussing with my hair," she protested.

A wide smirk on his face, Paxton said, "That is a new way of doing your hair, isn't it? I like the loose curls."

"I didn't know you kept up with the latest styles," she said flippantly, feeling self-conscious over the special pains she was taking with her hair.

He winked. "I don't, but I do have eyes."

"Perhaps I should comb it back and pin it up into a knot," she said and picked up a brush.

"No, you shouldn't." He gave her an impish grin. "You haven't looked so good in months."

Cornelia dropped her hands on her hips. "I'm not trying to look good, as you put it."

"Of course not." Paxton moved into the room and

113

perched on the bed. "I do like that frilly blouse. It gives you a feminine appearance." At her growing discomfort, Paxton changed the topic. "Isn't Locke supposed to be here shortly?"

"Yes, but you need to take your nap," she instructed.

"I intend to although I have to admit I'd love to see his reaction when he sees you." He ignored the tightening of Cornelia's lips and continued. "Perhaps Locke'll still be here when I get up. I do enjoy visiting with the man; he has so many fascinating tales to tell."

"Are you hinting that I should ask him to stay for supper tonight?"

"I hadn't thought of it, but I'm glad you did. Locke's unlike so many other people who have shied away from me since I returned from Europe, fearing I may contaminate them."

Cornelia cocked her brow. "As long as you are not attempting to play matchmaker, I suppose there'd be no harm in his staying for supper."

"Good."

Cornelia set the brush down and went to Paxton. "Let me help you to your room."

He waved her off. "I keep telling you that I am not a total invalid." He rose and went to the doorway where he paused. "While you're at it, why don't you put on that lavender ruffled skirt of yours? You look real pretty in it."

Cornelia rolled her eyes. "I wish you would stop it. I am not trying to make an impression on Locke Breckenridge. I am merely helping him learn to dance. Nothing more."

Paxton smirked. "Whatever you say."

"It's true," she insisted. "I am going back to Linley

114

where I belong once you are feeling better. I have no interest in another man and never will."

"Of course not. But put the lavender on anyway."

"Well, perhaps I shall. But only because it is an excellent dancing skirt and will make the lessons more realistic."

Paxton slowly turned, grunting as if he were in pain as he made his way down the hall toward his room. Once he was certain he was far enough away from Cornelia's room, he stepped up his pace. Cornelia had so needed someone to take care of to take her mind off her troubles with Linley that Paxton had decided not to tell her the good news. Despite his collapse two days before, he was not as ill as everyone thought, and it had helped Cornelia immeasurably to mother him. Now, though, he was having second thoughts. Especially since he had met Annie.

Paxton entered his room and lay down on the bed. For a long time he rested with his arms behind his head, staring at the ceiling, trying to figure out a way to make Cornelia believe that he was regaining his health so he would be free to start courting Annie and still keep Cornelia from packing up and returning back East.

Cornelia was standing on the porch when Locke arrived. Her hair, hanging in loose curls down her back, was tied with a lavender ribbon that matched one of the most feminine skirts Locke had seen since he left Leadville.

Framed against the rough-hewn lodge, Cornelia made his heart lurch. Despite the vow he had made to live as a hermit on the mountain, he found that

115

his mind drifted to the lady whenever he was away from her.

She had filled out since she had come to Estes Park and she was no longer so pale. Her daily walks in the sunshine had given her once sallow cheeks a healthy blush.

"Are you ready for that dance lesson, or are you going to stand there and stare at me?" she asked with a soft smile.

"Does it bother you?"

"Bother me?"

"My staring."

"Gentlemen do not stare at ladies," she scolded and turned to go back inside before he noticed that she had actually been enjoying the approval in his eyes.

"Not without good reason," Locke said, stopping Cornelia in her tracks. He liked her tiny waist, and from the gentle flare of her skirt, he could tell that she had a nicely rounded backside as well. With a few more pounds she would be indisputably most attractive.

Cornelia counted to five before pivoting around to face him once again. She chastised herself for secretly enjoying the harmless flirtation and stiffened her stance. She was not going to get into another verbal sparring match with the man. "And am I to assume that you feel you have good reason to stare?" she asked before she realized she had made a tactical error.

A wide grin slid easily over his lips. "I'd say I have very good reason."

A long silence ensued.

"Aren't you going to ask me what my reason is?" Locke prodded.

116

"Somehow I don't think that I should."

"Why?" he pressed. "Because you are afraid to hear that another man beside your ex-husband finds you attractive?"

"Locke, please. I am a married lady—"

"You are a divorced lady, Cornelia. Your foolish ex-husband let you go. That makes you free to accept compliments from other men."

"I don't know how to feel free to accept compliments when in the eyes of God I still feel married. I don't think—"

"Haven't I told you not to think? Cornelia, you are not married any longer, and in time you'll come to accept it." A look of frustration crossed her face, causing him to try to lighten the mood. "You might as well get used to compliments because I intend to bestow them on you on a regular basis from now on."

Cornelia sighed, growing increasingly uncomfortable with the direction the conversation was taking. "Perhaps the dance lessons aren't such a good idea after all," she finally said.

He sent her a coaxing smile. "You are not going to renege on your offer, are you?"

"I have never reneged on anything in my life!"

To Cornelia's utter shock, Locke bounded up on the porch, took her in his arms, and swung her around. "Good." He bent her backward, looking deep into wary green eyes. "I'll be over every day, so we will be the best dancers at the dance."

Her chest heaving, she said breathlessly, "I think you'd best let me up."

"Are you sure that's what you want?" he murmured.

"Of course I'm sure."

Reluctantly, Locke righted the lady. "Where are these lessons going to take place?"

"In the parlor. Annie and I have moved the furniture so we'll have plenty of room."

As Locke followed Cornelia into the house, he asked after Paxton and talked on about his books, but Cornelia wasn't truly listening. She was still reeling from their unexpected closeness.

"Well?"

Rudely brought back to reality by the tap on her shoulder, she started. "Pardon?"

"I asked if you'd read the book about bears that I loaned you."

"Oh, yes, yes, did. It was most informative."

"Then you'll be more careful about feeding the animals from now on?"

"Yes. There was a section on how animals forage, and I realize now that I shouldn't be feeding any of the wild creatures. I wouldn't want to be the cause of some poor animal starving to death during the winter just because I was being selfish and wanted to have a few minutes' pleasure feeding them."

"You know, you can get just as much pleasure out of watching them. I have a pair of field glasses in my cabin; I'll bring them next time I come. Then you can watch them to your heart's content while they romp."

"Thank you, I think I'd like that."

They entered the parlor, and Locke stood in the middle of the floor while Cornelia went to the piano.

"Isn't it going to be a little hard for me to learn to dance while you are playing that thing?" Locke asked. He held out his arms and embraced an imaginary partner. "I believe it is customary to have a partner with more substance."

"I am going to be your partner."

"Then I'll hum," he said and hummed a waltz, clumsily shuffling around the room, still pretending to be holding someone.

Cornelia watched his awkward efforts with amusement. As she observed him, it dawned on her that Linley never would have played the merry-andrew. Linley could not tolerate the thought of anyone laughing at him. The realization that Locke could so easily waltz about the room was cause for thought.

"Silly, you can stop now. Lord Dunraven has furnished the parlor with the most wonderful player piano I discovered last week. All I have to do is fit this roll in here," she said, struggling with the cylinder.

Locke was at her side immediately and took the paper from her hands. "Let me," he offered.

Cornelia stepped back and gazed at the ripple of his muscles beneath his shirt as he bent over the piano. Again, her mind did a comparison of Locke and Linley. Linley had never offered to help her with anything in the house. Of course, they hadn't been able to afford the popular household instrument, let alone the newly invented player piano.

"I've often wondered how it works. A friend back home has one, and we often used to speculate about it."

Locke glanced back over his shoulder. "It works through a system of bellows connected to a suction chamber by air ducts." He held up the paper roll. "The perforated paper moves across a tracker bar and when the hole comes into line a duct releases a valve and causes the hammer to strike a string."

Cornelia listened attentively to his technical explanation, marveling at the wealth of knowledge the man had and wondering about how he had come to

119

know so much. "You seem to know a lot about a lot of things," she said.

"I like to read" was all he answered, which left her no room to question him further. Instead, she said, "Ready?"

A waltz started on the piano, and Locke turned toward her with a broad smile on his face, his arms akimbo. He moved in front of her and said, "I'm all yours. Do with me as you may."

"Yes, well, the first thing you need to do is put your hand on my waist."

He beamed. "My pleasure."

"Take my other hand in yours," she instructed, fighting to ignore the tingling sensations his hand on her waist elicited in her.

The way he clasped her hand was like a caress and sent Cornelia's heart to thudding in beat with the music. His fingers entwined with hers, and he ran his thumb along the side of her hand.

She glanced up at him, then quickly looked away. "Start with your left foot and slide it to the left, then feet together before you take a step forward, understand?"

"Why don't we try it? Isn't there some kind of saying that practice makes perfect?"

"Until you are comfortable, look down at my feet and do what I do."

"I'd rather look into your eyes," he said softly.

"If I am going to have any success at all with you, you are going to have to be serious about what we are doing," she instructed, despite the forbidden pleasure making her senses reel.

"But I am. As a matter of fact, I haven't been as serious about anything for years."

"Yes, well . . ." she said, letting her voice trail off.

They tried a box pattern several times, going through the steps in awkward silence. "That is very good. Now, if we count one-two-three, one-two-three it will help with the rhythm."

"One-two-three," he counted.

"Very good." She held herself rigidly at a respectable distance despite the undeniable pull she felt toward him. "Ready, begin. One-two-three, one-two-three, one-two—ouch!"

"Sorry. I didn't hurt you, did I?"

"Besides the fact that I may have to do without that toe for the remainder of my life, no. Shall we try it again?"

"I'm ready when you are," he said and pulled her closer in his embrace.

Cornelia tried to pull back. "You can't watch your feet if you are holding me so close," she announced with great tact and control.

"I'll manage. Now, are you going to practice with me or renege?"

"I am going to practice. But not so close," she decreed and stiffly repositioned herself at a respectable distance. "Ready? Begin."

Locke smiled to himself as they glided around the room. He enjoyed her company, and she was beginning to loosen up a bit around him despite her efforts to keep a distance between them. He made a point to narrowly miss her toes so she would not declare him a success and discontinue his lessons. But it was hard remembering himself and not pulling the lady into his embrace, for she felt good in his arms and her lilac-scented hair beckoned him.

"Well, I'll be hog-collared," Annie said as she came into the parlor. "You two look mighty natural together."

Cornelia immediately broke apart. "I was just teaching Locke to waltz."

"What for?" Annie said to Cornelia's dismay.

"For the upcoming dance, of course."

"We do livelier dances than that. You know, foot-stomping music where a body can kick up her heels."

For the next two hours, Locke hid his disappointment as Annie took over the lessons and had them square dancing to allemande-left calls and swinging their arms to her hearty singing voice. Cornelia was openly laughing and seemed to be having a grand time, so Locke good-naturedly kept from suggesting that he would rather finish learning the waltz. He would have preferred holding Cornelia in his arms. Silently he vowed that next time he would send Annie on an errand into town.

Chapter Thirteen

For the next five days Locke showed up at the same time each afternoon. To Cornelia's delight he never came empty-handed. He brought books for her to read, and they often discussed them after his lesson. He brought samples of flowers, merely so she would become familiar with them, or so he said. And he always spent time with Paxton as well, which further served to endear him to Cornelia. In this, too, he was unlike Linley who, after he had learned about Paxton's illness, had ordered Paxton from his house and had demanded that Cornelia forsake her brother as well, even during their pending divorce.

The afternoon of the dance Cornelia spent more time than usual readying herself. As she raked the comb through her hair, she worried whether she was being selfish. Paxton had come to Colorado to get well, not to attend a social affair that afforded her the opportunity to dance once again after so many years. Swallowing her doubts, she tied a ribbon around her curls.

She twirled twice before the full-length mirror in her room before going to fetch Paxton. He was sitting at the window, gazing off at the distant mountains.

"Daydreaming?" she asked.

"Reveling in the surrounding beauty. You know, it makes me feel closer to God." At the look of alarm on her face, he added, "Don't worry, I'm not thinking about God in terms of my own mortality."

She forced a bright smile. "I didn't think you were."

"Yes, you did. We all have to die sometime, Sister dear. But I'm not anywhere near ready yet. Each day that I'm here, I feel stronger and more invigorated." He held out his hands, and she moved forward and grasped them. "You know, I have you to thank for that. I just wish there were something I could do for you."

"Being with you is more than enough," she said. "I love you." She hugged him.

He broke off and held her from him. "Are you ready to do a little toe tapping tonight?"

Cornelia smiled at his use of words. He obviously had been spending a lot of time with Annie.

"I'm ready if you are."

"Then what are we waiting for? Let's go meet the people of Estes Park."

"And join Annie. Isn't she going to be there with her father tonight?"

"Seven sharp. You think he'll take to a city slicker like me?"

"He won't be able to help himself," Cornelia said. "With your charm, he won't have a chance."

They pulled up near the junction of the Fall and Thompson rivers and stopped in front of the post office. Not far from the building, gaily colored lights swayed around a hastily erected pavilion from where lively music echoed. Cornelia collected the basket of goodies she had packed for basket supper, and they approached an empty bench on the edge of the dance floor.

When several people moved away, Paxton stiffened. "Ignore them," Cornelia suggested. She laid a blanket on the bench, and Paxton sat down.

"Don't worry about me, Sister dear. You go mingle and have a good time. I'm going to sit back and enjoy people-watching."

Cornelia squeezed his hand. "I'm going to stay right here until Annie and her father arrive."

"Have it your way. But I do not need to be babied."

"I never imagined you did."

She remained by Paxton's side all the same.

They were not at the dance more than fifteen minutes, listening to the music and watching the dancers fling their arms to the lively music, when Locke arrived. Cornelia noticed that he stopped and cordially greeted several couples before winding his way toward her. He was breathtakingly handsome in his jacket and string tie.

Locke removed his hat. "Evening. Nice night for dancing, don't you think?"

Cornelia could not hide a smile when he began to demonstrate his skills before her.

Paxton laughed at the big man's antics. "Cornelia, you had better hurry and join Locke before people begin to talk."

"Are you sure you'll be all right here alone?" she asked.

"I'll be fine. Now, run along and have a good time."

Before Cornelia could protest, Locke pulled her to her feet. The fiddler immediately stopped playing, and the next thing Cornelia knew, the tempo changed to a waltz. Locke gathered her into his arms, and with an expertise he could not have learned in just one week, he glided her about the floor.

"Did you arrange this?" she asked.

"The dance?"

"No, the waltz music. You made arrangements with the musicians, didn't you?"

He held her tighter and settled his chin in her hair. "I confess. I couldn't let our lessons go to waste."

The gurgling of the rivers flowing together combined with a gentle breeze swaying the colored lanterns that sent a variety of colors flickering around them. For five minutes Cornelia let the rest of the world fade into the background of her thoughts while she surrendered to the sensation of being in his arms.

"Where did you learn to dance like that?" she asked when the music ended and her mind took control again. "Certainly not from a few dance lessons a week before the dance."

"I'm a natural."

"Yes, a natural. Why didn't you tell me you knew how to dance?" she chided.

Locke shrugged. "You didn't ask."

"I certainly did."

"No, you assumed I needed to learn."

"So you let me teach you when all along you could have been giving me lessons."

"Angry?"

"No, how could I be after all the books and

flowers you've brought, not to mention the time you've spent with Paxton." Her face fell. "Some of the residents moved away when we arrived," she said. "We did meet a nice family—the Wrigleys," she added on a brighter note.

He put his arm on her back and escorted her toward where Paxton was sitting. "The Wrigleys are good folks. They rent cabins not far from your cottage. The ones who snubbed you are fools and not worth getting to know."

Cornelia had to blink at Locke's support. Linley had always lectured her about the importance of being in the right circles and saying and doing just the right thing so the right people would accept her. And here was a man who advocated that if people did not accept her, she should not concern herself with them.

By the time they weaved their way through the crowd and Locke introduced Cornelia to several of the homesteaders, Annie and her father were sitting with Paxton.

"Cornelia, this is Joe Mills, Annie's father," Locke said. "Joe has just started working at the telegraph office. So if you need to send a wire, Joe's the man to see."

A withered man not much taller than Annie thrust out a skinny arm. "Howdy, ma'am. I'm mighty pleased to make your acquaintance. My Annie has been tellin' me all about you."

Cornelia took his hand. His fingers were bony and heavily callused from years of scratching out a living. "You have raised a wonderful daughter, Mr. Mills."

"Joe, please, ma'am. And I know it. My Annie's the best."

"I agree," chimed in Paxton, who virtually beamed.

"She surely thinks muchly of you, too, young man."

"Pa!" Annie clasped her hands behind her back and rocked on her heels.

Paxton patted the bench next to him. "It's all right, Annie, it's a mutual feeling."

Annie dropped her eyes and fidgeted with her ruffle-trimmed calico skirt. "How about if we dig into the vittles I brung? Me and Pa brung a blanket so if you all want, we can set ourselves down by the river. That is, if it ain't too cold for you, Pax."

"Pax?" Cornelia echoed and grinned at her brother.

"I say somethin' wrong?" Annie blurted out, her eyes wide with innocence.

"No," Cornelia reassured the girl. "I used to call Paxton that when we were children, is all."

"Then you don't mind none?"

"Of course not." Cornelia bent down to pick up the basket. As she grasped the handle, Locke's fingers closed over hers, and their eyes met and held.

He slowly removed his hand, letting his fingers glide along hers, lingering. "I'll carry it."

Cornelia fought to force back the sudden unbidden thoughts that threatened her. "Thank you," she said and stepped away.

Locke and Joe billowed the blanket out and spread it along the riverbank, and they settled onto it. The ladies dished up the delicacies they had packed, and as they munched on bison strips, pickles, fresh bread, and an assortment of fresh fruits and melons brought into the Park from

128

the low-lying prairies, they watched the dancers.

After supper, Annie insisted that Paxton lay his head in her lap and cover up with another blanket she had her pa fetch from the buggy. Locke and Cornelia participated in the variety of dances, laughing and giggling as they tried to keep up with the fast-paced calls.

Cornelia was so enjoying herself that she did not see Sean McCurdy arrive and stand at the edge of the dance floor.

Sean's eyes followed the uppity piece and enjoyed the bit of ankle displayed when that bastard Breckenridge twirled her around. He fumed inside that she could so readily accept that outsider and yet snub him. Just as the Virginia reel was ending, Sean had an idea.

He stepped in front of Cornelia as she was leaving the floor with Locke. "How 'bout a dance?"

The man was leering, and Cornelia had no desire to dance with him. "Perhaps another time, Mr. McCurdy," she said politely. "I have been dancing for some time, and we were just about to return to my brother. But thank you just the same."

She started to pass him, but he grabbed her arm. "What's the matter? Don't you think I be good enough to dance with the likes of you?"

Locke pried the man's fingers from around Cornelia's arm, glaring at him. Cornelia put a staying hand on Locke's arm. "Please, people are beginning to stare."

The two men faced off, Locke narrowing his eyes into mere slits. Sean was shorter but heavier than Locke and returned the glare, staring up into Locke's eyes. Sean swallowed hard. He had no desire to fight the man over the uppity bitch, but he had a reputation to maintain. Slowly, Sean slid his hand into his back pocket and fingered the piece of iron he kept there. If Locke Breckenridge challenged him, Sean had no doubt who would arise the victor.

Cornelia was frantic. "Locke, please."

"All I want is a dance, Breckenridge. It be the least she can offer to the man who nursed the mountain cub she found back to health and sent the creature back to the wild this very morning. Or have you staked your claim on the *lady?*"

Locke tensed, every muscle in his body itching for a fight. At the moment, there was nothing he would have liked better than to pulverize McCurdy. Locke did not like the man. There was something evil about him, and Locke did not want Cornelia anywhere near the Irishman, let alone being touched by him.

"Well? You be staking your claim?" Sean repeated in an effort to antagonize Breckenridge.

"No, of course, he isn't," Cornelia said. In an effort to defuse the situation, she added. "It is all right, Locke. I suppose I can spare one dance."

Locke's gaze shot to Cornelia. "I don't want you dancing with the likes of McCurdy," he stated.

Cornelia's chin shot out. Despite the fact that she did not want to be anywhere near the Irishman, she did not want to be the center of attention on her first public appearance among the Park residents. Neither did she want two men fighting over her. So she said, "I believe we discussed the fact that I am a free woman able to make my own decisions. And at the moment I have decided to dance with Mr. McCurdy."

Locke's eyes flashed. "What I said was true, you

are free to make your own choices. Too bad you have not learned how to decide which ones are in your best interests and which ones are not."

Locke curtly bowed and left Cornelia standing on the edge of the dance floor with a gloating McCurdy.

Locke went straight to where Paxton was resting with Annie and gathered up his jacket.

"You aren't going to leave yet, are you?" Paxton asked, rising up on his elbow and seeing that Cornelia was merely going through the motions of a lively polka with the ranch foreman.

"Yeah, Breckenridge, we ain't seed much of you since you come to these parts. Why not stay and get better acquainted?" Joe suggested.

Locke's eyes trailed to Cornelia. "I think I've stayed long enough," he stated flatly. "Besides, I have a party to guide up Longs Peak tomorrow morning, so I need to be getting on home."

"You will come to the ranch after you get off the mountain, won't you?" Paxton asked.

"I've been neglecting things around my place," Locke hedged, edging toward his horse. He was angry with Cornelia and did not want to hear her explanation until he had had time to cool off.

"You mind if I come to your place then?" Paxton asked, trying to keep Locke talking until Cornelia returned. The music was ending and he noticed she was disengaging herself from McCurdy.

"You're always welcome."

"Have a safe trip up the peak," Paxton said as Cornelia was making her way toward them, followed by the foreman.

"You're not leaving?" she asked to Locke's retreating back.

"Most cowards turn tail and be running when the competition gets too rough, ain't that be right, boy-o?"

Locke clenched his fists, itching to take McCurdy apart piece by piece. Garnering all the reserve he could find, Locke slowly pivoted around and said between clenched teeth, "And most fools know when their company is not wanted. But then again, McCurdy, you always have had difficulty telling an invite from a slight." Locke barely smiled between his teeth, then nodded to Cornelia. "Good night, *Mrs.* Talbot."

Cornelia stepped between McCurdy and Locke to stave off a confrontation. She reached out her hand toward Locke. "Locke?"

He stopped, but he was too angry that he had let the likes of McCurdy get to him to look directly at her.

"Good night. Thank you for tonight. I had a marvelous time dancing," Cornelia said.

"With me," Sean added with a sneer that only Cornelia could hear.

Cornelia watched Locke mount his horse and ride into the night before she turned on McCurdy. "I have danced with you and now I wish to spend time with my brother. So if you will please leave us?" She dismissed him with a turn of her back.

The others stared at Sean. He considered himself a man who knew when it was best to retreat and regroup. And he did not want to chance Paxton Lloyd's telling Lord Dunraven negative things about him, so he smiled triumphantly. "Thank you for the dance. I shall be lookin' forward to you and me dancin' again real soon," he said with an innuendo of something more than dancing.

"I don't like that man," Annie said after he had gone.

"Oh, he's all right. Just seems to have taken a shine to you, Sister dear," Paxton observed in an effort to make light of what could have been a volatile situation.

"Well, I have no intention of dancing with him ever again," Cornelia stated. "You look fatigued, Paxton. I think we should be getting back." She picked up the basket she had brought.

While Cornelia was loading the basket in the buggy, Annie turned to Paxton and said, "I wonder why Locke didn't just up and belt that horrible Sean McCurdy in the mouth. He looked like he wanted to awful bad."

Joe rubbed his stubbly chin. "Suppose it might be because I heard tell he's already killed a man with them fists."

Chapter Fourteen

Paxton was wheezing by the time they reached the cottage and entered. Although tired, he felt exhilarated that he had been accepted by Annie's father so easily. Annie herself had never once left his side to dance with any of the young men who had approached her and asked. The only thing that bothered him about the evening was the way Locke had left Cornelia. Then there was the matter about what Joe had said about Locke having killed a man. Paxton wondered whether he had been wrong to encourage Cornelia to spend time with a man capable of killing another.

"I could just kill Locke Breckenridge for the way he acted tonight," Cornelia fumed, following Paxton to his room and plumping his pillows with a vengeance.

"Cornelia! I'm surprised at you," Paxton gasped. "I've never heard you talk that way before."

Cornelia was immediately contrite. "I am sorry. I don't know what has gotten into me lately. That was an awful thing to say, talking about killing another human being."

In an effort to lighten the topic, Paxton said,

"Sounds as if you're becoming accustomed to living out here in the rough West."

"No matter where one lives, there is no excuse for taking the life of another," Cornelia said staunchly.

Paxton cocked his brow, wondering how she would react if she knew about Locke's killing another man. Well, Paxton decided, he was not going to say anything before talking to the man.

Cornelia pulled back the spread, folded it, and set it on the trunk. "Enough of such talk." She puttered a little longer, smoothing the sheets before she looked up sheepishly. "Did Locke say anything about me dancing with Sean McCurdy?"

"So that is what's bothering you?"

"It doesn't bother you?" she protested.

"The look on your face gives you away, Sister dear. Are you taking a liking to the man, perchance?"

"I like Locke Breckenridge as a dear friend, nothing more, if that is what you are wondering," she said without the conviction she knew she should feel.

Paxton smirked. "I think you have answered my question to my satisfaction."

"Then you can answer mine."

"Yours?"

Cornelia pinched her lips. "Well, did Locke say anything about Sean and me dancing together or not?"

"No, he said that it was time to be getting on home since he is taking a party up Longs Peak tomorrow morning."

She hid her disappointment by turning her interest to the mountain. "Longs Peak?"

"Didn't he tell you that he serves as a guide around here on occasion?"

"He doesn't talk much about himself." She was dying to ask Paxton how much he knew about Locke Breckenridge, but she did not want her brother to think she had more than a passing interest in the man.

"No, he doesn't. Well, it's late and I best be getting to bed. Annie will be here bright and early and is expecting to spend time reading to me in the morning."

"Good night, *Pax*," she said.

He ignored the way she said his name. "Nellie, would you do me a favor?"

Cornelia stopped halfway out of the room and swiveled around. "Of course, what can I do for you?"

"It's not for me . . . exactly. It's for Annie. Do you think that you could give her a few hints on . . . on how to-to . . ." His voice trailed off. He was too embarrassed to lay the suggestion out in the open. He did not want anyone to think that he disapproved of anything about the girl.

"To take care of herself?"

Paxton lent her a grateful smile. "It is not as if I don't like her the way she is, because I do."

"Of course you do. Say no more," Cornelia said, sparing her brother the need to ask her to teach the girl about personal habits. Annie was the sweetest girl that ever walked the face of the earth, but without a mother to guide her, her feminine habits were sorely lacking. "Good night, dear."

Cornelia shut the door behind her and went to her room. First thing tomorrow she planned to start Annie's education. Annie had admired several

136

of Cornelia's dresses, so Cornelia decided to start with the girl's outer appearance. She hummed to herself. Before she was done, Annie would be transformed without ever realizing what hit her. She frowned when thoughts of Locke Breckenridge entered her mind. Tonight had not ended the way she had hoped.

Cornelia undressed in the dark and after slipping into her nightgown went to the window and looked out toward Longs Peak. The jagged mountain was silhouetted against the golden light of the moon, and Cornelia found herself intrigued, wondering what it would be like to climb to the top of such a peak.

The party of six men from Denver met Locke outside his cabin in the gray light of dawn. Locke assessed the reporter from the *Rocky Mountain News* and his cronies. Not one of them looked to be hardy enough to scale the peak like W.N. Byers, founder of the newspaper, who had unsuccessfully tried in '64 and then finally succeeded in '68.

Locke counted two potbellies, three double chins and one scrawny weakling loaded down with enough equipment to live on the mountain for a year, that was, if the man managed to lug the copious supplies up there in the first place.

Josh Pays stepped forward. "You ready to take us up the peak?"

"Not until you get rid of three-quarters of that stuff you've dragged with you."

"Why, I've never heard of such a thing. We engaged you to guide us to the top of the mountain, not lecture us. We were outfitted by the best sports

137

salesman in Denver," Gilbey Hansocker sputtered, placing a meaty hand on the precious purchases.

"If you gentlemen want me to guide you up the mountain, then you have a decision to make. Either get rid of all that needless baggage, or you can get someone else to guide you. I'll be inside while you talk it over. You've got ten minutes to let me know what you've decided."

"A negative report from my paper could destroy any business you hope to build," Barton Falk announced.

"Falk, I suggest you get busy—" Locke looked at his watch "—you now have only eight minutes."

Locke went inside and poured himself a cup of coffee. He ought to send that group packing, but truth was that he needed a challenging climb to get a certain lady off his mind. He certainly didn't need the money, nor did he have any plan of establishing a guide business—although the thought of sharing the beauty of the peak with others on a regular basis intrigued him.

Within five minutes the raspy voice of Falk hailed Locke from the cabin. Locke stepped outside and smiled in triumph at the load of discarded equipment. "Well, gentlemen, looks like you are nearly ready to go. Just need to get rid of a few more things."

Despite the grumbling, Locke picked through the gear. He put to one side everything that was not needed. When only a small percentage was left, Locke swung his own pack onto his back. "Get your packs and fall in behind me."

"Aren't we going to ride to the base of the mountain?" Gilbey Hansocker whined.

Locke looked back over his shoulder at the motley men. "A little exercise never hurt anyone," he said and kept walking.

Cornelia had risen before the sun came up, hurriedly dressed, and wrote Paxton a note so he would not worry about her. She went to the stable and saddled a horse, thankful that Sean McCurdy was nowhere in sight. Mounting the animal, she spurred it in the direction of Locke's cabin. She did not want any misunderstandings between them after the dance last night, although she refused to openly acknowledge to herself that it was important to her to keep their friendship.

She reined in the horse in front his cabin and nearly tripped over a bunch of ropes and an assortment of equipment. "Climbing gear," she said to herself. She went to the door and knocked. "Locke? Locke, are you home?"

No answer issued from the cabin, so she went inside. The cabin was empty. Disappointed that she had arrived after Locke had left, Cornelia went back outside and stared up at the foreboding mountain.

With the sunrise, the snow-capped Longs Peak loomed orange and pink above the clouds. And Cornelia again wondered about climbing the distant giant. She went over to the equipment and picked through it again.

"Howdy," Annie said, coming upon Cornelia.

"Good morning. What are you doing here?" Cornelia asked, surprised to see the girl.

"Paxton told me you headed in this direction when you left the cottage. Thought you might like someone to accompany you back," she said easily.

What she didn't say was that her pa had been worried last night by the way McCurdy had stared at Cornelia and told Annie to keep an eye out for the Eastern lady. When she had learned from Paxton that Cornelia had left a note informing him that she was coming over here, Annie had excused herself and hurried after Cornelia.

"That's thoughtful of you, but it wasn't necessary." Cornelia picked up a metal ring. "What is this for?"

Annie shrugged. "I dunno, some kind of mountain climbin' equipment, I reckon. Why?"

"Just curious." Cornelia tossed the ring back on the pile. Wanting to hide further questions about her curiosity over the equipment, Cornelia hooked her arm with Annie's. "Let's head back to the cottage. We can ride double."

"I got a horse in them trees," Annie announced and motioned toward the grouping.

Back at the lodge for the next three days Cornelia busied herself reading everything she could find from Lord Dunraven's library about mountain climbing. In the afternoon while Paxton rested, Cornelia spent time with Annie.

"Would you help me clean out my wardrobe?" Cornelia asked the scraggly-locked girl.

Annie shuffled her foot. "Me? I don't know nothin' 'bout clothes. I wouldn't know the first thing 'bout what to keep and what to get rid of?"

"Would you like to?" Cornelia asked. It was the perfect opening to help the girl.

"Don't know where I'd have a need to use such know-how," Annie said, but from the longing in her eyes, Cornelia could tell that the girl was anxious to learn.

"How about around here? I know Paxton has always enjoyed a pretty skirt and long curls. You know, your hair has a natural curl. With a couple of ribbons I bet you would send Paxton's head spinning."

Annie's eyes went wide. "You really think he'd ever look at the likes of me?"

"I think his head has already started to swivel. With a few finishing touches, he won't stand a chance."

"You don't mind none? I mean because I ain't one of them fancy ladies like he's probably used to."

"Mind? Annie, you are the most genuine young lady Paxton has ever taken an interest in."

"He's interested in me like Locke Breckenridge is in you?"

Cornelia slapped her hand on her chest. "Me? Annie, you must be mistaken. Locke and I are merely friends. He isn't interested in me the same way that Paxton cares for you."

"I may not be worldly wise, but I know when a man has a hankerin' for a gal. And Locke's definitely got a hankerin' for you." She crinkled her brow. "Even if he don't know it yet hisself."

Cornelia turned away from the girl and picked through her wardrobe, trying to ignore what Annie had said. But try as she might, she could not get the girl's words out of her mind.

"How about this blue one? It will match your eyes," Cornelia suggested, holding up a long-sleeved, powder-blue dress with a bow at the waist.

Annie's eyes widened. "You sure? I ain't never had a dress so pretty before."

"Of course I'm sure." Cornelia helped Annie into

141

the dress. The girl twirled around in front of the mirror, holding her hair up high on her head.

"Sit down in front of the mirror, and I'll style your hair," Cornelia offered.

Annie's face dropped. "But my hair ain't so . . . so clean."

"I have the perfect soap. It smells like roses. You'll love it." Cornelia grabbed the fragrant cake before Annie could say anything. Cornelia could not believe how easy Annie was making her efforts to transform the girl. "Come on, we'll go into the kitchen and I'll lather your hair for you."

"Gosh, I often wished that I had a ma or sister to share things like this with. I used to wash my hair in a rainbarrel at home, but Pa hollered at me that I was wastin' water, so I quit."

"You won't have to worry about that any longer. From now on, you are going to have the prettiest hair in the whole Park. And you can come over here and wash your hair as often as you like."

In less than a half hour, Cornelia had scrubbed Annie's filthy mud-colored hair to a shiny, warm brunette with gold highlights. Twisting strips of cloth around strands of her hair, Cornelia was satisfied that once it dried, Annie would look like a new person.

While they waited for Annie's hair to dry, Cornelia gave the girl a badly needed manicure and applied a thick layer of face cream to Annie's scrubbed cheeks.

"Cornelia, have you seen Annie—" Paxton started, barging into Cornelia's room only to stop dead in his tracks.

"Oh, no," Annie screamed and ran from the room.

"Annie, come back. I've seen Cornelia like that lots of times," he fibbed.

Annie peeked around the doorway, looking as though someone had smeared flour paste all over her face and tied rags in her hair. Paxton kept a straight face despite the urge to smile.

Cornelia took Paxton by the shoulders and gently shoved him from the room. "Now that you know where Annie is, you can go out on the porch and get some sun."

"By myself?" he protested. "I was looking forward to Annie reading to me."

"Well, you'll just have to read to yourself for a while."

"I can wipe this greasy stuff off my face and be there in a few minutes," Annie offered.

"No, you can't," Cornelia said. "All right, Paxton, out you go."

"Guess I have no choice since you put it that way."

Paxton kept his face impassive until he headed down the hall. Then he clasped his hands together, rubbing them in anticipation.

His sister was about to work wonders.

"It's a miracle," Annie squealed two hours later as she looked at the mirror marveling over Cornelia's efforts. "I look like somebody else."

"Nonsense. You look like yourself. And with the instruction I gave you, you will be able to do it yourself from now on. And you can keep the dress. It looks better on you than it ever did on me."

"Golly, I look like I fit my name. I look like a Annabeth, don't I?"

"You certainly do, and we can start calling you Annabeth if you'd like."

Annie thought a moment and wrinkled up her face. "No, I think I like just plain Annie better for every day. It fits. I'll save Annabeth for special occasions."

Cornelia hid a smile at the girl's reasoning, and she had to agree. Annie truly did "fit" the girl.

Annie gave Cornelia a grateful smile. "Now that you have helped me look so pretty, I can help you."

Cornelia was taken aback. "Me?"

"Sure. Pa waited until you went to put the supper basket in the buggy last night to say anythin', but I think you should know what I heard."

"What you heard?" Cornelia echoed.

"I ain't sure I ought to be passin' stories, but you ought to know. You got a right." At Cornelia's bewildered expression, Annie took a deep breath and blurted, "Locke Breckenridge is a killer."

"His past has nothing to do with me," Cornelia said without emotion.

"Just thought you should know," Annie said innocently and flounced from the room to show off her new appearance to Paxton.

Once she was alone, Cornelia sank onto the bed. She had been spending time with a killer? Instead of deciding never to let that man come near her or her brother again, Cornelia decided to confront him and find out why. It would have been easy to avoid him, but it wouldn't be fair. She remembered how people had treated her back home, finding her guilty without giving her a chance. She had sworn to herself that she would never do that to anyone. Secretly, she hoped Annie was mistaken since Locke Breckenridge was increasingly on her mind.

Chapter Fifteen

Having returned from the mountain, Locke trudged the last mile to his cabin. He was thankful that that bunch of exasperating tenderfeet, who nearly got him killed up on the mountain due to their unwillingness to follow orders, had decided to go directly to the Elkhorn Lodge. Locke was tired and needed some peace and quiet after enduring that group for three days. He was in no mood for company.

When Locke opened the door, he was met by the sight of Cornelia curled up on his bed with her head on her arm and sleeping soundly. Her hair had come loose and was spread around her like golden threads. One of his favorite books lay open on the floor next to his bed. Any other time he might have found the lady inviting, but he could not understand what she was doing in his cabin.

Despite the inclination to lie down next to her, because he was so tired, Locke sat on a chair and propped his feet up on the table. As the darkness of a moonless night overtook the cabin, Locke was slumbering peacefully.

Cornelia awoke to a room enveloped in blackness. Silently cursing herself for falling asleep, she got up and began to feel her way in search of a lantern. She had not moved very far about the room when her fingers came upon what felt like a warm, firm log covered with cloth. She felt her way up the object until she felt what seemed to be a knot in the log.

"Umm, what a way to be awakened," Locke crooned, causing Cornelia to jump back as if she had been burned.

"You! What are you doing here?" she demanded, startled.

"In case you've forgotten, I live here," he said. He got up and lit the lantern. Holding it up, he saw that Cornelia was crouched in a corner. "What are you doing here?"

She got to her feet and took a breath to calm her nerves. "I was waiting for you."

"Well," he smiled broadly, "you certainly found me."

"Please, that was a dreadful mistake," she said lamely. "I came here to talk to you. Why didn't you awaken me when you returned?"

"You were sleeping so peacefully I didn't have the heart. But you said you came to talk to me. What about?"

"I'm not so sure that I should have come," she said, losing her nerve. "Perhaps I should return to the cottage before Paxton is worried and sends out a search party." She began to gather up her shawl. "I'm ready to have you take me back."

To Cornelia's chagrin, Locke sat down. "Well, I'm not ready to take you. You came here to talk to me, so talk."

Cornelia hesitantly sat back down. It was obvious that he was not about to let her go until he heard what she had to say. "A couple of days ago Annie told me something about you that disturbed me, and if you must know, I came here to hear it from you."

Locke crossed his arms over his chest. "And just what might that be?"

She looked right into his eyes. They were such a warm brown that she could not believe that he could have harmed anyone. "Annie told me that you were a killer."

To her dismay, he did not deny it. She waited what she felt a reasonable length of time, then prodded, "Is it true?"

Locke's face hardened. "If you are asking if I've ever taken the life of another, yes, it is true."

"Oh, dear me," she murmured.

"Cornelia, it was not like it sounds."

"Do you plan to tell me about it?"

He studied her. He had not talked about it since it had happened, but despite himself, he felt a pull toward the lady. "Cornelia, as you know, I, too, was married once. Well, my divorce was also rather messy. Unlike you, my ex-wife was cheating on me. She even flaunted it in front of everyone." He stopped for a minute at Cornelia's gasp before he continued.

"Adultery has been going on since the beginning of time, Cornelia. By the time I found out about my *sweet* wife, I no longer cared. The trouble was she was not satisfied with a divorce, she wanted her lover and my money too. So she sent her lover to waylay me in an alley outside the opera house one night. We scuffled and I won. The only trouble was that the other man died. There never were any charges, but shortly after that, I decided that I needed a change, so I moved here."

"And your wife?" Cornelia asked, her heart going out for the man.

"She got her divorce, and I pay her alimony on the stipulation that she stays out of my sight. She left town shortly after the incident. I haven't the slightest idea where she went, and as long as she stays there, I will gladly continue the payments through my attorney."

"I am sorry," Cornelia said and laid a comforting hand on his arm. "I never should have come."

He closed his fingers over hers. "Cornelia, I'm glad you did. Perhaps now you can see that divorce is not such a bad thing sometimes. It is not the end of the world. People pick up the pieces and go on. You make a new and better life for yourself."

"My situation is different," she said weakly, feeling the warmth from his long slender fingers ooze through her entire being.

"Not so different," he murmured. He searched her face. Her cheeks were flushed. "You can't go back to a man like Linley Talbot."

"But my family."

"Your family can't live your life." His hands ran up her arms. "Why don't you admit the truth to yourself? You never loved the man. Cornelia, you have been the dutiful daughter all your life, Paxton told me so. Now is the time for you to break free. Start living your own life."

Cornelia stared up into Locke's face. It was a face she could so easily love. Her breath started coming faster, and she swallowed the urge to turn and flee into the night. "What is it you are suggesting?" she asked in a mere whisper.

"This," he murmured and bent his head to gently kiss her.

The joining of their lips sent spiraling sensations burning through her. Cornelia lifted her arms and encircled his neck. All rational thought and plans faded under the pressure of their kiss. Deftly, Locke's tongue nudged her lips apart and sought entry into her mouth.

Cornelia acquiesced, reveling in the soft texture of his lips and the heat of his probing tongue. Heat encapsulated her, and all the tenets she had lived her life by became dusty platitudes no longer applicable in her present situation.

Locke ended the kiss and held her from him, searching her face. "Cornelia, I want you. Come to bed with me and let me make love to you."

Her heart was beating so soundly that she could barely think. God, she wanted him, too. She could not deny it to herself or him. "Oh, Locke, I shall undoubtedly burn in hell, but I want you, too," she said, shaking her head no.

Instead of letting her practical side send her from him, Locke drew her into his embrace and began kissing her neck.

Cornelia threw back her head, her breasts peaking against his hard chest.

Locke lifted her high into his arms and strode directly to his bed. He set her down with a tenderness he had not known for years. Slowly, he nibbled at her lips, silencing any protests she might still have. He made his way down her neck, gently unbuttoning her blouse top and shifting it aside so he could taste the soft white flesh of her shoulders.

Cornelia was losing herself. She should put a stop to this madness, but she could not. Linley had

149

never taken the time to make love to her. Their couplings had always been hurried affairs, and until now Cornelia had thought that was the way it was supposed to be. Locke laid fiery fingers on her breast erasing all conscious thought until a knock at the door sent her bolting upright so fast that Locke was knocked to the floor.

"Oof!" he grunted with a thud. Rubbing his head, he looked up at her. "You are a lot stronger than you look. I hope you aren't planning to make this a continuing practice. This is about the third time I have wound up in a heap at your hand."

Ignoring his attempts at levity, she hurriedly buttoned her blouse top and straightened her skirt, which had ridden up. "Someone is at the door," she snapped. "Whatever are they going to think?"

Locke got to his feet. "They are going to think that you gave me a huge lump on my head if the throbbing there is any indication."

The rap sounded again.

"Hurry and answer it. It is probably someone looking for me." She scooted off the bed, grabbed the book she had been reading before she fell asleep earlier, and positioned herself at the rough-hewn table, pretending to read the thick volume.

Locke opened the door.

"Whatever kept you?" demanded Paxton, stepping inside. His eyes surveyed the room. The bed was rumpled, and his sister, with rather disheveled hair, sat at the table looking guilty as hell. "Aren't you going to greet your brother, Sister dear? I was worried about you."

"Do forgive me, I was so engrossed in this book —"

"That you didn't hear my pounding, right?" He

150

stepped up to his sister and uprighted the book. "You might try the conventional method of reading next time. You undoubtedly would derive much more from its contents. Or have you found a new method to read without your glasses?"

"Paxton—"

He held up a silencing hand. "No need to explain. I am happy to find that you are all right."

"Paxton, I came to find out about something Annie told me a couple of days ago."

Paxton cocked his brow. "Something Annie said," he repeated skeptically.

"She had to confront me about my being a killer," Locke said without emotion and started a fire in the stove.

Paxton sat down. "Why didn't you just ask me?"

"You? What do you know about it?" Locke demanded, trying not to get exasperated that his life was being laid bare so easily.

"Joe explained what happened. You may not spend much time with the residents of the Park, but there is little that escapes Annie's father. He has spent time in Leadville selling the furs he traps and heard the whole story."

Locke rolled his eyes and snapped, "Wonderful."

"Locke, I think it's great," Paxton said to Locke and Cornelia's chagrin.

"Paxton, I am surprised at you. How could you say something so dreadful?" Cornelia said, horrified.

"Not because I think that what happened was great, but because since you both have suffered at the hands of your ex-spouses, you have a lot in common."

"We have a lot in common without our ex-spouses, as you put it, having anything to do with it," Locke grated.

"How true. How true," Paxton crowed.

Locke had been furious, but now he threw back his head and laughed. Then he grew serious. "Paxton, while I told you that you are welcome at my home anytime, now is not the time. Whatever is between your sister and me is none of your business."

Paxton ignored him. "Speaking of business, I hear that you make periodic trips back to Leadville on business. I have been feeling much better lately and would love to accompany you on your next visit."

"Paxton, you are in no condition to be making any arduous trips outside the Park for some time," Cornelia said.

Paxton hid a grin. His sister had just taken the bait. "That may be true, but it shouldn't stop you from getting away for a couple of weeks. I have Annie to take care of me now, so there is no reason why you shouldn't accompany Locke."

"Only the best reason in the world," Cornelia said, having a hard time believing that her brother could even suggest such an outrageous idea. "A lady does not travel with a gentlemen unaccompanied."

She turned to Locke. His face was unfathomable. Paxton's showing up when he did managed to turn what had been a simple excursion to seek the truth about Locke's past into an incredibly complicated muddle. Cornelia waited for Locke to back up what she said, but he merely remained where he was.

Although Locke remained silent, he was busily

thinking about what Paxton Lloyd had just suggested. If that brother of Cornelia's hadn't come along, Locke would have made love to the lady. There was no doubt in his mind that she would not have stopped him. The worst part was that he now ached from his aborted efforts. Not only that, he also ached in another way as well.

Over the last month he and Cornelia Lloyd Talbot had gone from staunch adversaries to friends to more. He found that he wanted to explore their budding relationship further. What better way to do that than to get her away from Estes Park and any outside interference, he thought.

"Well, don't you agree, Locke?" Cornelia prompted, seeking confirmation of what she had said.

"Actually, it might do you some good to have a break. You could stay with my sister if you're worried about your reputation." What he did not say was that his sister had her own ideas as to whether she would accept guests.

"Sounds like a marvelous idea to me," Paxton chimed.

"I'll take the idea under consideration," Cornelia said, feeling outnumbered. "I think that it is time we leave, Paxton. Locke just returned from the mountain and needs his rest."

"Speaking of the mountain," Paxton interrupted her efforts to get him to make a timely departure. "How was it?"

"Paxton, we should get you back to the cottage."

"I am not a bit fatigued. Besides, since climbing the mountain peak is not a possibility for me, I should very much like to hear all about it."

Admitting defeat, Cornelia settled down to listen

153

while Locke told all about his adventure up Longs Peak. As she listened, her desire to climb the mountain grew stronger as did the thought of visiting Leadville. Although she knew a climb such as Longs Peak was out of the question for a woman, she silently considered accompanying Locke to Leadville. Could she take the chance, knowing what had almost transpired between them and surely would have if Paxton had not shown up on Locke's doorstep?

Chapter Sixteen

Once Cornelia climbed into bed, she could not sleep. Everything that Locke had told her kept circling in her mind, not to mention the intimacy they had shared. And she couldn't get what Locke had said about Linley off her mind.

She was no longer trying to deny the divorce, she thought to herself. It was very real. Too real. If anything, she was now angry inside. Angry at Linley for not believing in her, and angry at him for leaving her to face the world alone without the protection she had enjoyed as his wife. And angry at herself for the unbidden thoughts she had been having about Locke Breckenridge. Cornelia turned over and punched the pillow. Hot tears of anger rolled down her cheeks and dropped on the pillowcase until she had cried herself to sleep.

The sun was glistening gold through the window when she awoke. The morning always put things into perspective. She tucked the anger she had allowed herself to feel last night inside as she dressed and left her room to join Paxton for breakfast.

She gave him a peck on the cheek and took a seat. "The color has returned to your cheeks. You must be feeling better."

155

A wide grin spread to his lips. "As a matter of fact, I am," he said and took a bite of toast.

Cornelia recognized that expression. He looked terribly self-satisfied, just as he used to when they were children and he had done something that particularly pleased him. "It wouldn't have anything to do with a certain young lady, would it?"

"What about you and Locke?" Paxton asked, evading any further discussion about Annie. He was not prepared to discuss his relationship with the girl yet. "Have you given any more thought to accompanying him to Leadville?"

"As a matter of fact, I have."

"Good. When will you two be leaving?" Paxton forged ahead.

"I am needed here with you," Cornelia said. She immediately dropped her eyes and took a sip of juice.

Paxton waited patiently until she lifted her eyes again. He had no intention of allowing her to set aside her needs for his. And he had plans of his own that did not include Cornelia. "Cornelia, you are not going to sit at the table with your head down avoiding the topic until I defer to you, as you used to when we were children."

"I am not avoiding the topic," she retorted. "But speaking of our lives as children. That grin of yours a moment ago was just like when we were children and you were hiding something."

"We aren't talking about me, so don't try to shift the subject."

Cornelia glared at him for a moment. "I was not attempting to change topics."

"Then are you going to Leadville?"

She sucked in her cheeks. "I thought I already

answered that question. I am needed here with you."

"No, you are not. Annie can see to my needs for a couple of weeks."

Cornelia rose and set her napkin aside. "If I am not needed here, perhaps I should consider returning home."

"Sometimes you can be so obstinate. Why can't you accept the fact that Linley doesn't want you?" he blurted out.

Cornelia's face started to crumble and her breathing increased. Tears threatened to finish giving her away before she caught herself. "All right, Linley doesn't want me! Is that what you wanted me to acknowledge? Is it?" she cried.

"That's good, Sister dear, get angry. It's good for you. Get angry at that bastard Linley. Get angry so you can finally put aside all notions of sacrificing yourself for someone who doesn't deserve you and never did. Get angry!"

"I am angry! I am furious with him, if you must know." Spinning on her heel, Cornelia stomped from the house.

She was so angry that she ignored Locke's words of caution about walking in the forest alone. The weather was still crisp when Cornelia headed away from the cottage, but she was too chafed to go back and get a shawl. A branch caught on her sleeve, and she broke it off the tree. As she stomped along, she snapped the twig into little pieces, wishing it were Linley's neck.

At the edge of a swift flowing creek, she stopped and perched on a flat rock, pulling her knees up and circling them with her arms. She rested her chin on her knees and stared unseeing at the water as her mind replayed the tumultuous last six months of her life.

Sean had kept a safe distance so he wouldn't be detected when he saw the Talbot bitch storm from the house. He had been watching her for some time, but since the dance, he had been itching for an opportunity to get her alone. He didn't like teases and knew how to deal with them.

With great care, he moved from tree to tree, peering around the huge trunks so as not to lose sight of his quarry. There was no one out here to hear her call out if she proved uncooperative. But, of course, he had no doubt that once he mounted her, she would willingly fall victim to his charm. All the others had.

He waited until she stopped by the creek. He looked about to make sure no one would happen by. Then he slowly crept up behind her.

Locke reined in his horse at the front of the cottage Paxton and Cornelia shared next to Dunraven's lodge. All night after Cornelia and her brother had left, he had thought only of taking Cornelia to Leadville with him, and he had decided to make that trip soon.

"Morning, Annie, you look lovely this morning," Locke said to the girl sweeping the porch.

"Cornelia gave me this mighty fine dress and fixed my hair up real pretty. If you're lookin' for her, she ain't here. I saw her stomp off in the direction of the creek 'bout half a hour ago." She furrowed her brow and leaned on her broom. "Funny thing, not long after Cornelia headed out, I saw Sean McCurdy moseyin' in the same direction. Probably nothin' to it. He don't do much walkin' 'round though. He—Hey! Where you goin' in such a all-fired rush?"

Locke ignored the girl and ran toward the creek. He had warned Cornelia about going off by herself, damn her! If anything happened to her, he was going to wring her neck!

Ignoring the snagging limbs that seemed to reach out on purpose to impede his progress, he reached the water's edge in record time. Panting, he stopped to catch his breath. He scanned the area.

There was no sign of Cornelia.

At first he wondered if Annie had been mistaken in her directions, then his attention caught on a scrap of fabric snagged on a twig in the middle of the creek.

Wading into the rushing waters, Locke retrieved the fabric. It was a frilly handkerchief monogrammed with the initials CLT. "Damn it!"

Locke returned to the edge of the creek, bent down, and ran his hand over the ground. Disturbed leaves and dirt indicated that there had been a recent scuffle. Using all his tracking instincts, he methodically followed the trail that led toward a thicket off in the distance.

The bush shuddered, causing Locke to break into a full run. At a scream issuing from the brush, he frantically dove into the middle of the tangle and hit the ground, grappling with the thorny bramble that scratched and gouged into his face and arms.

"Cornelia!" Locke bellowed, continuing to fight his way through the underbrush.

To his dread three muffled grunts came from nearby. He tore his way out and came face to face with Cornelia.

"Sweet Jesus, woman," he said. He could not believe his eyes. He had risked life and limb in that damned thorny brush, and there she stood, a big smile on her face and a jagged rock in her hand.

McCurdy was lying on the ground out cold.

Locke stepped up to her and readjusted her torn sleeve. Picking leaves out of her mussed hair, he growled, "If that bastard hurt you, I'll—"

"I told you I could take care of myself," she said, despite being visibly shaken.

"I can see how you take care of yourself," he admonished, tucking her torn sleeve in at the shoulder and wiping the smudge from her cheek with his thumb.

McCurdy groaned, drawing Locke's attention to the man who now was leaning on his elbow, rubbing his forehead. Locke was lightning quick. He bent down and yanked McCurdy to his feet by his collar.

"You bastard," he snarled and punched McCurdy in the nose, sending the man sprawling backward.

Locke was not satisfied and went after the man. But McCurdy scooted backward on all fours, yelling, "Call him off, please. Call the madman off!"

Cornelia abhorred violence and McCurdy's already bloodied face was payment enough for his aborted efforts to corner her. She grabbed Locke's arm. "Please, let him be."

"Are you jesting? After what the man tried to do to you?"

"I didn't try to do anything," Sean growled, warily watching Breckenridge.

"You call Cornelia's torn sleeve nothing?"

"Locke, Mr. McCurdy did not tear my sleeve. I caught it on a limb after I left the cottage."

"Then what did happen?" Locke demanded, his frustration growing.

"I be trying to romance the *lady,* and she had a very demonstrative way of saying no, if you must be knowing," Sean sneered. He did not take his eyes off Breckenridge as he climbed to his feet and brushed off his clothes.

Locke cocked a brow, not entirely believing McCurdy's story. His fists clenched. "What happened, Cornelia?"

Cornelia's gaze shifted between the two men. Locke looked as if he could take McCurdy apart limb by limb. McCurdy's face wore a silent plea not to expose that he had tried to more than romance her. Ashamed, she did not want to lay out the details. Neither did she want Locke to think she had encouraged the Irishman after the way Locke had left the dance. Most of all, she desperately wished she had heeded Locke's advice and been more careful.

"Cornelia, it's all right. You can tell me what happened. I promise you, one way or another McCurdy is leaving the Park."

Noticing Cornelia's hesitancy, Sean said, "Tell him nothing happened. Tell him I be following you to protect you so I can be getting back to work. There's a lot to be doing at the lodge."

Cornelia swallowed hard but propped up her resolve. Despite having to recount the details, she had to make sure that he did not try to harm any more females in the Park. She just hoped that Locke would not misunderstand. "He t-tried to force himself on me. He pulled me away from the creek. W-We struggled and I managed to pick up that rock—" she pointed to the rock she had dropped "—and I blindly struck at him as he was trying to force me to kiss him," she cried, the story tumbling out once she started.

Sean took a step backward. "She be a lying bitch. She be begging for it for weeks, She—"

Locke cut him off with knuckles to his mouth. Sean again found himself on the ground. "Get up, you bastard," Locke demanded.

Filled with hatred, Sean sneered at Cornelia, "You be paying for this, you bitch."

Locke launched himself and proceeded to beat the man without mercy. Flashes of what Locke had told her about killing a man flashed before Cornelia's eyes, and she screamed, "Stop it! Stop it before you kill him."

Her screams brought Locke back to his senses. He gave McCurdy's body a shove and got to his feet. "Don't worry, he's not worth it."

"I should have listened to you," Cornelia cried. "Just look at your torn shirt sleeves, and you're full of scratches and bruises," she added in torment.

"I've had worse. But you might help me pick the thorns out of my arm. From now on, you are going to listen. I will be making a trip to Leadville in a couple of days, and you are going with me."

"But Paxton, I can't leave him alone. He—"

"He has Annie to look after him. Before we leave, I'll make sure McCurdy receives a one-way trip out of the Park. Annie's father will undoubtedly be more than happy to make sure that that bastard doesn't come back."

Cornelia looked down at Sean McCurdy. The sniveling coward remained on the ground, trembling. "It is not proper."

"Hah, I knew you weren't a lady. You be giving

162

it to Breckenridge," Sean sneered and immediately scrambled off, but not before the toe of Locke's boot connected square in the middle of his backside.

Cornelia was horrified that anyone could think such a thing. She swung around and started back for the cottage. Locke had started after McCurdy but let him go to catch up with Cornelia.

Sean stopped and picked up a fallen branch, prepared to defend himself since he couldn't run any longer in his condition. When he turned around, he saw that Breckenridge had given up the chase and was heading back toward the lodge at that bitch's side.

Panting, Sean watched them until they disappeared from view. He leaned against a boulder to catch his breath, throwing down the decayed branch. "Damn you, Breckenridge. And damn you, bitch," he puffed. His side pained him from the beating he had taken because of that bitch. And now he would no longer have that cushy position as Lord Dunraven's foreman. Hatred filled him, and he slid to the base of the boulder, trying to decide how to get revenge.

Locke caught up with Cornelia and grabbed her arm, swinging her around to face him. "Cornelia, what is wrong with you? I defend you and you get mad at me."

"You might have killed him," she cried. "Like you did that man in Leadville."

Locke was stung. His face hardened and he grabbed her arms. "I told you what happened."

She had hurt him. It was obvious. She was im-

163

mediately contrite. "I am sorry. It was wrong of me. What happened in Leadville was not your fault."

His features relaxed. "Since that is settled, I won't take no for an answer. You are going to accompany me to Leadville if we have to take Annie and Paxton along to satisfy you. So you had best get used to the idea."

Cornelia glared at him, her face heating up. "First you tell me I am a free, independent lady. Then you come along and boldly inform me that I have no choice in the matter. I am tired of conforming to everyone else's idea of how I should act and what I should do." To her chagrin, he smiled. "What are you smiling for?" she demanded.

"You. It's about time you're starting to fight for yourself. But that doesn't change the fact that we are going to Leadville."

Her face set, Cornelia said, "I have been out here long enough. If I decide to accompany you, I'll let you know." She plucked a thorn protruding from his arm.

"Ouch! What did you do that for?" he yelped.

"You needed it. Now, let's get you back to the cottage and tend to those scrapes and bruises." She ripped out another thorn.

She turned from him and marched off toward the cottage, leaving Locke no other option than to follow. He said no more about the trip, but his mind was made up. She was going to accompany him not only to have a break from her constant vigil over her brother, but to hear for herself from others what had happened when he killed that man — if he had to kidnap her.

Chapter Seventeen

Once they had returned to the cottage and gathered Paxton and Annie into the parlor, Locke tactfully explained what had happened with McCurdy. Then, over Cornelia's objections, Locke laid out his plan to take Cornelia to Leadville with him.

Paxton sat quietly and listened to Locke, every once in a while glancing in Annie's direction. Secretly, Paxton grinned inside at the idea of Cornelia accompanying Locke to Leadville. He had liked it the first time he heard it.

"Paxton, I don't think it is a good idea for me to leave you," Cornelia objected. "I came here to take care of you."

"Nellie, Locke is offering you a chance of a lifetime," Paxton insisted. "How often do you get an invitation—"

Cutting off her brother, Cornelia snapped, "I would hardly consider his edict an invitation."

"You can consider it anything you desire, but one way or another you are accompanying me."

"Why?" she demanded.

"Because we don't know what happened to McCurdy. And until he is located and sent packing, I want you safe."

"And who elected you my guardian?" she asked with sarcasm in her voice.

Locke's eyes trailed to Paxton and back to Cornelia. "Your brother and I talked it over and —"

"And you two decided, I suppose?" she grated out.

"Well, yes, Nellie," Paxton said quietly, sinking in his chair at the anger in her flashing eyes.

Cornelia swallowed her protests at the silent pleading in Paxton's expression. "Oh, for heaven's sake. Mr. McCurdy is no doubt long gone from the Park by now after the beating you gave him, Locke."

Annie had sat still with her hands in her lap, but when Cornelia continued to protest, she piped up. "I think it's a right good idea, Cornelia. You deserve a chance to get away." She cast Paxton a sheepish glance. " 'Sides, I can see to Pax however long you're gone."

Cornelia shifted her gaze between Paxton and Annie. While she knew they were concerned for her safety, it suddenly dawned on her that their urging her to go had little or nothing to do with her; they wanted to be alone. Cornelia thought about it a minute longer, then she glanced sideways at Locke. He had gotten to his feet and was standing with his back to her looking out the window. He looked so natural in this wilderness setting — a male animal, wild and untamed like the landscape. She could not deny that the thought of seeing Leadville intrigued her, especially with him.

"All right, I'll go." Locke swung around and their eyes held. "But not because you tried to bully me. This was my decision."

"Of course it was," Paxton offered and said no more. He did not want to chance her having a change of heart.

Locke's smile spread, but he was careful to keep the look of triumph from his face. Inside, he was glad that she made the decision to go with him; it saved him the trouble of having to come up with another method of persuasion, which she might really have objected to.

"You'll enjoy the trip," Locke said, "I have a few loose ends to take care of at my place before we leave. So we'll leave Tuesday morning bright and early."

Cornelia smiled weakly. "Yes, bright and early," she said, hoping she had made the right choice.

Paxton and Annie stood quietly on either side of Cornelia, watching Locke load Cornelia's things in the back of the wagon bright and early Tuesday morning.

Cornelia shifted uneasily. Unable to stand it any longer, she asked, "Are you sure you'll be all right without me, Paxton?"

Paxton dropped a hand on her shoulder. "I'll be fine."

"Are you sure? I don't have to leave you. It's not too late."

Paxton noticed Locke's head snap up. He liked the reaction. Paxton hugged Cornelia to him. "You are the best sister a man could ever have, but I will be fine here with Annie. I want you to go and have a good time."

Paxton held Cornelia from him for a moment before he gave her a kiss on the forehead. "Enjoy yourself, Sister dear."

Giving a half-hearted nod, Cornelia turned from her brother to Annie. "Take good care of Paxton."

"Don't you worry none, I'll have him in hollerin' shape when you return."

Locke moved to Cornelia's side. "Ready?"

"Yes, I suppose so." She gave Paxton a big hug.

Locke helped her climb onto the wagon seat and joined her. He snapped the reins over the team's rumps. As the wagon rumbled from the cottage, Cornelia turned and waved to Paxton and Annie standing on the porch returning the farewell.

Paxton and Annie waited until Locke and Cornelia were out of sight, then went back inside.

"You think we done the right thing, urgin' that Cornelia go with him to Leadville?" Annie asked as they entered the parlor.

Paxton went to the window, parted the curtain, and looked out.

"They're already gone if you're thinkin' to call her back," Annie said and perched on the arm of an overstuffed couch in the corner of the room. "Guess I could saddle a horse and go after them, if it's botherin' you," Annie added as an afterthought when he didn't immediately turn toward her and say anything. "Pax?"

He swiveled around to gaze at the girl. "Oh, sorry. guess I was deep in thought."

She leaned forward. " 'Bout Cornelia?"

"No. Us."

Annie fidgeted with her fingers and made a sudden study of a lint ball on the back of the couch. Dragging her eyes away from the bit of fuzz, she asked, "What about us?"

Paxton walked over to Annie and took her hands in his, pulling her to her feet in front of him. He gazed into her eyes. "That I find you a very, very special young lady."

"A lady? You really think of me as a lady?"

"A very pretty lady."

"Oh, golly," she squealed and threw her arms

168

around his neck. In her exuberance, she knocked Paxton off his feet and they both tumbled onto the couch.

Annie stared into his hazel eyes. He had the most beautiful eyes she had ever seen, and they reflected the greens and yellows of the leaves in the Park in summertime. Hesitantly, she reached up and smoothed back a lock of deep blond hair that had fallen over his forehead.

Paxton grabbed her hand and drew her fingers to his lips. He was about to kiss them when she pulled back.

"I don't know that we ought to be here like this," she said.

Paxton moved off her to the other end of the couch. "I am sorry, Annie. I guess I misunderstood. I thought that you felt the same about me as I do about you."

"Oh, I do. I do," she said openly.

He scooted toward her, but the look on her face halted his progress. "What's the matter then?"

Annie frowned. She did not want to hurt this wonderful man, but she believed in truth. "It wouldn't do neither of us no good if I took the sickness, too. I know a body ain't suppose to have no . . . ah . . . personal contact with anybody who's got your sickness."

He breathed a sigh of relief. "Is that all? Thank goodness. I thought that maybe you didn't return my feelings."

"Oh, no. I mean, yes. I do. I do," she reiterated.

Paxton shifted his eyes about the room, then moved to the edge of the couch. "Annie, if I tell you a secret, can I count on you not to tell anyone? And I mean *anyone,* not even your father."

Annie scrunched up her shoulders in delight. He

had to really care for her if he was going to let her in on some big, important secret. "I'd never let you down. I wouldn't think of ever tellin' anyone somethin' you told me, not if you told me it was for my ear alone."

Paxton reached out, took a gentle hold of her shoulders, and looked squarely into her eyes. How he loved the girl! "Annie, my sickness—"

"It don't matter to me none, I . . . I care about you anyhow."

Tears threatened to unman Paxton, he felt such joy. In an effort not to let her see the salty drops threatening to flood his eyes, he pulled her into his embrace. "Oh, Annie, you little angel, I'm not sick with consumption."

Annie pulled back. Her special man had tears in his eyes. She took a hankie from her pocket and dabbed the moisture. "Then what's wrong with you?"

Paxton sniffled. "A bad case of the ague. Remember when I was so sick and Locke brought the doctor?"

She tilted her head. "Yes, of course. I was so worried."

"Well, he has seen a lot of cases of consumption and informed me that I was ailing, but not with what we all thought. I've been getting stronger and have been feeling much better for several weeks. You don't mind, do you?"

"Mind? Silly, it's wonderful," she crowed before her face turned serious. "But why you been still draggin' about like a horse pullin' a felled tree then?"

"That's the secret. I don't want Cornelia to know."

Annie crinkled her forehead. "Whyever not? If I had been ailin' and then found out that I was right as the sun comin' up each mornin', I'd be up

170

on the mountain callin' it out to the whole Park."

"But that is just it. If I tell anyone that I am not sick, then Cornelia will return to Connecticut and try to get that bastard of an ex-husband back." Annie's eyes went wide. "I'm sorry, I didn't mean to talk that way in front of you. But there are no other appropriate words to describe that man after what he did to my sister."

"I don't mind none, my pa don't always use nice words, especially when he's out putterin' 'round the cabin."

Paxton smiled at her candidness. That was one of the things he loved about her. Feeling a complete sense of trust in the simple backwoods girl, Paxton said, "You know that Cornelia came to Colorado with me so I could regain my health, but what no one knows is that I'm not as sick as everyone thinks and the main reason I allowed her to talk me into coming here was because I wanted to get her away from Linley Talbot. He falsely accused her of adultery when all along that man was the one who had a string of lovers.

"The whole damned town turned against Cornelia and believed the worst. I couldn't stand by watching all her so-called friends snubbing her. Even all the pious church people whom Cornelia worked so hard for, volunteering so many hours for the good of the community, turned their backs on her.

"I had to do something. So, instead of telling my family that I wasn't as deathly ill as everyone thought, I let them think I needed to move to a dry climate and Cornelia, being the kindhearted person she is, insisted she accompany me so she could take care of me until I could get well." At her bemused expression, he added, "I was sick, Annie. I didn't lie about that. But not with consumption as everyone thought at first, honest."

"I believe you." Annie's heart went out to Cornelia. She was glad that the lady had made the decision to go to Leadville with Locke Breckenridge. "You don't need to worry none, I won't say a word."

He cradled her face. "I knew I could trust you."

Annie leaned forward, closed her eyes, and made an O with her lips. Then she waited. When nothing happened, her eyes snapped open. "Don't you want to kiss me?"

"Want to?" Paxton cheered. He did not waste another minute. With all the love in his heart, Paxton crushed Annie to him in a breathless kiss. To his utter delight, the girl responded with an overpowering vigor of her own. Paxton found the life being squeezed out of him, she was so exuberant. Finally, he was forced to break the kiss. "Wow!" he puffed. "When you kiss, you kiss!"

Annie's expression took on a serious glint. "Well, my pa's always said that anythin' a body learns is worth doin' a thorough job when you put that learnin' to use."

"Where did you learn to kiss like that?" he asked, intrigued by the girl's forthrightness. She was incapable of telling a lie, which had drawn him to her in the first place.

"It was out back of Pa's cabin when I was twelve. Jimmy Lee Hobart and me, well, we got to talkin' about what was so all-fired great about touchin' lips together so we tried different ways. You know, pressin' harder and longer."

Trying to keep his face impassive at the girl's extraordinary confession, Paxton asked, "And did you settle on the way we just kissed?"

"Oh, no." She giggled. "I ain't never kissed nobody like I kissed you. Kissin' you was special. What about you?"

"Me?"

"Yes. Where did you learn 'bout kissin'?"

Paxton took a deep breath. He had never been in the habit of discussing any of his amorous escapades. It was not a gentlemanly thing to do. Especially any of his early forays into the experimentation of youth. But Annie had so openly shared with him. "You really want to know?" he asked, hoping she was just being polite.

"I want to know all about you." She noticed his hesitation. " 'Course, only if you want to share with me. I'd never try to pull anythin' out of you, if you wasn't in the mood."

"Oh, Annie, I want to share everything with you."

She looked at him expectantly. "I'm so rightly pleased you feel that way, too. Well?"

"What?"

"Ain't you gonna tell me about the first time you kissed a girl?"

"Well, let me see. I first kissed a girl in Miss Oglevie's class at school when she left us alone to check on the rest of the class that had not come back after the noon meal. I was sitting behind her—"

"What was her name?"

"Her name?"

"Ever'body's got a name, Pax. Names are important. A name gives a body somethin' special. A name's personal. Sets a body apart of ever'body else. It means more than jes' callin' someone a girl or boy," she explained earnestly. "What was her name?"

He smiled at the wonderful girl. "Her name was Peggy Lynn Flint. She liked me and I liked her. So when the teacher left us alone in the class, it just seemed like the thing to do."

173

"Did you kiss her like you did me?" she probed.

He laughed. "Heavens, no. It was a quick peck. I have never kissed anyone the way I just kissed you." He hesitated since that was not entirely true, then quickly amended, "With my heart in it, I mean."

"I'm glad."

Long, silent moments lapsed. Paxton was thankful that she did not probe further as most females would have. And he was grateful for the knowledge that this special girl never would. She would always accept his explanations and be content. Secretly, he vowed never to let her be disappointed in him.

"Let's do it again," she suggested, breaking the silence.

Paxton needed no further coaxing. He drew her face to his and kissed her, deepening the kiss. Annie was just as enthusiastic and Paxton slipped his tongue into her sweet cavern and savored all her sweetness.

To Paxton's further delight, Annie was full of surprises. She removed his hand from around her shoulders and positioned it on her firm, full breast. Shards of heat cut through him and he began kneading her fullness until the center peaked against the heightened sensitivity of his fingers.

"Put your other hand on my bosom," Annie whispered against his lips as she tasted and explored his mouth.

"Oh, Annie," he moaned. He circled her breasts with his open palms as she leaned into him.

She began working the buttons down the front of her dress. But when she tugged on his hand and tried to slip it inside her shirtfront, Paxton pulled back. Panting and garnering all the reserve he could muster, Paxton said, "Annie, I want you more than I have ever wanted anyone in my entire life. You are the sweetest, gentlest, most open and wonderful girl I have ever known. But I can't—"

Annie's forehead furrowed in confusion. "Can't? I don't rightly understand. There somethin' wrong with your male parts?"

"Wrong? Good God, no, girl. I think for the very first time in my entire life everything is right . . . with every part of me. And it is all because of you." He cradled her precious face. "I think that I love you."

"You do?"

"Yes. As a matter of fact, I am sure I do. And I don't want to rush you."

"Pax, love. I love you, too. And we wouldn't be doin' anythin' that I don't want. But what about you? If you don't know how, I can help learn you," she offered in earnest. "Like you did me with book readin'."

To say that he was taken aback by her offer was putting it mildly. "You've done it before?"

She flipped her wrist. "Oh, no. But Pa and me raise hogs and we've had a few other farm animals so I got a pretty good idea 'bout *things*."

"Things?"

"You know. Things. The mating that goes on atween a man and woman. Things."

"Oh, those things," he said, fighting to keep to the same degree of seriousness that Annie had.

"Well, if you don't know how, I can show you."

Paxton swallowed a bubble of laughter, giving an instant's consideration to all the conquests he'd made in the past while he was in Europe. He was falling more deeply in love by the second. "I think I can manage to figure out how."

"Whew, that's good. For a minute I was a little

worried. Watchin' how it's done and doin' it ain't always the same thin'."

"No, it's not. But I think we'll manage without much difficulty."

"Good."

Not needing any further cajoling, Paxton rose. He took Annie's hand. He could not believe it when she sprang to her feet and led him into the bedroom. He was even more astounded that when he undressed her, she stood before him proud of her body. She was so different from the other women he had known. Silently, as he began to introduce his uninhibited angel to the world of love's sharing, he vowed that he would never let her go.

Chapter Eighteen

Cornelia's nerves were on edge as the wagon clattered out of the valley, heading south. In an effort to calm herself, she tried to focus her attention on the immense pines and aspens shadowing the sun and lending dark, feathery blotches across the ground the wagon rolled over. She could hardly believe that she was making a trip of this sort, let alone accompanying a man she had only known for a little over a month.

"I'm glad you decided to go to Leadville with me," Locke said as if he had been reading her mind, breaking the silence and interrupting her troubling thoughts.

"This is a new adventure for me," she said in a voice that questioned the sagacity of such an undertaking. "When will we board the train?" So we won't be alone together, she thought.

"We won't be boarding a train."

Her eyes widened. "But how are we going to get there then?"

"You're riding in how we're going to get there."

"I never dreamed when I agreed to accompany you that we would be traveling all the way to Leadville together . . . alone," she remarked, suddenly aware of his closeness. "How long is this trip going to take?"

He shrugged. "Several days."

"Several days!" she cried, her voice soaring an octave.

"Oh, no. No! I can't possibly spend that much time alone with you. You'll just have to turn the wagon around and take me back to Estes Park."

Feeling a surge of panic when he seemed to ignore her, Cornelia swiveled around to look over her shoulder toward the direction from which they had been traveling. When Locke still made no attempt to halt the team and redirect the wagon, Cornelia's dread mushroomed.

"Will you turn this wagon around?"

"No, I will not," he said flatly. "You agreed to accompany me, and I have to make this trip to Leadville. With McCurdy running loose somewhere in the Park, I can't in good conscience leave you there unprotected."

"I'd probably be safer back in Estes Park with Paxton than sitting so close to you for several days," she muttered, saying out loud what she was thinking.

"Beg your pardon?" Locke said although he had to smile to himself for he had heard her remark.

"Please turn this wagon around."

"Cornelia, stop worrying and let yourself relax so you can enjoy the trip instead of making yourself miserable."

"I am not making myself miserable," she complained.

"Well, you are coming close to making me miserable, and I intend to enjoy this trip. So sit back and enjoy the scenery."

Cornelia swallowed a retort and crossed her arms over her chest. They traveled for nearly an hour in tension-filled silence until Cornelia realized she was being foolish. From beneath the fringe of her lengthy lashes she sneaked a peek at Locke. The sun shone auburn through the wisps of mussed ebony hair dancing in the breeze. His features were strong, like the man himself. Yet she had to admit that there was also something tender and compassionate about the man despite the streak of stubbornness they shared, she thought with a slight smile.

"Why are you going to Leadville?" she finally asked.

She was coming around. For a while he feared the lady was going to pout all the way to Leadville. "Business," he answered.

"You've never said much about what you did before you came to Estes Park."

"No, I haven't."

Cornelia waited for him to continue. When he remained silent, she said, "Since I happen to be your captive, don't you think that the least you can do is tell me why we are making this trip?"

To Cornelia's chagrin, he threw back his head and laughed, "Captive? Cornelia, if you were my captive, I can only assure you that you would not be berating me and driving me nearly beyond myself with your infernal demands."

"Infernal demands?" she snapped. "Why I ever decided to start a civil conversation with you I shall never fathom."

Locke immediately was sorry. He had wanted to make this trip special. If truth be known, he had been back to Leadville only four times since the divorce, and the only reason he was going now was to discuss the deal to sell his interests in his supply business and talk to his lawyer. And he wanted to get Cornelia away from Estes Park and show her that there was more to life than duty and self-sacrifice. He hoped that she would come to realize that she did not need to return to a man who had not appreciated her.

179

"Well?" she prodded when he did not answer her. "Do you intend to be sarcastic the entire trip?"

"Cornelia, why don't we both take a deep breath and start over? Don't you think it would be much more enjoyable if we did?"

Cornelia swallowed all the questions she had concerning Locke and the reasons why he was making this trip, let alone the real reasons why he was insisting on her accompanying him. With great dignity, she took a deep breath. "All right, I am going to enjoy this trip."

"Good."

For the rest of the day they traveled slowly over the hills and valleys until they reached the old Half Way House located on the St. Vrain River near Lyons and owned by Chester Smead.

Chester had entertained many celebrated folks such as Anna Dickinson, Helen Hunt, Isabella Bird, and Lord Dunraven and had an easy way about him and a welcoming face with a broad smile. When he learned that Cornelia and her brother were staying in Lord Dunraven's cottage, he insisted that they stay the night.

"Thought you'd never ask," Locke said.

"You take care of the team, lad, while I take the lady inside and give her a hot cup of coffee," Chester suggested.

Cornelia surveyed the cabin with the swirl of smoke billowing out from the rock slab chimney. A huge leafless tree rose next to the chink-filled log cabin. A large black dog with a white bib lay snoozing near the door.

"Locke treating you the way he should?" Chester asked once they were inside.

"He is somewhat of an enigma," Cornelia offered.

"Lots of folks think so, but he's quite a man. Most folks don't know it, but last year when the Thompson River overflowed its banks and supplies ran low on account of being washed away, Locke quietly arranged to have plenty of food brought up from Denver. Made me promise not to breathe a word 'bout his good deed. He owns a successful supply business in Leadville, you know."

"What about Leadville?" Locke asked, coming into the cabin.

"Chester was just telling me what a bustling town Leadville is."

Locke shot the man a doubtful look but settled down on a bench near the table. Letting all questions drop, they engaged in a delightful round of conversation over a simple meal before bedding down for the night.

Cornelia breathed a sigh of relief that she was afforded some privacy. She had a room to herself, the men bedding down in front of the fire. Undressing, Cornelia could not help but reflect on Chester Smead's words about Locke's generosity and thoughtfulness. Again, she compared him to Linley who had never helped out others in all the time she had known him. She thought about this as she lay awake listening to the men talk companionably.

"First lady you brung this way, Locke," Chester observed. "She got a special meaning for you?"

"You've known me long enough to know better than to ask that kind of question."

Chester grinned from ear to ear. "True enough. But I'll be damned if you just didn't give me an answer."

Locke grunted in response. He turned his back to the man and heaved the blanket over his shoulder, effectively shutting out any more questions.

To Locke's chagrin, Chester gave a hearty laugh. "I knew I was right."

Cornelia was stunned by this revelation, and for a long time she mulled over everything in her head, unable to go to sleep. This new perspective on the trip ahead made her glad she had decided to accompany Locke. Her main concern was Paxton. Despite Annie's assurances that she would see to his needs, Cornelia felt that only she could tend Paxton properly.

Paxton lounged across his rumpled bed in the same state of dress in which he had entered this world. Beads of perspiration glistened on his lithe body, and he was filled with a glorious exhaustion.

"Ain't you goin' to get dressed before you catch your death and your sister blames me for not takin' better care of you?" Annie said, coming into the room with a tray. He made no effort to move. "You best put some clothes on. Pa said he'd be over sometime today to check on you. You wouldn't want him walkin' in and findin' you without a stitch on."

Paxton smiled and reached for the girl. "Put that tray down and come here."

"Pax, darlin', you'll tax your strength."

He looked down at his rising desire. "You're taxing something else by not joining me, sweet girl."

Annie's gaze dropped from the vision of his naked body to the floor. Then she set the tray aside, unbuttoned her dress front and let the plain cotton garment drift to the floor around her slender ankles. Proudly, she walked to him.

Paxton opened his arms and she went into them. "Annie, my love," he murmured.

His hands roved over the peaks and valleys of her smooth, satiny skin. He bent his head and suckled at her breasts, certain he had died and gone to heaven. Then he raised his head and looked at her puckered nipples glistening with moisture. Annie reached up and rolled his few chest hairs around her fingers.

"I like the feel of you," she cooed. "But I'm goin' to put some meat on them bones of yours. 'Specially now that I know it ain't an impossible task. I'm goin' to feed you till you've plumped out like a fatted calf."

"The only feeding I need right now is from your loving, sweet body."

"Then what you waitin' for?" she giggled and pulled him down on top of her.

To Paxton's delight, she encircled him and guided him into her woman's center. He groaned in ecstasy at the perfect fit. She was slippery, wet, and hot. As he moved, the friction built until he felt her explode. She circled his body with her thighs and nearly squeezed the breath out of him. She strained against him, her face glowing with pure rapture.

"Oh, Annie, Annie, Annie," he panted as his release grasped him and he poured his seed into her.

He lay atop of her, holding her and nuzzling her neck for some time until a conscious thought struck him. He propped himself up on his elbows and gazed into Annie's flushed face. He pressed gentle kisses to the tip of her nose and her lips, then said, "Wouldn't it be wonderful if we just made a baby?"

"A baby?" she gulped. "Don't be silly, you don't make babies until after you're married," she said with all seriousness.

Paxton rolled from her and stroked her flat belly. "Annie, sweet girl, babies can come anytime after a couple has made love."

She crinkled her brow. "That true?"

"You said you have seen the farm animals mate and then have babies. It is the same with humans."

A troubled expression shadowed her face. "I never thought of it that way. But if that's true, then I suppose we're jes' goin' to have to get married right quick."

Paxton swallowed a sudden lump in his throat. "Did you say *married?*"

"Yes, you know, in front of a preacher readin' a Bible and guests come to see that everythin' is all legal," she explained, bemused that a man as worldly as Paxton Lloyd seemed to be so unlearned. Then it struck her. She bolted upright and grabbed her rumpled dress in front of her like a shield.

"You don't want to marry me. You jes' said that you loved me so you could bed me," she cried.

Before Paxton could deny her wild accusations, she threw on her dress and marched toward the door.

"Annie, wait!"

Annie was so mortified she did not stop; she blindly ran from the cottage.

Paxton gave no thought to his lack of attire. He chased after her. He could not let her go without explaining. "Annie, don't go. I love you!" he bellowed.

Annie had stopped and was leaning against a projecting pine. Paxton darted in that direction. Suddenly, a deep male voice intruded into the scene.

"I'd say that it appears you forgot somethin', son," Joe Mills's voice boomed out.

Paxton stopped dead in his tracks. "Hello, sir," he gulped. "It — it is good to see you."

"Wish I could say the same. But I hadn't planned on seeing quite so much of you, son." He had been amused when he'd first sighted the naked young man before he'd had the opportunity to take in the whole picture and assess the situation. Joe turned to his daughter, who was visibly shaken.

"Annie, what you doin' standin' not more than ten feet from a naked man?" Joe demanded.

Chapter Nineteen

By the dark expression on Joe's face, Paxton was sure the elder man was going to kill him. The worst part about it was, as Paxton acknowledged, that the man had every right. If he were in Joe Mills's position, he would want to do the same thing.

Panic caused Paxton to come to life. He immediately attempted to conceal his state of undress by ducking behind a nearby watering trough. His heart hammered against his chest as he waited for the man to rout him out from behind the trough and squeeze the breath from him. Sweat poured down the sides of his face; he was too young to die.

As Paxton waited, his life paraded before his eyes. Beating down a dying man's thoughts, Paxton prayed the man would disappear.

Not hearing a word from the older man, Paxton finally garnered the courage and peeked eye level over the tub. Annie's father remained unmoved, arms crossed, toe tapping. Paxton swallowed hard. The man was not going to disappear as Paxton had been wishing. At least he had made no move to kill him. Paxton's gaze shifted to Annie. She stood by the tree, hanging her head.

"You comin' out from there? Or you plannin' to wait till dark?" Joe asked without a hint of amusement in his voice.

"Do you mind if I go inside and make myself respectable first?" Paxton pleaded.

"Is what you were doin' before I come 'respectable'?" Joe set forth with a cocked brow.

"Pa, please—" Annie begged. "We weren't doin'—"

"You weren't?" Joe said, incredulous. He may not have had much schooling, but he wasn't no halfwit. "And are you goin' to try to tell me you been standin' there at the base of that tree all mornin' and never once went inside or was aware that Paxton there—" he motioned in Paxton's direction "—is as naked as the day he was brung into this world?"

Annie had been studying the ground, but it was not in her to lie. She raised her eyes to look straight at her pa. "Pa, I—"

"Mr. Mills," Paxton interrupted, "Annie is the innocent party in all this."

Joe cocked a brow again. "Somehow I have my doubts that my Annie is all that innocent anymore."

"Why don't we go inside?" Paxton suggested, feeling a draft cross his backside with a cold foreboding.

Joe looked from his daughter to Lord Dunraven's guest. He shook his head. Pity, he thought, he had liked that young man. 'Course, he was staying with Dunraven whom Joe had no use for since the man had had his agent trying to buy up all the land in the Park a few years back.

"Might be a good idea if you got into some duds. Folks in the Park ain't used to folks runnin' 'bout like you're doin', even if you are a guest of Dunraven's."

Paxton did not waste another second. He made a dash into the cottage.

Annie hid a smile at the flash of milk skin that probably never had been exposed to the sun before the man's mad sprint.

"Daughter!" Joe's voice boomed out.

Annie immediately dropped her eyes and shuffled toward her pa. She was afraid to look up now that she stood directly in front of him. She knew that guilt was written all over her face. All he would have to do was take one look at her, and he'd know she'd been mating with Paxton.

"Annie, before we go inside and have a little talk with the lad in there, is there somethin' you want to tell me?"

"Ah, Pa, don't go blamin' Paxton," she pleaded, drawing circles in the dirt with the toe of her shoe. "It was all my fault. One minute I was kissin' him, then the next . . . well, I just sorta . . . ah . . ." Her voice trailed off.

"No need, child," Joe said, shaking his head. He put a hand on her trembling shoulder and ushered her toward the cottage. He wanted to blame the Lloyd boy and rant and rave and give him a good thrashing with his belt. But Joe still remembered Annie's ma and how they had come to be blessed with Annie shortly after they had stood before a preacher. Young 'uns had such strong drives that ruled their bodies instead letting the brains God gave them take the lead.

"You ain't goin' to forbid me to see Paxton again, are you, Pa?" Annie asked, her voice quivering as they went inside and sat down on the couch.

Joe leaned forward, resting his chin on his palms "He's an outsider."

"You didn't seem to think so at the picnic, Pa," Annie said in Paxton's defense.

"What about the fact that they're stayin' at Dunraven's place?"

"Pa, despite the way you feel about Dunraven's

agent tryin' to get hold of all the land in the Park, I work for Lord Dunraven," Annie reminded her father gently.

"Just 'cause we need the money, don't mean I have to like you comin' here day after day. Let alone your takin' up with someone the likes of Dunraven and his kind," he blurted out.

"I know you don't cotton to Lord Dunraven. But, Pa, Paxton ain't here to take hold of nobody's land."

"No, I suppose you're right. But the lad is sick, Annie. You shoulda knowed better than to get mixed up with someone who's got the sickness."

While Paxton had been buttoning his shirt, he had been listening just around the doorway. He was astounded to hear that Lord Dunraven was not held in high esteem throughout the Park as he had been led to believe by the tales Dunraven had told him in Europe.

Paxton had been waiting for Joe Mills to forbid his daughter to see him again. Despite the homesteader's apparent displeasure he had not sent Annie home. Most of all, Paxton was astounded that Annie continued to defend him, considering her upset over him. Paxton hoped it meant that the man would allow him to court his daughter since she seemed to want it.

Paxton listened a short time longer, then decided that he could not put off facing Joe Mills any longer. After all, a gentleman did not allow a lady to brave a parent's wrath alone.

"Ah, hem." Paxton cleared his throat and stepped into the parlor. He could feel heat flush his normally pale cheeks. Standing rod straight despite the threat of his knees knocking, Paxton raised his chin in a proud line. "Sir, I want you to know that if there is any blame to be affixed here today, it is to be borne by myself alone. Your daughter is an innocent party."

Joe caught sight of Annie's flinch when the lad said

that she was innocent. Then he noticed the thin man stand straighter. He had to admit the lad had spunk considering that he didn't look strong enough to defend himself should Joe decide that a good beating was warranted.

"Hell, come over here and sit down before you faint away. You don't look like you are goin' to be able to hold yourself up much longer, and I ain't got any inclination to be havin' to tote you off the floor."

Hesitantly, Paxton took a seat next to Annie.

His action gave Annie cause to hope that Paxton was planning to declare himself to her father. "Pa, it was somethin' we both wanted, and I'm not ashamed to say so."

"That true, lad?"

"Ah, well, I mean, ah . . ." Paxton's voice failed him. This had to be one of the worst, yet one of the best days in his entire life, and Paxton did not know what to say to the girl's father under the circumstances.

"Paxton?" Annie said with a beleaguered cry. "Don't you have anythin' to ask my pa?"

Despite his throat's threatening to constrict and cut off his air, Paxton managed to gasp, "Yes. Why don't you like Lord Dunraven?"

"Ohhh," Annie wailed and ran from the cottage.

Joe shot to his feet and shook a finger at Paxton, who had slumped lower than a varmint in his seat. "Lad, I would of bet money that you had more gumption in you. I'm sorry for Annie's sake that you don't."

Before Paxton could recant his question and redeem himself, both father and daughter had gone, leaving him more miserable than he had ever felt in his entire life.

* * *

Cornelia also was feeling miserable and, in addition, tremendously guilty that she had thoroughly enjoyed the trip to Leadville after all. Locke had been the perfect gentleman, pointing out places of interest and describing how the various towns they passed through had sprung up. Each night they had either stayed at an inn or with one of Locke's many friends.

Despite herself, as they reached a hill on the outskirts of Leadville, Cornelia secretly wished that he had tried to kiss her. She could still feel the taste and whispered softness of his tender, coaxing lips.

"Well?" Locke said.

Cornelia's attention snapped from her musings. "What? I'm sorry, what did you say?"

"I said what do you think of Leadville? It is the second largest town in Colorado. Must be nearly twenty-five thousand people living here now. It's a rip-roaring place although efforts have been made in the last few years to civilize it."

Cornelia surveyed the bustling town. Numerous horse-drawn wagons rumbled along the dusty road. The streets and walkways were literally crammed with humanity. Hardrock miners, bedraggled families, and an assortment of men, women and children crowded the town, all seeming like ants to Cornelia, the way they were scurrying about.

"Some people call it Cloud City," Locke said.

"Why is that? Because it must be over ten thousand feet in elevation?"

Locke shrugged. "Never thought to ask why. The elevation does lend a rather giddy atmosphere though."

"Is that why you left?" she found herself asking. Then, before she could stop herself, she added, "Or is it because your ex-wife is still here?"

"I told you that my ex-wife left town. Last I heard

she had taken the train east. Haven't the vaguest idea where, if you're wondering."

"I'm sorry. I should have remembered, and I shouldn't ask such probing questions."

"Ask anything you want. Folks in town are likely to tell you all about it anyway. My divorce was only overshadowed by Tabor's, and he flaunted the mistress he replaced his wife with." When he noticed the bemused expression on her face, he said, "I hope it won't bother you."

"Why should it?"

"I thought because of your own divorce, it might offend you."

"Locke, nothing anyone could say about you is going to change my opinion of you."

Locke's head snapped around. "I'm not going to press you for an explanation. I think I'll just take it as a compliment."

"In that case, I won't make an effort to explain. I'll allow you wonder."

"Touché." Laugh lines whispered out from the corners of his eyes, but Locke kept his silence. The trip had transformed the lady. She was more open now and seemed to feel freer around him. He knew she did not totally trust him; he did not expect her to yet. But in time she would.

"Where does your sister live?" she asked, moving the subject to safer ground.

"Off Harrison. You ready to meet her, or would you rather go to a hotel?"

Cornelia's head snapped up. "She is expecting us, isn't she?"

"Yes, but I haven't told you much about her. Perhaps we ought to have something to eat before we descend on her. Hungry?"

"I could eat a little something," she said, wondering

what reason he could have for not simply going to his sister's. Surely she would offer them something when they arrived.

Locke snapped the reins over the horses's rumps, and they headed in to town. As they rumbled down the street, Cornelia watched with fascination the hectic pace of life in the mining town and the size and number of businesses. What really amazed her was a complex of buildings on Harrison.

"I see the opera house has caught your attention," Locke said.

"An opera house? Out here?"

"Why not? Some tout it as the best theater west of the Mississippi."

"From the outside I can understand why," Cornelia remarked.

"Would you like to see the inside while we're here?"

"Very much."

"Then I'll see what I can do."

They stopped outside an unassuming restaurant. Locke helped her down, which sent strange sensations along every nerve in her body. When he did not immediately remove his hands from around her waist, she forced a smile, adjusted her hat, and said, "Thank you for your assistance. Aren't we going into the restaurant?"

"Of course. Where did you think we were going?"

"Inside the restaurant," she said weakly and followed him inside.

They sat down and ordered. Cornelia felt surrounded by an electrifying force. Despite its drab exterior, the interior of the tiny building was alive with energy. People bustled from table to table, a harried waitress bussed huge trays of food, and clusters of people gulped down their meals and hurried about their business.

She had grown up in a small town where everyone knew everyone else. Life had been static, cut and dried. It moved along at an appointed pace, seemingly indelibly set in a routine as unchanged as the main thoroughfare itself. Here she was in an atmosphere in which she felt caught up in the frenzy. Her neighbors back in Whitneyville would have looked down their noses at the way these people lived, but, for some reason, Cornelia felt alive and free among the throngs. With the feeling of euphoria, a strange affection suddenly hit her. It wasn't just this town that made her feel so alive, it was also the man sitting across from her at the table.

Chapter Twenty

Their order arrived and they began to eat. Locke was pleased that Cornelia's appetite had increased and she was filling out even more. Gone were the dark circles from under her eyes. Gone were the gray hollows of her cheeks, replaced by a healthy blush. Gone was the drab brown hair; a lustrous honey-brown shone with a golden cast in its stead. And gone were the dresses that had hung loosely from her shoulders. Nicely rounded curves now hinted at the delights hidden beneath the fashionable dress.

"Are you planning to eat that toast, or are you going to spend the entire meal watching me?" Cornelia asked, eying his plate.

Locke shoved the plate toward her. "Be my guest."

"Thank you. I was hungrier than I realized," she said as she buttered the burned crusts and heaped them with preserves.

Locke sipped his coffee while she polished off her meal and half of his before she was done. "Feel better?"

Cornelia dabbed at the corners of her mouth with her napkin. "Much. Now, what was it you wanted to tell me about your sister?"

194

Locke leaned his elbows on the table. "Why don't we stroll about town first?"

Cornelia was beginning to lose patience. He seemed to be stalling and she was determined to find out why. "I think you had best tell me now." Her lips thinned at the grinning man. "Locke Breckenridge, if telling me we would stay with your sister when we arrived in Leadville just so I would accompany you was a ploy, I warn you, I am going to be most upset."

Locke's grin spread, then he rubbed his chin. "Well, at least you are giving me a chance to present my case before you lose your temper with me."

"I have never lost my temper with you," she snapped. "I have always been even-tempered."

"Even-tempered? More like ill-tempered," he laughed.

"That's not true." Yet she knew she had been a shrew. "If you are trying to focus the subject on me instead of explaining about your sister, it is not going to work. I think it is about time that you explain. And I do hope that you truly have a sister."

Locke scratched his ear. The moment of truth, which he had been postponing was here. "I have a sister all right. It is just that Lamantha is different from most women."

Suspicious, Cornelia asked, "Different? How?"

Locke rolled his eyes. Bringing Cornelia to Leadville with him had seemed like a great idea at the time. Now, sitting across from Cornelia, Locke wondered what would happen when Lamantha got hold of her. He had wanted Cornelia to be more independent, think for herself, and come to realize that she deserved more in life than running back to a man who had had the stupidity to let her go in the first place. Somehow, exposing Cornelia to Lamantha might end up getting Locke more than he had bargained for.

"I am waiting," Cornelia prodded, her impatience coupled with growing dread. "I am sure she is *not* that different that you cannot describe her. She doesn't have two heads or anything, does she?"

"I wouldn't be so sure." Cornelia lifted her brow, warning Locke that he had better get on with it. "Lamantha hates men."

"What?" Cornelia questioned, not quite certain how to factor his explanation.

"Lamantha has little use for men. She is a hard-nosed old prune who will probably try to turn you against all men. So I thought that maybe once you heard the type of woman Lamantha is, you would rather stay at the hotel with me."

"With you?" she asked suspiciously.

"You would have your own room," he said.

"How generous of you. I think I might just enjoy staying with Lamantha."

"Well, there is a slight problem with that, too," Locke admitted.

"A slight problem? How slight?" she said in a tone clearly displaying rising displeasure.

A grin of guilt lifted the corners of Locke's lips. "She doesn't exactly know you're coming."

"I see. Did you tell her that you were coming to Leadville?"

"She knows that I need to check on my business. She also knows that I have been planning to sell the warehouses. Since I've never stayed with her, there was no reason to let her know when I'm coming."

"You two are amiable, aren't you?" she probed, fearing the answer.

"She tolerates me because I am her brother, but I am

the wrong gender to be considered a friend."

"Then you do visit her when you're in town." .

"She runs my warehouse business, Cornelia."

The thought of a woman running a business that would normally be run by a man intrigued Cornelia. She found that she wanted to meet this lady. She also had to silently admit that she wanted to talk to the lady because Locke's sister could tell her more about Locke although after listening to Locke's explanation, Cornelia wondered what Lamantha Breckenridge would have to say about the enigma of a man sitting across from her.

"Even though she does not know I am coming, you do visit her, so I would like to meet the lady."

"Would you like to check in to the hotel first before going over to Lamantha's?" he asked.

He was trying to manipulate her, and Cornelia was going to have none of it. He had already manipulated her into accompanying him under false pretenses, and she should leave him. However, she did not feel so adventurous all alone in this large city and decided to alter Locke's plans a bit.

"No. I think I should very much like to meet your sister first."

Locke shrugged. "Suit yourself." He paid the bill and ushered her back to the waiting wagon.

They drove to Lamantha Breckenridge's home in silence, each lost in thought. Until they stopped outside a smart two-storied, white plank house encircled with a picket fence. The yard had been manicured to perfection and planted with perennials set out in perfect rows and bursting with color.

"This is it," Locke said and helped Cornelia down. "It is the perfect place for Lamantha."

"Your family home?" asked Cornelia, impressed by

197

it's neatness.

"No. We were army brats. Never really had a home to call our own. Always followed our father. Until our parents were massacred near Fort Laramie."

"I'm sorry."

Locke put his hand on Cornelia's back and with the other hand opened the gate and ushered her into the yard. Stepping stones spaced perfectly with Cornelia's gait led them to the porch steps. They mounted the four steps and crossed the porch to the front door. Cornelia stood rigidly while Locke knocked.

A tall woman of square stature, considerably older than Locke, with a sunburned face creased like a surveyor's map answered the door. Her black hair shot liberally with gray streaks was pulled back into a severe bun.

"Lockforde, what are you doing here?" Lamantha's loud voice boomed out.

So, Lamantha Breckenridge definitely had not been expecting them, Cornelia thought, standing behind Locke. Locke dutifully gave the woman a peck on the cheek, and the woman stiffly stepped back, not returning his greeting. Then her eyes settled on Cornelia.

"Whom do you have here?" she asked. Her gaze perused Cornelia from head to toe, and Cornelia felt a chill as the cold assessment rolled over her. When Locke did not answer, Lamantha asked, "And who are you, young woman?"

"Miss Breckenridge—" Cornelia offered a gloved hand "—I am an acquaintance of your brother's."

Lamantha's eyes shot to Locke. "She's not from around here. Where did you two meet?" she grilled him.

Locke smiled at his sister, unperturbed. "You might invite us in before you set about with your interroga-

198

tion, Lammy."

Her straight brows shot together. "Humph! Come in, won't you?" she said harshly. She stepped aside and allowed Cornelia and Locke to pass, saying to Locke's back, "I thought you would have learned by now not to call me Lammy."

Locke ignored the woman and leaned over to whisper into Cornelia's ear. "Ignore my sister, she'll come to grow on you."

Like a wart, Cornelia was tempted to say. But that was uncharitable, and she made up her mind not to be judgmental. They entered a neat, small parlor and were shown to a flowered settee.

"You might as well sit."

"Thank you," Cornelia said in a small voice.

Cornelia looked about her. The room was formal to a fault. Not a thing was out of place. Undoubtedly, Lamantha Breckenridge would cane the person who dared to touch, let alone move, any of her treasures.

"You find the room interesting, young woman?"

"I find it immaculately decorated," Cornelia said, not allowing the forbidding woman to daunt her. "And my name is Cornelia Talbot."

"Well, Miss Tal—"

"It is Missus," Cornelia corrected, keeping her back stiff.

"Yes, well, Mrs. Talbot, why has my brother brought you to Leadville?"

"You believe in being blunt, don't you, Miss Breckenridge."

Lamantha raised a brow, and Cornelia held her breath expecting the worst. "And you seem to be capable of holding your own." An unexpected grin broke the tight line of her mouth. "I like you, Cornelia, if I may call you that."

"Please do." Cornelia relaxed a bit.

"And you may call me Lamantha." Her gaze drifted to Locke and back to Cornelia. "You are not afraid of me like that ex-wife of my brother's. 'Course, that one never came to see me. Thought she was too good, that one. Lockforde hasn't brought many of his female acquaintances to visit me."

As if an idea had just struck her, Lamantha turned to Locke. "Go to the kitchen and fetch us a pot of tea. I want to talk to this young woman without your hovering over her like a protective suitor."

To Cornelia's surprise, Locke did not protest. He winked at her, then rose, gave his sister a brotherly salute, and disappeared around the corner.

For what seemed like a half hour, Lamantha Breckenridge cross-examined Cornelia. Cornelia felt as though she were under a microscope, but she answered every question as candidly as it was asked. When the questioning finally abated, Locke's sister knew her life story. Pleasantly surprised that the woman did not show any emotion when Cornelia told her the truth of her own divorce and the reasons for accompanying her brother to Colorado, she was further pleased that Lamantha Breckenridge said nothing when Cornelia told her about accompanying Locke to Leadville.

Cornelia only had the opportunity to ask a couple of her own questions about Locke when he finally reappeared carrying a tray holding a silver tea service.

"Did I take long enough, Lammy?"

"Hardly adequate. But I suppose the time you allowed us must suffice," Lamantha returned.

"I imagine you two can probably use something to quench your thirst. Especially you, Cornelia. My sister has a way of making her guests feel as if they have just attempted to scale a mountain without a canteen. I'm glad she did not drive you from the house with her winning ways."

"Lockforde," Lamantha said in a disapproving voice that bespoke her displeasure. "Don't stand there speaking nonsense while the tea gets cold."

Locke laughed and set the service on the table by his sister. He sat next to Cornelia and with ease rested his arm across the back of the settee behind Cornelia.

She tried to ignore him, but she felt the rush of heat pass her cheeks on its way upward. She wondered what Lamantha would say about Locke sitting so close to her when the woman looked up from pouring the tea. To her further embarrassment, she noticed Lamantha's keen eye did not miss a thing.

"Lockforde, aren't you sitting a trifle close to Cornelia?"

"Not unless you would prefer that I sit on the floor," he said.

"Perhaps that would be preferable," she stated and handed Cornelia a cup. "My brother does not always believe in observing proper decorum. Of course, my dear, my brother often makes a point of doing things to annoy me. Always has. Never grew out of the habit. He knows how I feel about men and constantly makes a habit of reminding me that I have never been wrong about them."

Cornelia listened attentively as the woman poured out her untempered opinions and shifted as far away from Locke as possible unobtrusively.

Once they had had their tea, the conversation seemed to wither as if their allotted time was up and they were now expected to depart. Well, Cornelia was not going to a hotel without mentioning that she had planned to stay with Lamantha although Cornelia was not certain that was being wise.

"I suppose you two must be on your way," Lamantha said before Cornelia could open her mouth.

"Actually, Locke mentioned something about the possibility of remaining here as your guest," Cornelia said.

"My, my, you are nearly as direct as I am," Lamantha said without a smile. "But that is quite impossible. Lockforde knows I never entertain overnight guests. Even my dear brother has always taken a room at a hotel. You see, Cornelia, I have lived alone all my adult life. My house is quite adequate for my needs, but much too small to share with others, even for a few days. Of course, I do hope we shall have the opportunity to meet at one of the restaurants while you are here."

"I told you my sister is different," Locke said, waving off Lamantha's frown. "She likes her privacy."

"You should have told me," Cornelia said as sweetly as possible although she would have liked to wring his neck at the moment.

Locke shrugged, refraining from reminding her that he had done just that before they had descended on Lamantha. If it was important for Cornelia to give his sister a different impression, he was not going to say otherwise.

As they left Lamantha's house, Cornelia tried to analyze why she was so upset at the thought of sleeping under the same roof as Locke Breckenridge, albeit in separate rooms. She had to admit she was drawn to him. Perhaps it was because they shared the common bond of a painful divorce. Or perhaps it was because they both enjoyed the walks in Estes Park. Or perhaps it was because he had not tried to force himself on her. Or perhaps it was because she liked his sister despite the strangeness about the woman. Whatever it was, Cornelia could not deny the electricity that arced between them as she sat next to Locke while they drove to the hotel. She wondered what the next week would hold. They would be thrown together constantly, and Cornelia felt a growing attraction.

Chapter Twenty-one

Locke pulled up in front of the Claredon Hotel, and they went inside to check in. Cornelia hung in the background as Locke stepped up to the desk clerk to register. Locke signed the register and turned it toward the man dressed in somber, formal black.

"Mr. Breckenridge, sir, would you and the lady prefer one of our suites?"

Cornelia was horrified to hear the man assumed that she was a woman of easy virtue. Her first inclination was to turn and flee, but she caught herself. She was no longer the same lady she had been back home. She was strong and would stand up for herself. Locke had not set the man straight, so she had to take the initiative. She stepped up to the desk next to Locke.

"The lady will require separate accommodations," she said starchily. She picked up a pen and signed the register.

"Beg pardon, ma'am. I thought you two were together."

"We are," Locke said at the same time that Cornelia said, "We aren't."

Both men settled questioning gazes on her, making her feel terribly conspicuous. Cornelia looked around to see if any of the other guests was listening. She straightened the bow at her throat and set her features. "Mr. Breckenridge and I are acquaintances, but we are not that type of acquaintances."

The men's brows raised in unison. "I mean, we are merely casual acquaintances."

"Lady, it is not the policy of this establishment to inquire into the type of relationship its guests share," blustered the clerk. He bent his head and busied himself over filling out their registration cards.

"Sir," Cornelia protested, not satisfied to accept the man's remark. "I am a respectable woman."

"Yes, miss," the man said in a doubt-filled voice.

"It is missus."

He looked at the line on which the woman had signed the register. "Will Mr. Talbot be joining you then?"

"Mr. Talbot?" she croaked, taken aback.

"Yes, your husband?"

Locke had been standing idly by, but he did not like the tone of the man's voice toward Cornelia. His features set in stone, he loomed over the man, which caused the man to shrink and his shoulders to hunch.

"I believe the lady explained that we require two rooms. Is there a problem that I need to take up with the manager of this establishment?" Locke asked darkly. "Or perhaps I should discuss your policy with Horace Tabor. I am sure the man who built this establishment would find the manner in which you treat its guests most interesting."

The man loosened the tie at his throat that had suddenly become too tight. Everyone was aware of Horace Tabor's own affair with Baby Doe and the messy divorce that ensued and his marriage to the loose woman. Therefore, should this man chose to tell

Tabor, the desk clerk was sure that he would be forced to look elsewhere for a job. "No, sir. No problem at all." He turned to Cornelia, his face contrite. "I beg your pardon, ma'am." He reached for two keys and set them on the counter. "I think you will find these are two of our finest rooms."

"Good," Locke said harshly. "Have a bellboy see the lady to her room."

"Yes, sir."

While the desk clerk snapped his fingers and was directing the young boy to collect their bags, Cornelia pulled Locke aside. "You aren't going to your room now?"

"Don't worry, Cornelia, I'm not running out on you."

"I didn't think you were," she said although deep inside, she had to admit to herself that since Linley had deserted her, the fear had crossed her mind.

"I told you before we left Estes Park that I had business to tend to, so while you get settled in your room, I shall meet with my lawyer about a business matter."

"It isn't necessary for you to feel a responsibility to entertain me."

"I don't feel it is a responsibility. It is my pleasure. I'll meet you in the hotel's dining room for supper at six sharp," he said and left her standing in the lobby before she could react. Yet as she watched him disappear out the main entrance, she could not combat the rush of warmth that filled her breast. Her heart still beating double time, Cornelia followed the boy to her room.

Locke went directly to his lawyer's. He was shown into the man's plush office. Carter Hunnicutt rose from his desk and offered a bony hand. "Ah, Breckenridge, what brings you back to Leadville? Last time you were here, you led us all to believe that you would not be returning anytime soon." Carter's expression grew concerned. "I hope there is not any problem with the way my firm has handled your business?"

"Carter," Locke said, shaking hands and taking a seat. "I don't have any problems with your firm. My problem is with Margaret."

"We have been sending her monthly stipend to the address she left with our office," Carter said defensively.

"I have no doubts that your office has handled everything correctly, Carter, so relax. The problem is with Margaret's greed. She has decided that she is not getting enough money. She wants more." Locke handed Carter the letter Lamantha had slipped to him earlier.

Carter set his spectacles on his nose and perused the scrawling swirls across the pink stationery. "This is absurd. You were more than generous, considering the circumstances," objected Carter, who had personally handled the details of Breckenridge's divorce. He studied Locke's face. "You are not considering giving that money grubber more, are you?"

"I told you at the time that I didn't care what you had to offer her. I want her to stay out of my life." What Locke declined to say was that he did not want her to come to Estes Park, especially now that Locke had met Cornelia Talbot. Knowing Margaret, he knew she would delight in trying to ruin his fledgling relationship with Cornelia.

"And?"

"And if it means giving her an increase, give it to her. And send her a letter explaining that if she tries this again, I will cut her off, and she'll have to learn to fend for herself."

"But she is engaging in blackmail," Carter sputtered, outraged. "I don't think it is a good idea. As your legal counsel, I must strongly advise you to reconsider."

Deciding to put an end to their conversation, Locke rose to his feet. "There is nothing to reconsider. Pay her," he said with finality.

Carter was not satisfied to let the subject drop without a last-ditch effort. He rose to his feet. "Your sister has a vested interest in your business. What will she say to these exorbitant demands?"

Placing his fists on the large mahogany desk, Locke leaned closer, face to face with the man. "Carter, you have handled my legal matters for years. And while I realize that you are only interested in my financial welfare, what I do with the business profits is my business, not my sister's. Who, incidentally, knows better than to question me. So I warn you, if you want to continue to represent me and handle my business interests, which by the way means a tidy sum each year for your firm, meet my ex-wife's demands."

The bony lawyer stiffened, holding up his palms. "It is your money, Locke."

"Then do what I ask. And don't forget to warn her what will happen if she tries it again. Good day, Carter." He turned to leave, then stopped and pivoted around to face the man. "Oh, I nearly forgot, I have been considering selling the business; draw up the necessary papers."

"You needn't concern yourself further," Carter said to Locke's back. "I'll handle everything personally," he managed to get out just as the door slammed behind Locke.

Carter sank back into his chair once the big man had gone. He did not want to lose Breckenridge's business, but letting that scheming hussy get away with such blatant blackmail almost seemed like sacrilege.

Locke hurried back to the hotel to dress for supper, confident that he was done with Margaret. The last thing he needed was to have her show up. Cornelia was gun-shy enough as it was without being frightened away by his scheming ex-wife. Entering his room, he slung one of the fresh towels left on the dresser over his shoulder and went into the bathroom to shave.

Lathering his face liberally, Locke was scraping the razor over his chin when someone tried the knob on the bathroom door leading to the next room. He was wiping his face when he called out in muffled tones. "It's occupied. You'll have to be patient."

Standing in front of the beveled mirror, Locke tied his tie, ran a brush through his ebony hair, and splashed on a liberal amount of cologne. The doorknob rattled again, but Locke ignored it this time. He was looking forward to the evening with Cornelia. He had spoken with the restaurant manager and made arrangements to have everything perfect. Grabbing his coat, he headed toward the dining room.

The manager met Locke at the entrance and ushered him to a private table in a far corner. "Does this meet with your specifications, sir?"

Locke handed the man a coin. "Yes, it is perfect. Is the champagne on ice?"

"It is ready to be delivered as soon as the lady arrives, sir."

"Good. Be sure not to leave Mrs. Talbot waiting

when she arrives. Usher her right to the table," he instructed.

"You needn't worry, sir, everything is all set," the man said and scurried off to wait for the lady.

Locke sat at the table waiting. He was beginning to wonder if Cornelia had decided not to have supper with him after all when a vision in shimmering satin appeared at the entrance. Locke's breath caught. He knew her figure had been filling out; he had noticed it this morning over breakfast, but he had not realized what a beauty the skinny woman who had fought him at the train station in Denver all those weeks ago now was.

Cornelia was decked out in a champagne creation that Paxton had insisted she bring along. The capped sleeves were shot through with silver threads that gleamed in the light. The bodice of her gown clung to her like a second skin, whereas the skirt, beaded with crystals, billowed around her like a frothy cloud.

As she approached Locke, the look on his face told her that he was impressed, and it gave her a good feeling although she had argued with herself over the appropriateness of wearing such a gown.

He stood and helped her with her chair. "I was afraid that you had changed your mind," he said, taking a seat across the small, intimate table.

The waiter arrived with the champagne and was busy uncorking the bottle as Cornelia said, "I must apologize, it took longer than I had anticipated."

"Well worth the extra effort, I might add," Locke stated.

"I'm afraid I have been forced to share connecting accommodations, and the occupant was most uncooperative," she said, wondering as a strange fleeting light flickered into his eyes that caused her to withhold any further comment. She thought instead of his last comment. Compliments were a new experience for her, and she found that she enjoyed them. Linley had not paid her many, saying it was a wife's duty to look her best at all times and to maintain the family position in the community.

The evening's meal was a delight to Cornelia. Locke treated her like royalty, attentively listening to everything she said, and sharing anecdotes about his and his sister's youth. Cornelia gained a better understanding of Lamantha Breckenridge as Locke explained she had been like a mother to him and had sworn that once he was on his own, she would never again take care of another. She would care only for herself and she had kept to that. At first Cornelia thought it selfish of Lamantha, but as he described how bighearted the harsh woman really was, Cornelia found she liked and respected the older woman.

"Care for dessert?" Locke asked once they had finished the main course.

"I really shouldn't."

"Why not?"

Cornelia looked down at her empty plate. She had eaten every bite of the prime rib dinner. Her head snapped up when she heard Locke scoot back his chair.

Holding out his hand, he said, "Come on, I know where we can get the best ice cream in town. It's hand cranked, and often the owners put the patrons to work making their own. You game?"

To Cornelia's surprise when she hesitated, Locke bent her arm and made a big production of feeling her muscle. "Well, perhaps you can't man the handle," he announced with a challenging grin.

Cornelia pulled her arm back. Then, to Locke's delighted surprise, in front of all the decorous patrons of

211

the formal restaurant, she posed and flexed her muscle. "I bet I can make the largest dish you can eat."

"I'll take that bet."

Ignoring the censuring stares of the shocked diners, Cornelia cast Locke a big smile. He grabbed her hand and led her through the dining room toward the exit. She felt giddy and girlish and appreciated, and for the first time in her life, she did not care what others thought of her.

Chapter Twenty-two

Cornelia practically had to run to keep up with Locke as he led her down Harrison Avenue three blocks to a side street. Cornelia stumbled and would have fallen if Locke had not swung around just in time to catch her.

In the warm yellow glow from the storefronts, their eyes fastened on each other for a long moment until two couples passed by and their laughter intruded into the heightening tension between them.

"You all right?"

"My heel must have caught," Cornelia said and looked down at the separation in the boards along the sidewalk.

Locke offered his arm. "Forgive me, I shouldn't have been in such a rush."

"Nonsense" — she took his arm — "I'm just as anxious as you are to enjoy a big dish of ice cream."

"A woman after my own heart," he said. As quickly as the words escaped his tongue, Locke turned away and focused his attention on their progress toward the ice cream parlor. He had not intended to say such a thing.

Cornelia walked alongside Locke quietly, but her mind was spinning over what he'd said and her breast tightened. Enjoying the company of a man who was not her husband certainly was not an acceptable mode of behavior, but in these surroundings Cornelia did not care. She felt free and, she had to admit, a little wicked. Besides, it felt wonderful to be so unfettered.

They entered the crowded store. Clusters of wrought-iron tables stood in front of a large glass window. Four people near the counter were cranking ice cream buckets while joyous knots of young men and ladies watched and laughed.

Cornelia noticed the heaping dishes of ice cream that people were enjoying with relish. Many people were clearly engaged in courtship rituals, and she found herself wanting to pretend that she and Locke also were courting. Holding Locke's hand, much like other couples watching the workers, was such a natural feeling, so Cornelia made no attempt to retrieve hers.

"If you two would like to join us, we've made plenty," said a mustached young man looking up at them from his position on the floor next to the wooden ice cream maker.

Locke sent Cornelia a look of challenge, then glanced down at the young man. "Thanks, but the lady and I have a bet going."

At the look of confusion on the young man's face, Cornelia added, "This man doesn't think I am strong enough to turn the crank until I've made ice cream."

To Cornelia's delight and surprise, the group they were standing with began a rousing round of wagering. Locke accepted the bets, and soon he was offering odds. To Cornelia's further delight, Locke was betting against himself. He had faith in her, something Linley had never shown.

A roly-poly store owner brought out all the ingredients. Minutes later, Cornelia found herself the center of attention, and she started to panic; young ladies did not step into the limelight, they were supposed to remain in the background. She started to turn away.

"You're not conceding defeat, are you?" Locke whispered. "I have a lot of money riding on you."

Fighting to suppress the urge to flee, she asked, "How much?"

There was a twinkle in his eyes. "Nearly a dollar and a half."

"Since I would not want you to lose your money until I've won our bet, help me tie back my shawl."

Locke's fingers made short work of her shawl.

"Just one minute," the owner called out. He untied the apron he was wearing and offered it to Cornelia. "I would not want you to ruin that gown. Such a gown I have never seen in my shop before."

Cornelia blushed with pleasure at the compliment while Locke took the stiff white garment and tied it around her waist. "What are you waiting for?" he asked when she stood there staring at the waiting ice cream maker.

She turned to Locke, a twinkle in her eyes. "I was just thinking that our stakes should be higher than your eating the largest dish I can make."

Locke cocked a brow. "That is, if you can manage to make enough ice cream to fill a dish."

The gleam of challenge in his eyes egged her on. "I'll make more than enough."

"You want to go for higher stakes? Like a bowl of ice cream?"

To Cornelia's glee, the crowd delighted in urging

215

her to exact more of a forfeit from Locke, should she win.

"You should pay something other than enjoying the fruits of my labor. What are you willing to offer?" she asked.

Locke's gaze roved over her face and settled on her full lips. If she knew what he was thinking, she would probably flee back to her brother in Estes Park and make arrangements to take the first train back east.

"And what forfeit will you pay if you can't make enough ice cream to satisfy my appetite?" he challenged.

One of the men standing next to a buxom blonde shouted, "A kiss. She should pay a kiss."

Cornelia's head snapped around to look at the couples. They were all in agreement. Caught up in the excitement, Cornelia had to admit that she would like to kiss Locke again.

"Okay," she said before she could stop herself. "But what will you forfeit?"

"A kiss?" he offered.

The ladies giggled, and Cornelia felt a blush climb her cheeks. If he only knew how tempted she was to take his offer. But, of course, propriety would not allow such a thing. "I think that you should come up with another offer."

He spread his arms akimbo. "I'm at your disposal. Name your terms."

A variety of suggestions buzzed around the tiny room until someone called out, "Hush, let the lady speak."

"If I win, you must agree to take us all on a picnic," she said to cheers.

Locke bowed. "My pleasure."

Surrounded by so many friendly people, Cornelia let go of her inhibitions and basked in the ferment as she got caught up in the revelry. She turned the crank until she thought her arms would fall off. Gradually, the mixture started to take on the texture of ice cream. Locke even offered to allow her a break, but she refused. Despite the desire to experience another kiss with Locke, she could not afford to lose without trying her best. How could she allow him to kiss her in front of all these people? Still, she was having so much fun.

Finally, she had produced a bucket of rich ice cream. Then all eyes turned to Locke as the owner brought in a king-sized mixing bowl, and Cornelia dished up as much as she could fit into the huge bowl. The cold mixture ran down the side of the glass, and Locke reached out, swiped up the drip with his finger, and savored it.

"This is great," he said and dipped his finger into the mixture. Offering it to Cornelia, he asked, "Want a lick?"

She looked at the long slender finger held out to her. "Our bet was that you must finish it all."

"You don't know what you're missing," he said with a grin of deeper meaning. With smooth deliberation, he suckled the sweet frozen cream from his finger, all the while gazing at her with an intensity only broken by a flirty redhead.

"I'll pay the forfeit for her, if you'd like," the shapely redhead cooed and offered Locke a spoon.

Cornelia felt a stab of jealousy but quickly suppressed the urge to step in between Locke and the redhead. Instead, she said, "Waiting until the ice cream melts means you forfeit, Locke."

While Locke started to eat the gigantic bowl of

confection, Cornelia helped the owner pass out dishes to the group, and everyone ate while watching Locke.

Cornelia was astounded as the man dipped into the ice cream with relish over and over. She could not believe that anyone could eat that much frozen dessert in one seating, but Locke seemed to be doing it effortlessly.

"Are you ready to pay your forfeit?" Locke asked, holding the last spoonful.

She took the bowl from him and motioned to all the eyes watching. "In front of all these people?" she whispered.

"I think it is only fair, considering the huge stomachache I'll probably have to suffer earning it." Locke was not about to admit that ice cream was one of his favorite foods and devouring the bowl had not taken much effort.

He stepped directly in front of her, took the bowl out of her hands, and gave it to the disappointed redhead. Then he clasped his hands behind his back and rocked back and forth on his heels. "I'm ready when you are."

Cornelia looked around her. She expected to note condemnation. To her delighted surprise, the men wore grins and the ladies had expectant expressions.

"You aren't planning to welsh, are you?" Locke asked.

"No, of course not."

"Well then?" He puckered his lips.

Cornelia took a deep breath. She had no choice, she told herself. But if truth were known she secretly wanted to pay the forfeit although not quite so publicly. Her face heating, Cornelia raised up on her tiptoes, placed her hands on

Locke's shoulders, and gave him a quick peck.

"That couldn't hardly be considered much of a forfeit," the shapely redhead said. She gave Cornelia a quick shove, circled Locke's neck, and was fully prepared to give him a big kiss. To her chagrin, Locke held her at bay.

"Thanks for the offer, but no thanks," he said.

"Your loss," she snapped. To snickers from the others, she stuck her nose in the air, pushed through the crowd, and left the store.

"We're going on a picnic tomorrow," said one of the young men. "You are welcome to join us," he offered.

"Thanks, but we have plans," Locke answered. He settled all bets as Cornelia accepted congratulations and envious remarks from the group.

Once they had left the ice cream parlor and were heading back toward the hotel, Locke took her hand in his. Cornelia glanced down at their entwined fingers and felt a warm glow. A breeze blew past her neck giving her a chill, and she shivered, causing Locke to release her hand. He took off his jacket and wrapped it around her shoulders, then took her hand again.

"Thank you," she said, awed by his consideration. She could feel the warmth of him radiating from the coat, and it gave her a giddy feeling.

Back at the hotel, Locke insisted on escorting her to her room. When they stopped in front of her door, Locke hesitated a moment before he took her key and opened the door.

Cornelia stepped inside the door and turned to Locke. "Thank for you the wonderful evening," she said and took his jacket off her shoulders to hand it back to him. "I had a marvelous time."

Locke took her hand rather than the jacket. "It was my pleasure. But you still owe me that forfeit."

Looking up into his face, she said, "I kissed you in front of an audience."

A couple about the age of Cornelia's parents passed them in the hall, craning their necks, the woman huffing her outrage. Then, to make matters worse, the woman stopped farther down the hall and openly stared.

Cornelia, feeling embarrassed, quickly pulled Locke into the room. Locke kicked the door shut with his boot heel.

"I always believe in collecting on debts owed," he murmured in a husky voice.

"You do?" Cornelia rasped in a whisper as he pulled her into his arms.

"Always. Especially when the debt owed is from a certain special lady," he murmured. With the crook of his index finger, he lifted her chin and bent his head.

"We shouldn't be here like this," she pleaded half-heartedly to his lips.

"No, I suppose not." He gently kissed her. Her lips were soft and warm, silently inviting further exploration. Without wasting the moment, Locke deepened the kiss.

The sensations exploding inside her were more than she could control, more than she wanted to control. Shivering waves engulfed her, and despite her long-held resolve to return to her ex-husband and get him to take her back, Cornelia could not deny all the pent-up feelings that Locke had awakened and was releasing within her.

A hunger was also awakened within Locke. After two years of living as a recluse in Estes Park and swearing off all women, Locke's urges exploded. He explored her lips with a light-headed passion.

Cornelia leaned into him and followed his lead.

"Oh, yes," he murmured against her lips. His hands drifted up and down her back and toyed with the downy hairs on the back of her neck.

"Locke," she moaned, helpless to stop the heightening pleasure that dulled any further thoughts of protest. She was still in a daze when she felt him bend down and swoop her up into his arms.

Her childhood dreams of being carried to an incredibly romantic wedding bed flashed before her eyes, and in her state of growing rapture, Cornelia let her imagination entwine with the reality of being alone in a hotel room with this man.

In a dreamworld, she felt herself being set on a cloud-soft bed and electric fingers rove along her body, sending her senses streaking across the sky like lightning bolts. She did not protest when he expertly unfastened the tiny satin buttons, and his heated fingers delved inside her chemise to settle on a cresting nipple.

Locke slowly divested Cornelia of the remainder of her clothing, dropping each garment next to the bed. She was giving herself to him totally, offering him all of her self without protest as he explored every peak and valley, every curve of her body.

"You are so beautiful," he murmured as he dipped his head to suckle on her reaching nipple.

Cornelia had no resistance within her to fight even if she had wanted to, which she did not. She had already been conquered, and she surrendered without a thought to any future consequences. All tense muscles relaxed as he touched them, and when his fingers stroked into her, she lifted her hips to meet every stroke.

When he stopped the mind-bursting rhythm with his fingers and palm of his hand, Cornelia opened her eyes to watch him peel off his clothing and drop it next to hers.

She was enthralled by his muscular body and reached up to touch his chest dusted with curling hairs. She moved down his stomach, and his muscles contracted at her touch.

"What are you trying to do to me?" he uttered, wedging his knee between her thighs.

"What are you doing to me?" she responded. Her voice was an amalgam of pleasure and longing.

"I'm making love with you," he whispered hoarsely, and Cornelia's heart soared. He had said "with" her, meaning they were sharing themselves. He was not merely using her to sate his lust, she thought as sensation replaced consideration.

Slowly, with the greatest of care, Locke lowered himself into her all the while reassuring her with soft words. She was ready for him, wet and willing. And as he began that age-old rhythm, she met his every stroke until he was plunging into her and trying to hold himself back until she had reached her release.

Cornelia's sensibilities screamed as the tension built until she lost total control and her body jerked with the most incredible pressure and pulsing shivers that spread out from her feminine core down her thighs and arms. She strained and pressed herself to him, wrapping her legs around him and crying out his name.

Locke groaned and burst into her with a powerful eruption. The force of his release caused him to kiss her with all his bottled-up passion.

Not wanting her to cradle his weight, he shifted to her side and held her to him. "What are you thinking?" he asked.

Cornelia gazed into his heavy-lidded eyes. "I never realized that making love was supposed to feel like that," she said honestly.

"It feels like that and better," he said tenderly, wanting to hold her like this forever.

"Umm," she moaned and closed her eyes. She was cocooned in a warm lethargy, and for the first time since she was a little girl, she felt that the whole world belonged to her.

Chapter Twenty-three

For a long time after Cornelia had fallen asleep in his arms, Locke remained awake encased in a warm glow. He had been drawn to Cornelia Talbot for weeks, and he had been wanting her as a man. But he had never imagined that making love to a woman could prove so emotionally fulfilling.

Whores had eased his needs after he had married Margaret and discovered that she was only interested in his money. With whores, he had not had to worry about an heir although he wanted a family. And once his precious Margaret had shown her true colors, he had decided not to take the chance that she would conceive and try to parade another man's child as his son.

As dawn was turning the night into shades of wispy gray, Locke rose. He scribbled Cornelia a note, then dressed and returned to his own room. Taking her feelings into consideration, he had left. Once in his own room, Locke went into the bathroom to wash up.

A cuddling warmth surrounded Cornelia when she awoke. She was holding a pillow. Still sleepy, she reached over to touch Locke. He was gone. A smile came to her lips. He had had enough consideration for her to leave before that spying couple would be up. She reached out and hugged the pillow he had laid his head on. His manly scent clung to the pillowcase and brought back reminiscences of last night.

On the table next to the bed, a note leaned against the lamp. She scooted up and grabbed the plain white hotel stationery.

> My Dearest Cornelia,
> I considered presenting you with breakfast in bed, but thought better of it. I'll be waiting in the lobby for you.
> > Love,
> > Locke

Cornelia's breath caught when she read the salutation, and she realized that what they had shared last night meant more than just a physical experience to both of them.

In a rush to dress, Cornelia grabbed a towel and a fresh gown and went to the bathroom door. It was locked. She could hear the person on the other side of the door gargling. Impatient to meet Locke, Cornelia combed her hair using a small hand mirror. She paced the floor a few more minutes then tried the door again.

It was still locked. She rattled the knob, but no one responded. She was about to throw on a dress and go down to the desk clerk and demand another room when she heard the click of the lock. She swung the door open ready to give her neighbor a good talking-to, but no one was there and no one answered when she knocked on the door leading to the adjoining room. Determined to request a change of rooms, Cornelia hurried through her toilette and headed down the stairs.

She was almost to the desk when Locke intercepted her. "Ready for breakfast?" he asked, his eyes twinkling.

The brilliance of his smile caused previous thoughts of changing rooms to shift in order of importance. "I'm famished."

They had breakfast at a small café at the end of town, and then Locke spent the rest of the morning showing her around town and taking his sister out to lunch. Lamantha was true to character and declined Cornelia's invitation to spend the afternoon shopping while Locke tended to business. She changed her mind when Locke announced that he was considering selling his interests if he could spend time touring with his managers.

Not only did Lamantha spend the afternoon with Cornelia, but the elder woman was most cordial. "You must think I'm an old bag," she said suddenly as they were coming out of a dress shop.

"Oh, no," Cornelia said. "I suppose I thought you felt I am a loose woman for accompanying your brother to Leadville without a chaperone."

"Cornelia, banish the thought," protested Lamantha, who thoroughly believed in speaking her mind. "I am just thankful he got rid of that fortune seeker he married."

"Locke doesn't talk much about his ex-wife," Cornelia ventured.

"It was quite a scandal. Not as big as the Tabors, of course. Actually, I like to think the girl was crazy about Lockforde until she realized that his assets were tied up and she would not be living in the manner she had hoped for. She was a splashy little thing. Always hung around with Baby Doe. So when Baby Doe hooked Horace Tabor, naturally Margaret had to come up with someone to keep her in the same league.

"You see, despite the fact that my brother is an exceedingly handsome man, he has always worked very hard. He'd always led a simple life until he married and his wife started demanding that they keep up with the Tabors. So Lockforde worked doubly hard for her, and, of course, while he was working, the spendthrift was busy shopping and partying until he caught her in bed with another man. It close to destroyed him."

The rest of the afternoon Lamantha continued to relate all the sordid details of the nasty divorce, and as Cornelia listened, she came to understand more about Locke.

When they returned late in the afternoon burdened with packages, Locke was sitting on Lamantha's porch. "Looks like you two bought out the town," he observed, rising to take Lamantha and Cornelia's burdens.

Lamantha waved him off. "Nonsense. I practically had to force this one to buy anything for herself. She's definitely not like that ex-wife of yours."

Locke was pleased that Cornelia had passed Lamantha's inspection and the dear old crow was warming to her. They spent a half hour discussing the details of Locke's plans to sell his business interests. Then after Lamantha turned down his invitation to attend the opera with them that evening, she saw them to the porch with, "You wear that gown tonight that I insisted you buy.

Oh, and stop by before you leave town."

To Lamantha's surprise, Cornelia gave her a big hug. When Cornelia stepped back, Locke stepped forward. "You might as well get used to it, Lammy. You never know when you may be seeing Cornelia again."

Cornelia and Lamantha wore bemused expressions, but Locke had no intention of attempting an explanation. His feelings for Cornelia were too new.

Locke was arguing with the desk clerk over changing rooms when Cornelia descended the staircase.

Words failed him when he sighted her. She was a vision in the lime-green, beaded chiffon. He never thought that she could have surpassed the way she had looked the night before, but with her hair piled high and woven with sparkling beads that matched her gown, Cornelia Talbot would make any one proud.

"You look beautiful tonight," he said, moving to her side.

Cornelia beamed. "Thank you." She wanted to tell him that he was the one who looked *beautiful* in his tuxedo. He was so tall with his shiny black hair and brown eyes with silver flecks that danced when he looked at her.

Cornelia almost wished that Linley could see her with Locke now. The memory of how he had yelled at her that no man would ever look at her much less want to escort her anywhere still hurt, but that was a matter that she chose not to deal with now. She was having a wonderful time with Locke, so much so that she was falling in love. And she refused consider that it could not last.

Locke offered his arm, and they ambled back up to the upper floor and along the walkway to the adjoining theater. It was a nice touch, allowing guests of the hotel private access to the opera house.

Cornelia looked around in awe as they entered the opera house. She was astounded at its grand scale and impressed with the wrought-iron seats adorned with red velvet cushions. Her vision trailed toward the ceiling.

"It's canvas," Cornelia observed.

"Helps the acoustics," Locke said.

Several of the couples they had met in the ice cream parlor greeted them, and Cornelia felt the belle of the ball when the ladies complimented her on her attire.

They were about to take their seats when the shapely redhead from the ice cream parlor approached. "I'm surprised to see you here this evening," she said cattily, hanging on the arm of a fancy young man. She turned to her escort and said, "One would have thought they would be tucked away in some hotel room somewhere the way they were carrying on last night."

Cornelia was mortified, and Locke's eyes blazed. "Peters, I suggest you find your seats before it becomes necessary for you to see *the lady* home before enjoying the performance."

The redhead expected her escort, who managed the biggest warehouse in Leadville, to stand up to the stranger. "You aren't going to allow him to talk to me that way, are you?"

"Lydia, the man is my boss," he snapped, pulling a now daunted young woman away from Locke and Cornelia.

She looked back over her shoulder. "You mean he is the one who was married to the infamous Margaret?"

"Hush!"

"I apologize," Locke said once the couple had moved out of earshot. "I am afraid I have a rather notorious reputation in this town."

His remark made her feel good. "If we were in my hometown, it would be me whom they were whispering about," she remarked.

Locke just smiled. He had been livid, but now he was glad since the incident had helped Cornelia put her own situation into a better perspective.

They took their seats, and Cornelia looked about her as they waited for the evening's entertainment to begin. "Who sits over there?" she asked, directing Locke's attention to the curtained booth a short distance from them, close to the stage.

"That is for Tabor and his second wife. You know, he built this place as a monument to provide Leadville with culture and entertainment in dazzling style."

"His second wife?" she repeated.

"Tabor divorced his first wife in a scandalous divorce. Folks around here still don't accept the woman. He even lost a bid for the senate due to his remarriage. But Cornelia, your situation is not at all similar," he added.

"I suppose not," she said half-heartedly, remembering Lamantha's recounting of the tale earlier.

The music began and the curtain rose, curtailing further discussion of Tabor. Cornelia settled back and glued her attention to the stage. It was a rousing production of the farce *Who's Who,* and she greatly enjoyed herself.

Once the show was over and everyone was pouring out of the theater, a young woman not much older than Cornelia rushed up to Locke. Her face had character, and she was dressed in the latest fashion from New York, a pelisse draped over her arm. Her hair did not conform with the accepted style, and her inquisitive eyes sparkled.

"Mr. Breckenridge?" the young woman inquired.

"Yes?" Locke answered and looked to Cornelia. Cornelia's attention was immediately captured by the fine cut of her clothes.

"Allow me to introduce myself—" she held out a gloved hand "—I am Miss Carrie Simington. I understand from Mr. Hunnicutt that you reside in Estes Park and serve as a guide on occasions."

"Yes," Locke answered reluctantly.

"I am interested in engaging your services for a climb up Longs Peak. I have been reading accounts of climbs by Mr. Byers, founder of the *Rocky Mountain News,* Miss Anna Dickinson, and, of course, Miss Isabella Bird. And I am most anxious to make the climb myself."

Locke's attention shifted to Cornelia at the sudden intake of her breath. Miss Simington's attention also shifted to Cornelia. She held out her hand, "Miss?"

"Mrs. Talbot," Cornelia responded. "But please, call me Cornelia. I have been captivated by Longs Peak for weeks. It would be an experience of a lifetime to climb to the top of such a formidable mountain."

"Wonderful, yes. I am so happy that I have gained an ally so soon. And you, of course, my dear Cornelia, must call me Carrie. Do you reside here in Leadville?"

"No. I brought my brother out to Estes Park for his health. I am visiting this marvelous town as the guest of Mr. Breckenridge," Cornelia said, then dropped her eyes.

Locke was not sure he liked the turn the ladies'

conversation was taking. "Excuse me, Miss Simington—"

Her attention immediately shifted to Locke. "You must also call me Carrie. I won't detain you two any longer this evening, but I would be most happy if you both would accept my invitation to take breakfast with me tomorrow morning at the hotel, so we can discuss the matter of Longs Peak in detail."

Locke hesitated, but Cornelia stepped forward. "We would be delighted—" She turned to Locke "—wouldn't we, Locke?"

Locke glanced from one woman to the other. "With the gleam in your eyes, what choice do I have?"

"None, of course," said Carrie Simington, ignoring his reluctance and chattering a little longer before she rejoined three friends who had been patiently waiting nearby.

Locke stared hard after the eccentric young woman as she left the theater. Something about her gave off a signal to Locke that she meant trouble. Once she was gone, his attention shifted to Cornelia, who also had been watching Miss Simington stroll from them. There was a new gleam in Cornelia's eyes that he had not encountered before. It gave him pause for thought.

Up until a few minutes ago, Cornelia had demonstrated only a passing interest in the mountain, and he had thought nothing of it. But now, with Cornelia's newfound independence and the instant friendship she seemed to have formed with Carrie Simington, not to mention her exposure to his staunchly independent sister, Locke had a distinctly uneasy feeling in the pit of his stomach that he was about to encounter even more changes in Cornelia.

Chapter Twenty-four

Locke managed to dispel a nagging sensation of portending prophecy as he escorted Cornelia to the restaurant where they shared a late supper while Locke listened to Cornelia babble excitedly about her first venture to an opera house and meeting Miss Carrie Simington.

"Care to take a stroll before we call it a night?" he asked after he paid the bill.

"It's late." She had a hundred questions she wanted to ask after meeting Carrie Simington, but she decided to wait. He had not seemed too pleased with Carrie's request, and Cornelia had ideas of her own.

Her heart's pace took on a new beat and all thoughts about Longs Peak disintegrated as Locke escorted her toward her room. She lingered at the door, hoping he would kiss her.

Locke did not need any encouragement. "Why don't we go inside, just in case that same couple is lurking in the hallway tonight?" he suggested.

She returned his smile. "We certainly wouldn't want them to get the wrong idea." Or the right one, she thought wickedly.

Cornelia did not hesitate. She rummaged through

her bag and located her key, which Locke took from her. He let them inside and, without turning on any lights, he gathered her into his arms. "I have been waiting for this moment all day," he murmured against her lips.

"So have I," she admitted, unable to say otherwise.

Locke's kiss was raw from anticipation and filled with passionate hunger. Cornelia met his probing tongue with her own. Her tongue flicked out and slipped into his mouth to savor the taste of him.

In answer to her sweet torment, he bore her to the bed and joined her there. Cornelia was breathing hard when he left her to light the room.

Cornelia leaned up on her elbows. "What are you doing?" she asked in a heavy voice. "You aren't leaving, are you?"

"Not unless you want me to."

Inhaling to put words to her thoughts, Cornelia breathed. "Turn the lights back off and come back."

"I'll be right there. But I'm going to leave the lights on. I want to see you, so I'll know every inch of you. And I want you to know me."

The room was dimly lit when he returned to stand next to the bed. Slowly he shed his jacket, then his tie and then began to work the buttons on his shirt, all the while keeping his eyes fastened on her.

Cornelia watched their lover's ritual with unrestrained fascination at his corded torso. His tapering fingers went next to his trousers. Without hesitation, he slid them down his strong thighs. When he stood up, he sprang free, causing Cornelia's breath to catch at the size of him.

"Now it's your turn, my angel," he murmured.

He offered his hand. Cornelia put her hand in his and soon found that they had exchanged places. He was lying on the bed with his head resting on his arms, waiting for her to peel off her clothing for him as he had done for her.

She glanced over her shoulder at the light glowing softly on the nearby table. She had never done anything like this before. Linley had always been in a rush. Her gaze trailed back to Locke. The expression on his face was warm and filled with love and stilled all her doubts.

With trembling fingers, Cornelia slid the cape from her shoulders. She unhooked the back of her dress, but before she could slip out of it, Locke was standing at her side. "I'll finish it for you," he whispered against her ear as he stroked the milk white of her shoulder.

The gentle persuasion in his voice caused her to surrender the last of her inhibitions, and she burned with need as he stripped the layers from her. Unable to stand still, Cornelia swiveled to face him and ran her fingertips along his chest, reveling in the heated feel of him. She leaned into him, and her nerves sizzled as naked flesh pressed against naked flesh.

Locke gasped in a breath at the reeling sensations that claimed him. He set her on the bed and began an exploration that carried such sweet torment that he ached to unfetter his passion totally. Yet, for her sake, he held himself back.

Cornelia was astounded when his moist lips played across her breasts and settled on a nipple to suckle with such rhythm that she thought she would be driven totally wild. She ached for release as the pressure built within her loins, and she pressed herself against him.

While continuing to devour her breasts, Locke rode his hand over her flat stomach and glided it through her woman's nest to come to rest at the core of her being. Igniting fingers dipped into her, sending her writhing and rocking against his hand until she cried out in panting little breaths.

"Oh, God, Cornelia, I want you," he moaned.

"I want you, too."

Raising up, he positioned himself over her and plunged into the woman's depths of her. With precision timing, he used long, slow strokes to build the tension, withdrawing and pausing until she lifted her hips to draw his length back into her. Over and over he plunged as he watched the excitement grow on Cornelia's face and ecstasy take hold of her.

Cornelia lost control and wound her thighs around him. She dug her nails into his back as she clung to him, instinctively pounding herself against him time and time again, demanding all from him. The jarring thrusts exploded into mindless rapture so fierce that Cornelia's entire being was racked with an intense exultation.

Feeling Cornelia's climax caused Locke's body to burst forth, and he jerked, straining with the glorious surges until he was completely spent.

After he had returned to earth, he watched Cornelia slowly drift back to reality. Her face was flushed, and sweat had dampened her hair until it stuck to the sides of her head. Her lashes fluttered open around pupils heavily dilated, causing him to shift to his side and gather her into a protective embrace.

Lying within the circle of Locke's arms, Cornelia could feel the intensity of his need to hold her now just as much as the intensity he had brought to their lovemaking. A thought struck her: She had never made love with Linley as she and Locke just had; she had only done her duty. The more she considered it, the more she realized that this truly was her first love. She had just given all of herself, shared everything she had to share with the man holding her. Then a second thought hit her, and she wondered if he was experiencing any of the same feelings. She smiled to herself; the way he had made love to her, with such giving richness, she was sure he was.

She reached up and stroked his hair. The thick strands curled around her fingers, and her mind shifted to thoughts of children. If they had children together, they would be beautiful, she thought with a smile. Then her smile turned to anguish as she remembered how she and Linley had tried to conceive for four years, only to learn she was barren. Forcing herself to set any notion of precious babies aside, she finally fell into the numbing void of sleep.

For a second night, Locke remained awake for a long time. After his divorce, he had sworn never to allow his emotions to control him where another woman was concerned. He was losing sight of that oath. And if he were honest with himself, he would admit he was falling in love. The woman he held in his arms had given herself to him in a way no other ever had, and he silently vowed to protect her from any further harm, even if it meant from himself as well. With troubling thoughts, he tenderly kissed her cheek and slid from the bed. He had some serious thinking to do about Cornelia Lloyd Talbot, and he could not think clearly while holding her in his arms.

By the time Locke went downstairs and entered the dining room for breakfast, Cornelia was sitting with Carrie Simington and Lamantha. He came up short and stood watching the three women sitting with their heads together. Cornelia was animated as she spoke to Carrie Simington, and even Lamantha smiled, which gave Locke cause for concern; his sister had not been given to smiling much since she was a girl.

Fearing what the threesome might be concocting and surprised to see his sister, Locke ambled over to the table. "Mind if I join you, ladies?"

Lamantha's smile faded. Despite her love for her brother, he was still a man; she had no use for anyone of Locke's gender. "I believe you were invited," she said.

"Glad to see that you were too, Lammy," he said to his sister as he gave her a peck on the cheek and sat down.

Lamantha bristled. "I had an unexpected visit from the ladies earlier this morning and decided there would be no harm in joining them for a meal. And don't call me Lammy."

"I think the pet name is delightful," oozed Carrie, who had insisted that she meet Lamantha after hearing Cornelia talk about her. "I love animals, you know."

"Lockforde, Carrie was telling us that she actively supports the Society for the Prevention of Cruelty to Animals," Lamantha announced.

"Perhaps you might consider getting actively involved as well. I'm sure all male animals could benefit," Locke teased.

Lamantha looked down her nose at her brother, then picked up a water glass, ignoring her brother's humor at her expense.

Carrie turned a brilliant smile on Locke. "I am so glad to have met your sister and Cornelia. They have been regaling me with so many stories about you that I feel I know you personally. It always is good to feel a personal connection with the person who is going to become a part of my life, even if only temporarily." Then her attention swung back to Lamantha. "And Lamantha dear, the Society could definitely use your help if you are interested."

"You could use the practice," Locke said. "You might even find that not all male animals will try to bite your hand."

Cornelia hid a grin behind her juice at the sparring between brother and sister. Lamantha had confided in her how much she loved her brother, but how she could not tolerate men. So Cornelia understood the good-natured bickering. Carrie Simington simply seemed to ignore it. Cornelia watched Locke's easy smile as he spoke to Carrie and could not help but be reminded of his gentle, fiery touch last night.

Out of the corner of his eye, Locke noticed the flush creep up Cornelia's cheeks and wondered if she was thinking about last night as he was. She had been so innocently wild in his arms that although he tried to keep his attention focused on what Carrie Simington was saying, his mind continued to replay Cornelia's passion.

"So you agree?" Carrie probed when he failed to answer her.

"Agree?" he said absently.

"We were speaking about the climb I intend to

make up Longs Peak. May I assume that since you made no objections, you are agreeable to my terms and will accept the stipend I am offering to engage your services as a guide?"

Rudely brought back from his musings about Cornelia, Locke straightened his back. "No, you may not assume anything."

"Locke," Cornelia interceded, "Carrie is being very generous."

"Lockforde wouldn't quibble over the money," Lamantha added. "It has to do with his principles. Although at times misplaced, my brother has always held to his beliefs, you see, Carrie."

"Mr. Breckenridge . . . Locke, surely you must be aware that I will not be the first woman to make such a climb of the mountain?" Carrie protested. "Anna Dickinson was the first lady, and Miss Isabella Bird also made the climb. Both quite successfully, I might add."

"You mentioned them last night," Locke returned, feeling that he was a minority of one in his opinion.

"Then what is the problem?" she inquired.

"Yes, what is the difficulty?" Cornelia seconded.

To Locke's chagrin, his sister also had to add her voice to the chorus with, "Yes, do tell us, brother dear, what seems to be your problem?"

"I don't have a problem," Locke retorted. Hell, he now could understand how Custer must have felt at the Little Big Horn. Those women had him outnumbered and, he had to admit, outflanked. Despite it, though, Locke was not going to surrender.

"Then you will consent to serve as my guide?" Carrie asked. Her face filled with hope as she leaned forward in her seat.

Hell, he thought again, the other women were also staring at him, as were four others at nearby tables. He shot to his feet. Retreat was the only safe avenue at the moment. "No, I will not consent to be your guide."

Before Carrie Simington could mount another argument, Locke turned to Cornelia. "I believe I promised to show you the area around Leadville today. Are you ready?"

Cornelia glanced, wide-eyed, up at Locke before she looked to the other women. All faces were expectant. Locke expected her to accompany him, and she desperately longed to be with him despite his male pigheadedness. Locke's sister and Carrie Simington's expressions bespoke displeasure with Locke's refusal to serve as Carrie's guide. And Cornelia could not understand why he was refusing.

"Cornelia, are you going to spend the day with me or not?" Locke asked. He could see indecision in her eyes. From her expression, he could tell she was being pulled in two directions. Despite his annoyance, he understood that Cornelia had to try out her newfound freedom, she had to be the one to make the choice. Yet he could not help but feel a moment of triumph when she set her napkin aside and rose beside him.

His victory disintegrated into ashes when she merely smoothed out her skirt and sat down again at the table. With a mischievous grin, she looked up at him, her eyes sparkling. "Perhaps we will be able to spend the whole day together tomorrow. The ladies have invited me to attend a lecture with them."

"Well, since I know where I stand, I think it is time for me to leave you ladies before you have me scalped for refusing. I'll see you tonight at supper, Cornelia," he said and left before they could berate him further.

As he headed out toward his warehouses, Locke's uneasy feeling in the pit of stomach from the night before was turning to dread. Dark thoughts surrounded him over what could become an impasse between Cornelia and himself despite his conviction that she had to make her own choices. He had worried that Carrie Simington was trouble, and now he knew he was right. Cornelia had sided with the woman and his sister, much as he might have expected, but he had not actually expected her to remain with them. Worst of all, he wondered what kind of ideas those two would attempt to imprint in Cornelia's mind today.

Chapter Twenty-five

Cornelia felt a stab of regret as she watched Locke saunter from the restaurant. If truth were known, she would rather have spent the day with Locke, but he was being unreasonable and she had a duty to protest such treatment.

"Cornelia," Lamantha said, drawing Cornelia's attention back to the table. "It is not necessary for you to remain if you wish to go with my brother."

Cornelia was shocked to hear Lamantha suggest such a thing. And surprised that she had been so transparent. "But I thought—"

"What, my dear, that I detest all men including my brother?" The lines on the older woman's face softened. "Lockforde's behavior is senseless, but despite the fact he is a man, my brother is the exception."

"And you certainly needn't concern yourself about me," Carrie added. "Locke Breckenridge hasn't seen the last of me yet. So please, feel free to join him."

"I made the choice to remain," Cornelia protested.

"Yes, you did," Carrie observed, "but I only hope

it was for the right reasons. I am a firm believer in going after what I want, often that is the only way to get it, heaven knows. Furthermore, if you aren't interested in that gorgeous hunk of man, I might very well be. I would not let grass grow beneath my slippers if he sparked my interest, the way he seems to have yours."

Cornelia noticed that Lamantha looked horrified at Carrie's forthright statement. Cornelia opened her mouth to speak, but Carrie gestured to silence her. "Oh, now, don't try to deny it. Everyone can tell the way you two look at each other, that you communicate without words."

Cornelia did not respond. She was too busy absorbing what Carrie had said. When she came to Colorado, she had intended to return to Connecticut and win back Linley. But now going back to Linley did not hold the same urgency. In fact, she no longer thought much about returning to Linley, and she knew that Locke Breckenridge was the reason. A grin of reason-come-to-light sparkled across Cornelia's face. "I think I shall join Locke after all. But I shall return in time for the lecture late this afternoon."

She jumped to her feet and started toward the exit.

"Cornelia dear, we'll meet in the lobby," called out Carrie, who was grinning broadly. Conquest still fresh on her face, she shifted her gaze to Lamantha. She noticed that the older woman was thoughtfully staring in Cornelia's direction. "Well, my friend, what do you think of my handiwork?"

Lamantha gave a small laugh. "I think that young lady already had her mind made up before you said a word." To Carrie's crestfallen face, Lamantha added, "But I also think that if she hadn't, she would not have stood a chance up against you. I couldn't have done a better job myself."

Carrie brightened and she sat straighter. "Well, in that case, why don't you accompany me to the Society this morning, and I'll see what I can do for you? There is a man there that I think just may change your mind about all males."

"Don't count on it," Lamantha blustered.

Carrie tore a roll in half and buttered it. "Do not worry, I won't."

Carrie popped the warm crusty bread into her mouth. Behind her look of sheltered innocence, she was planning her next move.

Cornelia tried not to look as if she were rushing as she left the hotel, but she worried that she had tarried too long at the table. Out on the street, the bustling population was busy plying their trades and hurrying to their destinations. She looked up and down the teeming thoroughfare, but no one fitting Locke's description was about.

She turned to go back inside the hotel to rejoin Lamantha and Carrie but decided against it. This was her first trip to a large city as an independent woman, and she determined to browse about on her own. She went back to her room, gathered up a parasol, and returned to the street.

Strolling along Harrison, Cornelia felt a surge of pride. She had made her own decision about how to spend the day. She stood taller due to feelings of worth and stopped to gaze in shop windows.

"You lost?" a deep male voice asked. "Perhaps I can help."

A shiver of dread filled her breast. Some man was going to accost her since she was unaccompanied. She took a deep breath and swung around to face him.

It was Locke. And the infuriating man was grinning.

"What are you doing here?" she demanded, trying not to appear visibly shaken.

"I might ask you the same question since you informed me you were going to spend the day with my sister."

She raised her chin. "I changed my mind. What is your explanation?"

With flourish, Locke put a hand over his heart and hung his head. "I have none, I'm afraid. I had the entire day just to wait until tonight when we could be together again and I was merely aimlessly roaming the streets waiting."

She boxed his arm. "Don't be silly."

"Alas, the lady considers me silly," he echoed to the sky. "What am I to do but accompany her for the day and try to humbly prove my devotion."

"If you are done with the theatrics, you can give me a tour of the countryside," Cornelia said. She tried to keep the obvious pleasure out of her voice, but she knew by his grin that she had failed.

He offered his arm and directed her toward the buggy he had hired for the day. "Your carriage awaits you," he said, making a grand gesture.

Cornelia shook her head with befuddled amusement as he helped her onto the seat. "What has you so . . .?" Her voice trailed off as the most appropriate word to describe his sudden antics escaped her.

"Exuberant?" he supplied. When she nodded in agreement, he joined her and added, "Probably because I am glad you changed your mind and decided to spend the day with me after all."

"Aren't you being a little presumptuous?" she said archly.

"Not at all." He slapped the reins over the piebald's rump.

"Actually, if you must know, I did decide to spend the day with you, but you had already gone," she admitted. "If I hadn't already made that decision, I would not be sitting here with you now."

He smiled to himself. "No, of course not."

They drove through town, heading west toward Turquoise Lake. Cornelia marveled at the magnificent scenery, far-reaching pines, and darting deer. They crossed a rushing stream, and Cornelia begged to stop so that she could dip her fingers into the icy waters. She laughed freely as he stopped the buggy.

Cornelia jumped down and splashed at Locke. In defense, he caught her up in his arms. As he did, he was filled with a deep longing for her. He had never known anyone with her ability to enjoy the simple things in life.

Cornelia stopped laughing and gazed deeply into those warm brown eyes with the dancing silver flecks. He was beckoning her to kiss him, and needing no further encouragement, she tipped her head back. He held her chin tenderly and pressed a sweet kiss to her lips.

Pulling apart took great willpower on Locke's part. He would have liked nothing more than to whisk her off to the dense grove of trees nearby and make love to her. "We'd best get back into the buggy before I'm unable to continue our journey."

Cornelia did not have to ask what he meant. She had felt his arousal pressing against her belly as he kissed her. "Yes, I think we should be on our way."

Once they were resettled, they traveled along the rutted road leisurely covering the two miles to the lake.

"It's magnificent," Cornelia cried when the lake came into view.

Locke was caught up in her excitement. "The perfect spot for a picnic, don't you think?"

"A picnic?" She looked behind the seat. There sat a large wicker basket. Leaning over, she opened the lid and found a wide assortment of fruits, cheeses, breads and wine, lay side by side, along with several other dishes. She turned back to Locke, her face a mass of confusion and disappointment. "You did expect me to accompany you all along."

"Cornelia, we made plans to spend the day together before you had breakfast this morning with my sister, if you'll remember. I had the hotel staff pack it before I joined you. If you hadn't changed your mind, I was going to have to eat the entire contents by myself." Her face relaxed, prompting Locke to say, "And speaking about eating, I didn't get any breakfast, so I'm starved. Why don't we stop under that tree and enjoy the food before I'm forced to start nibbling on you."

"An interesting notion on your part," she said. "I could be tempted to explore it."

"So could I, except I'm truly starved." His stomach rumbled right on cue, which caused Cornelia to grab up a chunk of bread.

248

"Here"—she stuffed it into his mouth—"you can nibble on this until we get set up."

Locke attempted a reply, but his mouth was full and it came out garbled, which caused Cornelia to burst out in another round of laughter.

The sound of her unrestrained laughter cast the net about Locke's heart more tightly. He knew he was in danger of conceding defeat to the strong feelings he had about the lady. In an effort to fight the battle of his senses, he spread a blanket under a tree and took up a position a safe distance from Cornelia.

The remainder of the day, Locke devoted himself to Cornelia: he watched her wade in the lake; holding her hand, he walked by her side over the many trails crisscrossing the shore; he made her a bed of leaves and spread his jacket over it for her to lie upon; he studied her while she dozed; and he marveled at how easy it was to be with her.

The distant screech of a hawk soaring overhead awoke her. Her eyes flew open and she bolted upright. "Oh, dear, what time is it?"

"Not quite two," he said, looking at his fob watch.

In a rush, she began scooping up the remains of their picnic. "Please, we must hurry. I have to be back at the hotel by four-thirty. I told Lamantha and Carrie I would meet them in the lobby."

"We wouldn't want to keep Lamantha and Carrie waiting," Locke grumbled.

Cornelia ignored him. She tossed the blanket on top of the basket in the buggy and waited for Locke to help her onto the seat. He finished unhobbling the horse and came to her side. When he put his hands around her waist, she stroked the side of his cheek.

"Thank you for the marvelous day. I have not enjoyed myself so much in years," she said. Up on her tiptoes, she kissed him.

Locke was not about to settle for a simple peck although his better judgment warned him to release her and step away. But Locke was not listening to the voice that assailed him of his past pain. He was too enthralled with Cornelia. He kissed her back soundly until she pushed at his chest.

"We must be getting back." She caught sight of another couple who had come to spend the day at the lake. They were openly staring at them. "Besides, we are making a spectacle of ourselves."

"With just one kiss?" He leaned toward her with a mischievous grin on his face. "Since they seem to need something other than each other to occupy their time, why don't we give them a real spectacle? They might even learn what a real kiss is all about."

Cornelia was on the road to independence, but she was not that free from restraint. "Not from us, they won't," she said flatly.

Locke shrugged, then turned to directly face the watching couple. "I'm afraid if you are hoping to learn how to kiss, you'll have to learn from someone else. My lady just isn't cooperating. Sorry."

The couple turned away and focused their attention toward the lake.

"Locke, how could you!" Cornelia snapped, mortified by his comment.

On the way back to town, Locke was careful to keep the conversation on neutral ground. Cornelia seemed to forget about his offense quickly, which

250

pleased him no end. Margaret had often held her anger for days and made life with her miserable. The more time he spent with Cornelia, the more he realized how different the two women were, and the more he felt himself drawn to the incredible woman at his side.

After they had made arrangements to meet in the lobby at seven, he dropped her off in front of the hotel and watched her disappear inside. The day had been almost too perfect, which warned him that something was bound to occur to mar the perfection of the time they spent together. He had to figure out what so he could prepare to deal with it.

Chapter Twenty-six

Cornelia's face was flushed and she was overly animated when she met Locke in the lobby to go to supper. She was a virtual bubble of enthusiasm, babbling on about Carrie Simington and Lamantha and their ideas about life and their viewpoints about the world. He was pleasantly surprised that neither woman had seemed to try to poison Cornelia. He knew that Lamantha had no use for men, and although Carrie Simington had not said anything concerning her feelings, she was single and hardly intent on changing her status.

"You haven't told me what the lecture was about," he said.

"Animals. Carrie is trying to get people involved in more humane treatment of animals."

"Were there many people there?"

Cornelia's face dropped. "No, but some good did come out of it. The ones who were there gained a new awareness, and Carrie introduced Lamantha to one of the male workers."

"I wouldn't count on anything coming out of that."

A conspiratorial grin captured her lips. "I won't."

"Good," he said. "You know how Lamantha feels about anyone male." But he did not miss that look. Thank goodness they would be leaving Leadville soon, or Cornelia would undoubtedly try to play matchmaker. Knowing Lamantha, Locke was sure it would be disastrous.

"Ready to go?"

"Yes, I'm famished."

He took Cornelia to an intimate, little out-of-the-way restaurant where they were met by the whiskered owner and ushered to a corner table adorned with candles and hovered over by a tailed violinist.

"I'm glad you enjoyed your day," he said, reaching across the table to run his finger along the edge of her gloved hand. The feel of the soft velvet conjured up the texture of her velvety skin, which he longed to savor later. The reflection of the candlelight flickered in her eyes, reminding him how she had burned for him last night. He had to beat down the urge to whisk her back to the hotel.

"It was perfect," she said.

He poured Cornelia a glass of champagne, filled his glass, and offered a toast. "To continued perfection."

A surge of warmth lit the inner recesses of Cornelia's body as she joined Locke in the toast. She took a big gulp and then made a toast of her own. "May the rest of the trip be perfect as well."

Locke watched her over the rim of his glass—the flutter of her lashes against rosy cheeks, the innocent enthusiasm that animated her face and made her eyes light up. He watched her remove her gloves. If she only knew what a sensuous thing it was to see her push each glove down her arm, then pull one velvet finger at a time. He wondered if she knew how desirable she was.

She sipped more of the effervescent liquid, the bubbles tickling her nose. All through a meal of sumptuous seafood, Cornelia could not get her mind off the incredible time she was having in Leadville. She had proved she could stand on her own two feet; she had discovered that she was not a pariah since she had made friends who knew about the divorce; and she had found love.

The notion of what love could really be like made Cornelia anxious to return to the hotel and be held in Locke's arms. With that in mind, she quit dawdling over her meal and gulped down the rest of the champagne Locke had poured.

The violinist played one last hauntingly beautiful piece before Locke tipped the man and helped Cornelia on with her coat. Out in the evening air, Cornelia wrapped her coat closer around her neck as the evening had turned chilly. Locke took her hand and held it securely in his as they strolled back to the hotel in companionable silence.

Back at the hotel, Locke secured both keys from the desk while Cornelia waited by a potted plant. Her head was buzzing, and she knew she had drunk too much champagne. It was also a heady feeling.

Locke held out Cornelia's key. "Your key, ma'am. Or would you like me to open the door for you?" he asked.

Feeling emboldened by the champagne, a coy grin came to her lips. "Perhaps I should take your key and open your door for you," she offered.

"A lady opening a gentleman's door for him. That would be novel." Novel, he thought, but her response when she learned where his door was would not be novel. Inside, that earlier feeling of foreboding gripped him.

"Women are not helpless creatures. We are quite capable."

"I've never doubted it," he said. He could see his sister's hand behind Cornelia's stand. "But I prefer to play the gentleman."

To Locke's chagrin, Cornelia stood her ground. "Play? I do not want to play, sir. I want show you how capable I am."

"Fine. Then tomorrow you may drive the team."

"Fine," she said in triumph, but she was not sure whether she had actually won anything or not. To be certain, she asked, "I have risen victorious, haven't I?"

Locke rolled his eyes. He wasn't sure exactly what she was talking about. One thing he did know—he could have wrung Lamantha's neck at that moment. Why the hell did Cornelia have to go and pick this particular moment to exert her independence. "Yes, you have risen victorious." He offered his arm. When she stood as still as a tree on a windless afternoon, he urged, "Now, give me your arm, so I can escort you to your room."

He had not thought she had drunk too much champagne, but as they ascended the stairs, it became painfully visible that her condition was rapidly deteriorating. She swayed against him and giggled at the slightest thing.

Once they reached her room, he turned the key in the lock and shoved open the door. Cornelia just stood there like that same infernal tree, smiling.

"Aren't you going to come in and make love to me?" she asked.

If there had been the slightest breeze in the hallway at that moment, Locke would have been blown over. Then he realized it was the alcohol talking. "No, I think you need to sleep it off."

"But I don't feel like sleeping," she protested and began to fiddle with the buttons on his shirt.

Locke stepped back. "Cornelia, you don't know what you're doing."

"Are you so sure?"

"Lady, if I wasn't, let me assure you, you may very well have found yourself on your back by now," he grated out. He could not deny she had aroused him. But hell, for some damned reason, he could not take advantage of the situation.

Cornelia tried to focus on what he was saying, but her head was beginning to pound. She put her hand to her temple as the door began to tilt.

Locke caught her just as she was about to collapse into a heap. Carrying her to the bed, he threw back the covers and set her down carefully. Once he had lit the light, he went to the bathroom door. It was locked. He had to smile to himself. She was conscious of her personal safety. Unlocking the door, he moistened a cloth for her head.

She mumbled something unintelligible when he put the cloth on her forehead. He pulled up the spread, but she was wearing such a beautiful gown, he decided to remove it.

Once he had her tucked in nicely, he crept from the room and returned to his own room. For the third night, he could not sleep. Each and every side of Cornelia Lloyd Talbot, Locke discovered, was more tantalizing and fascinating. Finally he punched the pillow, turned over and willed his mind to wipe her from his consciousness.

Cornelia awoke with a head that felt like the size and shape of the Rocky Mountains. Her mouth was dry and felt as though it was coated with sand. She sat up and then realized she was only wearing her chemise. Her gown was neatly laid over the chair next to the bureau.

Wanting a drink of water, she got up, rubbing her eyes, and went to the bathroom door. The knob turned. Confused because she thought she had locked it, she slowly opened the door. Suddenly her head snapped up.

Locke was standing there in front of the mirror shaving, and he was naked down to the waist.

He ceased his efforts and smiled at her. "Good morning. Sleep well?"

"Yes, but I didn't realize you would still be here," she said, trying to clear her head.

At that, his earlier sense of foreboding grabbed him. He had forgotten to lock the door leading into her room. Swallowing hard, he thought fast. "Just thought I'd shave before leaving."

She smiled weakly. "All right."

She turned to leave him to his morning ritual, then she saw the open door to the next room. At first she paid no attention to the clothes folded neatly on the chair and shifted her attention back to Locke.

He was shaving.

She tilted her head in bemusement. Shaving? Razor? Shaving mug and soap? Clothes folded on the chair?

Cornelia walked to the doorway and peered into the room next to hers. A familiar jacket on the chair and boots on the floor next to it caught her eye. She pivoted around to stare at Locke. Suspicion was beginning to overtake her, and her mind became all too clear.

"You never did tell me what floor your room is on," she said.

Damn, he had forgotten to close the door. "No, I didn't." He held his face straight, but he could see the emotions crossing Cornelia's face.

She crossed her arms over her chest. "Well?"

He reached out his hand in an effort to escort her back into her room. "Why don't we go sit down?"

Cornelia flung her arm back. "I don't want to sit down. I want you to explain that!" She pointed a finger toward the adjoining room.

"There is nothing to explain," he said. Seeing the building stormcloud by the way she stood before him and in the rising pitch of her voice, Locke wiped the remaining shaving soap from his chin in preparation for the coming battle.

"Nothing to explain?" She swept her hands out and raised her eyes to the ceiling before she pinned him with a stare of furious disbelief.

"Cornelia, you are getting upset over nothing."

"Nothing? Nothing! You are trying to tell me that connecting rooms are nothing?"

"The desk clerk misunderstood, is all."

With a snort, she said, "If it was a simple mistake, why didn't you tell me? Or was it because you planned to seduce me all along?"

258

"I did not plan anything. What happened between us had nothing to do with which hotel rooms we're staying in."

Cornelia desperately wanted to believe him. But he had to have known they had adjoining rooms and had not bothered to bring it to her attention even after she had mentioned the problems she was having with the person next door and had insisted that they have rooms on separate floors so people would not get the wrong impression.

She had been standing there glaring at him; he reached for her. She stepped back, shaking her head. "Cornelia—"

Cornelia took a deep breath but tears began to well in her eyes. "No, don't. Don't touch me. I don't believe you." Visions of the men who had tried to seduce her, thinking she was an easy mark, materialized in a taunting parade before her eyes. "Just because I was accused of adultery, you thought you could take advantage of me, didn't you?"

All he could say was "No."

"I wish I could believe you."

"Cornelia, I admit I should have told you about the rooms when I discovered what had happened. But I did not plan anything. And there has been no harm done."

"No harm done? You lied to me," she cried.

"I did not lie."

"Oh, no, only the simple sin of omission."

Locke attempted to calm her down, but she was no longer listening to him; all she could think was how utterly naïve she had been to believe that anyone could care for a divorced woman such as her-

259

self. Unable to stand there and let him see her break down in front of him, Cornelia turned, threw on a dress, and fled from her hotel room.

"Cornelia!" Locke called out, chasing after her down the hallway. He ran to the top of the stairs, but she was rapidly disappearing down the staircase. "Cornelia, wait!"

That same nosy couple who had stared after them two nights ago was ascending the stairs. Locke groaned. That couple would undoubtedly compound his problem since they had seen her fly past them.

In a huff of shock, the woman spat out, "I knew there was something strange about that young couple, Abraham. Didn't I tell you?"

"Yes, dear," the man said mechanically. Behind the woman's back, he shot Locke a sympathetic look.

Locke slung the towel back over his shoulder and cocked his brow. "What's the matter, lady? Haven't you ever seen a half-naked man before?"

"Well, I never!" She hooked her arm with her husband's. "Come along, Abraham. We do not have to be subjected to such people!"

Locke stood and watched the woman drag the man down the hallway. Then he returned to his room and plopped down on the bed. He punched the mattress. "Damn it!"

He went to the connecting door and swung it open wide. Cornelia was bound to return soon. She had nowhere else to go. Once she cooled off and stopped to think rationally, she had to realize that it was nothing more than a simple mistake.

He got up and paced the room, chiding himself

for not stopping her. He went to the window, pulled back the curtain, and looked out on the street below, abustle with humanity. Somewhere out there, in a frenzied state, Cornelia was down there among them.

When Cornelia had not returned hours later, Locke began to worry. Throwing on a rawhide jacket, he hurried from his room to look for her.

Chapter Twenty-seven

Nearly blinded by tears of shame and self-recrimination, Cornelia ran from the hotel. Out on the boardwalk, she stopped. She had no idea where to go. Two men jostled her as they shouldered their way among the crowd. They stopped, offered their apologies, and asked if she required assistance.

Cornelia looked at their expectant faces. "No, no, I'm fine," she cried. "Just fine."

Despite looks of disbelief, the men tipped their hats and hurried on their way. Cornelia watched them. She was not going to lean on others. Moving along with the crowd, Cornelia walked aimlessly.

Her mind was racing with how she had been totally foolish to believe that Locke Breckenridge was different. He was unabashedly like all the others, only smoother in his approach.

She wandered about all day, and the sun was sinking low in the sky when she stopped and became aware of her surroundings. At first glance nothing looked familiar.

It would be dark shortly, and she was lost.

Feeling frantic, she looked around for a familiar landmark until her vision settled upon a small, neat house that was all too familiar.

Cornelia swung around. The last thing she wanted was to seek help from Lamantha Breckenridge. With quickened steps, she hurried away from the white picket fence.

Lamantha walked out onto her porch, a watering can in her hand. As she bent over to talk to her precious plants, she caught sight of a familiar figure. "Cornelia? Cornelia Talbot," Lamantha called out.

Cornelia stopped. Despite her inclination to keep going, she could not be rude to the woman. Looking a little sheepish, Cornelia pivoted around and walked back to the older woman standing with her hands on her hips.

"Well? What are you doing out this way all alone, without hat or gloves? You look as lost as a mangy pup."

Cornelia did not want to involve Lamantha since she certainly could not tell her the truth. "I'm afraid that I was in such a hurry to take a stroll before the sun went down that I didn't bother with the usual accessories." She inched away. "I should be getting back to the hotel before it gets dark."

"You'll do no such thing, young woman. You just come on in this house."

"But—"

"No buts. I won't take no for an answer." Lamantha held the door open. "Now come on in before you let all the heat out. I can't afford to heat the outside, you know."

Dutifully, Cornelia complied. She was caught and had no choice. As soon as she could, she would make a graceful exit.

Seated in Lamantha's tidy parlor, Cornelia waited for Lamantha to descend on her with a thousand questions. Lamantha Breckenridge was an astute observer and skilled at ferreting out the truth despite all efforts to hide it.

Lamantha waited for the girl to tell her how she had managed to be standing in front of her home. She didn't believe for a moment Cornelia's story about a stroll. By the look on her face, Lamantha was sure there was a problem between the girl and Lockforde. Although Lamantha did not believe in interfering in her brother's life, God knew she should have said something when he brought home that floozie Margaret. This girl, Lamantha liked.

"Are we going to sit here stiffly waiting for the other to speak, or are you going to tell me what's going on?"

Cornelia tried to look relaxed, but every nerve in her body tensed. "I don't know what you mean."

"Yes, you do," Lamantha countered. "I may be getting older, and my eyesight may not be what it used to be, but I am not totally blind or senile. You look troubled." She moved to the edge of her chair. "It's Lockforde, isn't it?"

Cornelia had tried to keep her gaze straight. At the mention of Locke's name, her gaze faltered.

Lamantha straightened. "I thought so. What has the boy done?"

"Nothing, really," Cornelia lied.

"Your being in front of my house and the expression on your face is not *nothing*. Furthermore, it isn't going to solve anything if you keep whatever's bothering you inside. Eats at one's insides." Lamantha placed a comforting hand on Cornelia's arm. "I'm not going to judge you, girl."

Cornelia's heart pounded, and before she could

stop her tongue, she blurted, "He is just like all other men."

"He?"

"Locke."

Lamantha patted Cornelia's hand. "If that brother of mine hurt you, he's going to have to deal with me."

Cornelia shook her head. "He didn't hurt me. It's just that . . . that . . ."

"Say no more. I think I understand."

"I'm not a loose woman the way they think back home," Cornelia cried. "I'm not. I was a good wife, but no one would believe me." Lamantha's abrupt kindness caused a floodgate to open, and Cornelia's entire story poured out.

"Well, I'll be. Those folks back in Connecticut ought to be downright ashamed of themselves."

An urgent pounding at the door interrupted them.

Lamantha rose and offered Cornelia a hankie. "Don't you go worrying. I'll get rid of whoever's at the door, then we'll have a nice, soothing cup of tea."

Lamantha closed the sliding double doors behind her and went to the door. She pushed back the lace curtains and peered out. Locke was standing on the porch rubbing his neck. The boy looked worried as he paced back and forth. Lamantha smoothed the bow at her neck and opened the door.

"Why, Lockforde, what brings you to my door?" she asked, leaning her hand across the entry.

To Lamantha's utter surprise, Locke did not stand on convention. He gave her a peck on the cheek and pushed past her.

"Lockforde!" she bellowed.

265

Locke stopped and pivoted around. Lamantha was standing like a sentry, ready to defend her territory.

"From the way you are standing, I think you know why I am here, Sister dear. Where is she?"

"She?"

"Don't try to pretend that you don't know who she is. It is not·your style, Lamantha."

Lamantha's lips tightened, and she lifted her chin. "*She* is in the parlor." Locke advanced, but Lamantha grabbed his arm. "Wait, Lockforde. Cornelia is pretty upset. Perhaps it would be best if you give her some time. Now, why don't you come to the kitchen with me, have some refreshment, then go back to the hotel."

Locke peeled her fingers from his arm and dropped his fists on his hips. "I am not going anywhere until I talk to Cornelia."

"Need I remind you that this is my house?"

"And need I remind you how you came by it?"

She stiffened.

They had never spoken of Locke's generosity because Locke knew his sister needed to be independent. He had simply instructed his banker to see that Lamantha's account never dipped below a set level. And he had employed her to run his business, knowing it would give her a sense of pride. Now he wanted to bite his tongue at the injured expression on her face.

He reached out and touched her sleeve. There was a moment of unspoken bond between brother and sister, a moment when understanding reached between them despite the words they had exchanged. "Lamantha, I must speak with Cornelia," he said softly.

She waved off his hand. "Oh, all right. I'll wait in the kitchen. But if you upset her further, you'll answer to me, you understand?" she said gruffly.

"Completely." She turned from him and swished off toward the kitchen. "Lamantha?"

Her hands clasped in front of her, she looked back. "Yes?"

"Thank you."

"Humph." She shook her finger at him. "You just mind my words."

Locke waited until she had disappeared and then went to the parlor doors. He slowly opened them and stepped inside the room. Cornelia was standing at the side window, staring out.

"Cornelia?"

Cornelia swung around. Her face was bathed in pain. "You! What are you doing here?"

Locke wanted to go to her but remained where he stood. "I was worried when you didn't return to the hotel, so I came looking for you."

"Oh?" she said skeptically.

"You weren't with Carrie Simington, and I looked in all the store windows. I figured that —"

"I didn't have anywhere else to go?"

"No. I figured that since you were a level-headed woman you would know where to go." He took a step toward her, but she stepped back. "You needn't worry, I am not going to try to grab you."

Her heart was drumming, but she deigned to stand her ground. "I am not worried."

She took up a position in a lone chair, and Locke sat down on the settee across from her and he leaned forward. "I did not mean to hurt you or deceive you, Cornelia."

"No? What did you mean to do? Use me?"

267

"No! For your information, you are not the only one who has been hurt. Lots of people have suffered."

"Including you, I presume."

"Yes, including me. My ex-wife only wanted what I could give her." He told her all about Margaret, leaving nothing out, and Cornelia listened attentively. Her hurt and anger began to fade.

"Just because you have also felt used, it doesn't give you the right to go around using others, does it?"

He stared directly into her eyes. "Is that what you think I was doing when we made love . . . using you?"

She gazed back into those warm brown eyes. Only sincerity shone in the depths. She dropped her eyes for a moment, studying her hands in her lap, then returned his gaze. "No, I suppose not."

Lamantha had been listening at the crack between the double doors. She had had a sneaking hunch that that was the problem between the pair. A smile hovered about her lips; she was glad they were resolving their differences. Locke rose and perched on the arm of Cornelia's chair and took her hand. He looked as if he was going to kiss her, and Lamantha could not have that in her parlor.

"Well, it looks as though everything is settled," she said, barging into the parlor.

Locke and Cornelia immediately broke apart. Locke lurched to his feet and Cornelia fussed with her skirt.

"Yes, I suppose so," Cornelia admitted with a sheepish grin.

"Well, good. I did not want to have to put you up for the night," Lamantha barked out in her usual abrupt manner. "You know how I feel about having company."

"Yes, we know, Sister dear."

"Well, then you also know that I rarely send folks away without first having some of my fresh-baked cookies."

The woman had not offered Cornelia cookies the last time she was here, but she sagely kept her silence. She had come to like the gruff woman whom she now knew had a hard exterior but a heart as soft as satin.

Cornelia jumped to her feet. "Let me help you."

"That's what I had in mind. I don't know if I can trust my brother alone with you in my parlor. Come along. You can carry the tray."

"Why don't we enjoy them in the kitchen? It's more homey that way," Locke suggested.

"Who said anything about homey?" asked Lamantha, who had already started toward the kitchen. "I always entertain guests in the parlor."

"I'm not exactly a guest. And, unless I'm wrong Cornelia has become almost like family."

Lamantha did not miss his observation but decided against commenting on it. "No, you're not a guest, and you aren't wrong about Cornelia either. But that doesn't change my mind. So sit back down and stay there until we return," she instructed.

Locke saluted. "Yes, ma'am."

"It's about time you showed a little respect," she huffed. "Come along, Cornelia."

In the kitchen, Cornelia helped put the cups and saucers on a tray and watched while Lamantha took oatmeal cookies out of a jar and arranged them on a gold-ringed plate.

"I'm glad you two made up," Lamantha said, looking up.

Cornelia looked directly into the woman's lined face. Realizing how much Lamantha thought of her after her remark about family, Cornelia relaxed. She was glad to have someone to talk to. "You know, don't you?"

"Know?"

"What the problem was."

"My girl, I am not an ostrich with my head buried in the sand. I know the feelings between a man and woman can sometimes be stronger than what polite society demands. Now, don't go hiding your face. I may be an old maid, but I am not oblivious to love."

At the word "love" Cornelia swallowed hard. She had not thought that it was so apparent to anyone else. "Don't you think that is a rather strong word?"

"Not at all." She looked at Cornelia out of the corner of her eyes. "Not if that is the emotion we're talking about. It is, isn't it?"

"Please don't say anything to Locke," Cornelia pleaded. She was beside herself with worry that the woman would up and ask Locke to declare himself when he probably did not feel as strongly about her as she did about him.

"I don't have to say anything to my brother. He is as smitten by you as you are by him. All you two need to do is admit it openly to each other. I would think that both of you should be able to." She raised her brows. "If not, I might just have a few suggestions."

A hesitant smile captured Cornelia's lips. Lamantha Breckenridge was the last person that Cornelia would have thought would ever be interested in getting her brother to admit to such feelings.

"I think that if Locke is truly interested in me he will announce his intentions when he's ready," Cornelia said. Yet beneath her expression of self-assurance, she felt like a young girl experiencing the flutter of first love. Excitement filled her with a strange twinge of anticipation as she took the tray and followed Lamantha Breckenridge back into the parlor.

She was so close to finding love that she felt like skipping. Then the realization hit her. She truly knew nothing of the courting ritual that led a man to declare his feelings. Linley had been picked out for her, and there never had been real love between them.

Cornelia took a seat a respectable distance from Locke and watched as Lamantha served, but her attention was on Locke and whether he was going to tell her that he loved her or not.

Chapter Twenty-eight

Cornelia sat next to Locke as he directed the wagon toward the hotel. The twilight surrounded Locke with an iridescent glow, filling his profile with shadowy peaks and valleys and giving him a dark, questioning appearance. He was not an easy man to read, Cornelia thought. He had carefully skirted Lamantha's leading questions and left the old dear shaking her head.

Unable to stand the silence and wondering if he had any intentions of declaring himself, Cornelia asked. "What are you thinking?"

Surprised by her question, Locke turned to look at her. *What am I thinking? I am thinking how much I love you.* "Nothing, really," he said. "Why do you ask?"

Cornelia smiled despite her disappointment. "No reason. When will we be returning to Estes Park?"

"Aren't you enjoying your stay in Leadville?"

"Oh, yes. But I've been wondering how Paxton is getting along. I am concerned about him."

"How about tomorrow morning, then? Think you can be ready?"

"Of course." She hesitated a moment, then added, "I told Carrie Simington that she could ride

272

along with us when we return. You know that she is interested in climbing Longs Peak."

He rolled his eyes. "How could I not help but know. That is all the woman talks about." Doubt came over Locke's features. "She hardly looks strong enough to make such a climb."

"Why? Because she is a woman? You don't think a woman is capable of such an undertaking?"

"I did not say that," he grumbled, wishing that the subject of Carrie Simington had not come up.

"But you don't think she should accompany us either, do you?" she pushed.

"She probably doesn't even get out of bed until after noon, and we'll be pulling out at dawn."

"If that is your main concern, I guarantee that she'll be ready."

Locke rolled his eyes again. He did not want to get into another argument with Cornelia tonight. Not after they had just made up. "If it will make you happy, Carrie Simington can ride with us back to Estes Park," he said.

"Good. I already told her you didn't mind."

Locke shook his head. He should have known. Although he did not relish having the eccentric woman along, Locke secretly admitted that he was happy with the change in Cornelia. She was no longer a scrawny woman unsure of herself. Colorado had transformed her. "But if she isn't ready to pull out at dawn, we're going to leave without her."

"You needn't worry. I'll even stay with Carrie tonight." She noted Locke's lips tighten. "Just to make sure that we're both ready and waiting outside the hotel for you in the morning."

"Yeah, sure. Just to make sure that you're both ready," he echoed in a grumbling voice. Cornelia's staying with Carrie Simington was not what Locke had had in mind for their last evening in Leadville.

"What other reason would I have?" she asked in an innocent voice.

"I can't imagine," he muttered.

Cornelia smiled inside. His negative reaction gave her great satisfaction. It was a good sign . . . a good sign indeed.

"You had something else in mind?" she said before she could stop herself.

Locke's face brightened considerably. Without hesitation, he pulled the wagon over to the edge of the road. After tying off the reins, he reached out and curled his hand around hers. Drawing her hand to his lips, he said in a husky whisper, "I'd like to wake up with you beside me." He kissed her knuckles. "Have you wake up with me beside you."

Cornelia was sorely tempted to let Carrie make it to the outside of the hotel by her own devices. Locke's ministrations were mind numbing, chipping away at her strong sense of duty. Reluctantly, she pulled her hand back.

"Just a thought, is all," he said, accepting defeat gracefully.

Cornelia gave him a warm smile, trying not to show that in another second her resolve would have crumbled. "A very nice thought though. A tempting one."

She had again caught his undivided attention. A hopeful expression lit his face in the slight glow of twilight. "You mean I gave up too easily?"

"No. I mean that you know how to make me feel . . ." the words trailed off. She had almost admitted that he made her feel wanted and desired as Linley never had. To add to Locke's esteem in her eyes, he did not push her. Smiling inside, Cornelia switched her attention to the scenery ahead as he spurred the horses back into action; she did not see a thing.

They had not traveled far when he pulled up on the reins and abruptly maneuvered the wagon around.

Cornelia grabbed the edge of her seat at the sudden jarring. "What are you doing?"

"Since we will be leaving tomorrow morning, we should go back and say good-bye to my sister. If we don't, there will be hell to pay when we do see her again."

"Oh," she said. But inside his comment about "we" seeing Lamantha again meant only one thing to her: Locke's future plans also included her. Cornelia's heart began to race so fast that she was sure it would reach Lamantha's house long before the wagon did. Sitting up straighter and prouder, Cornelia wondered what Linley would think if he could see how much she had changed.

Linley sat in his lawyer's spacious wood-paneled office, wondering what his little perfect wife would think if she could see how much his life had been transformed since he had unloaded the little paragon of virtue. Life had been one big round of parties with Margo. They stayed out late, made love with a passion he had never known, and slept past noon each day, lounging the day away until the next party.

The lawyer cleared his throat, which brought Linley back from his daydreams. Linley's attention snapped up. Wilbur Morrison was thumbing through a jumble of papers.

Linley tried to remain calm although after he'd received that message from the lawyer, he had been

275

hopping mad. He crossed and uncrossed his ankles as he waited for Morrison to finish shuffling through the enormous stack of papers cluttering his desk.

"Ah, here it is." The emaciated lawyer picked out the folder he had been looking for and opened it. "Seems that Cornelia neglected to sign the final divorce papers before she left town, Linley," he said without expression.

"I know that!" Linley snapped. "If you will recall, I was the one who informed you of that little detail, which, incidentally, you neglected."

"Yes, well . . ."

"Why haven't you gotten her signature on the papers yet, Morrison?" Linley demanded.

"I have been waiting for you to let me know where Cornelia went. It is merely a formality"—he pulled a sheet out of the folder and thrust it toward Linley—"once you get her signature on the document."

Linley took in a breath, then threw up his hands. "Merely a formality the man says." Linley came out of his chair and slammed his hand down on Morrison's desk. "How can it be a mere formality when the little mouse isn't available?"

Morrison bristled back. "I told you weeks ago to get the information I needed to complete the divorce," the lawyer said in his own defense.

Linley calmed down. "I stopped by her folks' place to find out where she had gone, and the old woman was as sweet as chocolate candy to me. Invited me in and fawned all over me. Guess that old crow thought I might be having a change of mind."

"And I suppose you did nothing to dispel her misconceptions, did you?"

Linley smiled at that. "Didn't want to ruin her day."

"Of course not. Did you perchance find out where your wife—"

"Ex-wife, Morrison," Linley intruded. "Ex-wife."

"Need I remind you again that until you have succeeded in getting Cornelia's signature, she is still legally your wife?"

"No, dammit!"

"Well? Did you find out where she went?"

Smoothing the side of his hair back, Linley picked up a paperweight from the desk and studied his reflection. "With my charm you have doubts?"

Morrison got up and went to the map on the wall. His fingers roved over the chart of the United States. "Well then, where do I send the papers?"

Linley joined Morrison at the map. His stubby fingers pinpointed an area in northern Colorado. "There, outside of Denver. A place called Estes Park."

While Morrison continued to drone on about all the details and legalities involved with sending the documents to Cornelia and procuring her signature, Linley sauntered over to the window and looked down toward the street.

Margo was pacing back and forth next to the carriage. She was a fine specimen of womanhood, he thought as he surveyed her buxom figure. She had curves a man could lose himself in. Then he noticed the pout on her full lips and her gloved fingers drumming on her forearms in an impatient rhythm as her heels beat against the wooden boards of the sidewalk in an angry rhythm. Patience was not one of her virtues. Linley laughed to himself. Margo did not possess many virtues; she was much more inclined toward debauchery—one of the things he liked about the woman.

"Linley, even after you have divorced Cornelia, you know that you are not eligible to inherit your father's estate until you have produced an heir," Morrison said, interrupting Linley's thoughts.

Linley turned away from the window and resettled himself in the lawyer's leather chair. He tented his fingers as he watched the greedy little attorney return to his desk. "You needn't concern yourself about my producing an heir. I already have that neatly planned out."

Morrison looked doubtful. "With the lady you have been squiring about these last weeks?"

"The very same."

"You will forgive me, Linley, but she hardly appears to be the motherly type."

"Thank God, no, Margo isn't. I already was saddled with one of those."

"Then how do you propose to produce an heir? I can't quite imagine Margo having any interest in having a child."

"Money is a great convincer."

"But doesn't she have her own income?"

"She got a nice settlement from her ex-husband. But with her expensive tastes, she has already gone through a healthy portion of it. I have my doubts that the fool she was married to is going to continue to be quite so generous to any further demands for more money. And we know how expensive her tastes are."

"So?"

"So the lure of the size of my inheritance will insure her cooperation. Besides"—Linley grinned with self-satisfaction—"I'm sure it won't be long before we have a little announcement to make. You see, we have been putting special effort in that department every night, if you know what I mean."

The lawyer ignored Linley's bragging about his male prowess. Most folks already knew of the arrogant man's lusty forays in the bedroom with Margo. "But even after you have the child and your inheritance, won't the child change the way of life you two have grown so accustomed to?"

"Once I have met my fool of a father's demands for an heir, my mother can raise the brat for all I care."

"Yes, well, just make sure you have met all the conditions in the will before you dump the child."

"You needn't concern yourself, you'll get your share."

Morrison grinned. "I am glad we understand one another. Now, there is the little matter of the debts you have been accruing with Margo in your pursuit of, shall we say, pleasure?"

"You can say anything you want."

"Zenas Joshaby stopped by to see me the other day. He is getting impatient. Perhaps you should pay him a call and reassure him."

Linley's face darkened at the mention of Joshaby. "All my debts will be paid as soon as I inherit."

"Cornelia did not want the divorce. What if she refuses to sign the papers?"

"She won't," he said with conviction. Linley had not given that a second thought. Suddenly, he was not so sure. He remembered how stubborn Cornelia could be and how much she had wanted to keep their marriage together. Cornelia could ruin everything for him.

"You don't look convinced. Perhaps you should consider getting her signature in person. She might be less inclined to refuse."

Linley's thoughtful expression faded and was replaced with an evil gleam, that took even the lawyer's larcenous heart aback. "You know, Morrison, it just might be amusing for Margo and me to make a trip to Colorado. I'm sure Margo would find such a trip rather entertaining."

"No doubt she would," concurred Morrison. He could almost count the money he was going to collect for legal fees.

Linley rose. "I'll talk to Margo and let you know."

"Very well. I'll have the papers readied."

Linley left the lawyer's office feeling much better than he had when he entered. He was even smiling when he joined Margo.

"Well, did you straighten everything out?" she whined in that little girl voice she used to get her own way.

"Almost," he said, helping her into the carriage.

She smothered his face with kisses. "Then can we have some fun now?"

He ran his fingers over the generous swell of her breasts, then leaned forward to instruct the driver, "Take us to the Stag and Hound, driver."

"But the party isn't supposed to start until after nine tonight," she protested. "Why are we going out there now?"

"Business."

She turned from him and folded her arms over her chest. She detested having to wait while he saw to such dreary matters as dumping that prude of a wife and then dealing with that lowlife of a man who owned the Stag and Hound. She wanted to have fun.

The carriage rumbled out of town into the countryside toward New Haven while the occupants of the carriage remained silent. Linley did not notice the lush summer grasses and the trees plump with leaves. He was busy planning.

Margo also ignored the landscape. She was too busy planning a little revenge on Linley for forcing her to accompany him on one of his boring little business ventures. Perhaps she'd tease him tonight with a particularly seductive pose, let him start panting after her, and then plead a vicious headache. She liked the power she had over him with her body.

Pity that ex-husband of hers never succumbed to her attempts to use her charms to manipulate him. He was more of a man than Linley by far. But Linley and she were two of a kind. They both used others and each other to get what they wanted. Once Linley received his inheritance, they would make a good match, Margo was sure of it.

The carriage pulled up in front of an old converted barn. It was quite unimposing from the outside, situated as it was out in an old pasture. Once inside, all misconceptions about the remodeled structure fell away, and Margo stood in awe of the utter opulence despite the fact that she had been there many times with Linley for an evening of gaming and forbidden pleasures.

Directing her attention back to the task at hand, Margo noticed Zenas Joshaby strut into the room, followed by his usual entourage of huge bodyguards. He gave her a lewd nod, then focused his attention on Linley. "Ah, Talbot, to what do I owe the pleasure of your visit so early in the day? Come to pay me what you owe me?"

Linley kept the glare from his face as he watched the barrel of a man's stomach shake when he laughed with amusement at his own joke. Linley was not amused, but he carefully pretended to go along with the joke. "If I did, Zenas, you'd be able to retire. And that wouldn't be nearly as much fun as you're having now."

Linley's laugh died in his throat when he noticed that Joshaby's expression was filled with contempt and displeasure. Linley sent Margo to the bar so she would not witness him having to kowtow to the fat pig. Linley hated having to bow down to such trash.

Once the men stood alone in the entryway, Linley said, "You know that as soon as I receive my inheritance, you'll get your money."

Zenas rested his meaty hands on his belly. "While I have been a patient man, I am not that patient. What about that wife of yours? You told me she had a little money of her own. Get the cash from her."

Linley was starting to sweat. He had heard stories that men who did not pay their debts to Joshaby ended up with shattered extremities and worse. "I divorced Cornelia. You know that."

"Heard that the divorce wasn't final yet. The law says that a husband's debts are his wife's."

"But she has left the state," Linley blurted out. He started to feel desperation closing in on him.

"You could send her a letter telling her you might consider a reconciliation if she helped you out. You said she fought against the divorce, didn't you?"

"What if she ignores the letter?"

"The sum you owe me is large enough to follow her for it. Unless, of course, our luscious Margo has that kind of money."

The words "our luscious Margo" conjured up sordid pictures of Zenas's after-hours entertainments. The man had been getting bolder with his suggestions, and now Linley feared that he would not be able to turn him down much longer if he did not come up with the money. Worst of all, Linley feared that once Joshaby introduced Margo to the wild sexual forays he had in mind, Linley might lose her before he managed to produce an heir with her help.

"I'll get your money," Linley sniveled, "even if I have to travel to Colorado and personally collect it from Cornelia myself."

The merest smile left Zenas's puffy face. "You're not thinking about trying to run out on your debts now, are you, Talbot?"

"You know me better than that," Linley said.

"I do know you pretty well, don't I? And since I know that the only way you are going to be able to pay me in the near future is to collect from your soon-to-be ex-wife, I think that you should go and personally collect from her."

The relief that had come over Linley's face at the man's suggestion quickly dissolved when Zenas added, "And just to make sure that you don't go getting the urge to remain in Colorado after you have collected from the little woman, I am going to send along a couple of my boys to keep you company."

Linley's gaze shifted to the gorilla-sized men smiling at him as they cracked their knuckles. Damn Cornelia for putting him in such a situation! As he finished his business with Joshaby, he kept thinking that Cornelia would pay for what she'd done to him.

All the way back into town, Linley mulled over his conversation with Zenas Joshaby and what he now knew he had to do. He glanced over at Margo. She was still pouting over being dragged from the Stag and Hound before she was ready to leave. He would enjoy wringing the money out of Cornelia, so traveling to Colorado would no doubt prove to be a most interesting as well as profitable trip. Now all he had to do was to convince Margo that making the trip with him would be as amusing for her.

Chapter Twenty-nine

Ladened with an armful of flowers, Paxton paced back and forth outside Annie's cabin. For over two weeks, she had refused to see or speak to him after he had not stepped forward and offered marriage as she had expected. Now he was getting desperate. Her father had been disappointed in him, but at least Joe had not tried to stop him from convincing Annie to come out and talk to him.

Taking a deep breath, Paxton approached the simple rough-hewn cabin door. He had knocked to no avail before, but this time he was determined to stand and pound against the door until Annie answered it.

He took another deep breath, bunched up his fist and knocked.

No answer.

Paxton clenched his teeth, undaunted this time. He knocked harder. His tone urgent, he implored, "Annie, I must talk with you."

Still no answer.

Resolved not to leave this time without seeing Annie, Paxton hammered on the door. The door shuddered against the onslaught. "Annie, I'm not leaving until you come out and talk to me," he bellowed like the wounded suitor he was.

No answer.

He beat against the door again, harder. Not about to give up, he was about to try again when the door squeaked open a sliver. "Annie! Annie, please open the door and come out so we can talk. Please." Then in a softer voice, "I brought you some real pretty flowers. They smell awful nice. I know you'd like them. Ah, come on, sweet girl, open the door so I can see you again and talk to you," he pleaded in utter desperation.

Slowly the door squawked on its hinges and opened a little wider. Paxton was so excited at the prospect of finally speaking to Annie that the bouquet tumbled from his arms. Busying himself with gathering up the blossoms, he crooned, "I'm so glad you changed your mind. I was beginning to worry that I never would get to gaze into those beautiful eyes or hear that sweet voice of yours again. You know that I think you are the prettiest little thing alive in the entire Park. No one can compare to you," he offered as he scooped up the last of the flowers. When he shifted to grab the last bloom, his eyes fastened on bare feet standing in the doorway. The whites of his eyes bulged, and he gulped back the next compliment standing ready on the tip of his tongue. Trailing his gaze up the thin ankles and higher still, Paxton felt the lump blocking his windpipe expand in size.

To Paxton's utter horror, Joe Mills's craggy face grinned down at him from the doorway. The old man gave a hearty laugh. "Them's some mighty pretty words, son." He rubbed a stubbled chin. "I always knowed I had a mighty handsome pair of peepers, and nobody ever complained about these scratchy old vocal cords of mine, but I never would of thought that I was considered pretty." He rubbed his nose. "Let alone being the prettiest thing in these parts."

Slowly, Paxton straightened and cleared his throat. Embarrassment colored his usually pale cheeks, and he fought for something clever to say, but nothing saved him from utter mortification as he stared into Joe Mills's wide smirking face.

"You brung me flowers, son?" Joe asked.

"Ah, no. N-no, sir," Paxton stammered, not sharing in the old man's amusement at his expense. "These are for Annie. I've got to see her, Mr. Mills. I've just got to."

The older man's grin faded, and he stared at Paxton as if he were assessing him, which caused Paxton to want to run. This was too important, though, and despite his fear that Joe Mills might be sizing him up for a pine box, Paxton held his place. While Joe Mills had always been most cordial to him, Paxton had not spoken directly to the man since he had come upon Paxton buck naked a couple of weeks ago. Joe had to know what Annie and he had been doing, and that worried Paxton all the more.

"What you got to say to the girl?" Joe questioned, cocking a brow. He liked Paxton Lloyd and understood about what happened between a pair in love. But Annie was his flesh, and he intended to see that the boy came to the right conclusion with respect to his only kin.

"You goin' to spit it out, or you goin' to keep standin' there with your knees knockin'?" Joe said when Paxton continued to cower before him, silent. At least the boy hadn't turned tail and hightailed it out of there.

Paxton forced down the clog in his throat and willed his knees into a slower beat. "Sir, Annie and I had a misunderstanding that we cannot work out unless we talk," he hedged. He could not tell the man what he intended to talk to Annie about since Paxton was sure that Joe Mills would get his shotgun out and either march him to a preacher or fill him with buckshot. While Paxton loved Annie, he was not sure he was ready for a wife.

Joe's face lost any hint of benevolence, and a serious frown drew his brows together. "You decide how you're goin' to settle that *misunderstanding* of yours?"

From the look on the old man's face, Paxton could tell that the man knew exactly the source of his problems with Annie. "Sir, no kind of decision can be made unless Annie and I talk."

Joe crossed his arms over his chest. "I see."

"Then will you let me in to talk to her?" Paxton asked hopefully.

Joe moved aside, and Annie stepped into the doorway. Paxton gasped when he saw her. She was even more beautiful than he had remembered. Her hair was tousled, and the dress Cornelia had given her hung nicely on her shapely frame. He ached inside to take her in his arms and kiss her.

"Annie," he whispered, his throat choking up again. He was so excited that, without thinking, he thrust the bouquet forward so hard he inadvertently shoved it into her face, causing her to sneeze.

"Ah-choo!" She sneezed a second time and pushed the offending flowers out of her face. "Paxton, what are you trying to do—smother me?"

"Me? Oh, no. No, never! I'm sorry, Annie," he said and hesitantly tried to offer her the crushed petals again.

She made no attempt to take them.

Joe laughed at the boy's awkwardness and then sagely disappeared inside the cabin to change out of his robe, leaving his daughter alone with Paxton.

"What did you want to talk to me about?" Annie asked after she saw that her father had gone.

He tried a third time to hand her the flowers. This time he silently pleaded that she take them. To his relief, she accepted the offering. The expression on her face showed that she was pleased despite her efforts to demonstrate how upset she was with him.

"Will you walk with me while we talk?" he asked. He had to get her away from the cabin so she wouldn't turn and order him out of her house if she had a mind to. "Please, Annie."

He looked so earnest that Annie was sure he had changed his mind and was going to ask her to marry him. After all, after they had bedded, they had to be wed. A good girl just did not run around bedding men; a girl only bedded the man who would call her his wife. Her pa had drilled that into her from the time she was a young 'un, and she was determined to hold true to it. She nodded her consent.

"Whew, I'm glad," he said in a rush and offered his arm.

They strolled in silence out behind the cabin among the towering aspens. The leaves quaked in the breeze, and Paxton wondered if that foreshadowed what was to come since he was also quaking—inside.

Churning everything he wanted to say over and over in his mind, Paxton silently practiced his words, but nothing seemed to fit the situation. They walked until they came to a fallen log. There Annie spread her simple blue skirt and plunked down.

She patted the place next to her. "Come, sit so you can say what you got to say."

Paxton swallowed hard. He had to say it right, or he would risk losing the girl, and he did not want to do that.

"Nice day, don't you think?" he uttered, folding his

lithe frame next to her on the log.

"I reckon," she answered, shuffling the toe of her shoe through the thick bed of fallen, decaying leaves and pine needles.

With slow deliberation, he took her hand in his and rubbed his thumb along the side of her finger as he gazed into her eyes. They were wide and expectant. "I've missed being with you and seeing you, Annie."

"Have you?"

"You know I have. Haven't you missed me?"

"Should I?" she answered evasively again.

"I hope so."

Silence.

Paxton waited for Annie to say something, but she did not. She was not making this easy for him. "Annie, about a couple of weeks ago — "

"What about it?" she asked, taking back her hand and setting it in her lap with the other one. She looked away and shut her eyes, holding her breath. He had to declare himself; he just had to!

"You were awfully upset when you left."

She crossed her fingers and looked back at him. "I'd say I had a mighty good reason to be, wouldn't you?"

"Oh, gosh, Annie, I'm sorry your father had to come along and see me that way. I would never want to do anything to upset you or cause you any trouble. Honest."

Her heart thundering in her chest, Annie bolted to her feet and swung around to face him. "Is that all you got to be sorry about?" she cried.

He stood up and put his hands on her shoulders. She was trembling. "I am not sorry that we made love, if that's what you mean, because I love you, Annie."

Tears threatened to blur her vision when Paxton said he loved her, since she loved him more than she had loved anyone — excepting of course her pa and dearly departed ma, and that was a different kind of love.

"Annie, please, let's sit back down. We need to straighten things out," he pleaded.

Annie was shaking so that she was sure that if she did not sit, her legs would buckle out from under her and she would make a spectacle out of herself. So, without a word, she gingerly nestled back on the log. As Paxton took a seat next to her, she crossed and recrossed her fingers and prayed with all her strength that he was going to make an honest woman out of her.

Paxton slipped his arm around her quivering shoulders and brushed his lips against her temple. She went rigid, warning him that he had better proceed cautiously. With great care, he turned her to face him. "Annie, what happened between us was very special."

"Special enough to last us a lifetime?"

"It'll always be special to me, sweet girl."

Her lips thinned. "But is it special enough?"

"Enough?"

Growing impatient with his thick skull, Annie gritted out, "Enough to do right by me?"

"Right by you?" Paxton gulped.

"Paxton Lloyd, either you're more dense than an owl in the daylight, or you're no better than them riverboat gamblers Pa told me about what takes a woman's virtue and leaves her to a life of bein' one of them painted women."

Paxton was horrified by her outburst. He didn't think she even knew about such things, let alone could even consider, for a moment, that that could be her fate—not a girl like Annie.

"Well, are you goin' to just sit there and not even open your mouth?" she cried.

"Y-you could never be like one of those soiled doves," he sputtered. "You are—"

"I am no better," she cried. "You bedded me, and you ain't got no mind to wed me, do you, Paxton? Do you?"

"Ah, I . . ."

"I thought so. You, you—" she thrust out her hands and shoved Paxton backward as hard as her strength would allow, sending him spilling over the log onto the ground with a thud"—you mule's behind!"

Not waiting to see if Paxton had been hurt, Annie bounded to her feet and fled.

Paxton was momentarily stunned by the force with which he had been propelled backward. "Annie! Annie!" he called out when he had regained his senses, but he was surrounded by the silence of the forest; Annie was gone.

His feet in the air with legs draped over the log, Paxton struggled up on his elbows. As he attempted to angle his legs from the log, he fell backward. Momentarily ceasing his efforts to right himself, Paxton dropped his head back against the bed of leaves and let out a disgruntled moan. He had bungled everything. Annie would probably never forgive him now. He rubbed his temples. The worst part about the whole mess he had gotten himself into was he was not sure he would forgive himself for hurting Annie. Affixing his attention up at the brilliant blue Colorado sky, Paxton thought of the letters that had just come from his parents and prayed that Cornelia was having better luck with Locke than he was with Annie.

Chapter Thirty

Cornelia could see her breath against the early morning chill as she and Carrie Simington waited outside the hotel for Locke to bring the wagon around. Although it was still officially summer, the summer warmth was beginning to wane, hinting that another season had nearly passed. She bundled her hooded cloak up closer around her neck.

"I am so excited and so happy to be accompanying you back to Estes Park," Carrie chirped, seemingly oblivious to the cold. She hugged herself. "I have wanted to climb Longs Peak ever since I read about Anna Dickinson's account of the climb. This is just ever so exciting," she gushed. "Locke Breckenridge has a reputation for being one of the best guides in the area. I simply know the climb will be everything and more than I expect with him along."

Locke pulled up with the wagon, saving Cornelia from having to inform the lady that Locke had no intention of serving as her guide.

Cornelia shivered, causing him to say, "Why didn't you two wait inside?"

"We would not think of having to make you wait," Cornelia said.

Locke gave her a spare smile, recalling his complaints that the Simington woman's presence would probably cause them undue delays. "As soon as I get your bags loaded, we'll be off," Locke grumbled and threw the three carpet bags on top of the supplies in the back of the wagon.

"But what about the rest of my luggage?" Carrie chimed in a plaintive voice when Locke turned to help Cornelia up onto the wagon seat.

Locke glanced at the wagon, already over half full, and back at the eccentric lady. "Rest of your luggage?"

"Why, yes, my trunks are in the lobby." She stepped forward and presented her arm, smiling coyly. "You can help me up first though."

Locke rolled his eyes. He had gone to Estes Park to get away from women, and here he was surrounded! He felt a glimmer of how Custer must have felt, and a foreboding of what the trip back to the Park was going to be like hit the pit of his stomach. He was certain he would not get even a moment alone with Cornelia. Accepting defeat, Locke helped the woman up and went to fetch her luggage.

His back aching, Locke finally managed to load the last of the four heavy trunks. The poor horse; it had its work cut out on this trip. To judge from her luggage, that Simington woman was probably planning to move to Estes Park permanently. When he climbed up next to Cornelia, the two women were conversing companionably. Locke gritted his teeth. He had not received so much as a "thank you."

When they continued to remain seated in the wagon in front of the hotel, Cornelia finally tore herself away from one of Carrie's fascinating adventure tales and turned to Locke. "Is something the matter?"

He gave a shrug, keeping his expression bland. "Not at all." *Nothing that heaving Carrie Simington's luggage and person out of the wagon wouldn't remedy.*

"Then why are we just sitting here?" she questioned further.

Tonelessly, he said, "Haven't the faintest notion. Sitting here isn't my idea."

A bewildered expression dropped over her face. "Then we might as well get started."

"Sounds good to me," he answered and continued to sit with his hands balled inside his pockets.

Cornelia turned to Carrie, who merely widened her eyes. She apparently did not know what the delay was either. Cornelia turned back to Locke. "Well, what are we waiting for then?"

"You."

"Me? Why me?"

"You don't remember?"

"Remember what?"

A wide grin made his face shine. "You rose victorious," he said and handed her the reins.

At first, Cornelia did not understand, then it hit her. She had wanted to demonstrate how capable she was. With a burst of laughter, she closed her gloved hands around the reins. "I shall drive, although a day late. If I recall, I was supposed to do this yesterday."

As the wagon jerked into motion, Carrie watched the pair share a private moment of laughter together. Although she was dying to discover what was so amusing, she kept her peace. She had learned enough about Cornelia to know that the woman deserved happiness, and at the moment she seemed to have found it. As for Locke Breckenridge, she thought he was a bit too much on the grumpy side for her taste.

All day, the threesome endured the jerky wagon ride over the rough road. The horse tested Cornelia at every opportunity, and she nearly ran them off the road into a ditch twice when the stubborn animal got it into its mind to change course.

By nightfall, Cornelia breathed a silent sigh of relief when Locke directed her to the side of the road. She relinquished the reins without protest.

"My, my, this has been a long day," observed Carrie, rubbing the back of her neck. "It will feel good to stop for the night. A soft bed is just what I need."

Locke cocked a brow and snapped the reins over the horse's rump. "Well, you had best get comfortable where you are because we have several hours ahead of us yet."

"But it is getting quite dark."

"You aren't a child. I think you can handle it."

"I suppose if I were an exhausted child of yours, you would still insist on continuing," Carrie announced.

Locke's gaze shifted to Cornelia, and he winked before turning his attention back to Carrie. "The children I plan to have will love the outdoors and probably beg to hold the reins."

Cornelia was stung by his plans for a family. She had always wanted children and silently mourned her barren womb. Forcing her thoughts away from Locke's comment and its ramifications, she refocused her attention on Carrie's continuing protests at Locke's travel plans. She knew Locke intended to make the return trip in as short a period of time as possible, and now she too was in a hurry.

The trip back to Estes Park was made in record time. Every time Carrie brought up her plans for her visit to Estes Park, Locke pushed the animal all the harder. Every night they drove way past dark until Carrie appeared exhausted and Cornelia had to swivel around on the seat in an attempt to find a comfortable position.

It was early afternoon of the fourth day when the valley cradling Estes Park came into view from the top of the ridge high above. Without warning, Carrie bolted to her feet and nearly fell out of the wagon. Locke grabbed her around the waist and pulled her back down on the seat just before she lost her balance.

"What the devil are you trying to do, break your neck?" Locke grumbled.

"Heavens, no. It is just that everything is so . . . so beautiful, and I am most excited."

"Well, just be 'excited' from your seat," Locke mumbled none too politely. He ignored Cornelia's silent look of annoyance at his less than gentlemanly behavior toward the Simington woman and spurred the team forward.

The sooner he unloaded Carrie Simington, the better!

"Where can we drop you?" Locke asked as they descended the ridge.

"Oh, didn't Cornelia mention it? The dear girl has graciously offered to let me stay with her and her brother," Carrie said all aflutter.

Locke cast Cornelia a decidedly annoyed frown. "Evidently, Cornelia neglected to inform me."

"Isn't it wonderful?" Carrie enthused, putting her palms to her cheeks.

"Yes. Wonderful," Locke answered unenthusiastically.

Noting the dark look alight on Locke's face like a rain cloud over the Rocky Mountains, Cornelia quickly interjected, "Locke, it makes sense. Carrie and I have become such fast friends and have so much in common that having her stay with Paxton and me will make my sojourn here all the more pleasant."

"Yes, you two have a lot in common," he mumbled under his breath. "And I'm sure the rest of your visit to Estes Park would be boring without her."

"Beg your pardon?" Carrie asked.

Cornelia shot Locke a look of warning, causing him to say, "I just agreed that you two do have a lot in common. Your presence is certain to liven up Cornelia's visit."

Carrie interlocked her fingers and talked excitedly as Locke grudgingly turned the horse toward Lord Dunraven's.

While Cornelia made every attempt to listen attentively to what Carrie was saying, Cornelia secretly wondered about Locke. She sneaked a peek at his profile. His nose was proud and straight, reminding her of the man himself. His full lips were set in a rigid line, the color on his cheeks was high. His figure was robust and rock hard from living a rugged life at his cabin. The muscles in his arms bulged, straining as he worked the reins, along with the muscles in his strong thighs shadowing through his trousers as he worked the foot brake. He had an inner strength as well as an outer strength. Despite the longing in her heart for the man, she now knew that their relationship could never come to anything. Locke deserved the family he longed for, and she could not give him one.

By the time they pulled up in front of the cottage, Cornelia was anxious to see her brother again. She had been away nearly a month, and she had worried about Paxton's health since she had left. Belatedly chiding herself that she would never be able to forgive herself if Paxton had taken a turn for the worse, Cornelia was startled when she sighted Paxton sprinting across the yard without the benefit of his cane.

"Paxton," Cornelia shouted, shocked to see him move so agilely. "Paxton!"

At the sound of the familiar voice hailing him, Paxton stopped in his tracks. Suddenly realizing that he had not had to think of his pretended illness for weeks and had grown lax in his behavior, Paxton swung around and walked slowly over to the wagon. With a sheepish grin, he raised his gaze to Cornelia. Her face held a bewildered frown.

"What are you doing outside?" Cornelia asked.

"I'm feeling much better, Sister dear. Thank you for asking," he said with a grin. He turned his attention to Locke and the attractive woman with them. "How was the trip, Locke?"

Locke shot a disgruntled frown toward Carrie, then answered, "It had its moments."

"I can see that it must have been more than you bargained for by the lovely visitor you and Cornelia have brought back with you." Paxton made a quick bow, focusing his attention on the lady. "The name is Paxton Lloyd. Cornelia's brother." He offered his hands to help her down. "It is an honor to make your acquaintance, Miss?"

Carrie flashed the man a bright smile. "Miss Simington. Carrie Simington. Your sister has graciously invited me to stay with you two while I'm here in Estes Park."

"Pleased to make your acquaintance, Miss Carrie Simington."

Annie, who had come to talk to Paxton at her pa's insistence, shrank back behind a towering tree when she caught sight of Paxton openly flirting with a strange woman. Swallowing against the threatening tears, Annie felt as if she had been wounded.

When Paxton offered his arm to the woman Annie gasped and slid down the trunk of tree until she was curled into a ball. Chiding herself for even allowing her pa to convince her to give Paxton another chance, Annie remained hidden by the tree, quietly sobbing and bemoaning her foolishness. Despite the crushing pain she felt, she continued to listen.

"Let me show you where you will be staying, Carrie," Paxton crooned. He offered his arm and started to lead Carrie toward the house when Cornelia's sharp tone stopped them.

"Paxton, are you perchance trying to avoid me?"

Paxton stopped halfway to the house. Cornelia's voice had cooled considerably. He had hoped that in all the excitement over her return and being busy with her visitor, Cornelia would forget about what she had seen when they arrived and not ask probing questions.

"Paxton?" Cornelia called again.

"Paxton, I think your sister is calling you," Carrie

300

whispered. "I'm afraid you are not going to be able to avoid her any longer."

Casting Carrie Simington a look that denoted guilt, Paxton shrugged. "I fear that you are right in your assessment despite my valiant attempts to escape my sister's clutches."

Unlinking his arm from Carrie's, Paxton pivoted slowly around to face Cornelia. She was now standing next to the wagon with Locke at her side. Her arms were crossed over her chest, her face set, her brow cocked. From the look of determination in her eyes, she was not amused by his attempts to charm Carrie Simington in order to avoid her questions. Thank God, Annie was nowhere near, or he would have had double trouble.

"Paxton, I asked you a question," Cornelia said much too sweetly for Paxton's comfort.

"Did you?" he gulped.

Cornelia rolled her eyes and sucked in her cheeks. Paxton was hiding something. She could always tell when he was trying to keep something from her. "Let's not play games, Paxton. We aren't children any longer, and even when we were, you never were successful in keeping things from me."

"Well, there was that time down by the river when you nearly caught me smoking Father's pipe. You never did get that out of me. Then there was the time—"

"Enough of your evasive tactics. I think you owe me an explanation," she said. "Oh, and I knew all about the pipe."

Paxton opened his mouth to admit that he was no longer ill but was saved by the snapping of a twig that drew his attention toward a tree next to the house.

"Who's there?" Locke called out in a harsh voice and started toward the noise, worried that Sean McCurdy could still be lurking nearby as his fear for Cornelia's safety returned.

To Paxton's utter horror, Annie hesitantly stepped from behind the tree. Her shoulders were slumped and she hung her head, keeping her eyes fastened on the ground.

"Annie? Annie, what were you doing behind that tree?" asked Cornelia, bemused by the girl's unusually subdued behavior.

Paxton's breath fled him, and he gasped. Choking, he started toward the trembling girl. By her look, Paxton knew she had witnessed his efforts to charm Carrie Simington and had totally misunderstood. He had to explain. About ten feet from her, he reached out a hand. To his growing horror, she stepped back.

"No. Don't come any closer," she hissed.

"But, Annie, you don't understand," he said in a pleading voice. He swallowed back the fear attempting to close his throat. Before him wasn't the sweet girl he knew and loved. Before him stood a wild creature, wild eyed, ready to fight if cornered.

"Don't I?" Annie's eyes trailed to the woman and back to Paxton. "I may not be city bred, but I ain't deaf or blind. I got eyes. I can see that you were nuzzlin' up to her." Annie motioned to Carrie.

"But, Annie, I can explain."

He took another step toward her.

She took another step backward.

"You can explain until you're old and your tongue shrivels with your lies, but not to me. I ain't goin' to listen," she sniffled. Not waiting to give

302

him further opportunity to embarrass her, Annie swung around and fled.

"Annie! Annie! Wait!" he hollered.

To Paxton's further chagrin, Cornelia said, "Since you seem to be ready to do some explaining, why don't we leave Locke to see to getting Carrie settled. Then you and I can go into the house, and you can explain what is going on to me."

Paxton looked to Locke and Carrie to rescue him; they merely shrugged. With all the enthusiasm of a man about to be sentenced for a crime, Paxton motioned for Cornelia to lead the way. She walked past him, her heels sinking into the ground. With a sigh, he followed her into the house, dreading the conversation that was to come.

Chapter Thirty-one

Not taking his eyes off Cornelia, Paxton followed her into the parlor. With great trepidation, he noted her straight back as she seated herself on the couch. There was nothing relaxed about her features, which now seemed to exude a new strength he had not noticed before. Her lips were set in a tight line, and her eyes snapped with fire. Certain that he was going to face a most unpleasant interview, Paxton gingerly sat down on the piano bench facing Cornelia and waited.

"Paxton, what has been going on while I've been gone?" she asked.

The set of her features warned him she would brook no excuses. Paxton swallowed frantically, trying to come with a way to forestall the inevitable. He searched his mind for some way to transfer the subject from himself.

By the way Locke had hovered over her outside by the wagon, Paxton was sure that Cornelia's resolve to return to Linley was weakening. He had to buy more time for himself.

His gaze caught at a nearby table, and a sudden idea came to him. He rose, went to the table, and picked up an envelope. Waving the missive, he smiled. "A letter came for you from home."

Cornelia flinched. Prior to going to Leadville, she had been anxiously awaiting news, but now a sense of foreboding grasped her.

Her reaction took Paxton by surprise. She seemed so uneasy. Her shoulders slumped, and she was biting her lower lip. There was no longer any doubt in his mind something had happened while she and Locke were in Leadville.

"Cornelia, are you all right?" he asked and went to sit beside her. While he was grateful that the attention had shifted from him, he was concerned at the effect the letter had on her, and he chided himself for not reading it first.

"I'm fine." She waited, and when he made no effort to give her her mail, she held out her hand. "The letter?"

"Oh, oh yes, the letter. I'm sure it's nothing. Why don't I read it for you since you don't seem to have your spectacles with you?"

"They are in my reticule." She rummaged through her bag and pulled out her glasses. Setting the wire-rimmed eyeglasses on the bridge of her nose, she huffed out, "All right, hand me the letter."

"I have always liked those winkers on you, but you might try getting them on straight." He adjusted the glasses. "There, isn't that better?"

"Quit trying to stall and give me the letter."

Paxton attempted to keep his voice light and airy. "I could never say no to you, Nellie. Here you are."

Cornelia cast him a frown and turned her back as her trembling fingers worked the envelope flap.

"It's from Mother," she announced with a sigh of relief. She had feared it would be from Linley.

"I'll just leave you alone to read it in peace," Paxton announced, inching his way from the room.

Cornelia's head sapped up. "Don't leave. We have not had our talk yet."

"Yes. Our talk," Paxton groaned and took a seat. "Why don't you read Mother's letter aloud since I seem to be a captive audience?"

Cornelia raised her brow at his referral to himself as a captive but decided to ignore it. "It is addressed to me, but I suppose you are as anxious as I am to hear news from home."

Cornelia settled back and began to read:

My Dearest Daughter,
Your father and I miss your brother and you very much. I hope you are taking good care of our Paxton. Give him all our love. I know you must be anxious to hear about Linley, so I shan't waste time with the usual news first. You will be thrilled to learn that Linley came to see me, and I am certain that he is having a change of heart. He asked about you and said he has been thinking a lot about the divorce. He wanted to know exactly where you went. Isn't that simply grand? I am certain that you two will be reunited and everything can get back to the way it should be. Now, for what has been going on here at home since you left . . .

Visibly shaken, Cornelia removed her spectacles

306

and set the letter aside but continued to stare at it.

"Aren't you going to finish reading it?"

"Here" — she handed him the letter — "you can read it for yourself."

His heart went out to her. He could not bear the thought that she might still be giving even a moment's consideration to returning to that bastard. And he could wring his mother's neck for her well-meaning interference. He had gone to Europe to escape her, but Cornelia had not been so fortunate. Now the woman was reaching across two thousand miles to meddle again.

He patted Cornelia's hand in understanding. "Cornelia, you don't have to go back to Linley," Paxton said in a quiet voice. "You can stay out here in Colorado. You have made a new life for yourself. Out here, you won't be under anyone's thumb." The sadness in her eyes caused him to add, "From what I've seen, you may very well have a future here . . . with Locke."

To his utter shock, Cornelia flew to her feet. Tears welled in her eyes, and she was wringing her hands. "I don't have a future out here with Locke," she cried. "I don't."

Paxton jumped to his feet and gathered her into his arms before she could flee. Stroking her hair, he cradled her against his shoulder while she sobbed.

"There, there, everything will be all right." He held her from him and studied her red, swollen face. "From what I've seen, I'd say that Locke cares for you and you care for him."

Snuffling back a sob, Cornelia wiped the tears from her cheeks. "That is just it. I think that he does care about me. And I have to put a stop to it before our feelings grow any deeper."

In an effort to ease the tension and allow Cornelia to compose herself, Paxton made a grand display of feeling her forehead and taking her pulse. "No fever. Your color is good. Strong heartbeat. You don't appear to be sick."

She gave him a peck on the cheek. "Thank you."

"Me? What for?"

"For being here for me."

"Then, let me be here for you, Cornelia. One would think that you would be jumping for joy rather than being Miss Gloom and Doom. I just don't understand, but I'd like to help if you'll let me."

Cornelia shook her head and smoothed her hair back. Her gaze trailed to the ceiling as she fought back more tears. "That is just it, you don't understand."

"Then by all means, let's sit back down so you can enlighten me."

"I can't unburden my troubles on you. I'm here to help you get well. You aren't here to take care of me," she insisted, her voice cracking. "Go see to Carrie's comfort. We'll talk about you and Annie later." Breaking free of Paxton, Cornelia lowered her head, hurried past Locke down the hall to her room, and threw the lock on the door so to collect herself in private.

"Cornelia!" Paxton called out from the doorway.

Noticing Cornelia's state, Locke swung around and barged into the parlor, blocking Paxton's exit. "Where do you think you're going?" he demanded.

Bemused, Paxton shrugged. "To see to Carrie Simington's comfort."

"The woman's already settled. Said she was going to take a nap."

The gruff tone of Locke's voice startled Paxton. "Is there something I can do for you?"

"To start with, you can tell me what you said to upset Cornelia."

Backing out of Locke's reach, Paxton immediately took up a position on the couch and held a needlepoint pillow in front of him for protection. His gaze roved over Locke. There was no doubt that if Locke had the inclination he could break him in half. He watched in horror as Locke put a boot up on the couch and leaned forward toward him.

"All right, Paxton, what happened?"

Paxton swallowed hard. "Nothing, truly."

Locke put his face in Paxton's. "It did not look like nothing."

"She received a letter from home," Paxton hedged, leaning back until his head was against the couch. He could not tell Locke that her upset seemed to have something to do with him since Paxton didn't understand it himself. Until he found out, he could not break the confidence that he and Cornelia had shared since childhood.

"What was in the letter?" Locke demanded.

"Don't you think that's personal?"

"I don't give a damn if it's personal. If the contents upset Cornelia, I want to know."

"What is it you want to know?" Cornelia asked, returning to the parlor.

Locke swung around toward Cornelia framed in

the doorway. He took his foot off the couch and relaxed his stance. Paxton's gaze went between the pair. There was only concern in the big man's eyes, while his sister's expression held despair.

"He just wanted to know when Lord Dunraven would be back."

"Standing over you with his foot on the furniture?" she asked in disbelief.

"He was adjusting his sock," Paxton blurted out.

"I see. When will Lord Dunraven be returning?" she asked in order to keep the conversation away from herself.

"I was just telling Locke that Dunraven returned from his trip to Grand Lake while you two were gone and had to leave for Ireland. He said to tell you that he was sorry he could not remain but that we are free to stay here as long as we like."

Cornelia looked doubtful, causing Paxton to say, "I am getting quite exhausted after all the excitement of your return. I think I shall go to my room and rest. If you'll excuse me?" He gave Cornelia a peck on the cheek and whispered, "Whatever is bothering you, now's your chance to work it out while you two are alone." Then he nodded to Locke and quickly made his exit before the opportunity passed.

Paxton headed down the hallway toward his room until he was certain that they had lost interest in him. Then he changed course. He had to go talk to Annie and straighten out their latest misunderstanding before she decided never to speak to him again. As he crept back past the parlor he could hear Locke's voice. Although he did not believe in eavesdroping, he stopped and craned his ear to listen.

"Cornelia, your brother said you received a letter from home and were quite upset about it."

"I was not upset," she insisted, making every effort to remain detached from the feelings surrounding her. "And he had no right to tell you that."

"You were in a state when you passed me in the hall a few minutes ago, and on the journey back from Leadville you didn't seem yourself either. It was as if you were withdrawing from me."

"The letter was from Mother," she said to avoid discussing her actions toward him. "Mother seems confident that Linley is going to have a change of heart."

Locke felt as if someone had just taken a chisel and hammer to his heart. "You aren't thinking of going back to that man, are you? A man who discarded you." Not after what we shared, he thought.

Cornelia clasped her hands in front of her to keep them from trembling and giving her away. "Linley was my husband. We took vows to death do us part."

Locke felt utter desperation engulf him. He could not believe what he was hearing. He had been so careful to stay away from all females after Margaret, and now when he had fallen in love, it was happening again. Only this time he had a rival two thousand miles away standing between them.

Locke squared his jaw. He loved Cornelia, and he was not going to allow her to ruin her life!

"The way I heard it, you were the only one who kept those vows." Her gasp did not stop him; it only spurred him on in his efforts to convince her to make the right choice. "Paxton told me how the man used to run around and how he then did not stand by you when you needed him."

"Linley had his family's name to consider,"

"What about your name, Cornelia? From what I know about the man, he doesn't deserve to scrape the mud off your boots. And never did. You yourself have to admit that you have changed since coming to Colorado." He raked his fingers through his hair. "My God, what makes you think you could be happy returning to a man who treated you the way that bastard did." He shook his head. "No. I am not going to allow you to go back to him and ruin your life."

His last sentence got her dander up. "*You* are not going to allow me?"

Locke crossed his arms over his chest. "That's what I said."

In an effort to stand her ground, Cornelia mimicked Locke and crossed her arms over her chest. "And just exactly what gives you the right to make any decisions concerning how I lead my life?"

"I have every right," he spat out with hard-fought-for restraint.

She moved directly in front of him, put her hands on her hips, and looked directly into those angry brown eyes. "I asked just what makes you think you **have any** say in how I live my life?"

She was **so close** that he felt mesmerized by her presence **as he** inhaled her scent of rosewater. Her eyes burned, and he felt himself consumed by them.

"Well?"

Her harsh tone intruded into the fantasy image that had held his senses enthralled. "What?"

"I said, what makes you think you have the right to dictate what I should do with my life?"

The pressure building him inside burst, snapping his restraint. Like an eagle swooping down on its prey, he grabbed her shoulders. "Dammit, because I love you, that's why. I love you. Do you hear me? I love you."

Chapter Thirty-two

The room rotated, giving Cornelia a sense of lightheadedness. Her knees started to buckle, and Locke caught her up in his arms. She was enslaved and breathless by his simple declaration of love. She lifted her face to his and saw how much it had cost him to say the simple words that held such far-reaching meaning.

She felt fiery fingers thread through her hair and draw her to him as he tilted forward and crushed his mouth on hers. He kissed her long and hard, his arms gliding up and down her back, pressing her to him as if his declaration would meld them together for all time.

She did nothing to discourage him or pull away. She wanted to revel in his arms, to feel truly loved and treasured if only for a few moments. She could feel his heart pounding against her chest, feel his sex pressing against her. She crushed herself to him more tightly, wishing that there was no outside world to intrude and destroy this moment of happiness.

Determined to hold fast to the feelings of being in his arms, Cornelia slid her fingers inside his shirt. His flesh was afire as she ran her hand over his bunched muscles.

"Cornelia—" he groaned at her touch.

She cut him off with a kiss. Then into his mouth, she begged, "Make love to me."

Locke glanced at the open door. "I'll lock the door." Paxton made quick work to take his leave before Locke shut the door.

He swept her up and set her on the couch. He joined her and began kissing her. First, the top of her head, her eyes, her nose, lips, and chin. Then he dropped to the creamy flesh along her slim throat and continued his descent until he pushed aside her shirt front and suckled at her breasts.

Cornelia trembled with pleasure as he divested them of the clothing separating their bodies and took them to the heights of passion. He teased and tantalized with a compelling urgency, coaxing and forcing her to respond to his every desire.

Cornelia brought her own hunger to the union. She sampled and explored him, trying to memorize every inch of him. She welcomed his tongue's invasion, following his lead and savoring him until he laid her back and joined their bodies.

Fiercely, the pressure built within her as he ignited her senses and sent them blindly erupting in spasms so strong she held him to her with all her might.

Afterward, nibbling on her lips, he murmured, "Isn't there something you have to say to me?"

Her eyes popped open to look directly into the heavily dilated eyes smiling back at her. "Say?" she responded weakly and inched away from him.

"Yes." He propped himself up on his elbow and

toyed with the lap robe she had covered herself with. "When a man declares himself to a woman, who hopefully shares his feelings, she usually proclaims hers."

Cornelia broke away and dressed quickly. "Mine?"

"Yes. Your feelings. Toward me," he said, sliding into his clothes effortlessly and unlocking the door as Paxton was passing it again. Something had stopped him from going to see Annie, and now he bent down to listen again.

At Cornelia's long silence, Locke's smile vanished. "Cornelia, you can't deny you have feelings toward me."

She lowered her eyes, but he moved forward and raised her chin with the crook of his finger. "Cornelia?"

"No. No. I can't deny my feelings for you. I do love you. But it doesn't matter."

Worry troubled his brow. "You aren't still thinking of going back to that ex-husband of yours? Not when we love each other."

"I wasn't thinking about Linley," she said quietly.

He heaved a sigh. "Thank heaven for that."

Before she had a chance to say another word, he grabbed her hand, sat her back down on the couch, and kneeled in front of her. He cradled her palm in his, tenderly rubbing a thumb along the soft skin. She opened her mouth, but he shushed her.

"Hush, and let me speak before I lose my nerve. When my marriage broke up, I never dreamed I would find someone who could fill the void in my life. I was convinced that I was going to spend the rest of my life alone. And I did for over two years. Then you came into my life. Cornelia . . ."

As she listened to his open declaration, she marveled at how tender he could be and thought what a fool his wife had been. This man would be true; she could see it in his eyes, hear it in his voice. She desperately wished that she could accept his proposal and begin a new life out here. But she was barren and could not give him the children he wanted to have someday.

Linley had never wanted a family except to inherit his father's estate, and she had been sure that, had he worked, he could make his own fortune although he had often cruelly reminded her that it was her fault they did not live according to the station of life he had been born into. And she had obligations to her family, she rationalized. But, she thought staunchly, she would never regret their few stolen moments together.

". . . I think it was meant to be for us," he was saying as she pulled her attention back to the present. "And if Lamantha liked you, we can't go wrong," he added on a lighter note. "So I would be honored if you would be my wife."

Cornelia had feared he had been leading up to a proposal. Panic overtook her and she tensed and remained speechless, unable to form the words to decline such an eloquent offer.

Locke waited, sensing something was wrong. In an attempt to salvage the situation and save himself from being an utter fool if the lady wasn't ready yet to admit that she would marry him, he said drolly, "Perhaps I should try the other knee?

I'm not well versed in proper procedure in times such as this."

Paxton had given them enough time alone, he figured from outside the door. He had listened to the hesitancy in Cornelia's voice at Locke's proposal. Paxton made a loud noise and entered the room in an outlandish display of fumbling through his pockets. From the conversation he had had with Cornelia, he feared that she would turn Locke down, and he had to forestall such a folly.

Locke glared at Paxton and quickly got to his feet. Cornelia cast Locke a glance of sympathy, although she was relieved at the intrusion, and went to her brother.

"Are you all right?" she asked, deliberately fussing over him in an effort to escape having to decline Locke's proposal. "Shall I help you back to your room?"

"I think your brother is quite capable of maneuvering himself back to where he came from," Locke announced darkly.

Cornelia shot Locke a distinctly anguished frown. "Paxton needs me. We'll have to talk later," she said in a hoarse whisper and helped him back toward his room.

"I need you too," Locke said in a clipped voice as he watched the pair disappear down the hall. "And whether you know it yet or not, you need me. You are not going to escape me to be controlled by that family of yours again. Soon you will come to realize we are going to be together. Then you will be mine, and I'll allow you the freedom you deserve," he said to himself, and stuffing his hands in his pockets, he left the cottage in a state of undaunted frustration. At least he had not been refused.

Locke was fifty yards from the cottage, mulling over Cornelia's strange behavior, when he decided that a little detective work was in order to find out what was going on with Cornelia. Putting aside any notion of wrongdoing that spying conjured up in his mind, Locke headed back to the cottage. If he was going to help Cornelia realize the right choice, he needed to be informed.

Inside the cottage, once Cornelia had Paxton settled on his bed, she turned to leave but was halted by the urgency of his voice.

"Cornelia, stay, will you?"

She pivoted around and took up a position on a chair near the bed, carefully composing her features to hide the anguishing thoughts whirring through her mind. "Is there something troubling you?"

Paxton rolled his eyes. "That's an understatement. There are any number of things causing me grief at the moment," he said, thinking of his difficulties with Annie, the lie he had been living to keep Cornelia in Colorado, and now the problems he could sense with Cornelia and Locke.

"Problems with love?" she asked, her smile fixed. Anyone who had witnessed the scene with Paxton and Annie knew there was trouble between them.

Paxton propped himself up on a plump pillow. "We seem to be a family of personal calamities in respect to love, don't you think?" he offered with nonchalance, watching for her reaction.

Cornelia flinched.

"I thought so. Since we both seem to have more than our share of dilemmas, why don't we put our heads together and see if we can come up with a viable solution?"

A look of utter misery came over Cornelia. "I wish it were that simple," she said dejectedly.

"Nothing worth having is ever simple, Sister dear. I'll tell you what, I'll go first. Once you hear the jumble I've made of things, it might be easier for you to realize that your position may not be so dreadfully unsolvable."

Cornelia nodded although in the back of her mind there was no doubt that her position was without solution. People married to have children, to carry on the family name, to perpetuate the race. People did not wed merely for love. Her very own mother had drummed that into her head after her father had arranged her marriage to Linley.

Paxton gave her a sheepish grin. "I have a confession to make, and I want your promise before I do that you will forgive me."

Cornelia looked confused at his strange pronouncement. She could not imagine what he could confess that would require such a vow.

"Do you promise?" he prompted, a boyish hopefulness lighting his usually ashen complexion.

"You know I would forgive you anything," she offered with sincerity.

"Good," he said on a more serious note, "because this is one trespass you are not likely to find that easily forgivable."

"In that case don't keep me in suspense."

Paxton eyed her for a moment, trying to chose just the right words so she wouldn't have to go back on her word.

"I am not as sick as you may believe."

"I can see that you have made great strides since I have been gone."

"No, that is not what I'm talking about." He took a deep breath; the time had come to 'fess up. "When you agreed to accompany me here, you thought I had consumption. Well, I thought so too at first. But as it turned out, I learned that I was actually suffering from a severe case of the ague and had been run down from the high life I had been living in Europe. The symptoms were similar, so I let everyone believe I needed to come to Colorado so I could get you away from Linley and Mother . . ."

As Paxton continued his confession, the truth of it began to dawn on Cornelia. He had been lying to her all along; he had let her worry and fret until she had stood up to their mother and insisted he come to Colorado. She thought it all through, mulling over all the implications of what her brother had done before a wee smile hinted at her lips.

Paxton took her hand once he had finished his tale. "You aren't annoyed with me, are you?"

She laughed at the absurdity of it all. "My greatest crusade has been in vain, and I haven't saved you for Mother after all. I wonder what she'll say when she finds out."

"She need never know," Paxton said, hopeful that he was being easily absolved of his sin. "You don't hate me, do you, for lying?"

Cornelia rested a hand on his shoulder. "How could I ever hate you? You are my brother and thought you were doing what was best for me," she said softly.

Paxton breathed in a deep sigh of relief. "Thank God. I was so worried. You can't imagine how hard it's been pretending. I was afraid that Doc Jones was going to tell you truth."

"You know, now that I think about it, he did have a rather strange look on his face when I asked him about you. But what about all those coughing spells?"

Paxton looked sheepish. "They were real enough at first; I forced them later on. I've always been on the thin side, so looking haggard didn't take much effort."

"I'm glad you are not ill," she said.

"It has all worked out for the best because now you need never return to Connecticut. Cornelia, we can both stay here and start new lives. We can both be happy," he said and then blurted out the whole mess with Annie.

Cornelia listened to Paxton's misery before she said, "It sounds like a rather simple solution to me. All you have to do is marry Annie, that's all she wants, Paxton. After all, you said you love her. She is obviously devoted to you. Money won't be a problem; you can start painting again for a living. So what are you waiting for?"

Paxton stopped to think, and it suddenly hit him like a landslide of boulders. "Nothing, I guess. I'll do it! I'll ask her to marry me." His bright mood dimmed. "All I have to do is get her to listen to me."

He was surrounded by his own contemplations until he noticed that Cornelia's face held a deep sadness. "Cornelia, why didn't you accept Locke's proposal? It is crystal clear that you two love each other. You're both free." When she said nothing, he forged ahead. "It's time Mother quit living our lives and pay attention to her own marriage. So if she's the reason you feel you must return to Connecticut, put it out of your mind."

"Mother's not the reason."

"You can't be thinking about Linley?" Paxton asked, horrified at the thought.

"It's not Linley either."

He grabbed her arms, prepared to pull the answer out of her if necessary. "Then what?"

"It's me," she admitted and dropped her eyes.

"You? I don't understand. What is stopping you?"

Cornelia could feel the bubble of tears nearing the surface and fought to keep them from erupting and robbing her of her dignity.

"Cornelia, this is your brother you are talking to. The one whom you've pulled out of more scrapes than anyone could imagine. We're always pulled together. You don't have to pretend with me. Let me help you, or at least share your burden this time," he urged. "It's my turn to support you after all you've done for me."

"Paxton," she began hesitantly, "do you know why Linley divorced me?"

"Because he thought you were cheating on him."

"That, yes. But after thinking about it, I think the real reason was because I-I am barren."

"What?"

"I can't have children, and in order for Linley to inherit from his father's estate, he must produce

323

an heir. I can't have children. Do you understand?" she cried. "Even though I love Locke, I can't marry him because I can never give him the children he wants and deserves," she ended, sobbing.

"How do you know it's you? Linley never did like children."

She covered her face with her hands. "Stop trying to make excuses for me."

"All right, no excuses. But your solution is almost as simple as mine," he offered cheerfully.

She glared at him and waited. How could there be a solution? When he did not offer an explanation, she wiped her nose and dried her eyes. "All right, Mr. Magician, let's see you wave your magic wand and solve my problem."

"You remember all those poor street urchins we passed after we got off the train in Denver, on the way to the hotel?"

Cornelia pictured all the scrawny children who had given her pause when they had first arrived in Colorado. "Yes."

"Well, you and Locke can adopt a dozen to raise. Giving birth to a child is only one facet of being a parent. The most important thing is rearing a child and giving it love. It doesn't truly matter who gives birth to it; it will be yours the same as if you had birthed it."

Locke had been listening closely for nearly an hour as brother and sister had poured out their troubles and shared secrets. Although he wished that Cornelia had had enough trust to confide in him, he now understood what was keeping her from accepting his proposal.

The doorknob to Carrie Simington's room turned. She was up from her nap. The last thing he needed was to have that woman discover him eavesdropping and blab to Cornelia. Cursing his luck, Locke was forced to leave his position without hearing the rest of the conversation.

With the quietness of a cat, he slipped into Cornelia's bedroom across the hall from Paxton's and climbed out the window. As he headed back to his cabin, Locke's mind was filled with Cornelia's concealed pain and thoughts of how much he wanted a family. Settling down near a stream to think, Locke spun everything around in his mind. He loved Cornelia . . . and he wanted a family.

Chapter Thirty-three

The first chill of evening was settling on the ground by the time Locke left his perch by the stream and headed toward his cabin. He had reached a decision, and all he had to do now was to make Cornelia understand.

He had spent hours surrounded by the silence of the forest. Two young fawns had scampered nearby, reminding him of playful children and a long-held desire to have a family. Being out among nature had given him time to think clearly. Locke always had been considered a methodical man, not given to impetuous decisions. So, although there never really had been but one choice all along, he had considered every option.

By the time he neared his cabin, Locke had concluded how he was going to proceed with Cornelia. As he broke the clearing in front of his rustic home, he stopped.

The front door had been flung open, and yellow light spilled out on the steps. Pulling out his gun, Locke moved under the front window with the stealth of a thief. With great care, he angled up enough to peek through the glass, then gave a huff, and shoved his gun back in its holster.

He stomped around to the front door and

barged into the room without preamble. "What the hell are you doing here?"

At the harsh question, Paxton swung around. "It's about time you returned." A sudden spasm grabbed him, and he doubled up.

"You can stop the theatrics, I overheard you and Cornelia talking."

It was another minute before Paxton was able to oblige Locke. "I'm afraid that while I may not be afflicted with consumption, I do have a bit of a cough," Paxton said in response. The thought crossed his mind to ask what Locke had overheard, but he squelched it since he was already in a rather precarious position, and Locke looked none too happy to see him.

Not wasting time on formalities, Locke grated out, "What do you want?"

"Mind if we sit first?"

The aroma of coffee perking filled Locke's nostrils. "Since you have already made yourself at home, it seems to make little difference what I mind."

"Coffee? I made a fresh pot."

"Get to the point."

Paxton gingerly sat on the bed and watched as Locke turned a chair around and straddled it, then proceeded to glare at him. "I came on Cornelia's behalf."

"What's the matter, can't Cornelia speak for herself?" Locke said, annoyed that the man was getting involved in what should be a personal, private discourse between Cornelia and himself.

"I am quite capable of speaking for myself, as you so eloquently put it," Cornelia said.

Locke swung around. Cornelia stood framed in

327

the door, the warm yellow light creating an arc of gold about her. The vision made him speechless, bringing him back to his senses only when she stepped inside the cabin and turned on Paxton.

"When you disappeared from the cottage, I had a distinct uneasy feeling you might show up here," she said with reproof in her voice. Then she pinned Locke with a stare. "What has Paxton been telling you?"

Paxton could have sworn he saw sparks fly off Cornelia's tongue, she was so angry. When Locke did not immediately offer an explanation, Paxton's gaze shot to him. Locke had gathered to his feet facing her, his features hard set into a scowl. Gingerly, Paxton eased off the bed. Holding himself away from the pair, he inched his way toward the door.

"Where do you think you are going?" she demanded just before Paxton could make good his escape.

"Let him go," Locke answered for Paxton, who had lost his tongue.

Paxton nodded and started to leave again until Cornelia snapped, "Stay where you are."

"Get out of here," Locke barked.

Cornelia swung around. "Then I am going with him."

Before Cornelia had a chance to take more than two steps, Locke was behind her and grabbed her arm. He was seething, and Paxton did not need further encouragement. He fled the cabin.

"Let go of me," she growled like a cornered animal.

"I let you go once back in Leadville, and I am not going to do it again. You are going to sit down and talk to me if we have to remain sequestered here until spring."

The words out, Locke ushered her to a chair. "Sit down."

Cornelia wasn't sure whether she should be grateful to Paxton for forcing her to face Locke, or whether she should be furious with Paxton and even more furious with Locke, the way he was strong-arming her. But one way or another, there would be a resolution of the situation before she left.

"All right, I am sitting," she spat. "Now what?"

"Now we talk," he returned, pulling up a chair and sitting down directly across from her.

"About what?" she demanded. Despite a secret longing to empty her mind of all the secrets she held, she could not let him think he was going to get away with acting the frontier bully.

"About us."

"What about us?"

Locke raked his fingers through his hair. She was acting like the pushy broad he'd first met back in Denver.

"I asked you to marry me, if you will remember," he grated out.

"I remember," she practically shouted. "How can I possibly forget?"

"What are you trying to say? That you are trying to forget?" he shouted back.

Paxton had stopped behind the first tree and listened until he heard raised voices. He smiled to himself. It was a good sign. The pair was just angry enough to get everything out into the open before they realized what they were saying. Then their problems could be resolved, and he would get a new brother-in-law; he was sure of it. Feeling quite content with his handiwork for one day, Paxton bundled his jacket up around his neck and headed back toward the cottage, whistling as he headed toward the horse tethered nearby.

"How can I possibly forget when you are yelling at me?" she shouted.

"Me yelling at you?" he bellowed, throwing up his hands.

"That's what I said."

"I have never 'yelled' at a woman in my entire life," he shouted. "That is until you came along."

"Until I came along! What gives you the right to start sounding like a wounded boar now?" She kept her voice at his level.

"Because I love you, and you are not making it easy!"

"Well, I love you too!"

Locke bolted from his chair and stomped around the cabin. "Then why don't you just accept my proposal, for God's sake? You would think that I am in the habit of offering myself daily, the way you act."

"The way I act?" She got to her feet and stood directly in front of him, glaring. "And just what is wrong with the way I act?"

He glared back. "That is an easy one to answer. You act like you love me; you tell me that you do. Then you up and leave me hanging after I propose. That's what wrong with how you act!"

She huffed out a breath of indignation, threw her balled fists on her hips, and thrust her face into his. "Well, I shan't leave you 'hanging' any longer."

"Good."

"Yes, good."

For a long moment, they sparred off at each other in bristling silence. "I thought you weren't going to leave me waiting any longer?" he snorted.

"I'm not!" She was so livid that the secret she had carefully harbored from him barreled to the end of her tongue and leaped off. "I did not accept your proposal because you want a family, and I can't give you one."

The instant she finished her tirade, she felt her anger begin to crumble and her shoulders slumped.

"Don't quit on me now," Locke spat, afraid she was going to retreat from him.

Her eyes shot to the ceiling, and she bit her lip. "Oh, don't you understand? I can't marry you because you want children and I am barren. I can't have children," she said with a sob.

"Did you ever think to ask me which was the most important to me?" he said in a softer voice now that the truth was out into the open and they could deal with it.

"People marry to have children."

"Maybe they do, maybe they don't. Did you ever think to ask me why I intend to marry again?"

She compressed her lips and turned from him. "No."

He was right behind her, circling her in his arms, his breath warm and inviting on the back of her neck as he nuzzled his face in her hair.

"Why don't you ask me, Cornelia?"

"I can't."

"Ask me," he whispered, holding her tight against him.

She was thankful he did not attempt to make

her face him, for she was certain she would cry if he did. When he held her, she almost felt that everything would be all right.

"Please ask me," he murmured again.

She could not force herself to ask the question that would end the sweet time she had had with him. More moments passed until what she had feared occurred. She found herself being pivoted around to face him.

Locke raised her chin until their eyes met, hers filled with hesitation and dread. "Ask me," he ordered softly. "Ask me."

"All right. Why do you intend to marry again?" she barely whispered in a strangled voice.

His heart sang as it soared. "Because I love you more than life itself. I overheard you talking to your brother earlier, and it doesn't make any difference."

She pulled out of his embrace. "You were spying on me?"

"Didn't you hear what I just said?" he said in disbelief.

"Yes, I heard you and I am delighted. But you had no right to listen in on Paxton and me!" She forged ahead in a steamy voice.

"For your information, I proposed marriage to you, so I had every right," he returned with the same exasperation in his tone.

"I haven't accepted."

"What do I have to do—"

"You might try proposing again," she said in an even voice.

"I may need my head examined for wanting such an exasperating woman. But, dammit, I love you and you are going to be my wife!"

332

Cornelia hid a smile at his proposal. "Well, since you put it so eloquently, I accept."

He bent his head to kiss her. She ducked. "With one stipulation."

He looked suspicious. "Stipulation?"

"Yes. I'll accept your proposal," she shouted, "on the condition that I enjoy the same right to make decisions for myself."

Locke recalled Paxton telling him how her mother, then her ex-husband had ruled her life. He had already decided their marriage was not going to be like that. "Done."

"Good. Then that's settled," she exclaimed. "But you still had no right to eavesdrop!"

"All right," he roared back, "I had no right. But at least, you finally admit you're going to be my wife. And if you want children, we'll adopt a houseful!"

"Good," she spat.

In response, he bellowed, "Good."

For a few more moments they stood and stared at each other, out of breath. Then they both started to laugh until tears were running down their faces and they thought their sides were going to split.

"Oh, God, I love you, woman," Locke said after he recovered himself.

Cornelia's exuberance faded and her tears of laughter were replaced with tears of immeasurable joy.

"What's the matter, aren't you happy about our engagement?" he asked, confused with her sudden change.

She sniffled. "Of course I'm happy. I just can hardly believe it, is all."

He kissed her forehead. "You better believe it."

"Oh, Locke, all during my marriage to Linley, we tried to have a family—"

"Shh, you don't have to tell me about it. It's not important. It doesn't matter."

"But it does matter. If we are going to put it behind us, I have to tell you."

"All right. But why don't I pour us a couple of cups of coffee, and then you can tell me everything."

Grateful for this wonderful man, Cornelia took a seat at the table and watched him gather the cups and pour the coffee. She still could not believe her good fortune although the pain of not being able to give him children lingered deep within her heart. Firming her resolve to accept his love as a gift from God, Cornelia forced herself to tuck the pain away.

Without the slightest reservation, Cornelia related the whole story of why Linley had wanted a family and her failure to give him one. He asked about the divorce, and she told him every detail. Not once did he look startled or disappointed in her, which caused her love for him to grow all the more.

By the time she finished sharing her life's story, the coffee was cold and she was exhausted. She watched Locke go to the coffeepot as if he knew she needed fortification.

As he poured, she said, "There is one more thing."

He refilled his cup and sat down.

"That letter I received from Mother. She said that Linley had paid her a visit, and she hinted that he may be open to a reconciliation, and wanted to know where I had gone. Oh, Locke, you don't think he would consider traveling here, do you?"

Locke's face turned dark, and all humanity seemed to leave him when he said, "It won't do him any good if he does."

"But what if he tries to cause trouble?"

"If he does, he will be sorry because he will have to answer to me."

Cornelia was startled at the venom in his voice. At the same time, she was thankful that there was little chance of Linley ever giving serious consideration to coming to Colorado and wanting her back.

Chapter Thirty-four

Paxton was sitting on the porch, listening to Carrie chatter when Locke and Cornelia drove up in his wagon. He glanced at his watch, then at the sun. It rode high in the sky. He stepped off the porch, his shadow almost directly beneath him.

"Morning," Paxton said, a smirk on his face as Locke helped Cornelia down. "Or should I good afternoon?"

"You shouldn't say anything," Locke grated.

Undaunted, Paxton grinned. "Fair enough."

Carrie rushed to join Paxton and hovered over Cornelia. "I missed you last night, Cornelia. At first I was worried when I discovered you weren't anywhere to be found in the cottage, but Paxton assured me that you were quite all right."

Cornelia looked up at Locke, then back at Carrie, a bright smile on her face. "Yes, I was 'quite all right."

"Anyone can see that. You are virtually glowing," Carrie chirped.

Paxton scratched his ear. "Yes, a healthy glow, Sister dear." When Cornelia did not volunteer the reason for her happiness, Paxton prodded, "Well, do you two have an announcement to make?"

Locke cocked a brow. "You have a lot of nerve

336

for someone who ought to be concerned for his own health."

For an instant Paxton thought he perceived a threat but relaxed when he saw that Cornelia was making a futile attempt to suppress a smile.

"I should be angry with you for trying to interfere, but instead I think I will give you a big kiss," Cornelia announced and planted a kiss on Paxton's cheek.

"Does all this mean what I think it does?" he asked.

"Yes," Cornelia answered.

"I knew it. I knew getting you two together would work," he crowed and pumped Locke's hand.

Carrie stood watching the whole scene with bemusement. "I do not understand. What is going on?"

Locke slipped his arm around Cornelia's waist and pulled her to his side. "Cornelia has consented to be my wife," he announced, pride evident in his voice.

"I was wondering when you were going to get around to asking her. It certainly took you long enough. Lamantha and I knew it was just a matter of time back in Leadville. I simply must write and let her know she was right all along."

"No doubt my sister suggested you keep an eye on the situation just in case everything did not work out the way you two decided it should."

Carrie shrugged off his annoyance. "Well, it did. And I am most happy for you. When is the wedding?"

Cornelia and Locke looked at each before Cornelia said, "We haven't set a date yet."

"How about right after Locke guides my expedition up Longs Peak?"

Locke's expression turned dark. He opened his mouth to inform her he was not going to serve as her guide when Cornelia laid a hand on his arm.

"Carrie, I think you should know that Locke has no intention of guiding you up to the summit of Longs Peak."

For weeks as summer gave itself up to fall, Locke held firm to his resolve. Despite all Carrie's machinations, he refused to be moved. He ignored his sister's letters on Carrie's behalf, put up with Carrie haranguing him nightly, and disregarded Paxton's urgings that he relent so they all could get some peace and quiet.

Locke had half expected Cornelia to join the crusade on Carrie's behalf, but Cornelia had not been feeling well, which further determined him not to leave her side. She was not getting better, and he was plagued with a nagging suspicion that McCurdy could be behind it, the way the man had vowed revenge against Cornelia. Although McCurdy had not been seen in the Park, Locke quietly kept a vigil over Cornelia.

Locke had sent the doctor out twice, and both times Cornelia refused to see the man, locking herself in her room. The doctor had finally left a bottle of medicine with instructions that Locke humor her and merely keep watch over her and let him know if she worsened, since a woman with so much fight in her could not be too ill.

Locke was leaving the cottage after seeing that Cornelia returned to her bed to rest when Carrie cornered him by his horse. "Why are you being so obstinate?" she demanded.

"I'm not being obstinate, as you put it. I am simply not going to guide you up the mountain."

"Why?"

"I told you. You aren't strong enough to make such a climb."

"Why? Because I am a woman?"

"I just told you why. Your gender has nothing to do with it. Besides, Cornelia has been under the weather, and I have no intention of leaving her."

"She only has a little tummy upset."

"Look, if you want to make the climb so bad that you ignore common sense, then get someone else to guide you," he said with finality. Not waiting to listen to any further arguments, he swung up into the saddle and spurred his horse toward his cabin.

Frustrated, Carrie watched him ride away, then turned back toward the house. To her surprise, Cornelia was standing at the window. She hadn't put much effort into eliciting Cornelia's aid, not wanting to bother her but Carrie was getting desperate. If she didn't make the climb soon, she would have to wait until spring, and she had no intention of spending the winter here. She also intended to have Locke as a guide.

Carrie waved to Cornelia and headed toward her room. Locke adored Cornelia, and Carrie was sure that if she got Cornelia to support her, he would have to relent.

Without knocking, Carrie squeaked open the door. Cornelia was bent over the chamber pot. "Oh, dear, your stomach is still bothering you. Perhaps you should call in the doctor. You do not seem to be getting better."

Cornelia wiped her mouth and slide the pot under the bed. "It is just some bug. I told Locke I don't need a doctor, and now I am telling you: I do not need a doctor."

339

"You can be stubborn," Carrie said. "Why don't you want to see a doctor?"

"I don't need one. Carrie, why are you trying to force a doctor on me?"

"I was just thinking."

Cornelia settled back into bed. "What were you thinking, Carrie?" Cornelia asked. It was obvious that the woman was up to something.

"Actually, I was thinking that once you are feeling better, you might consider making the climb up Longs Peak with me. I recall that back in Leadville you showed an interest in the mountain."

Cornelia slapped her hand to her mouth and waited until the latest wave of queasiness passed. "Carrie, even if I were interested in going up the mountain, I am not up to it now. And besides, Locke already told you he was not going to guide you."

"Locke doesn't have to be the guide," she fibbed. She wanted the best, and that was Locke. "As soon as you are feeling better, I'll engage someone else." Carrie went to the door. "And to make sure that you are well soon, I am going to find out where the nearest doctor is located and see that he looks in on you."

"Carrie!"

The click of the door shut off Cornelia's protest. Cornelia started after the woman, but a new wave of nausea overtook her, and she rushed back to the chamber pot just in time. She lost the remaining contents of her stomach. If she weren't so fatigued, she would go after Carrie, but she did not have the strength.

Carrie looked back over her shoulder, expecting Cornelia to try and stop her from summoning a doctor. Cornelia had not followed her, which made

340

Carrie all the more determined to have someone examine her.

"Oh, Paxton, here you are. I have been hoping to talk to you."

"I've been over visiting Joe Mills."

"Every day?" she asked.

His lips tightened. "Yes, every day. And I shall continue to go over to Annie's cabin daily until she agrees to talk to me. Carrie, if you want to talk to me about convincing Locke to be your guide, I'm afraid it is no use. The man is not about to cave in; he is not going to guide you up the mountain. I have done some climbing in the Alps while I was in Europe. Will I do?"

"Thank you for the offer, but Locke is the best, and I have my heart set on him."

Paxton shrugged. "Good luck then."

Carrie took Paxton by the arm and ushered him into the parlor and closed the doors. Actually, I wanted to see you about Cornelia."

"What about Cornelia?" Paxton asked, edging down on the couch.

Carrie settled next to him and placed her hand over his. "I'm worried about her. She has been under the weather for weeks and refuses to see a doctor."

"Cornelia's always been fearful of doctors," he said. Thoughts of the pain she had suffered when she broke her ankle as a child reminded Paxton of why Cornelia had shied away from doctors since then. The doctor had nearly crippled her for life when he bumbled setting her ankle.

"She is not getting well on her own, so it is time we do something to help her. Who is the nearest doctor?"

"Doctor Jones, about five miles toward town."

Carrie jumped to her feet. "Hitch up a buggy. I am going to pay Doctor Jones a visit."

In less than a half hour, Paxton had the buggy ready in front of the cottage. "Want me to drive?" he asked Carrie as she headed toward him.

"Certainly not. I am quite capable." She ignored his efforts to help her up onto the seat. Once she was settled and had a good grasp on the reins, she said, "You stay here and take care of your sister until I return with the doctor."

"I was going back over to Joe Mills's place," Paxton said.

"The man can wait until I return," Carrie instructed and laid the whip to the horse's rump.

Paxton watched the buggy wheels kick up dust as she drove from the yard. The fine powder made him sneeze and caused him to double over with spasms. As he was straightening up, he thought he caught sight of a shadow lurking behind a shrub.

"Annie! Annie! Is that you?" he called out.

No one answered.

Paxton went to the shrub, but no one was there. He knelt down and ran his hand over the ground. The leaves had been disturbed. He looked around the cottage, but there was no sign of anyone. If Cornelia didn't need him, he would have hurried over to Annie's place. He was sure she must be coming around, since he was sure it was she who had been spying on him. Anxious for Carrie to return, Paxton went inside the house to check on Cornelia.

Carrie drove the horse at a steady clip over the rough dirt road. She caught sight of the mountain peak standing proud in the distance. She was concerned about Cornelia, but she also had to conquer that mountain before she moved on to her next adventure.

Not far from town, Carrie slowed the horse. There was a fork in the road, and Paxton had not told her which one to take. Off in the distance a rider came toward her. Saved from making a mistake, Carrie stood up in the buggy and waved at the stranger.

"Thank goodness," she said when she recognized Locke.

Locke shaded his eyes against the sun. "What are you doing out here?"

"I am on my way to fetch the doctor for Cornelia."

Locke had been annoyed by the woman's presence, but news that Cornelia had finally agreed to see a doctor softened him toward the eccentric woman. "Cornelia finally agreed to see Doc Jones?"

"Not exactly."

Worry creased his brow. "She's not worse, is she?"

"Well, no. But I think it is time we force her to see someone."

"I sent the doctor out twice, and she refused to unlock her door, if you'll recall."

"I think she is feeling poorly enough now that she won't put up such a fuss this time."

"For once we are in complete agreement." Perhaps having Carrie stay with Cornelia had its advantages after all, Locke thought.

Breaking into Locke's ruminations, Carrie said. "Well, what are you waiting for? Direct me toward the doctor's house."

"Go back to the cottage; I'll go for the doctor."

Carrie began to protest, but Locke cast her a look that brooked no argument. "All right, but do not tarry."

Locke rolled his eyes and reined his horse toward Doc Jones's place.

When Locke returned to the cottage with the doctor in tow in record time, Carrie was pacing back and forth on the porch. "It is about time," she chirped. "Do hurry, Doctor."

"Any change?" the doctor asked.

"Well, Cornelia has finally agreed to see you."

"She must be feeling worse," the doctor said.

"She does have a green tinge to her."

"I see."

Locke had listened to all the talk he could tolerate. He grabbed the man by the arm and ushered him to Cornelia's door. "You're here to take care of Cornelia, not to visit with Carrie."

The doctor raised his brows at Locke's impatience, remembering how the man had forced him to drive all night to look in on the woman's brother only to discover that Paxton Lloyd had a case of the ague.

Locke knocked and received a "come in" from the other side of the door. He started to enter, it was the doctor's turn to take his arm. "Wait in the parlor while I consult with my patient."

Locke scowled at the man but nodded his consent and left the doctor to his patient. But Locke was not about to wait in the parlor; he hovered near the outside of the door.

Cornelia was sitting on the bed holding her hand over her mouth when Doc Jones entered. "Well, what seems to be the problem?"

Cornelia was hesitant at first, but the doctor's gentle bedside manner won her over, and she described her symptoms and allowed him to examine her.

Anxious to get relief from the strange malady, she watched him put his stethoscope back in his black bag, then sit back in the chair next to the bed, and cross his legs.

"Well?" she urged.

"You have no idea what is causing your illness?" he asked.

"I thought at first I might have eaten something to make me ill. But I have been very careful for the last few weeks."

"I see."

Cornelia sat up straight on the bed and crossed her legs. "Since you obviously don't know, I shan't waste any more of your valuable time."

"Young lady, I know what is *ailing* you."

"Well then, would you mind letting me in on it."

Doc Jones was taking a long time, and Locke was getting impatient outside Cornelia's door. He stopped and raked his fingers through his hair. He was just about to start another round of pacing when Cornelia's scream of "no" issued from her room.

On the other side of the door, a glimmer of astonishment flickered into the doctor's eyes before he caught himself. "You, young woman, are definitely pregnant."

Chapter Thirty-five

Cornelia's scream brought Locke crashing through the door. He rushed to Cornelia's side, followed by Paxton and Carrie.

"Are you all right?" Locke asked, searching her face. He clasped her shoulders. "What's going on in here?"

Cornelia was sitting on the bed, her hands clasped over her mouth, her eyes filled with disbelief. She looked to be in shock, causing Locke to swing on the doctor.

"If you hurt her, you'll answer to me."

Doctor Jones cleared his throat. "I-I can only assure you that—"

"I am fine, Locke," Cornelia interceded.

"Then what's going on?"

"Yes, do tell us," Paxton and Carrie chorused from the background.

Cornelia studied the worried faces. "The doctor got a needle out of his bag and was trying to give me a shot." She said sheepishly. "I'm sorry if I frightened all of you. You see, I am deathly afraid of needles. Please, I won't scream again."

Paxton opened his mouth to comment, but Cornelia's silent plea stopped him. "Come on, Carrie, we'll go back to the parlor. Locke, why don't you join us so the doctor can finish without further interruption."

"I think that is a good idea," the doctor seconded.

"Please, Locke," Cornelia urged. "I'll be fine now."

Locke thought she was behaving rather strangely, but he grudgingly said "all right" and closed the door behind him.

The instant Cornelia was alone with the doctor, she scrambled to the edge of the bed. Trembling, she forced herself to say, "Doctor Jones, there must be some mistake. It can't be. It is impossible."

"I am afraid it not only is possible, but I'm ninety-nine percent certain. You have all the symptoms. You, young woman, are pregnant."

She ran her palms down the sides of her face. "How?"

Doc Jones looked surprised. "You mean to tell me you have no idea how babies are conceived?" He scratched his head. "I haven't ever had this conversation with a grown lady before, but I suppose if you really don't know I ought to explain it to you."

"No, no." She blushed. "I mean, I know how babies are conceived. But I can't be having one," she said, incredulous.

"You not only can, but you are," the doctor insisted.

"But I'm barren," she said and hung her head.

"Young woman, I don't know who told you such a ridiculous thing, but you are not barren. I've brought hundreds of babies into this world, and believe me, I know when a woman is in a motherly way. You aren't very far along. I'd say about a month by the symptoms. When was your last monthly?"

Cornelia thought about it. She hadn't kept track; there had been no need since the divorce. Then it hit her. "Oh, my goodness, it's been at least two months."

Cornelia didn't know whether to laugh or cry. She cradled her queasy stomach. Never once had she considered her nausea as symptoms of pregnancy, but when she appraised all the symptoms carefully, she realized the doctor must be right; she was pregnant with Locke's child.

Snapping out of her reverie, she grabbed the doctor's hands. "Are you sure? You couldn't be mistaken, could you?"

"I'd say in another eight months you will have your proof."

She gasped and jumped up, twirling around the room. A baby! She and Locke were going to have a baby!

"Once you settle down, might I suggest we go tell the father-to-be?" the doctor suggested. Everyone in the Park was aware that Cornelia and Locke had been keeping company, so it really came as no surprise to the man. Babies often didn't wait for marriage certificates.

"Doctor Jones, I'd like to be the one to break the news," she said. "Would you mind not saying anything to anyone just yet?"

"Well, of course, I can understand you will want to be wed first," he said. "You can rely on my discretion. Now, I suggest you keep a tin of crackers by the bed and nibble on them before you rise in the mornings. That'll help settle your stomach. And

348

don't worry, this *sickness* of yours will pass, and you'll feel rightly real soon."

Cornelia hugged the man. "Thank you. Thank you. I can't tell you how happy you've made me."

"Young lady, I had nothing to do with your present condition."

"Thank you anyway."

Cornelia watched from the window as the doctor fielded questions. He was a sly old fox, she thought, listening to him inform Locke, her brother, and Carrie that there was nothing to worry about. Before the man drove away, another wave of nausea grasped her, and she rushed back to the chamber pot. Only this time she hardly noticed the gripping spasms. She was too ecstatic. She was going to have Locke's baby.

What Paxton had said was all coming true: She was better off away from Linley and her mother. She was actually going to be happy with Locke and a family of her own in Colorado.

Linley scowled at Margo's flat belly. He had been pumping her nightly for months until recently without result. Of course, an heir was only secondary. He enjoyed sticking it to her. She was incredible in bed, never failing to come up with innovative positions. She was the total opposite of his barren ex-wife, and Linley knew he would never tire of Margo—even after he got his heir off her.

The thought of an heir and his inheritance caused his scowl to deepen. Margo was proving to be difficult. He had never known a woman whose monthly lasted so long, but since they had visited the Stag and Hound and he had announced that they would be going to Colorado, she had denied him her favors. He knew it was out of spite; it was her way of getting revenge. She did not want to go to Colorado and had let him know it in no uncertain terms.

"Come on, Margo. If you don't get a move on, we'll miss the train."

She lay back against the mounds of pillows and crossed her arms over her chest, effectively cutting off Linley's hungry view of her ample breasts through the sheer fabric of her nightgown. "I don't care. I am telling you, I don't think it's a good idea. Furthermore, I don't want to go to Colorado; it's such an uncivilized land."

"And I have told you over and over again, nothing can go wrong."

"You had better be right," she warned.

"I am," he reassured her. "And we won't be gone for very long."

"Yes, I know, just long enough to squeeze the little bit of money your ex-wife has out of her. Why not just let her have it?"

"Would you rather Zenas Joshaby broke both my legs?"

Margo's gaze shifted to his growing crotch. "As long as he doesn't harm your more important parts, I'd just as soon remain in Connecticut."

He was beginning to lose patience. "You know we can't be married until I get her signature on those damn papers."

She gave him a coy pout. "True."

"Wouldn't you like to have a little fun in Colorado?" he coaxed, now that she seemed to be weakening.

"Well, I have to admit it might be interesting to see your wife squirm."

"Then hurry and get dressed. After I tend to my business, we'll see that Joshaby gets his due, and then you can have all the fun you want."

Margo grudgingly admitted that there would be no deterring their trip to Colorado, but they would leave when she was ready and not before. She reached up and pulled Linley's face down to her breasts. "It's been too long. Why don't we work on that little heir of yours first?"

Linley tore the flimsy fabric from Margo's body and slurped hungrily at her breasts, his hands roving over her smooth flesh. "You've denied me for too long," he said and clamped his teeth on a nipple.

She let out a little yelp. "Well, I'm not denying you any longer."

Careful not to let him see her gaze shift to the time, she watched him stumble out of his clothes in a heated rush to mount her. As he drove into her, Margo bit his shoulder and began to meet his pounding thrusts. They would go to Colorado, but it would not be today.

Cornelia still could not believe her good fortune as she dressed to go into the parlor and break the news to Locke. They were going to have the family they both wanted. She thought about all those years with Linley when her efforts to conceive had come to naught. She could not understand how now it had suddenly happened without trying. She finally came to the conclusion that love had played a major role. That was it. She loved Locke so much that God had answered her prayers.

She was so filled with excitement and wonder as

351

she slipped into her shoes that she did not hear Carrie enter the room.

"My, my, you seem to feel better already," Carrie gushed. "Doctor Jones must be a miracle worker."

"Yes, I guess he is."

"Oh, that is wonderful. Since you will be good as new soon perhaps we can make our climb before it is too late in the season," Carried enthused.

Cornelia went to her window and looked out at the magnificent mountain, so seemingly unapproachable in all its flaming grandeur. She had given a great deal of thought to the expedition with Carrie after the woman had suggested it. Of course, that was before she learned she was pregnant.

Cornelia swung around to inform Carrie that a climb would be out of the question now. Carrie rushed forward and hugged her.

"Oh, you can't imagine how much this climb means to me," Carrie announced. "Most men do not think women are capable or strong enough, your Locke among them, but we know better, don't we?"

Cornelia listened to Carrie and realized she was right. Locke had said all those things back in Leadville and in the last few weeks in Estes Park. Cornelia had discovered since bringing her brother to Colorado that she was strong and capable. He had promised when they were engaged that he would not stand in the way of her independence, and Cornelia had to admit she wanted to climb the mountain with Carrie.

"Yes, I suppose we do," Cornelia agreed.

"Then you'll make the climb with me?" Carrie asked. She held her breath as she waited for Cornelia to respond. She knew Cornelia's newly found freedom was important and hoped that she had said just enough to make Cornelia agree to go with her.

Cornelia thought a moment longer. She was only a month pregnant. Surely it couldn't harm the child she carried, and it would make a wonderful story to tell the child someday. Locke could serve as their guide, which would make the expedition safe. She was sure he would relent after she reminded him of his promise. A smile came to her lips.

"All right. We'll climb to the summit together." Another bout of nausea hit her. "Right after I am feeling better."

"Right after you are feeling better what?" Locke said.

Cornelia startled, and Carrie stepped back. "Oh, Locke, I'm glad you're here. I have something to ask."

"Why do I get the distinct impression that I am not going to like whatever it is you are going to ask me," he said. His eyes trailed to Carrie and back to Cornelia. Those two were up to something.

"Doctor Jones told you that my illness is nothing serious, I heard him," Cornelia said.

Locke's brows drew together. "Yes," he answered. He was thankful that McCurdy had had nothing to do with it and relieved that the doctor had said her illness would soon pass, but a sense of foreboding continued to plague him.

"Well, since I feel better already, I was thinking . . ."

That could be dangerous, he groaned inside when he noticed Carrie's bright countenance.

". . . I intend to go up the mountain with Carrie," she blurted out.

Carrie watched Locke's face turn stormy dark

and promptly made her exit. Paxton was just entering the room, and she pushed him back and shut the door. "I think it would be wise if you and I were out of earshot."

At that moment Locke bellowed "what" and Paxton decided that Carrie was right; it was the wise who did not put themselves in front of a raging frontier bull. "I think you're right. Let's go for a walk."

As they left the cottage, they heard Cornelia's voice rise in harmony with Locke's.

She was glaring at him. "I am going to climb Longs Peak with Carrie."

He ignored her glare. It took all he had not to shout when he replied, "You are not."

"Oh, yes I am," she announced. "I am a free and independent woman. And in a few days when I am feeling better, I am going on Carrie's expedition."

They were nose to nose, those eyes fighting a silent battle in a stare-down. Each expecting the other to relent and look away first.

"You are engaged to me, and I say you are not going."

"Need I remind you of your promise that you would not interfere with my choices?" she snapped.

"No," he conceded.

She kept her glare even with his. In rebuttal to his flat unreasonable declaration, she gave him an ultimatum. "Then you can either serve as our guide, or you can let your male pride get in the way and remain here until I get back."

Secretly, she hoped his male pride would not keep him from relenting. She knew if he headed the party, all his fears for her safety would come to naught.

"Why are you being so stubborn?" he grated out in a soft reproof.

"Because this is something I must do."

"What? Prove to yourself that no one is ever going to control you again? Cornelia, I'm not like your ex-husband," he added, hoping to reason with her since putting his foot down had only served to make her more determined than ever.

Cornelia balled her hands on her hips. Fighting down another urge to vomit, she said quietly. "Then prove it. Take us up the mountain . . . please."

She looked so imploringly beautiful, and when she used that soft sultry voice, he knew he had lost. She was going to go with or without his approval. She would go without him, and he could not let her go with anyone else.

"All right, dammit, I'll take you up the damned mountain. But I want you to know that I think you will be sorry. Carrie Simington isn't strong enough, and you have not been well."

She ignored his final objections and threw her arms around his neck. "Thank you. I knew you would not let me go without you. When do we leave?"

Locke walked to the window and glanced at the mighty peak. It was late in the season, and he didn't like it. He didn't like it one bit. "Oh, hell, as soon as you are ready. But don't say I didn't warn you."

Chapter Thirty-six

Once Cornelia was aware of the reason for the nausea and supplied her room with an ample inventory of crackers, which she nibbled on before arising, she began to feel better. She knew it was too early, but when she felt right below her belly, she could have sworn she noticed just the slightest swelling. Her cheeks took on a new glow, and her world seemed close to perfect except for Locke's silent disapproval of her expedition with Carrie.

Although Locke said nothing further, Cornelia was sensitive to his exasperation by the tight set of his lips and his clipped answers in response to her questions about what to pack.

"If you are set on going through with this, get rid of everything but what you can carry, and make sure you take your warmest clothes because you're going to need them."

He went to the door, needing to go outside and cool off before he broke his vow to accept her foolishness.

"Locke, Carrie and I will be ready tomorrow morning."

"Yeah, sure," he grunted.

Her voice stayed his departure again. "Oh, and Locke, Paxton has requested to go along. I told him we could use his help. He has been trying so hard to make up for lying to me. And with Annie still refusing to talk to him, I think it would be good for him if he went along with us."

Locke sighed. "What's one more?"

"He has done some climbing in the French Alps," she defended Paxton.

"Great, just what I need, someone who thinks he's an expert. Oh, what the hell, be ready to pull out at dawn," he said and left, shaking his head.

Cornelia rushed to the door and caught sight of the dappled sun glinting his ebony hair auburn. He was rubbing the back of his neck as he walked away from her. Despite the way he felt, he was going along with her. Her heart filled with love. "Locke?"

He swung around, shading his eyes from the sun. "Yeah?"

"I love you."

Despite his acute frustration with the woman, a tender smile came to his face. "Love you too, Nellie."

Humming, Cornelia went to hunt up Carrie and Paxton and inform them that they would begin the ascent tomorrow morning.

There was a light blanket of frost on the ground when Locke arrived at the cottage with a wagon to transport Cornelia and the rest of the party to the base of the mountain. He loaded their belongings in silence, merely grunting when first Cornelia, then Paxton tried to engage him in conversation. He was in no mood to pretend to humor anyone. All he

357

wanted was to get the damned climb over with, but even as he spurred the horse toward the lofty peak, he could not get the sense of apprehension out of his mind.

Cornelia sat bunched up against Locke as the wagon moved slowly toward the mountain. She could feel the warmth of Locke's leg and longed to have him put his arm around her. She noticed Paxton and Carrie on the other side of her. They seemed lost to their own thoughts.

"How long do you think it will take?" Cornelia asked, attempting to break the silence again.

"What?" Locke grunted.

"The climb. How long will it take?"

"Three days."

"Oh."

"Do you like my outfit?" she asked, determined that he was not going to remain silent the entire trip. "Paxton borrowed the clothes from Joe Mills."

Paxton's head snapped up when he heard his name. But he and Carrie had decided last night not to irritate Locke further than he already was, so Paxton sagely kept his remarks to himself.

Locke looked her over. He had to fight hard not to smile at her preparations. From her heavy boots and baggy trousers to the old leather shirt and three or four waistcoats over it, she looked as if she was prepared to brave a blizzard. "Suppose you'll do."

"Thank you, I think."

When he made no further response, she refocused her attention on the mountain, which seemed to be growing grander as they neared its base. She was spellbound by the splintered gray crest sprinkled with patches of snow.

At the base of the mountain, they transferred to

358

the saddle horses Locke had arranged to have waiting. Cornelia watched as Locke packed each horse with camping gear, quilts, foodstuffs, and water for three days.

"What are you waiting for?" he asked when Cornelia did not immediately mount her horse as the others had done. "Have a change of heart?"

She had been feeling a little queasy, but his brusque tone made her fight down the urge to seek respite for an hour or two until it passed. She took a cracker out of her pants pocket and chewed it with a vengeance. Choking the dry crumbs down, she walked over to the horse. "I'm ready now. Help me up, will you?"

Locke laced his fingers and gave Cornelia a boost up, then mounted his own stallion. Heavily loaded, they rode for hours through grassy meadows, fording streams, making abrupt ascents and descents. The winds whipped up as they climbed, and distant thunder and lightning added to the magnificent mountain canvas painted in changing hues of rustic pines, golden aspens, cottonwoods, and jagged boulders brushed in reds and blues and greens and grays.

They stopped to rest the horses, and Carrie and Paxton settled down to rest. They both looked quite done in to Cornelia. "Are you two feeling all right?"

Paxton nodded his head. "Just gotten a little soft after not doing much these last couple of months."

Cornelia patted his shoulder in understanding. "How about you, Carrie? You look as though you are ready to give out."

Putting her hand to her ashen cheek, Carrie forced a weak smile. "Nonsense. I'm fine."

"If you insist," Cornelia said and went to join Locke.

Locke was standing with his back to them next to a trickle of a stream fringed with splinters of ice, his foot up on a rock.

"The trail looks as if it gets steeper from here," Cornelia remarked.

"It does." He pointed out the path they would be taking, describing what lay ahead in detail. "Can't you see that this is no place for you and Carrie Simington? The weather looks as if it might take a turn for the worse. Have you noticed those clouds off in the distance? Can you imagine what it is like up on the mountain in a storm?"

"Locke, please, can't we make the best of it?"

Locke rubbed a hand over his mouth. "Cornelia, this climb is a mistake. Just look at your brother and Carrie. Neither one is in any condition for such an arduous trip. You haven't been feeling well either. And if the weather does turn ugly, God only knows if I'll be able to get you all off the mountain in one piece. Why can't you just admit it was a bad idea so we can turn back before a tragedy occurs?"

"Nothing is going to happen," she insisted. "Besides, Carrie would never agree. You know how much this means to her."

He let out a sigh. "In that case, go tell your *hardy* trailblazers to mount up."

"Can't we rest just a little longer?"

"Not if you want to reach the summit." He went to his pack, pulled out some jerky, and handed it to her. "Pass this out. We won't be making camp until evening," he said and walked away.

They rode on up the steep trail, through thick virgin forests that thinned as they continued upward.

Cornelia tried to focus on the tumbling waterfalls, the plains below and the gorges that framed them. Despite the glorious scenery, her mind kept drifting back to Locke.

They made camp in a clearing with a view of the grand crater side of the peak. Snow lay thick in its crevices, and Cornelia shivered. She guessed the temperature had already dropped below freezing. It was colder than she had anticipated, and she wrapped a quilt around her shoulders and over her belly, to protect her unborn child.

She was sitting before the huge fire Locke had built with a chunk of bread and boiled beef when Paxton joined her. "I've been meaning to ask you about your aversion to needles," he said and took up a place next to her.

"Isn't the view magnificent from here? It would make the perfect model for you to paint."

"Don't try to avoid me, Sister dear. Needles have never bothered you. What's going on?"

Subconsciously, her hand went to her belly and she looked down. "I don't know what you're talking about."

His eyes followed her line of vision, and he noticed the protective way she was holding her stomach. "I think you do. You aren't pregnant, are you?" Cornelia's lip trembled. "Oh, my God, you are, aren't you?"

She slapped a hand to her mouth. "Don't tell Locke. He would never let me make this climb if he knew."

"I'm going to be an uncle," he announced to the stars. He knew she had been mistaken when she'd told him she was barren.

"Shhh!"

"You can't keep this from him. You have got to tell him. Maybe going back isn't such a bad idea after all under the circumstances. Carrie is exhausted. My God, the woman has already turned in for the night. Why not just tell Locke. He'll make the decision so Carrie won't be upset with you."

She shook her head. "No."

"You either tell him, or I am going to."

"Not until I make this climb."

"Tell him," Paxton argued.

"I can't do that!"

"What can't you do?" Locke demanded as he joined them.

"Nothing," Cornelia insisted. "There is nothing I can't do now that we are going to be married."

She was withholding something from him. She scooted over and leaned into him, and his ire faded. He draped his blanket over her shoulders. "You are impossible."

"One of the things you love about me?"

He rolled his eyes, the silver speckles glittering gold in the firelight. "Right."

"Well, I'm for bed," Paxton announced. He rose. "I'll leave you two." He directed a stare at Cornelia. "I'm sure there are a lot of things you two have to discuss before morning." His gaze grew more pointed. "Until morning, Cornelia."

Cornelia pinched her lips; Paxton was serious. "Goodnight, Brother dear."

"What did he mean by all that?" Locke wanted to know once they were alone.

Cornelia studied his face. It was so full of his love for her that she was sure he would have to understand. She expelled a breath. If she didn't tell

Locke tonight, Paxton was going to in the morning. He would be furious if he found out from someone else. She had no choice.

She took his hand in hers and drew it to her lips. She kissed his palm. Then looking up into his expectant face, she took a deep breath. "Locke, I have something to tell you." Suspicion filled his eyes, and she wished she had told him about her pregnancy before.

"It's about time," he said. He knew she had been hiding something; he had felt it in his gut.

She had opened the door, and now there was no turning back. She had to tell him. She took another deep breath and swallowed hard, trying to think of the best way. But as the tension built, her head began to pound until she blurted it out rapid fire, "I am with child."

"You're what?" he questioned.

He just sat there calmly. She had expected him to be furious, which would have been better than the emotionless statue that sat next to her.

"I said I am going to have a baby. Your baby."

"You're sure? I thought you couldn't have children."

Annoyed by his response, she snapped. "Yes, I'm sure. "I was as surprised as you are."

She waited for a further reaction as she watched the play of emotions dart across his face.

"I see. And just when did you plan to inform me that I am going to become a father? After the child is born, possibly?"

He spoke softly, but Cornelia knew he was now livid with her; she could see it in his tight jaw and narrowed eyes.

"I had been meaning to tell you, honestly, but the

363

opportunity did not seem to present itself."

His restrained fury unleashed, and he echoed with an incredulous roar, "The opportunity did not seem to present itself!"

"Well, at least you are finally showing some emotion. I would have thought you would be overjoyed," she snapped.

Locke threw up his hands. "My God, I *am* overjoyed! But you should have told me before we started on this expedition. First thing tomorrow morning, we are heading back. I am not going to have the mother of my child endangering herself and the child by climbing to the summit of Longs Peak."

"That is exactly why I didn't tell you," she bit out.

"Well, you did."

Cornelia looked about. He had awakened Carrie and Paxton, and they were looking their way. "Please, can't we discuss this in private without disturbing the entire camp?"

"There is nothing to discuss."

She knew she was on shaky ground. She had been wrong for not telling him, but she just couldn't turn back now. "How about a compromise, or are you going to renege on your promise?"

"Don't try to throw my promise back in my face at a time like this. I love you. I shall always love and respect you. But when you take unnecessary chances with our baby, I am not going to stand idly by, do you hear me?"

"Yes, I hear you," she retorted. "I'm sure everyone can hear you."

"Good," he said on a harsh note. "Then everyone knows we are heading back tomorrow morning."

His point made, he softened. "When is our child due?"

She glared at him until her temper calmed. "About eight months. I never guessed my 'illness' could have anything to do with being pregnant until Doctor Jones examined me. I thought I was barren."

"So that's what all the screaming was about that day."

She shrugged. "I was shocked. I had wanted a baby for so long. It is still difficult to believe."

Locke suddenly reached over and embraced her. He kissed her so gently, so tenderly that Cornelia wanted to cry with joy. Then he slipped his hand to her belly while he gazed into her eyes. "Cornelia, I could take you over my knee for not telling me about the baby sooner." With great emotion, he added, "You can be stubborn and pushy, but so help me God, I love you. As soon as we get back to Estes Park, we'll be married. How does that sound?"

"It sounds wonderful," she answered.

But as he held her, murmuring how happy he was about having a baby, her mind was churning, and she wondered how he would feel toward her if he knew what she was thinking.

Chapter Thirty-seven

Long after Cornelia had turned in next to Carrie, she lay awake. She looked over at Carrie. This climb had meant so much to the woman, and Cornelia too hated to think that she would have to quit the trek. She mulled everything over in her mind again until she had reached a decision. Locke had been so happy once he had announced they would be turning back that she almost felt guilty for what she was about to do.

"Carrie," Cornelia whispered. Her breath came out like a white cloud, it was so cold. "Are you awake?"

Carrie rolled over and looked at Cornelia. "Yes. I'm truly thrilled for you," she said less than enthusiastically. "I heard Locke tell you that we would not be continuing up the mountain." Then in an anguished voice. "Oh, Cornelia, must we give up the expedition?"

"You don't have worry about going back tomorrow morning," Cornelia answered. She knew what had been on Carrie's mind; it was the same thing that had been on hers.

Carrie propped herself on her elbow. "You mean Locke has had a change of heart?"

"Not exactly."

"What exactly?"

Cornelia looked around. The full moon illuminated the camp. She could see Locke and Paxton clearly. They both slept soundly, letting out soft snores that emboldened her.

"You really want to climb to the summit, don't you?" Cornelia said.

"Of course. More than anything."

"How would you like to be the first woman to climb to the summit without benefit of a male guide?"

"We don't know the way."

"I managed to glean detailed directions out of Locke yesterday while he was describing what to expect on the way."

"But your pregnancy?" Carrie set out. She was worried about Cornelia's scheme, but the excitement at the prospect of reaching the summit surged through her veins.

"I am only a month along. My unborn child will hold the record for being the youngest to make it to the summit of the American Matterhorn."

"The American Matterhorn," Carrie echoed. "Longs Peak has been called that. All right. When do we go?" Carrie suppressed a giggle. She felt giddy at the idea. Cornelia had captured her adventurous spirit.

"Now."

They exchanged conspiratory smiles and silently gathered their things, all the while keeping one eye on Locke and Paxton. Once all preparations had been completed, they managed to lead the saddle horses away from camp without alerting the men.

It was utterly freezing, and Cornelia experienced

another twinge of guilt before she recalled how she had been the meek wife. Determined not to be led around again, she firmed her nerve and spurred the docile horse up the trail. But chagrin soon claimed Cornelia at the lava beds when she discovered that they would have to abandon the horses and continue on by foot. Taking everything they could carry, the two women forged on.

Locke had felt such contentment after hearing that he was going to become a father and they would be turning back in the morning, that he had retired and slept more soundly than he had in years. As the pink streaks of morning crossed the sky, Locke realized he had overslept. Normally, he would have been up before dawn, ready to pull out. But, of course, it was not crucial this morning since they would be returning to Estes Park.

Locke yawned and sat up. Paxton was snoring. Locke looked over toward where Cornelia and Carrie had made their beds. It had been so cold last night that the two women had totally burrowed under their mounds of blankets. In no hurry to awaken them, Locke rose and began gathering firewood for breakfast before they started down.

"Morning," Paxton said when Locke returned with an armload of wood.

"Morning."

Paxton glanced to where Cornelia had bedded down. She was still asleep, so he decided it was the perfect time to make sure she had told Locke the truth. "Cornelia talk to you last night?"

"She told me about her little secret, if that's what you're getting at," Locke answered without looking up as he tossed wood on the fire.

"Just found out myself about the baby last night," Paxton said. "Congratulations."

"Thanks." Locke thought to question why Paxton had known about the baby but thought better of it. He knew brother and sister were close. "We'll be heading back to Estes Park right after breakfast. I don't want Cornelia to take any chances in her condition."

"Have to admit, I'm glad," Paxton offered. "The weather doesn't look too good off in the distance."

"Why don't you wake Cornelia while I put the coffeepot on?"

Paxton nodded and strolled over to where the women slumbered. He crouched down next to her bedroll. "Cornelia, it's time to get up."

No response.

"Cornelia?"

He shook the mound of blankets.

A sickening sense came over him when his hand sunk in the soft hill. He pulled back the blankets and his eyes went wide. "Locke! Locke!"

At the urgent tone in Paxton's voice, Locke rushed to join Paxton. "What's wrong?"

"They're gone."

Locke let out a string of curses as his eyes roved over the blankets rolled to make it look as if the women were asleep. "Dammit! I should have known she accepted going back too easily."

A loud roll of thunder shook the ground, and Locke swore again. Rushing to break camp, he ordered, "Get down to Joe Mills's place and bring help."

"But can't we both go after them?"

"Chrissake, they don't know the trail; they'll

likely get lost, and we don't have a lot of time. You see that storm brewing? If it hits the mountain, the weather will drop to subfreezing temperatures, and they'll never be able to survive if we don't get volunteers up here to help find them first."

"Right." Paxton swallowed hard. "Right. Don't worry, I won't let Cornelia down."

"Just get going," Locke ordered. Not waiting for Paxton to collect himself, Locke mounted his horse and rode off in the direction he had noted the tracks led.

Paxton's heart raced with fear for his sister as he spurred his horse down the mountain. The animal stumbled and Paxton nearly lost his seat, but he could not afford to fail Cornelia this time as he had when her marriage had been arranged for her. If he hadn't gone to Europe, Cornelia would have had him to stand up for her when Talbot had offered for her. Now she was taking her life in her hands to prove her independence, and he could not let her perish trying.

The sun was high overhead when Paxton charged up to Mills's cabin. He reined the horse to a halt and promptly tumbled off the animal's back with a thud.

Annie and Joe had heard the urgency of the pounding hooves approach the house and ran outside to catch sight of Paxton hitting the ground.

Thinning her lips, Annie marched out to where Paxton sat in a daze, rubbing his head. "If you think that by acting like you are hurt, you will get my attention you're wrong!"

"Maybe next time, I'll have the horse kick me in the head," he groaned and crawled to his feet.

"Hopefully, that would elicit a more favorable response," he added and stumbled past her.

Annie's mouth dropped open at the sharpness of his tone as she watched him weave by her and approach her pa.

"Joe, there's trouble on the mountain." Paxton held his head, swaying as his vision blurred.

Joe caught Paxton as he tottered precariously. "Annie, put that pride of yours aside, and help me get this boy into the house."

Annie had had all she could do not to go to Paxton when she had seen him fall off the horse, and she needed no further encouragement. Rushing to his side, she put his arm around her shoulders.

"No, no, you must help," Paxton muttered as they supported his weight and helped him into the house.

"Let's get him into your room, gal. He needs to rest."

Over his mumbled protests, they managed to get him on the bed. Annie rushed to get a damp cloth for his head while Joe unfolded a blanket to cover him with.

His head clearing, Paxton blurted out. "No, don't bother with me. You have got to hurry and get some men together. Cornelia needs help."

Joe stopped his efforts at the urgency in the boy's voice. "What you talkin' 'bout, boy?"

"Cornelia and Carrie Simington sneaked away from camp last night and went up Longs Peak alone. Locke sent me for help. Please, we've got to find them."

Paxton tried to rise, but Joe shoved him back down. "You ain't goin' nowhere till that bump on your head goes down. Annie'll see to you till it

371

does. Now, tell me all you know, so I can be of some use."

Annie returned and stood in the doorway while Paxton explained what had happened. All the while she listened, her eyes kept trailing to him. She had missed him so much she ached inside just looking at him.

When she noticed her pa rub the back of his neck, her mind spun with his advice about Paxton. Although her pa didn't have much book learning, he was rightly smart when it came to the business of living. He had told her that getting Paxton to declare himself was as simple as fishing. Paxton had already taken a nibble and set the hook, even if he didn't know it yet. Now all she had to do was to let him flounder around until he got tired of fighting and then reel him in.

"Annie," Joe said, causing her smile at what he had advised to fade. "See to the boy. Boy, you get some rest."

"But Cornelia's my sister. I have to be there to help her."

"Rest first. Then Annie can bring you up to where we set up base camp in a couple of hours. And don't you go worryin' none, we'll have them ladies found safe and sound by the time you two meet up with us." Reluctantly, Paxton nodded his consent. "Smart boy. Meanwhile, I'll get a few of the men together and head on up the mountain."

Joe winked as he passed Annie. "Simple as fishin'," he whispered.

"Yes, Pa," she said and hid a big grin behind her hand.

Instead of going right to Paxton's side and putting the damp cloth to his brow, she fumbled through a drawer and plunked an old hat on her head first.

"Why the devil did you put that thing on for?" Paxton asked of the beat-up old cotton hat with hooks stuck in around the base of the crown.

"Just thought it was time I go fishin', is all," she answered. She sat down on the edge of the bed and laid the cloth across his forehead.

"I don't understand."

"Don't rightly expect you do, but you will."

Paxton grabbed her hand before she could pull away. Although he was worried about his sister, he could not let Annie get away from him now that he had the opportunity to straighten everything out with her.

"Please don't leave, sweet girl. I've been trying for weeks to talk to you."

Annie's hand went to her favorite fishing cap as she bolted to her feet. "If you got nothin' more 'n excuses to offer, I ain't got no time to listen."

It took all the strength she could muster to turn and walk away from him. She was almost to the door when he called out.

"No! Wait! Don't go. Please."

She stopped but did not look at him. Her heart was hammering so fast that she thought she was going to faint.

"Annie, I can't stand not being with you," he blurted out. "Please, come back and talk to me."

Let him flounder until he tires, then reel him in. The words echoed in her mind as she pivoted around to face him. Clasping her hands in front of her to still their trembling, she slowly walked back toward the bed. *Let him flounder until he tires, then reel him in.*

"You ready to be reeled in yet?"

"What?"

"I meant, you got a real hunger yet?"

"Oh," he said and accepted what she explained at face value. "Actually, my hunger is for you." Annie's gaze dropped, and he took her hand before she had a change of heart and decided to run from him. "I've missed you so much. I guess I didn't realize how much I truly cared for you until you weren't around me anymore. I can hardly stand not seeing you and touching you. I miss holding you and hearing your laughter. I miss just being near you. Oh jeez, Annie girl, all I've done is think of you. I can't think of anything else. So I have come to a decision."

"A decision?" she echoed, tensing.

"What I mean is, I-I, ah . . ." He choked up and his voice trailed off.

Annie plunked down on the bed beside him. Silently, with hopeful eyes, she encouraged him to declare himself before she was forced to take drastic measures.

"What you mean is?" she prompted and nodded her head as if she were leading a band.

Paxton swallowed. "What I mean?"

"Paxton Lloyd, you are the damnedest fish I've ever tried to land."

"What?" he questioned, confused by this sudden obsession with fishing.

"Oh, never mind." She bounced to her feet with a frown and ripped the hat off her head, shaking it at him. "I don't got all day to stand here while you sit there funnin' with me."

"I don't know what that stupid hat and fishing has to do with anything. But I love you—"

"You've said that before. But it don't change nothin'. You can't drink milk from a cow that don't belong to you. You got to get your own, and then the milk will be twice as sweet."

"You mean, I should marry the cow?" he asked.

She scowled at him. "You callin' me a cow?"

He stood up until he was eye to eye with Annie. "I'm not calling you anything, sweet girl. But if you would accept, I'd like to call you my wife."

Without reservation, Annie threw her arms around his neck with such vigor that she knocked him back on the bed, landing on top of him.

"Ouch!" Paxton exclaimed and pulled a hook from her hat out of his arm. "Those hooks can be dangerous," he complained.

Annie grabbed the hat, and looking down at him, she rained smacking kisses all over his face. Suddenly, she ceased kissing him and stared into his eyes.

"You are askin' me to marry you, ain't you?"

Paxton leaned his head back and laughed, then wrapped his arms around her. "Yes, my Rocky Mountain Girl, I am asking you to marry me."

"It's about time."

"Well, will you?"

She sat up and plunked the hat back on her head. "Okay, you can ask me now," she announced.

He pulled her back down and cradled her face. "Will you marry me, Annie?"

"That's a silly question, what do you think I been waitin' for all these weeks? Of course I will. The sooner, the better."

Paxton had expected another shower of kisses, but instead she bobbed back up, pulled the hat off, and tossed it across the room.

"Now do you mind telling me what that was all about?"

Annie shrugged. " 'Course not. Pa said that gettin' you to propose marriage was like going fishin'. So I let you flounder around, not talkin' to you until you got all tuckered out. Then I just reeled you in."

"And the hat?"

"My favorite fishin' hat."

She was so sincere and serious that Paxton had to beat down a bubble of laughter at her incredible tale as he rubbed the spot on his arm where the hook had pricked him. Quietly he vowed to always let her think that her father's advice had worked. Then he thought about it for a moment and wondered if it actually had.

"Pax?" she questioned. "You look like your mind is a hundred miles away. Are you worryin' about your sister?"

The mention of Cornelia brought Paxton out of his happy musings about Annie. He bounded off the bed with Annie close behind.

"Where do you think you're goin'?"

"To help find Cornelia. And don't try to stop me. I feel fine now."

She grabbed her coat and one of her pa's hanging on the hook near the door as they passed. Thrusting the garment at Paxton, she said, "Put this on, you'll need it. Cornelia is goin' to be my kin too and needs *our* help."

Chapter Thirty-eight

Locke drove his stallion hard as far as the lava beds. There, at the expanse of large and small boulders, he found the women's horses. A loud clap of thunder reminded him that he did not have a lot of time to locate them before the storm could move in. Dismounting, he checked the two animals.

After a brief survey of the area, he picked up their trail and tracked them to the notch. He left the horse and made his way along the knifelike ridge, past chasms that framed mirror lakes fringed with lush forests far below.

By the time he had made his way past the "gate of rock," the black stormclouds were almost overhead. The afternoon had turned bleak, and the temperature was plummeting. The freezing wind had picked up and howled around him. As he climbed, he scanned the crevices below, fearing he would find Cornelia lying broken on the jagged rocks.

He rounded a bend and saw Cornelia clinging to a four-foot ledge jutting out from the rugged trail winding just out of her reach. Carrie was huddled beneath a blanket on the trail seven feet above her. His line of vision scanned the mountain. Above them were four thousand feet of towering, ice-encrusted rocks cloaked in forbidding majesty.

"Cornelia?" he bellowed, fearing she had been hurt or worse.

"Locke," she answered in a voice quivering with fear.

"Locke! Thank God," Carrie screamed hysterically as she came out from beneath her blanket. "Hurry. You have to help her. Please hurry. Please."

Ignoring his own safety, Locke rushed up the trail. As he reached Carrie, the first flurry of snowflakes were starting to fall.

He peered over the edge. Cornelia was half sitting, half lying along the narrow tier. "Cornelia," he rasped out, "Are you all right?"

Sniffling back sobs that threatened to overcome her, Cornelia looked up into those warm brown eyes. She had half expected him to lecture her for pressing on after he had decided to turn back last night, but his face was only filled with concern.

"I'm a trifle cold," she answered and brushed the coat of white from her hair. "Please hurry and help me off this ledge. I would prefer not to spend the night here," she added with a measure of bravado she did not feel.

"Don't worry. And don't try to move. I'll have you safe in a few minutes."

"I am safe," she insisted. "I simply slipped and seem to be stuck."

Locke sat back on his haunches and shook his head. She was frightened but refused to show it. Not wasting a moment, he rummaged through the bag he had strapped to his back.

"I hope you won't be too upset with us," Carrie managed, wringing her numb hands.

He sent Carrie a disgusted look, then went back to work uncoiling a rope and working it into a slip knot. "Upset? I ought to wring both your necks. You two could have been killed."

"I know, and I am truly sorry. I know I am going to be breaking a confidence, but I am going to share a secret with you. Climbing the mountain means more than just conquering the summit to us. It is a symbol—"

"Yeah," he grumbled as he worked to get Cornelia off the ledge. "It could have symbolized both your graves."

"Please understand. Conquering the mountain for Cornelia means that she will finally be able to surmount and triumph over her fears of the past. The mountain is like the obstacles standing in the way of her happiness. Once she has shown she can ascend the peak, there is nothing that can come along in her life that she cannot meet head on and prevail over. Don't you see?"

He finished tying a knot around his waist and, handing her a section of rope, glared at her. "What I see are two women who could have lost their lives on this silly mountain. Now wrap this rope around your waist, and hold on to my legs while I lean over the ledge and try to get Cornelia off it in one piece," he directed without sympathy.

Carrie dropped her eyes and said no more. She silently followed his orders and prayed as he knelt down.

"Cornelia, grab this rope and slip it around your waist. I've made a knot, and it will tighten

379

as I pull you up. Just hang on. You hear me?"

"I hear you, but my hands are so cold I don't think I can hold on to the rope."

Without hesitation, Locke removed his own gloves and dropped them to her. "Put these on."

Cornelia's fingers were stiff, but she managed to slide the fur-lined gloves over them. "Good girl. Now slip the rope over your head. Good. You ready?" Cornelia nodded. "Okay, carefully stand up."

She looked down, and all her bravado fled. Below the ledge was a sheer five-hundred-foot drop. "I can't. I'll fall," she cried. A scream echoed up her throat, and she fought to beat it down.

"You won't fall; I've got you. I'm not going let the mother of my child go that easily," he said with laughter in his voice in an attempt to calm her.

At his tone, Cornelia forced a brave smile. "I warn you, if you drop me, I won't marry you."

"You have nothing to worry about then. I have no intention of allowing you to renege on your promise to be my wife."

The snow was coming faster, and Locke could not work his fingers as the temperature fell rapidly. After two attempts, he realized he was not going to be able to get her off that ledge before his hands went completely numb. He stopped and surveyed his options. Settling on the most feasible, he turned to Carrie. "Guess if my bride won't come to us, we're going to have to go to her."

"No! I can't go down there. Cornelia slipped and was lucky to have landed on that ledge," Carrie cried.

"Shut up and stop blubbering. We don't have time. Pretty soon, we're all going to be frozen if we don't do something and now."

In soothing tones, Locke explained to Cornelia that they were going to have to come down to her and all descend together. She looked so forlorn, almost as if she was about ready to give up.

It was much easier to lower Carrie to the ledge and shimmy down the rope than to pull Cornelia up in the wind and snow. It took him only a few minutes to spread his slicker over them. It required all three of them to keep it from blowing away, or he would have hugged Cornelia to him, he had been so worried about her.

"What are we going to do now?" she hollered to be heard over the howling wind.

"Catch our breaths, and then get off this ledge before nightfall," he yelled back.

"I can't! I can't!" Carrie screamed. "We'll all be killed if we try to move off this ledge."

To Locke's surprise, Cornelia slapped the hysterical woman, and she calmed down. "Carrie, I'm sorry," she apologized. "But we must listen to Locke, or we shall be killed."

Carrie just shook her head. "You needn't worry further."

"Good. Now listen carefully," he said. "One at a time, we are going to tie this rope around our waists. I'll go first. There are some rocks jutting out from the ledge leading down to a ridge. From there, if we are very careful, we will be able to hold on and inch our way back to the trail."

"But the snow, the wind!" Carrie cried. "We'll never make it."

"We have to. It is our only chance," Cornelia admitted.

"That's right. Remember it. It is our only chance. We must get back to where my horse is. It is carrying enough supplies to survive the night, and there isn't any time to waste. Ready?"

Each took a turn tying the rope. Locke let go of the slicker, and the wind whisked it away. Snow swirled around them, nearly blinding them in its freezing white torrent.

It felt like an eternity as Locke plastered himself to the side of the cliff and used the rocks sticking out from the rock face to inch his way around to the ridge. Cornelia watched in horror as his foot slipped, and he grabbed at the rocks, catching himself before the mountain could claim him.

The trail—and safety—was three feet on his right. It was now or never. Locke took a deep breath and launched himself toward the boulders. He grappled with the footing and finally managed to crawl onto the trail.

"I made it," he yelled at Cornelia. "Now it's your turn."

Cornelia and Carrie embraced, and then Cornelia began to move toward the ridge. A gust of wind caught her, and she screamed as she lost her footing and plummeted down the precipice.

Locke braced himself and held on. He glanced up at Carrie. Despite the woman's fright, she had held her position, and between them, they broke Cornelia's fall. She dangled at the middle of the rope. With superhuman strength, he pulled her up until he could reach out and grab her.

"Oh, God," he said, kissing her scratched face,

"I'd never let you go. But now you must help me with Carrie. Can you do that?" Cornelia was shaking. She nodded. "Good. Just sit down behind me and hold on to the rope. Okay?"

By the time Carrie could be coaxed to start toward the ridge, the snow whipped about them in blizzard proportions. She closed her eyes, said a prayer and put her foot out onto the rock. Locke's hands gripped the rope, and he guided her along until she reached the ridge.

"Now I want you to jump to me, and I'll catch you. We both have hold of the rope, so you can't fall."

Carrie filled her lungs with air, pinched her eyes shut, and launched herself.

Locke grabbed her.

It was another half hour before they were back on flat ground and almost dark by the time they reached his horse. Nearly frozen, Locke managed to make camp, and they crawled into the shelter to wait out the night.

Carrie sobbed herself to sleep almost immediately. Locke took Cornelia into his embrace and held her.

"I guess I should have known better," she admitted.

"Frankly, I don't know what I am going to do with you."

She cuddled deeper into his embrace. "Just love me."

"I do." He nuzzled his chin in her hair. "I do."

"Locke," she whispered. "I'm sorry. But I had—"

Shushing all further efforts to explain why she had had to disregard his warnings and attempt the climb without him, he held her until she fell asleep from exhaustion. As the wind whistled outside, Locke remained awake thinking about what Carrie had said back up on the trail above the ledge. Finally, he, too, fell asleep with his arms closed tightly around Cornelia.

The sun rose bright, glaring cold against the blanket of snow around them when they left their shelter. The storm had passed almost as fast as it had come, leaving the mountain sheathed in a pristine white.

Cornelia rubbed her arms in the bitter cold. "I suppose we should be on our way back," she announced.

Carrie was right behind her and, looking longingly to Locke, waited for him to order them to break camp.

He made no effort to start picking up.

"I know I undoubtedly will require Doctor Jones to make a thorough examination of my head. But since you two made it this far, it'd be a shame not to finish the climb."

He barely had a chance to get the last word out before Cornelia hugged him. "You won't regret it." She looked at Carrie. "Will he?"

"I sure hope not. Let's get outfitted and finish conquering this damned mountain," he announced. What he did not say was that Carrie's telling him how important reaching the summit was to Cornelia decided him to forge ahead last night.

Five hours later, they had scaled the last five hundred feet after many stops to catch their breaths every few minutes. Standing on the summit, a nearly level acre of boulders with steep sides cascading downward all around them, Cornelia rejoiced at her victory as she gazed out from her mighty loft.

Locke came and circled his arms around her as she took in the unrivaled vistas below them. "You won," he said softly, recalling the secret Carrie had shared with him.

"Won?"

"Yes. This is your victory. Now nothing or no one in your life can ever force you to submit meekly. You have proved you are strong enough to surmount any obstacle in your path. From this day forward, you'll be able to meet whatever happens head on and conquer it."

She cast him a strange look, then her gaze trailed to Carrie. For an instant, she thought about an earlier conversation with Carrie. Carrie was busy studying her surroundings. "Have you been talking to Carrie?"

He kissed her forehead. "Cornelia, you are a winner. Never forget that," he said, evading answering her.

She leaned against him, viewing the awesome sight from the summit and let her question drop. "No, I shan't."

It was late afternoon by the time they had collected Cornelia's and Carrie's horses. Not long after they had mounted and were riding through the drifts of snow, they encountered the search party.

Paxton caught sight of the three riders and spurred his horse forward. "Cornelia! Cornelia! My God, are you all right?"

He pulled up alongside his sister. "We were so

worried about you. Why did you go and pull a dumb stunt like that? You could have been killed," he lectured her.

Cornelia listened quietly, sneaking a peek at Locke. He had not berated her as Paxton was doing, and her heart swelled that she was so lucky to have Locke's love. "As you can see, I am quite fine, as is Carrie."

Paxton's gaze shifted from Cornelia to Locke to Carrie as the other riders reached them.

"Any casualties?" one of the men asked.

"No. I'm happy to report that the two mountaineers are none the worse for wear," Locke announced to the group of five men.

Cornelia noticed Annie among the men and her gaze shot to Paxton. "I see you and Annie must have made up."

Paxton beamed. "Looks like there may be a double wedding, Sister dear."

Cornelia congratulated them. "I am so happy you two have worked out your difficulties."

Paxton's chest puffed out with pride, then he sobered. "I'm sorry you didn't have the chance to climb to the top of the summit, but I'm sure you now realize what a mistake it was to attempt it."

"But we did climb to the top," Carrie announced. "And it was simply grand!"

All eyes shot to Locke in disbelief.

" 'Fraid it's true. They were almost there by the time I reached them. I merely accompanied them the rest of the way after the storm passed," he explained.

Cornelia and Carrie shared knowing grins and

silently thanked Locke for not divulging their near mishap, or his heroics. Cornelia knew Carrie was grateful, and Cornelia quietly jotted down in her memory another thing she loved about Locke. He was allowing them to retain their glowing success without glorifying his own part.

"Well, I'll be," Joe said, scratching his head.

The group exchanged small talk for another fifteen minutes before one of the men suggested they head back to Estes Park before it was too late to ride down to the base of the mountain before dark.

As they rode, Carrie chattered on in a steady stream to the five men about how she and Cornelia had conquered the mountain. Paxton and Annie rode together, and Locke and Cornelia brought up the rear.

"Now that we're on our way back, why don't we hunt up a preacher tomorrow morning and get married?" Locke suggested. "I don't want anyone counting when we announce our expected blessed event," he added.

Cornelia was filled with such pride for having scaled the peak and with such total love for the man who had made her success possible that she reined in her horse and slid off the animal's back.

Uncertain what he was about to face with her now, Locke motioned for the others to continue down the mountain without them. He joined Cornelia, who had seated herself on a rock and was waiting for him.

"Something wrong with getting married tomorrow?" he asked as he approached her.

Her face was implacable when she said, "As a

matter of fact, there is. I would much prefer it if we found a minister tonight."

He breathed a sigh of relief. "Chrissake, woman, you had me wondering what obstacle we were going to have to overcome next," he said as he joined her on the rock.

"No more obstacles," she announced in between kisses.

"While I would love to remain here kissing you, we had best head back before we end up spending another night up on the mountain," he suggested and pulled her to her feet.

Arm in arm, they strolled back toward the horses. "Would that be so bad?" she said.

"I can't think of anything better than being alone with you. But first I am going to get you back to where it is warm."

He helped her remount, and as he swung into his own saddle, Cornelia said, "For the first time in my life my world is perfect. From now on nothing can mar my happiness."

Chapter Thirty-nine

The moon had already risen by the time they said good-bye to the men in the search party. Paxton had insisted on seeing Annie home. He had winked at Cornelia and announced that he probably would not be back until morning since he had a lot to discuss with Joe.

Once they reached the cottage and had a chance to clean several days' worth of mountain soil from their bodies, they sat down in the kitchen to a warming pot of coffee. Not waiting to drain her cup, Carrie stood up and thanked Locke. She was exhausted and proclaimed plans to sleep quite soundly for at least a week.

"I guess it is my turn to thank you," Cornelia said as she cleared away the dishes.

Locke watched her move about the tiny kitchen. "You don't have to thank me."

"But I want to . . . properly." She took his hand and led him toward her room.

To her surprise, he stopped and swung her around to face him. Then he took the crook of his finger and lifted her chin until she was staring into his eyes.

"Cornelia, what are you doing?"

She snaked her arms around his neck. "What do you think?" she breathed.

To her further surprise, he removed her arms. "I am not sure what to think."

"Locke, today I learned more than just being able to surmount the obstacles that are put in my way on top of the mountain. I also learned that if I want something, the best way to get it is to go after it—not to wait, hoping it will come to me." Then with a soft whisper, she murmured, "Lockforde Breckenridge, tonight I want you."

Locke grinned. "I can see that taking you to the summit definitely has its advantages." He rubbed his chin. "Let me see, which mountain should we climb next?"

She leaned into him. "I know exactly which challenge I intend to take on next," she said and kissed him.

Locke lifted her high into his arms and took her to her room, closing the door with the heel of his boot. "Lady, I am no challenge. You have already conquered me." He set her down on the bed and began to unbutton her shirt.

She batted his hands away and sat up, pushing him down in her place and leaning over him. "Tonight, I want to show you how much I've learned."

He cocked a brow. "I have a better idea. Tonight, we'll take turns. You kiss me, and I kiss you," he suggested, reaching up to sensuously stroke the side of her cheek with the back of his hand.

Cornelia felt her heart screaming *yes* inside her chest. Matching his actions, she ran her hand up his cheek. It was stubbly with three days' growth of whiskers. "How can I argue with that?"

He pulled her to him and nibbled on her upper

lip. "No arguing tonight, Nellie." He finished working the buttons on her shirt and slid the garment from her. Cupping her breasts, he stared into her eyes and watched her reaction. "I like to know that I am pleasing you," he whispered in a husky voice.

Cornelia trembled when he coaxed her nipples into tiny peaks between his fingers. With shaking hands, she followed his lead. She worked the buttons on his shirt free and rubbed his chest, letting the wiry hairs covering him slip between her fingers.

Locke groaned and pulled her down until her breasts brushed back and forth against his chest. "I love the soft feel of you."

He positioned her next to him, then peeled away her skirt. Slowly, he removed each shoe, massaging her feet and kissing her ankles as he rolled her stockings down her legs. Her hips lifted of their own accord so he could strip the last of her clothing away. She lay still while he appreciated her with his eyes, but inside she was throbbing with desire for him.

"I want to see you, too," she breathed and reached for him.

"Your command is my wish." Without wasting a moment he undressed and straddled her.

His erection nested in her woman's curls, pressing against her when he bent over and kissed her. Cornelia's mind swam with delicious thoughts as his tongue recaptured hers in a lover's rhythm over and over. Hungrily, their mouths met and tasted in drugging sensations while his hands enticed and enslaved her body to respond to his.

In seemingly endless, burgeoning tension, his fingers memorized her body as he moved about her. Promising and coaxing, outlining every inch of her, he left a trail of fire everywhere he touched.

Out of control, her body took on a mind of its own, responding wildy when he delved inside her. Riding his hand, she caught her breath time and time again. On the brink of a blazing wave that threatened to engulf her, she closed her eyes and clamped her thighs together, straining for release from such sweet torture.

When she looked up at him, his eyes had darkened. He brought his hand to his lips. "You taste so incredibly sweet; I'll never be able to get enough of you."

"We're supposed to take turns tonight," she reminded him.

She slid her hands down the tense muscles of his chest, over his flat belly, and around the rigid, satiny male part of him. He throbbed in her hand, and she delighted in his response to her. She wanted to give as much as she received. She increased her stroking until he let out an animal growl and shifted her onto her back.

"Do you know what you're doing to me?" he asked.

Staring up into eyes heavy with passion, Cornelia knew. "The same thing you are doing to me," she whispered.

His hand rode down her breasts to her belly. There, he stopped and leaning down, his hands gripping the sides of her hips, he kissed the beginnings of the gentle rise. Then playfully nipping at the dark curling hairs, he angled up to her navel. "Prepare for a wild ride, junior," he murmured.

With a joyous tear-filled smile, she kissed the top of his head. "I think he is ready," she said hoarsely. "At any rate, I am."

"God, I love you," he said fiercely, changing the mood.

He positioned himself over her and eased inside of her. Ever so slowly, he began to move, building the tension, prolonging their release.

His strokes were slow and deep, withdrawing and hesitating before sliding back into her. Cornelia matched each stroke until she wanted to explode. She attempted to increase the measure, but he controlled each movement until she could barely stand it any longer. "Please," she begged into his ear.

Locke's head snapped up, and his lips came down on hers with unparalleled desire. He thrust himself into her, engulfing her in a wild and primitive tempo until the frenzied pace released spasm after spasm of gripping explosions. Immediately after her release, his body jerked, and he poured himself into her, panting against her ear.

Cornelia's body cradled his until their breathing slowed. Then he moved to her side and nestled her in his protective embrace. Letting his hand lazily trail to her belly, he announced, "I hope you held on tight, junior. Because before you make your entrance into this world, you are going to be expert."

Cornelia giggled and kissed his neck before she closed her eyes. For the second night as she drifted off to sleep, she thought how perfect her world was and that nothing could ever again mar her happiness.

An insistent knock at the door brought Cornelia suddenly awake. She sat up and looked around. It was late morning. Locke had thoughtfully left her sometime during the night. "I'll be there in a minute," she called out.

"Cornelia, I think you should come now!" Carrie

said as she continued to hammer at the door.

Cornelia hurriedly grabbed a robe and padded to the door. "What is the matter?" she demanded until she saw the worried expression on Carrie's face. "Come in." She stepped back and allowed Carrie to enter. "I thought you were going to sleep for a week."

"I wish I had," she mumbled. She was wringing her hands and walked over to the bed with her head down.

Cornelia waited for Carrie to unburden herself. When the woman made no effort to say a word, merely fidgeting with the corner of the quilt, Cornelia grew impatient. "Carrie, whatever it is, it can't be that bad."

Carrie's head snapped up, her eyes huge with worry. "I am afraid it is."

"Then don't just stand there. Tell me."

"I am afraid there seems to be a little problem waiting for you in the parlor," she hedged. She liked Cornelia and abhorred the thought that she had to be the bearer of such news.

"A little problem," Cornelia repeated. She was about to lose another measure of patience. "Exactly what is this *little problem?*"

Carrie slapped her hands to her cheeks. "Oh, I simply cannot bear to tell you. You'll have to see for yourself. It is in the parlor."

"*It*. All right, we'll go to the parlor," Cornelia said to humor the distraught woman. She started for the door.

"No, no, you must dress first," Carrie insisted. "And do hurry."

Cornelia shook her head. If she hadn't known how eccentric Carrie was, she would have been annoyed with the woman. Instead, Cornelia threw on a simple morning dress of striped green and ran a comb through her mussed hair. She swung out her arm. "Would you like to lead the way, or shall I?"

"Oh, dear, this is simply too dreadful," Carrie mumbled and swept past Cornelia.

Cornelia followed the muttering woman down the hall. They stopped outside the parlor. When Cornelia put her hand on the handle to enter the room, Carrie put her hand over Cornelia's.

"Remember, you have my complete support," she announced in hushed tones.

Bemused, Cornelia nodded. "Thank you, I think."

Without further hesitation, Cornelia swung open the door and entered the parlor. A man stood with his back to her, staring out the window. Cornelia cleared her throat. "Excuse me, are you here to see . . ." Her words caught in her throat threatening to cut off her air when the man turned to face her. "W-what are you doing here?" she gasped once her breath returned.

"Is that any way to greet your husband?" Linley said with a smug grin.

"Is he really your *husband,*" Carrie asked, her eyes wide.

"Miss Carrie Simington, this is my *ex*-husband, Linley Talbot."

"Pleased, Miss Simington," Linley said and stepped forward with his hand outstretched. "But I fear that my dear wife is quite mistaken in her referral to our relationship in the past tense. I *am* Cornelia's husband."

Carrie let his hand dangle in the air as her hands flew to her cheeks. "Oh, my." Her eyes shifted to

Cornelia, who had a look of disbelief on her face, and then to Linley Talbot. She could have sworn his grin was evil. "Well, I can see that you two must have a lot to discuss, so I shall leave you. Cornelia, if you need me, I'll be nearby," she said, backing out of the door. She bumped into a table, causing a figurine to totter before she managed to swing around and grab it. "Oh, dear, I am not usually this awkward," she chirped and shut the door behind her.

Once they were alone, Linley made himself comfortable on the couch and patted the place next to him. To his annoyance, Cornelia took a chair some distance away and sat with her back rigid. "You look well." He allowed his eyes to rove over her. "Gained weight in all the right places," he added.

"What do you want?" she demanded. Her perfect world was crumbling. But she deigned to meet this unexpected development in her life head on, she silently repeated to herself.

"How is your brother? Much better I hope."

"You didn't come to Colorado to ask about Paxton, Linley. Why are you here?"

The smirk spread from his lips to his eyes. "You've gained backbone. Colorado must agree with you." He got up and wandered around the room, fingering the knickknacks and running his hand along the edge of the piano. He looked at his palm. "Not a speck of dust. You always were the perfect little housekeeper."

Unable to stand the suspense any longer, Cornelia jumped to her feet. "Since you seem to have little intention of informing me as to the reason for this unexpected visit, I suggest you seek accommodations elsewhere until I have time to grant you a proper interview," she announced coldly and headed toward the door.

"Wait, *wifey dear.*"

Cornelia halted her exit. With her hands clasped tightly in front of her to still their trembling, her face set in cold stone, she pivoted around to face him. "I am no longer your wife, and you are not welcome here. Please leave."

Unaffected, he rested back against the cushions. "Guess it is good that I took one of those crude cabins down the road that those hillbillies, the Wrigleys, offer for rent since you are being so ungracious to your devoted husband." His smirk deepened. "Pity you didn't have so much spunk before the divorce. But I am sure you will be most happy to learn that you are indeed still my wife," he said with a lewd smile.

The tension in Cornelia's body increased. "I don't believe you."

He gave her a look of fabricated sympathy. "Afraid it is quite true. I suggest you sit down. You look like you are ready to fall down. Tch, tch, tch. Don't tell me you aren't happy about the news I brought?"

Carrie nearly fell over as she listened at the door. Her heart aching with fear for Cornelia, Carrie lifted her skirts and ran toward the stable. She wasn't sure whether she should ride to Joe Mills's cabin and fetch Paxton or whether she should ride for Locke. All she knew for sure as she frantically saddled a horse was that she had to get help.

Chapter Forty

Carrie spurred the horse onward along the road, ignoring the chill in the pine-scented air. Patches of snow from the storm two days before bunched by the side of the road and decorated the colorful changing leaves of the aspens.

At the fork in the road, she stopped.

To the left, the road led toward Joe Mills's cabin where she would find Paxton. She looked to her right. Locke's cabin was off that road. Whom should she summon? Who would be the most help to Cornelia? At the sound of a horse heading her way, Carrie's head snapped up.

The rider drew up short when he saw her, and she momentarily wondered why he swung around and galloped off the road into the trees, but she was too preoccupied to give more than passing consideration to the incident. Deciding who would be the most help, Carrie gave the horse a swift kick and reined the animal to the right.

Out of breath by the time she reached Locke's cabin, she slid off the horse screaming, "Locke! Locke! You have got to help. Oh, please, help!"

Hearing the desperate cries for help, Locke grabbed his gun and ran out of the cabin. Carrie immediately launched herself into his arms, surprising the hell out of him.

Holding her at arm's length, he demanded, "What the devil is wrong? Is it Cornelia?"

"Yes, oh yes. Please, you must come with me," she cried. But he was already saddling his horse as she spoke. She watched his furious efforts to ready the horse and decided that it would be prudent if she spent the next few days in town and alerted Lamantha to all the new developments.

Not waiting for an explanation, he leaped on the horse's back and lit out of there as if the devil himself were chasing him.

Locke reached the cottage in record time. A strange horse stood tethered out front at the post. Fear surrounded his heart. Disregarding all care, Locke leaped off his horse and barged through the door.

"Cornelia!" he bellowed, stomping through the cottage and into the parlor, gun in hand.

"What's wrong . . ." His voice trailed off when he took in the scene before him, and he shoved the gun back into his holster.

Cornelia looked as if she was on the verge of tears, sitting with her hands trembling in her lap. Across from her sat a stranger with a complacent grin on his face.

Locke immediately disliked the man.

"What's going on here?" he demanded. His face softened when his gaze settled on Cornelia. "Carrie came to get me in a panic and said you needed help."

Linley's smug grin never once left him as he surveyed the little scene. So his little mouse of a wife had found herself a male friend, he thought with satisfaction. Now she would have to be cooperative, and he could have a little fun before he and Margo left this godforsaken place. But he did not like the dangerous look of the big man.

"I am quite all right," she lied. "This man was just leaving." Her gaze shot to Linley. "I'll see you out."

"Oh, but I'm not going anywhere," Linley said and remained seated. The big man took a threatening step toward him, and Linley held up his palms. "Now just calm down. You no longer need to play Cornelia's champion. You see, I am her husband, Linley Talbot, and I'll take care of her now. So you can be the one to leave anytime," he added with an egotistical grin and waited for the man to depart.

Taken by complete surprise, Locke reacted with the swiftness of a bobcat and grabbed Linley by the collar, hauling him to his feet. "You can't do this?" Linley managed to choke out as he was being unceremoniously dragged through the house by the scruff of the neck.

Locke kicked open the front door and tossed Linley out. He tumbled down the steps and landed in a heap in the dirt. He looked up in time to catch the hat Cornelia threw after him.

"I believe it is *ex*-husband," Locke snarled. "Stay away from Cornelia, or next time I won't be so sociable toward you," he added.

Linley sagely held his tongue as the pair closed the door behind them. Crawling to his feet and brushing off his attire, he grumbled, "You haven't

400

heard the last of me. And for this little insult, dear *wife,* it'll cost you double before I'm done." Hat in hand, Linley stumbled toward his rented horse to regroup.

"Psst, psst, psst" issued from the bushes, drawing Linley's attention briefly before he started to swing up into the saddle. "Psst, psst" came the sounds again.

Linley left his horse and cautiously inched toward the sounds. Before he could react to the rustle of leaves, an arm thrust out through the bush and pulled him into it. "What is the meaning of this?" Linley demanded.

"Hush! You want to be alerting them inside?"

Linley's eyes narrowed. He knew a man with a mission when he saw one. And the red-haired man was up to no good. A calculating grin spread his lips. "Unless you have something better to offer, I might be inclined to do just that."

The man thrust out a hand. "Sean McCurdy's the name. And I be thinking that the way you be leaving the house a moment ago, we might be of help to each other."

Linley cast Sean a big grin along with his hand. "Linley Talbot. Why don't we go back to my place? I think we just may have a mutual interest to discuss."

Escorting Cornelia back to the parlor, Locke held her until she stopped trembling. "It's going to be all right, honey," he crooned. "You don't have to worry about Linley Talbot. I'll take care of him so you will never be bothered by him again."

"Oh, Locke, I wish it were true," she said as she fought to retain her composure. "I wish it were that simple."

She was so shaken that Locke was tempted to locate Talbot and see that he was kicked out of the Park immediately. Then, what the man had said echoed in Locke's mind. "Cornelia, why did Talbot come here?"

She covered her face with her hands, then caught herself, and placed them in her lap. She was not going to return to being the meek woman she had been. She took a deep breath. "Linley says I did not sign the final divorce papers so we are still legally married. He showed me the papers, but when I attempted to take them from him so I could sign them and be done with him, he tucked them in his vest pocket and said he wanted something for his trouble first."

"I'll give him something for his trouble," he hissed and started to rise.

The threatening tone of his voice scared her. She grabbed his arm. "Locke, wait. The copy Linley showed me needed his signature, too. He said if I didn't cooperate he would withhold it." She pressed the other hand to her stomach, thinking about her child. Her child had to have a name, she thought desperately.

"What does he want, Cornelia?" Locke asked when all he wanted to do was to find Talbot and force him to sign the papers if he had to break his fingers doing it.

"My grandmother left me a little money when she passed on. I saved it despite his demands that I give it to him while we were married. Linley said that since we are still legally married, his gambling debts are also my debts, and I am obligated to pay them."

"Let me guess. His gambling debts come to exactly the amount of money your grandmother left you, right?"

Cornelia lowered her head in shame. "Almost to the penny."

"You aren't going to give him a nickel." He took her hands; they were cold. Rubbing them between his, he soothed, "Don't worry, I am not going to let him blackmail you."

"What is this about blackmail?" Paxton asked, coming into the room with his hand curled around Annie's.

"Nothing, really," Cornelia quickly said and went to hug Annie. "Annie, I am so happy for you and Paxton."

"Pax talked to Pa last night, and everythin' is all settled," she said with pride in her voice.

"Yes, it looks as though we're both going to be married," Paxton said. Although Cornelia attempted a glowing smile, it was too bright, and Paxton could tell she was covering something up. "Cornelia, something is wrong. What is it?"

"It's nothing," she insisted.

"Locke? What were you two talking about blackmail when we entered?" Paxton pressed.

All eyes shifted to Cornelia. "Your brother loves you, Cornelia. He deserves to hear it from you," Locke said as he encircled her quivering shoulders in his embrace.

"I'll go make coffee if you want to be alone," Annie offered.

"No, Annie, you might as well stay," Cornelia

403

said. "Sit down, you might as well hear it from me."

Once they were all seated, Cornelia spilled out the entire story about Linley. Locke held her hand, all the while silently fuming with what he was going to do to the bastard.

Paxton bounded to his feet, his face red with anger. "You aren't going to let that blackguard get away with it, are you?"

"I don't know what else I can do—" Cornelia began.

Locke cut her off. His fists clenched, he announced, "Well, I do! Quit worrying. Talbot is not going to get away with anything."

Cornelia's eyes went to Locke's fists. He had killed a man with those fists. And although he had been only defending himself against a man sent to attack him, Cornelia could not stop worrying. She had no idea how far Linley would go to get his hands on her money, but she did know that Linley must have been pretty desperate, or he never would have made the trip to Colorado. And while she felt nothing but contempt for Linley Talbot, she did not want anyone else to suffer because she had neglected to sign those divorce papers.

"She is going to suffer for not signing those damned divorce papers," Linley grated out in the small cabin he had engaged for himself and Margo. "If she had signed them when she was supposed to, we wouldn't have to be here now."

Linley dabbed at the cut by his lip that he had sustained when that man threw him out of the house. "What did you say the man's name is who so rudely escorted me from Cornelia's house?"

"Locke Breckenridge." Sean cast a glance at the two gorilla-sized men who stood silently in the corner with their arms crossed over their huge chests. They had not said a word, but Sean did not like the way they were staring at him.

"What is that man to Cornelia?" Linley demanded.

"Who cares?" Margo snapped and began to pace the room like a nervous predator.

"We have to care, dammit! The man is standing between us and the money to pay my gaming debts," Linley snapped.

"He be sweet on your wife," Sean supplied.

*"Ex-*wife," Margo sneered.

"Not quite yet, Margo," Linley reminded her.

"What is it?" Sean asked, confused. "Is the *lady* your wife or no?"

Linley cocked a brow. "She is."

"That is merely a formality," Margo said with a pout. "Furthermore, all we want is what is rightfully due Linley."

"Then why don't you be using those two—" Sean motioned to the men standing in the corner like sentries"—if that be all you're after?"

The larger of the two men stepped forward, disdain on his face. "We're only here to keep an eye on Talbot so he doesn't decide not to return to Joshaby, and that's all." His piece said, the man moved back to his position.

"Money was all I wanted until that bastard Breckenridge thought he could throw me out on my ear and get away with it. Now those two are going to pay." Suspicion overtook Linley and he probed, "By the way, what were you doing in those bushes outside Cornelia's house?"

Sean crossed his legs. He was not about to tell Talbot he had tried to rape the woman. "As I be telling you on the way over here, your precious wife cost me my reputation and a cushy job working for the earl. And me being made the victim to cover up for her sneaking around with Breckenridge . . ."

Linley listened to the rest of McCurdy's story without comment, but he did not believe a word of it. He knew Cornelia well enough to know that McCurdy was lying, not that it mattered. What did matter was that McCurdy wanted revenge, and so did Linley.

"Since we share the common bond of revenge, McCurdy, I think that we can come to terms that will be of mutual benefit to both of us."

"What about me?" Margo snapped, thinking about Locke Breckenridge.

"What about you, Margo? You're here at my request. I have told you that you'll have some fun. But you will have your fun after I am finished and not before."

At the vehemence in Linley's voice, Margo settled back in her seat with her back toward Linley, glaring blankly at the door. Her cheeks flamed in fury at Linley for speaking to her in such a tone in front of others, and she silently swore that he would be sorry.

As she waited, she was chagrined that Linley did not seek to atone for his outrageous behavior. She sneaked a peek over her shoulder. Linley had turned from her and was focusing his attention on what that crude Irishman, Sean McCurdy, was saying. She perked up her ears to listen to what the men were discussing. It never hurt to know what was going on just in case she might have use of the information.

"Since you have obviously been keeping watch over our *lady,* what do you propose we do once I have my money? Linley asked McCurdy.

Sean broke a calculating smile. "I be glad you asked, boy-o. Just so happens I be coming up with the perfect plan to repay the pair of them."

Chapter Forty-one

Carrie had sent word she would be remaining in town for a few days, Annie had gone home hours ago, and it was late in the evening as Cornelia listened to Locke and Paxton continue to discuss what Locke intended to do about Linley. Finally, when she could stand no more, she jumped to her feet.

"One thing you two seem to be forgetting is that this is my problem," she insisted.

"We are merely trying to help," Paxton said.

Cornelia's gaze swung to Locke. "And what about you? Are you going to tell me you also are only trying to help?"

"Cornelia, I am not merely trying to help. You are going to be my wife, and I want to take care of you. And in the morning I will take care of Linley Talbot. He will sign those papers," he said with deliberation that warned Cornelia he would not be swayed. "Talbot is not going to bother you again. Now, I don't want you worrying about him any longer. It's late, why don't we all get some rest?" he suggested.

"Good idea," Paxton seconded "How about you, Sister dear? You'll feel better in the morning. The morning's light always puts a different perspective on things."

Cornelia was getting nowhere trying to make them understand that it was her responsibility to deal with Linley. Neither man was about to listen to reason. So she hid her annoyance with a smile. "I suppose you are right."

Locke didn't like the way she so easily agreed. "I'll sleep on the couch, so I'll be nearby just in case the man decides to return. I settle this in the morning," he said.

Noticing Cornelia's look of shock, Paxton offered, "I'll get you some bedding, Locke."

Once they were alone, Cornelia forced down the urge to inform him that she intended to handle Linley. Instead she reached up on tiptoes and gave Locke a kiss on the cheek. "See you in the morning."

An unsettling feeling surrounded Locke while he stared after her as she left the room. He had dealt with Talbot's kind before and knew how to handle him. But he could not get the gut reaction out of his mind that Cornelia was up to something.

Without dressing for bed, Cornelia turned out the light and settled on her bed to wait until she was certain Locke had fallen asleep. She waited an hour, then crept down the hall and into the kitchen. She had just creaked the door and was about to slip out undetected when a deep warning voice stopped her.

"Just where do you think you're going?"

Cornelia swung around. Moonlight filtering in through the windows illuminated Locke leaning against the doorframe with an "I-knew-you-would-try-something" smirk on his face.

"Would you believe that necessary?"

He crossed his arms over his chest. "I might if you had taken a lantern and weren't fully dressed, instead of trying to sneak off into the night like a thief."

Cornelia huffed out a breath and pushed past him.

He turned and followed her back to her room. "Don't you have anything to say for yourself?"

She stopped outside her door. "Obviously you wouldn't believe any excuse I made up anyway, so why should I bother?"

He had to smile at her candor. He opened the door and swung out his arm; the expression on his face turned serious. "I said I would take care of Talbot. Don't try it again, Cornelia."

"You can quit worrying. You won't catch me trying to sneak out of the house again tonight."

Not totally assured, he cautioned, "Just see that I don't."

Fuming at the frontier bully, Cornelia shut the door and paced to the bed. Quietly rearranging the blankets so the bed looked as if she were sleeping, she hoped it would work a second time. Once she was finished, she went to the window. She was not going to be dictated to in such a way! She was sure he would not expect her to try sneaking out again so soon, so she threw open the window and climbed out. As she crept from the cottage and into the forest, she was pleased that she had outwitted Locke. Just then huge metal jaws clamped around her ankle, sending her sprawling to the ground in pain.

She was caught in a trap.

She tried to open it the way she had with the mountain lion cub when she had first arrived in the Park; this one held fast. Bleeding from where the jaws had bit into her flesh, she ripped a strip from her petticoat and wrapped it around her ankle.

She called out, but she was too far from the cottage. She was imprisoned until someone came along and freed her. Cursing her misfortune that she had been in such a rush to talk to Linley that she had not been paying attention to where she was stepping,

Cornelia tried to make herself comfortable while she waited.

She did not have long to wait. The crunching of pine needles and fallen leaves drew her attention to the light spilling through the trees. "Over here," she called out. "Over here. I need help."

"Well, well, who be it I've got me here?" Sean said in a harsh voice, holding his lantern high in the air. "This couldn't be better if I be planning it this way."

Cornelia's heart pounded when she recognized Sean McCurdy, and she frantically tried to pry open the trap again.

He crouched down near her with his arms crossed on his leg. "It won't be doing you no good, my little colleen. I set my traps to be holding on to what I be after. Funny, don't you think? When I be putting that trap here, I didn't think I be catching such fair game. Since I be catching you, guess that makes you mine." When Cornelia did not respond, he prodded, "What be the matter? Can't you be speaking now?" His expression turned so cold that it made Cornelia shiver. "You be having plenty to say last time we were together."

"Release me, and I promise I won't tell anyone I saw you," she offered.

"You won't be telling anyone anyway," he returned. He grasped her ankle, causing Cornelia to flinch. "What be the matter? Don't you like my touch?"

"My ankle hurts, is all," Cornelia managed as she fought to keep her wits about her.

"Much like that mountain lion cub, no doubt," he said.

"You were the one trapping those poor animals on the earl's land, weren't you?"

"So his lordship told you about that, did he? It be a nice side business until you be meddling and alerted the earl that there be traps on his land," he sneered. "You be ruining that for me too. But I be having a notion of how you can make up for the trouble you be causing old Sean."

He stood on the side springs and opened the jaws. Ignoring her throbbing ankle, Cornelia tried to scramble away. Sean was quicker. He caught her and dragged her toward his horse.

"Let go of me," she hissed, struggling despite the pain.

"Talbot said you be a meek little lamb. But old Sean be knowing better. That husband of yours be thinking I should wait until he be getting his money. But I be watching and waiting to get my revenge too long. You cost me an easy life, girlie. So I aim to be finishing what we started a couple of months ago by the stream before that bastard Breckenridge came along. I be going to teach you what it means to be a tease. You be going to have a taste of a real man now."

They reached his waiting horse, and he quickly tied her up despite her efforts to break free. "You won't get away with this!" she hurled at him.

"No? It's not too sure I'd be, if I were you."

"Locke will find you and you'll be sorry when he does."

"I be hiding out waiting and watching you since Breckenridge kicked me out of the Park, and no one has found me yet." McCurdy turned his back on her for an instant to untie his horse.

Cornelia screamed. "Help!"

"You bitch," he bellowed and swung around to silence her. They tumbled to the ground, and he clamped his hand over her mouth. "It be a good thing we be too far from your precious lover for him to hear you, or I just might be forced to change my plans," he sneered as he gagged her. "Now, get up."

He yanked her to her feet, tossed her over his saddle, and, after climbing up behind her, reined his horse around. "I be having the perfect little place to finish our business together, my little colleen." He waited, then said, "Aren't you anxious to be knowing where?"

He laughed since Cornelia was gagged and could not reply if she wanted to. "Well, I be going to tell you anyway. We be going to the last place Breckenridge will be looking for you. The bastard will be scouring the mountains for his precious woman, and all the while we'll be cozy in his own cabin. Brilliant, don't you be thinking?"

He gave another burst of hearty laughter and spurred the horse on faster.

Locke remained awake listening for Cornelia to try to sneak past him the rest of the night. He was cranky and feeling like a grizzly as he snapped the blankets into some semblance of order.

"Good morning. Sleep well?" Paxton asked as he joined Locke in the parlor. Then before Locke could answer, he added, "I hope you two don't mind if I don't stay around today. Annie's coming over later, and we are going for a long walk. I have a lot of time to make up for with her, and I don't intend to waste a minute. Besides, I'm sure you'll enjoy the day once you take care of Linley since Carrie sent word she will be staying in town for a few days. Cornelia have breakfast ready?"

"She's not up yet," Locke grunted and stacked the last of the blankets on the pile.

"That's not at all like Cornelia. She's always the first one up."

A warning sounded in Locke's head. "Well, we better have a look."

Right behind Locke, Paxton spied the form nestled in the bed when Locke opened the door. "Shh. She's asleep. She must have been exhausted after Linley's visit yesterday."

"Like hell!" Locke boomed, startling Paxton.

Locke stomped to the bed and threw back the covers. "I should have known, dammit! She got away with this on the mountain with those mounds of covers."

"The mountain?" Paxton questioned, confused.

"She and that Simington woman pulled that little trick back up on the mountain, remember?"

Shaking his head, Paxton muttered, "Yes, I remember now. But I still don't understand."

"It's simple. Your sister wanted us to think she was asleep in order to give her more time."

"More time?"

"She was determined to get to Talbot before I did."

Locke stomped to the window and leaned out before he turned back to Paxton. "She must have crawled out the window."

Locke was headed toward the door before Paxton managed to get out the words "Where are you going?"

"After her," Locke growled and stormed out of the house toward his horse. Cornelia had told him Talbot was staying in one of the cabins the Wrigleys rented, so he wheeled his horse in that direction.

Locke was furious as he drove his lathered horse the short distance to the rental cabins. Once he had roused old man Wrigley and learned that Talbot and some woman were staying in the cabin on the end, Locke headed there with determined strides. He was not going to let Talbot get away with blackmail.

Not about to knock and give Talbot the chance to cover himself, Locke burst through the door. "All right, where is she . . ." His question died in the air when it became apparent that the quaint one-room cabin was vacant.

He ran back outside and caught sight of two people strolling toward a trail leading to the woods behind the cabins. He headed in their direction only to come to a sudden stop about two hundred fifty feet behind the pair.

The woman with Talbot looked exactly like his ex-wife. She had the same shape; she was the same height; she had the same taste in clothing; and she had the same auburn-colored hair. His thoughts coming in spurts, Locke recalled what Cornelia had told him about Talbot. Talbot would be exactly the kind of man his ex-wife might latch on to.

His ex-wife and Talbot were two of a kind; they would be a perfect match. Each one was a money grubber who never gave a thought to anyone else. Margaret was an Easterner, so it made sense that she would head toward familiar territory after leaving Leadville.

Shaking his head, Locke called out, "Talbot, hold up." Locke stomped forward in an effort to catch up with the pair. "Hold up!"

They seemed to be ignoring him. It would be just like Margaret, he thought as he gained on them. "I said hold up, Talbot," Locke snarled.

"Ignore him," Margo hissed. She tightened her arm around Linley's.

"He isn't about to let us," Linley barked and stopped. Margo pouted and rigidly held her hands in front of her. Disregarding Margo's furious demeanor and her demands that they pay no attention to Breckenridge, Linley turned to face the man. "What do you want, Breckenridge?" he called back.

Locke drew to a halt. Talbot was facing him, but the woman still had her back to him. Locke erased the distance between them until he was standing not more than three feet from the pair. Ignoring Talbot's scowl, Locke questioned, "Margaret, is that you?"

Margo stiffened further when she heard her given name. She had not been called Margaret for a long time.

As the woman slowly pivoted around to face him, Locke's breath caught as he waited to see her face. His ex-wife was the last person he wanted or needed to see now!

Chapter Forty-two

The cool autumn sun glistened red across the woman's frizzy curls as Locke took in the whole picture of her, ignoring Talbot's demands that Locke explain himself. Locke stared into her face and heaved out his breath.

She was not his ex-wife.

"Most people call me Margo. But how did you know my given name?" the painted woman questioned.

Her eyes held appreciation. Though Locke was relieved that she was not his ex-wife, her actions reminded him of Margaret. Locke gave an indifferent shrug. "Good guess."

"Pity. For a moment I had hoped we had met before," she cooed.

"What do you want, Breckenridge?" Linley demanded. He did not like the way Margo was measuring the big man. She had voracious tastes, and Linley knew she would not hesitate to take Breckenridge to her bed if she had the chance.

"Where's Cornelia?" Locke charged without preamble.

"Don't tell me you have misplaced her," Linley said in a snide voice.

Ignoring the woman's presence, Locke grabbed the

417

little weasel by the throat. "I am not telling you a thing, Talbot. But if you don't want your face rearranged, you had better start talking. Where's Cornelia?"

Margo stepped back to watch. It was becoming apparent that Linley had misjudged his opponent and besides, she was enjoying this. Linley had mistreated her last evening in front of others so he was getting what he deserved.

"I haven't seen Cornelia since you so ungraciously saw me out yesterday afternoon."

"I don't believe you," Locke growled.

The two men sent by Joshaby to watch Talbot were just coming out of their cabin, spied the fray, and came running. Margo stepped between them and Linley. "It's all right, boys. Linley is merely making arrangements to collect what is owed him," she said with a coy smile.

To Linley's chagrin, the two men nodded and retreated to watch from their cabin before he could engage their help. "You'll be sorry for that," he hissed at Margo.

Locke took a tighter hold of Linley and shook him. "You in the habit of abusing women, Talbot?"

"No, no, never," he choked.

"Then if you don't want me to start abusing you, you had better tell me what happened to my future wife."

"I don't know, I tell you. My God, I don't know!"

"For once he is telling the truth," Margo offered in a bored voice and studied her fingernails.

Locke released Talbot with a shove and stood glaring at the man. Hell, Talbot was too afraid not to be telling the truth. Silent, Locke was relieved. He relaxed. Cornelia had not come to see Talbot after all. She must have gone for a walk although he could not quite understand why she had gone to all the trouble to hide the fact from him unless she was angry and wanted to be alone.

Noting the tension lessen in Breckenridge, Linley moved to Margo's side. He was not going to take the chance that Breckenridge might change his mind. "Why are you so worried about Cornelia?"

"What's it to you?" Locke shot back.

"It's nothing to me, really. It's just that I can't understand why anyone would care about a woman like her."

Locke took a threatening step toward Linley. Linley immediately moved behind Margo's skirts. "Now don't get upset, Breckenridge. If you want a woman who is barren and can never give you children, I guess that is your business. But I need to have a family," he rushed on, not noticing the change in Locke's expression. "A woman who can't have children, like Cornelia, deserves to be divorced."

Linley had expected to shock Breckenridge. So when Breckenridge threw back his head and laughed, Linley scowled. "What's the matter with you, Breckenridge? Didn't you hear what I said? Cornelia is barren. B-a-r-r-e-n.

"We tried for four years to have children. When I finally realized that she never could give me an heir, I was forced to come up with a plan to get grounds to divorce her," he blurted out in his efforts to show the big man what a mistake he had made to be interested in his ex-wife.

When Breckenridge's laughter died, Linley thought he had finally gotten through to the man. With a big smirk on his face, Linley stepped from behind Margo. "What are you standing there for? You should be thanking me. I have done you a big favor telling you about Cornelia's dark secret. Now you won't be tempted to make the same mistake I did."

"You had to come up with a plan to divorce Cornelia?" Locke asked. If he had not wanted to hear the details of Talbot's confession, Locke gladly would have punched the little weasel in the mouth right then and there.

Linley puffed out his chest, thinking how he had showed this Colorado hick how smart he was. Seeking to add to his glory by enlightening the man further, Linley said, "I sent Cornelia a note instructing her to meet me for dinner, then paid a gambling acquaintance from the Stag and Hound to meet her in my place and embrace her in front of the popular restaurant where I knew the town gossips regularly ate. Of course, with a little help, everyone believed the worst."

Locke's brow lifted. "Of course."

"All I had to do afterward was sit back and let everyone believe the worst—"

"Linley," Margo tugged on his sleeve, "I don't think you should say any more."

He flung his arm back. "Why not? I'm proud of how I got rid of the barren bitch." He turned to Breckenridge. "Don't you think I was clever?"

Barely able to contain himself, Locke gritted out, "Real clever. Tell me more."

"Everyone had always thought so highly of Cornelia. When they saw her embracing a stranger in public and later when she couldn't produce the note I conveniently had my man take from her, the town turned on her. Adultery is a sin, you know."

"How well I know," Locke said in a voice that should have warned Linley, had he not been so absorbed in his own triumph.

"I never would have divorced Cornelia if I could have gotten an heir off her. I need an heir to inherit."

Locke was so livid he could have killed the man with his bare hands. Keeping a tight rein on his emotions,

420

Locke asked, "What happens if you don't produce an heir?"

"I would be virtually penniless. But before you stands my future wife" — he motioned to Margo — "as soon as Cornelia and I conclude our little business. So you can see that won't be a problem. And since you now know the truth about Cornelia, you'll no longer want to stand in the way of our finishing our business transaction." As an afterthought, Linley advised, "If I were you, I would dump her."

Locke gave a curt nod. "If you were me," he echoed.

Linley swallowed hard, beginning to sense something was amiss. "Yes, unless, of course, you don't care if you have children or not and want a prude for a wife."

"Oh, I care about children," Locke said much too calmly to suit Linley, who started to sweat. "As a matter of fact, Cornelia and I intend to have a houseful. And we plan to start immediately."

"That is impossible," Linley scoffed.

"Oh, I don't think so. You see, Talbot, Cornelia is carrying a child."

Shock reverberated through Linley's bones. "Cornelia is pregnant with my child?"

"Think again, Talbot," Locke said in a deadly voice.

Realization hit Margo. "Linley, if Cornelia is pregnant and it is not your child, do you know what that means?"

"Shut up!" he shouted in a panic as the full force of realization hit him. "That is impossible. Cornelia is the one who is barren."

"Afraid not, Talbot. It appears to be your problem. Now it looks as if you'll never inherit a dime. Guess when you get back to the rock you crawled out from under you are going to have to start looking for a job," Locke stated in a pleased voice.

"No! No! I don't believe it."

Margo slapped her hands to her cheeks: "Oh my God, it is true. It's you with the problem."

"If you think you are going to get a dime out of Cornelia, you had better think again," Locke said menacingly. "While I'm here, you might as well go get those divorce papers so we can conclude *our* business dealings."

Linley ignored Locke. Linley's mind was spinning with how he could still gain control of his father's estate and get hold of Cornelia's money.

Shaking her head in disgust, Margo stalked away from Linley. He ran after her. "Margo, wait! Let's stop and think about this. I am sure I still can come up with a way to work this out. Please, Margo, wait!"

Not about to let that little weasel try to run out on him without relinquishing those papers, Locke went after Talbot.

"Locke! Locke!" Paxton yelled, running toward them with Annie in tow. "Locke!"

Margo stopped and watched the frantic man gallop past her, as did Linley, who was anxious to overhear what was so urgent.

"Locke, something has happened to Cornelia," Paxton puffed, out of breath. "Annie found this"—he held up a bloody length of lace from a petticoat—"next to a trap in the woods not far behind the cottage while she was on her way over this morning. It's Cornelia's."

"How can you be sure it's Cornelia's?" Locke asked. He took the strip, his heart pounding. Although it had not been proved, Locke suspected McCurdy was the one who had been setting the traps on Dunraven's land.

"I'd know Mother's handiwork anywhere," Paxton answered as he ran his hand through his hair.

Margo was watching the little scene unfold and moved closer. When she noticed the blood-soaked lace, she gasped and whirled on Linley. "This is your doing, isn't it?"

"Don't be crazy. I had nothing to do with that!" he swore. But deep down he had an inkling who did.

"No? Then what were you doing with that man last evening?"

"We had nothing to do with this," he insisted. Out of the corner of his eye, he kept watch on Breckenridge.

Hearing Margo's accusations, Locke swooped down on Linley, blocking his attempts to retreat. "What is she talking about?" Locke demanded of Linley.

His eyes huge, Linley's lips trembled but he remained mute.

"You better tell me, Talbot."

"I don't want any part of anything like this," Margo snapped. "Tell him!"

Locke pulled back his fist.

"Sean McCurdy stopped me outside Cornelia's yesterday, but . . " he ceased when Breckenridge swung around and raced toward his horse. "Breckenridge, I didn't have anything to do with what McCurdy is up to!" Linley hollered. He turned to Paxton. "You believe me, don't you?"

"The only thing I believe is that you'd stoop to any level to get what you want," Paxton snarled. He took Annie's hand. "Come on, Annie. Let's see if we can be of help to Locke." Then he looked pointedly at Linley. "Something stinks around here."

Linley burned as he watched the pair walk away. "Margo, I think I just came up with a plan to salvage my inheritance," he said to the woman.

She balled her fists on her ample hips. "It had better be good. Because this is your last chance." She toyed with an auburn curl. "You know Zenas Joshaby made me an interesting proposition before we left Connecticut. Perhaps I should take him up on it."

Linley grabbed her wrist. "You're mine, Margo. Don't forget it."

"Then you had better have a damned good plan because I have no intention of remaining with a pauper."

A calculating grin spread his lips. "Don't worry, Breckenridge doesn't know it, but he gave me the perfect idea." He linked his arm with hers. "Come on, let's go to Cornelia's place and wait until she returns."

"But you heard what happened. What if McCurdy harms her?"

"Then she won't be in an shape to put up much of a fight when I present her with my demands. Now, let me explain what I have in mind . . ."

Locke pushed his horse to the limit of the animal's endurance as he raced to where Annie had found the bloodied lace. Jumping out of the saddle, he spied the trap.

Locke scowled. "McCurdy, the bastard."

Fear for Cornelia and the memory of what that son of a bitch had tried to do to her grasped him. He knelt down and surveyed the area.

There was evidence of a struggle.

With methodical precision, he ran his hand over the ground, noting the scattered leaves and the indentations in the dirt. Locke followed the signs twenty-five feet through the trees and found depressions that a horse had recently been tethered there. The hoof prints headed south. Not wasting time and fearing the worst, Locke mounted his horse and followed them.

As he carefully tracked the trail, he vowed that if McCurdy harmed Cornelia in any way, he was going to kill the bastard with his bare hands!

Chapter Forty-three

Locke was confused at first as he traced the hoof-prints through the hills. The trail was leading toward his own cabin. Then it dawned on him: McCurdy undoubtedly thought that would be the last place Locke would go while Cornelia was missing. Locke gave a bitter laugh. If McCurdy hadn't left such an easy trail to follow, Locke wouldn't have returned to his own place.

Locke left his horse a short distance from the cabin and crept up behind it. A strange horse was tethered near the trough. With great care, he moved beneath a window. Waited. Listened for voices. Then peeked inside.

Cornelia was huddled on the corner of his bed, McCurdy standing over her. "You won't get away with this!" Cornelia spat at McCurdy.

"You be thinking not, my little colleen? I be waiting and planning. So I wouldn't be counting on that lover of yours to be saving you."

"No?" Locke said, suddenly framed in the front door. "I wouldn't be too sure about that, McCurdy."

Sean did not turn around. Instead he grabbed Cornelia, holding her like a shield.

Locke had started for McCurdy but stopped when he saw McCurdy was pointing a gun at Cornelia.

"How you be finding us so soon?" McCurdy demanded.

"You're sloppy, McCurdy," Locke said and waved the strip of lace in the air. "A child could have followed the trail you left. Why don't you let her go while you're still able to walk out of here?" His eyes went to Cornelia. "How is your ankle?"

"It is all right," she said in a quivery voice.

"Maybe you don't realize it, but I be the one with the gun, Breckenridge." Sean waved his Colt toward a chair. "Sit down before I be forced to put a hole in your lady."

McCurdy's hand was shaking, making him doubly dangerous. "Okay, I'm sitting down. Don't panic," Locke said in a calm voice.

"I'm not panicking!" McCurdy shouted. "You," he snarled at Cornelia, "pick up that rope over there and tie him up. I aim to be doing away with you two at my leisure."

Cornelia looked to Locke. "Do as he says, honey."

As Cornelia slid off the bed, Locke said to McCurdy. "Since you seem to have a mind to kill us, mind if we pray?"

Sean scratched his head. "You be wanting to pray?" he repeated in disbelief.

"Aren't you a God-fearing man, McCurdy?" Locke said.

"What if I be?"

"Then you shouldn't have anything against a man making his peace with his God."

Sean narrowed his eyes. "Suppose it be all right."

Locke stared straight into Cornelia's frightened eyes. "Cornelia, get my Beecher Bible. You know where it is. Where I keep the Beecher Bible. Go get it."

426

Cornelia was trembling. Her eyes trailed to the corner of the room before she flicked her gaze back to Locke.

"Go get it and bring it to me, Cornelia."

Sean was getting anxious, listening to the deliberateness in Breckenridge's voice. He stomped to Breckenridge and stood over him, waving his pistol. "What you being up to?"

"Nothing, McCurdy. Just waiting for my Bible."

While Locke engaged McCurdy, Cornelia inched toward the corner of the room.

Sean swung around. "What you be doing . . . Arrgh!" he grunted as Locke jumped him.

The gun blasted, which forced Locke to back off.

Cornelia screamed and grabbed the rifle behind her.

Sean was panting and as frightened as a cornered rabbit as he gained the upper hand. "What you be having behind your back?" he demanded of Cornelia.

"The Bible," she gulped out and continued to inch toward Locke.

"Show me."

Cornelia looked to Locke, her eyes wide. "Show him," Locke instructed with a nod.

McCurdy's gaze darted to Locke just long enough for Cornelia to raise the rifle toward the big Irishman.

"Pull the trigger!" Locke shouted.

McCurdy aimed and shot at Locke as Locke dived for cover; Cornelia squeezed her eyes shut and jerked the trigger. A blast issued from the rifle, knocking her backward against the wall. She hit her head, which caused her to crumple to the floor.

When she awoke, she was lying on the bed, and Locke was patting her hand. He stroked the hair from her forehead.

"How are you feeling?" he asked, smiling down at her.

She quickly sat up. "We're alive."

"Very much so."

"But he shot at you," she cried and felt up his arms.

"He didn't have very good aim."

"Then you are all right?"

"I'm fine."

"Thank God," she breathed out.

He chuckled. "Thank the Beecher Bible."

"Oh, Locke, I was so scared. At first, I didn't know what you were talking about. I thought you truly wanted to pray. Then I remembered the story you had told me about Beecher back in Kansas carrying a Bible in one hand and a rifle in the other." Her gaze trailed around the room and settled on McCurdy. He was tied to a chair, a gag in his mouth. She looked back to Locke.

Her eyes were troubled. "What's the matter, honey?"

"If you knew about the Beecher Bible, why didn't he?"

"We were lucky. He hasn't been in the country long."

"What if he had known?"

"Then we probably wouldn't be sitting here now." He leaned close to her ear. "Pity we aren't alone."

Ignoring McCurdy's shards of hatred silently directed toward them, Cornelia threw her arms around Locke's neck and hugged him.

Locke winked, left the bed, and tossed an old blanket over McCurdy's head. Then he returned to Cornelia. "Let me see, where were we?"

He took her face between his hands and was just about to kiss her when Paxton, followed by Joe Mills and Annie, burst through the door. Locke rolled his eyes and went to greet them.

"We followed the trail. Where's McCurdy?" Joe Mills questioned.

Locke thumbed toward the blanketed hill in the corner of the room. "Over there. Get him out of here."

"My pleasure." Joe threw the cover off McCurdy, cut the ropes from his legs, and yanked him to his feet. He shoved McCurdy toward the door. "You shoulda left the Park when you were free to go. Now you're headed for jail for a long time."

"He didn't harm you, did he, Cornelia?" Paxton asked.

"We was awful worried about you?" Annie put in.

Locke slipped his arm around her. "McCurdy took on the wrong lady."

"You mean that Cornelia bested the man?" Paxton said, surprised.

Locke chuckled. "With Bible in hand."

Paxton looked bemused. Annie noted the rifle lying near Cornelia, so she took over. "You mean a Beecher Bible?" At Locke's nod, she said, "A rifle, Pax."

His eyes wide, Paxton blurted, "You held a gun on McCurdy?"

"She pulled the trigger, too," Locke said.

Cornelia basked in the glow of triumph as Locke explained how he had been able to best McCurdy after Cornelia shot at him to throw him off guard. Although she had been frightened, she had overcome that panic to prevail over her own fears. Now all she had to do was to deal with Linley.

As if Paxton had read her thoughts, he said, "Cornelia, you'll be pleased to know that Locke took care of Linley this morning."

Locke had expected her gratitude, instead she swung on him. "What did you say to Linley?" Not waiting for an answer, she grasped Paxton's arm. "What did he say?"

"Well, I don't exactly know. I didn't arrive un—"

"You were there too?" she demanded.

"Just to get help for you," he said in his own defense.

"Cornelia, you can quit worrying about Talbot. I think he understands that he can't hurt you," Locke said. "Why don't we all sit down? I have something I think you should know about Talbot."

Cornelia was angry. But the tone in his voice caused her to bite back her words and sit down. "I'm sitting. What is it you have to tell me?"

"Cornelia, Linley admitted he paid the man whom you were accused of committing adultery with," he said, relating the whole tale.

Paxton gasped. "I'll kill that bastard!"

"No, Paxton," Cornelia said. "If anything, I should thank him. My life never would have been as happy as it is now if Linley hadn't divorced me."

Annie moved to the edge of her seat. "Just think, Pax, if Cornelia hadn't brung you to Colorado, we wouldn't never of met and fell in love."

"True," he crooned to his sweet girl. "Nellie, I guess everything has worked out for the best after all." There was a pause in the conversation, so Paxton suggested, "Why don't we go back to the cottage and celebrate our good fortune?"

"Why don't you two go on ahead? We'll be along in a little while. There are a few things Cornelia and I have to discuss first," Locke said.

Paxton's gaze shifted from his sister to Locke, then to Annie. "Come on, sweet girl, I think they need some time alone."

Once they had left, Cornelia turned to Locke. "Now that we are alone, what else did Linley have to say?"

Locke gave her the rest of the details about how Linley gained the divorce, his lady friend, and then hesitated before he finally said, "Cornelia, I told the man you are pregnant. It shut him up when he learned that he is the one with the problem. The bastard is going to have to work for a living because he won't be inheriting any money. He'll never get that child he thought he would with that floozy he has with him."

Cornelia patiently waited until he filled her in on all the details. "I wish you hadn't told him about the baby," she said and lowered her eyes.

He lifted her chin. "Cornelia, I am proud that we are going to be parents. You don't have to be ashamed. You aren't back in that small-minded town now. And you aren't going back. Furthermore, we're going to be married before anyone else knows you are going to have a baby."

Cornelia fidgeted with her fingers. Such a topic was taboo in polite society, and Linley was sure to run back to her hometown and blab to everyone who would listen. "Did Linley sign the divorce papers?"

"He will," Locke said with finality. Her skeptical expression caused him to add, "Cornelia, if you are worried about Talbot, you needn't be. He values the arrangement of his face too much to tempt me into rearranging it for him."

"I don't want you fighting over me," she said with a shudder and unconsciously let her eyes drop to his hands.

"If you're afraid because I killed a man once, don't be. I told you I wasn't looking for a fight that night. But I am not going to back away from one either. You are going to be mine, Cornelia. I protect what's mine. Linley Talbot is not going to cause you any more trouble, if he knows what is good for him."

431

"Linley, if you know what is good for you, you will take the next stage out of Estes Park and never look back," Margo warned as she packed her bag.

Linley jumped off the bed and started ripping her neatly folded garments out of her bag and throwing them on the floor. "I told you everything can still work out! Didn't you hear me!" he shouted.

Margo grabbed a chemise out of his hand. "I heard you. No doubt the whole Park heard you! I simply think that you are playing with fire. You do know what happens to people who play with fire, don't you?"

"Yes, Margo, baby," he retorted sarcastically. "They use it to burn their enemy's house down."

"You're a fool!"

"You'll eat those words." He picked up her hat and handed it to her. "Now, come on, we have an appointment at the telegraph office before we go pay Cornelia one last little visit."

Chapter Forty-four

Linley and Margo waited impatiently outside the closed telegraph office for over an hour until the clerk finally arrived.

"You're late," Linley announced in a condemning tone when the weathered, bony man arrived.

"Had me some important business to tend to earlier, mister."

"I hope it was as important as keeping your job. I have half a mind to report you," Linley said as he and Margo followed the clerk inside.

Margo rolled her eyes and muttered under her breath, "Half a mind is correct."

Linley ignored her, finished scribbling the message he wanted to send, and handed it to the clerk. Margo grabbed it out of the man's gnarled hand and read it. "Linley, you can't send this."

Linley ripped it out of her hand and gave it back to the clerk. "Send it," he said to the man and flipped him a coin. Dismissing the man's strange expression as he read the message, Linley took Margo's arm and unceremoniously escorted her from the telegraph office.

Outside, he grabbed her arms. "What are you trying to do to me? To us? Don't you want me to inherit what is rightfully mine?"

She shook him off and brushed off her sleeves. "Don't you ever touch me like that again, Linley Talbot."

He raised his palms. "All right. All right. I am sorry. But please, Margo, just a few more hours. Since Cornelia is in a motherly way, she'll be desperate to get the divorce now. So she'll have to cooperate."

"Well, I suppose it might be amusing to watch her squirm. After all, it is her fault I am here now." She took in an uncertain breath. "But I certainly hope you know what you are doing."

Linley's gaze caught at the two men who had been shadowing him everywhere he went. His knees twitched. "I do. I can't lose this time."

Margo rolled her eyes. "So you have said before, but this is the last time, I'm warning you."

"Quit worrying. Come on, let me help you up onto the horse. We'll ride on over to Cornelia's and finish up our business."

"Although I'd love to remain here in your cabin with you all day," Cornelia said as she rose from the bed and began to dress, "Paxton and Annie are waiting for us .back at the cottage. They will begin to wonder."

Locke got up and circled his arms around her from behind, kissing the back of her neck. "Oh, I don't think they'll be too surprised if we are a little tardy getting back there."

Scandalized, Cornelia swung around to face him. "Locke!"

He chuckled and gave her a peck on the forehead. "Oh, all right. But only if you ride on my horse with me so I can hold you on the way over there."

As they slowly rode back to the cottage, Cornelia snuggled within Locke's strong embrace. The day had cooled as dark clouds rolled in, blocking out the sun. Once again she felt that everything would be put to right with her world. With Locke at her side, Linley would not dare continue to hold the divorce papers over her head.

When they reached the cottage, Locke announced that he would see to the horse and join her shortly. Cornelia stood on the porch and watched him lead the horse toward the stable, then went into the house.

The smile on her face vanished when she entered the parlor. Linley and the woman Locke had described sat on the couch, their backs rigid.

"What are you doing here?" Cornelia demanded.

"Waiting for you, wifey dear. I'm glad to see that Breckenridge was forced to worry over nothing," Linley said with that same smirk he always wore. "I don't believe you two have been formally introduced. "Cornelia, this is Margo. The woman I plan to marry."

Margo held out a gloved hand. "Charmed."

"Well, I'm not. I know you two have been sneaking around for months." She turned on Linley. "What do you want?"

"I have a little proposition for you." His face lost its smirk, and an ugly snicker curled the corner of his lip.

"I'm not interested. Just sign the divorce papers and get out!"

"My, my aren't we getting rather brave? Now, sit down."

At the threatening tone of his voice, Cornelia took a seat.

"That's better," Linley said, sitting back and relaxing. He knew when he had the upper hand. "If you want this divorce, you are going to have to cooperate. If you don't, you can kiss my signature goodbye."

"You can have the money, if you'll get out now and never come back."

His smirk returned. "That might have sufficed before, but not now."

"Before?" Cornelia questioned.

"Yes. Before your lover so graciously informed me that you are in a motherly way, and that I . . . well, that I may not in fact be able to claim my inheritance without . . . shall we say, without your help."

"My help? I don't understand," Cornelia said, confused by what her pregnancy could possibly have to do with Linley's predicament.

"It's simple, really. All you have to do is return to Connecticut with me long enough for me to claim your bastard as mine so I can collect my inheritance money. Then you can quietly return to your lover and procreate a hundred bastards for all I care."

"No! That's absurd. Even if I might have wanted to help you once, I never would agree to such an outrageous scheme after what you did to me to get the divorce in the first place."

"The bastard told you." Linley shrugged off her

436

anger. "A mere necessity. There was nothing personal, you understand."

"Of course," she answered as she fought down the choler in her heart. "Well, I still won't do it!"

He glared at her. "You will if you ever want to marry Breckenrdige. Because if you don't, that precious child you are carrying will truly be a bastard, and I'm sure you wouldn't want that. Especially since I have already taken the liberty of telegraphing your mother and telling her the good news."

Cornelia gasped; her words fled, and her shoulders slumped. "You told my mother I am expecting a child?"

He circled his knee and rocked back and forth on the couch. "My child, of course." He paused to give her time to absorb everything, then added, "When do you wish to leave?"

"Locke will never stand for this," she blurted out.

"Who's going to tell him? You? And chance never being able to marry the man? I don't think so. You are brighter than that. Just tell him I brought news from home that your mother needs you. You can return with me until I claim my inheritance and then return here, and no one will ever be the wiser."

Horrified at such a suggestion, Cornelia's gaze swung to the woman. Margo bristled at the scorching look Linley's wife gave her. Disgusted with Linley, she stood up. "You needn't think I had anything to do with Linley's scheme," she snapped and marched from the room.

"Your friend obviously does not share your enthusiasm," Cornelia hissed.

"Maybe she doesn't share my enthusiasm now, but she will happily share my inheritance later. And if

437

you think that you can stall for time, don't bother. I want your answer now."

Locke met Paxton and Annie tending the horses in the barn as he led his horse toward a stall. Annie was currying one of the roans as she had since McCurdy had been relieved of his duties; Paxton was sitting on a keg keeping her company.

"Did you get everything settled with Cornelia?" Paxton asked and slid off the keg to greet Locke.

"She didn't put up a fuss when I told her I was going to handle Talbot this time," Locke answered and closed the stall door behind the horse.

"Thank heavens for that. Talbot is a slippery little bastard," Paxton said.

"Well, he's not going to cause Cornelia any more trouble." Locke's gaze shifted to Annie. "Cornelia's inside, why don't we go in and have some refreshments?" Locke suggested.

"I'm almost done," she answered. "Why don't you and Pax do some man talkin' while I finish up?"

Locke and Paxton settled on a couple of bales of hay not far from where Annie worked and visited while she finished up.

When they walked out of the stables, Locke spied Margo standing with her arms crossed over her chest, her foot tapping, facing away from the house. "What the hell?" Murder rose in his heart, and he took off running toward the woman.

Paxton started to follow, but Annie pulled him back. "It's between them, Pax. You'd be best to let Locke handle it."

"I suppose you are right, as always, sweet girl.

We'll give them some time before we return to the house. But I'd sure like to be there when Locke tears Linley limb from limb," he said and followed her back to the stables.

Locke reached Margo in record time and glowered at her. "What are you doing here?"

The murderous look in his eyes caused her to step back. "This wasn't my idea. Why don't you go inside and ask that idiot Linley?" she said quickly. Then spat, "Oh, and you can tell the fool that I have decided to leave him and return to Connecticut and accept Zenas Joshaby's offer." She swung around and marched toward her waiting horse.

Locke bounded up the steps and into the house. He stomped into the parlor. Cornelia was sitting very still, and Talbot sat with his legs crossed at the knee, his arms along the back of the couch.

Linley immediately sat up straight when he saw the fire spark from Breckenridge's eyes, and he recalled what Margo had said about playing with fire. He gulped down the urge to flee and held his position. "Hello, Breckenridge. I was wondering when you would arrive."

Locke started for Talbot until Cornelia called out, "Locke, wait. It's not what you think. Linley was merely delivering news from home. Mother is ailing and has requested that I accompany Linley back to Connecticut to care for her." At the darkening of his face, she added, "I won't be gone long."

"You won't be gone at all." He swung back to Talbot. "What are you trying to pull this time?"

"Nothing. It is just as Cornelia told you. I am only here to do her a favor."

439

"Then where are the divorce papers?" Locke demanded.

"I fear I did not bring them with me, but you needn't concern yourself any longer." His eyes shifted to Cornelia. "Cornelia and I have reached an agreement, I believe. Isn't that right, Cornelia?"

Locke's attention went back to Cornelia. She was awfully nervous about something. Her eyes beseeched him not to press her.

"Cornelia, isn't that right?" Linley pushed.

"Yes," she forced herself to rasp. "Yes, that's correct." She rose. "Now, if you will excuse me, I must go pack."

Linley rose to make a timely exit. "I shall be by to fetch you as soon as Margo and I have our things ready."

She was almost to the door when Locke grabbed her arm. "Oh, no you don't. No one is leaving this room until I have the truth."

In a pleading voice, she said, "Please, Locke, I must go with Linley, or he'll—" she slapped her hand over her mouth.

"Or he'll what, Cornelia? He'll what?"

The stress was overwhelming; Locke was not going to let it go; he would keep at her until she crumbled. She hung her head in defeat. "Linley said he won't sign the divorce papers so we can be married until I return to Connecticut long enough so he can claim our baby as his and receive his inheritance. Oh, Locke, he wired Mother that I am expecting and that it is his child. What am I going to do?"

Linley stepped back, but he was not quick enough. Locke whirled around, swung out his fist,

440

and laid Linley flat. Linley did not attempt to get up, hoping the big man would leave him be.

Locke had other ideas. An animal growl issued from him as he launched himself at the bastard and proceeded to beat the man to within an inch of his life.

"Bravo!" Paxton clapped, coming into the room. Annie and Joe trailed behind him. "It's about time someone beat the hell out you," he said to Linley, who lay on the floor moaning.

Cornelia just stood where she was, her hands covering her mouth. Now she was sure Linley would never sign the papers out of spite.

"Cornelia," Paxton said, interrupting her pained musings. "Joe brought out a wire from Mother."

"Oh, no!" she cried, shaking her head. Paxton handed her the telegram. "Oh, dear, she and Father are on their way here." The urge to flee was nearly overwhelming, but with Linley in a bloody mess on the floor, she was going to have to face her mother learning the truth. So she returned to the chair and sat down.

Linley was coming back around to his senses and tried to scramble away. Locke was faster. He grabbed Linley by the lapels. "Weasels like you never trust anyone. So they usually keep any incriminating evidence on them."

Despite Linley's attempts to protect his person, Locke riffled through his jacket pockets and pulled out the divorce papers. "Those are mine. Give them to me."

"You'll sign these damned papers, or I will give it to you." Locke brought his face close to Linley's. "Did Cornelia ever tell you that I once killed a man with my bare hands?"

Linley looked to Paxton. "He has," Paxton said glibly. "I'd sign the papers if you value that rotten, stinking hide of yours."

Linley looked at Locke. "Give me a goddamned pen."

Locke got a pen and threw it and the divorce papers at Linley.

Linley crawled to his feet and scribbled his name. "You're going to have some explaining to do to your mother," he scoffed. "If you don't believe me, ask him —" he motioned toward Joe — "since he is the telegraph clerk. I sent your mother the telegram before I came over here."

All eyes settled on Joe. "He was at the telegraph office this mornin'," Joe offered.

"Oh, no," Cornelia cried out.

"Don't you want to see your ma?" Annie asked and looked to Paxton.

"That's not it. It is simply that . . . that . . ." Cornelia's voice failed her.

"I am sorry, Cornelia. I suppose I should have told you about Mother's letter," Paxton said and took Annie's hand. "Mother insisted we return after I sent a wire and informed her I was feeling better and we both intended to be wed. According to the wire I got from Father, she threw a hissy fit. Well, you know how he has always let her run over him. I guess Father has finally decided she is going to quit meddling in her children's lives. He indicated that he had given her an ultimatum. He announced he was coming out to attend our weddings, and if she didn't come with him he just might remain in Colorado. Guess she's decided that she doesn't want to lose Father. So they

442

are both on their way."

"I don't understand. You invited them to our weddings?"

Paxton shuffled his foot. "Well, actually it was Annie's idea."

"And Mother is already on her way here?"

Paxton looked at his watch. "They should getting on the train any minute."

Cornelia looked defeated. "Then they had time to get Linley's wire, informing them that I am expecting and he is the father."

"The wire he sent?" Joe said, pointing to Talbot.

"Yes," Linley crowed. "The wire I sent to Cornelia's mother in time for her to get it before she boards the train." Even if Breckenridge thwarted his scheme and ruined his life, he at least had the satisfaction of knowing he had ruined Cornelia's. It was a small measure of satisfaction, but it gave him some solace through the haze of pain that was on his face.

"Oh, you mean this wire?" Joe pulled the crumpled paper out of his pocket and waved it in the air. "Somehow I just didn't have me the time to send it yet."

Cornelia broke down and cried with relief. Paxton and Annie looked bemused. As Cornelia wiped her tears to explain it to them, Locke grabbed Talbot by the collar.

Dragging Talbot out of the parlor and through the house, Locke snickered, "Evidently once wasn't enough for you, Talbot. You have to be thrown out twice before you get the message. Only this time you won't be returning." With a kick, Locke tumbled Talbot off the porch. As two huge men approached Talbot, Locke sneered, "By the way, Margo said she

443

was returning to Connecticut without you. Mentioned something about preferring a Zenas Joshaby to a loser like you."

Linley's retort stuck in his throat as he was suddenly grabbed off his feet and imprisoned in between the two men sent by Joshaby. "What are you doing? I'll get Joshaby's money."

"You have the money?" the larger of the men asked.

"Not yet, but I'll get it. Just give me a little more time. Please, just a little more time," he pleaded.

"You've had all the time you're gonna get," the smaller of the giants said. "Time you paid your debts." The man looked up at Locke. "He won't be bothering you no more."

"Help me! They're going to break my kneecaps," Linley cried. "You can't just let them hurt me! My God, I am Cornelia's husband," Linley screamed as the men were dragging him away.

"Ex-husband," Locke said.

Returning to the parlor, Locke brushed off his hands. Divorce papers in hand, Cornelia rushed into his arms. "I'm truly free now, if you still want me."

Locke rolled his eyes. "Want you? After what we've been through together, no one else will ever do. It would be too boring. Although I have to admit I'm ready to settle down and live without any more excitement while we build a new home."

"I love your cabin just the way it is," she said.

"Then we'll keep it, too."

The thundering sounds of a buggy storming up to the front of the cottage rent the air and ended their conversation.

Locke huffed out a breath. "My gawd, what else can happen today?" he grumbled as they rushed outside to see what was happening.

A white-haired, tall man with stooped shoulders approaching sixty stepped down from the buggy. He turned and fumbled with something in the back seat. When he finally faced them, he held a bulky box in his hands. He set it on its stand, fumbled a moment longer, then said, "Hold that pose!"

"Uncle Cornelius!" Cornelia cried and ran toward the man who was furiously taking pictures.

Locke looked at Paxton. "Cornelia's uncle, the famous photographer?"

Paxton shrugged. "I thought he would enjoy photographing the wedding of his namesake. So I wired him when I sent the wire to Mother. I knew he would want to be here for the weddings."

"Any other relatives coming that I should know about?" Locke asked half-heartedly.

"Well, as a matter of fact, Father's wire stated that they are bringing a few of the cousins."

Locke's lips tightened as more hooves raced toward the house. Carrie pulled up on the reins and stepped down from her carriage. Locke slapped a hand to his forehead as his sister Lamantha alighted after the Simington woman. "I should have known the Simington woman would inform my sister." He shook his head, marched over to Cornelia, grabbed her hand, and started walking away at a fast clip.

"Locke, the introductions—"

"Let Paxton and Annie handle it. They can explain everything to that horde and the ones that will be arriving. I came to these mountains to get some peace and quiet, not to be bombarded by a clicking shutter,

Lamantha's delving questions, and Carrie Simington's prattle about the next adventure she is planning."

"But my parents. They will be arriving shortly as well," she protested.

"Yes, and Paxton said they are bringing some cousins with them."

Cornelia smiled up at him and winked. "I only have eight."

"Eight? All the more reason for you and me to have a chance to spend some time alone together before we are surrounded."

"Locke, wait!" hailed Lamantha, who headed after him, followed by the entire entourage trailing after her and all talking at once. "I have news," she shouted over the others' voices. "Several of your business associates should be arriving soon. And there is someone from the Society I want you to meet, as soon as he arrives."

Throwing up his hands in defeat, Locke waited as they were about to be descended upon.

Cornelia reached up and kissed his ear. "Don't worry, we'll have a whole lifetime together once everyone leaves," she whispered. "Just us and at least six rowdy children."

"Peace be damned," he said as he hugged her. "Seven."

No matter the test that life
sets before us . . .

No matter the trial

446

We shall meet it head held high

And triumph with a smile. . . .

—Cornelia Lloyd Talbot Breckenridge
   Winter 1875

READERS ARE IN LOVE WITH ZEBRA LOVEGRAMS

TEMPTING TEXAS TREASURE (3312, $4.50)
by Wanda Owen

With her dazzling beauty, Karita Montera aroused passion in every redblooded man who glanced her way. But the independent senorita had eyes only for Vincent Navarro, the wealthy cattle rancher she'd adored since childhood—who was also her family's sworn enemy. The Navarro and Montera clans had clashed for generations, but no past passions could compare with the fierce desire that swept through Vincent as he came across the near-naked Karita cooling herself beside the crystal waterfall on the riverbank. With just one scorching glance, he knew this raven-haired vixen must be his for eternity. After the first forbidden embrace, she had captured his heart—and enslaved his very soul!

MISSOURI FLAME (3314, $4.50)
by Gwen Cleary

Missouri-bound Bevin O'Dea never even met the farmer she was journeying to wed, but she believed a marriage based on practicality rather than passion would suit her just fine . . . until she encountered the smoldering charisma of the brash Will Shoemaker, who just happened to be her fiance's step-brother.

Will Shoemaker couldn't believe a woman like Bevin, so full of hidden passion, could agree to marry his step-brother—a cold fish of a man who wanted a housekeeper more than he wanted a wife. He knew he should stay away from Bevin, but the passions were building in both of them, and once those passions were released, they would explode into a red-hot *Missouri Flame*.

BAYOU BRIDE (3311, $4.50)
by Bobbi Smith

Wealthy Louisiana planter Dominic Kane was in a bind: according to his father's will, he must marry within six months or forfeit his inheritance. When he saw the beautiful bonded servant on the docks, he figured she'd do just fine. He would buy her papers and she would be his wife for six months—on paper, that is.

Spirited Jordan St. James hired on as an indenture servant in America because it was the best way to flee England. Her heart raced when she saw her handsome new master, and she swore she would do anything to become Dominic's bride. When his strong arms circled around her in a passionate embrace, she knew she would surrender to his thrilling kisses and lie in his arms for one long night of loving . . . no matter what the future might bring!

Available wherever paperbacks are sold, or order direct from the Publisher. Send cover price plus 50¢ per copy for mailing and handling to Zebra Books, Dept. 3468, 475 Park Avenue South, New York, N.Y. 10016. Residents of New York, New Jersey and Pennsylvania must include sales tax. DO NOT SEND CASH.